Secrets in Our Cities

A Paranormal Urban Fantasy Anthology

The display type was set in Goudy Bookletter 1911.
The text type was set in Garamond.

Published by Rowanwood Publishing, LLC.
www.rowanwoodpublishing.com

First Edition

Introduction

We are the Just-Us League, an international group of friends dedicated to the craft of telling stories.

Though we come from diverse backgrounds and have different styles of writing, we share a common passion for storytelling.

Come journey with us as we prowl the cities and the backwaters in search of paranormal worlds that dwell alongside us. In this sixth installment of the Just-Us League Anthologies, we will tell you stories both fair and fell as we encounter zombies, fae, werewolves, dragons, and more. Each tale brings to life the supernatural with twists and turns beyond imagining. For your enjoyment, we have stories that tickle the funny bone and tug the heartstrings, stories that bring shivers of fear and the delight of wonder. After reading this book, we hope you will never see your own world in the same way again.

Without further ado, we present to you the *Just-Us League Anthology: Volume Six*. Please enjoy.

Sincerely,
The Just-Us League

Table of Contents

No Rest for the Werey

Katelyn Barbee

The cold water bottle pressed against my forehead does squat for my pounding headache. I set it on the edge of the desk, beside a messy stack of unfinished paperwork and yesterday's half-empty coffee mug, then rummage through a drawer. At the bottom, my trembling fingers brush against a smooth plastic bottle. I pull it out and shake it, the painkillers inside rattling. Excellent, there are a couple left.

After the change is like the ultimate hangover. You wake up naked in the middle of a field, head throbbing, unable to remember what happened, praying you didn't do anything stupid—or worse, criminal. But I wasn't covered in blood this time, and there weren't any news reports of beasts or dead bodies. That's always a good sign.

As I slouch back, my chair gives an ear-splitting squeak, making me wince. The mini fridge against the adjacent wall hums loudly, and too-bright fluorescent lights buzz. I cover my ears until the assault dissipates then pop a couple of aspirin. I don't have time for headaches, even if it will go away soon. Not with the first client of the day about to arrive.

An unfamiliar scent invades the air, originating from the other side of the long hallway outside my office—strong flowery perfume mixed with fresh and old sweat. Probably not Jimmy Wong, my first scheduled client. I inhale again, slowly. Undercurrents of street stink. Garbage and soggy cardboard. Smoke from Sal's hot dog stand on the corner six blocks away. Whoever they are, they've been walking for a while.

The smells intensify. Footsteps creep down the hall at a quickening pace. They're remarkably quiet and lack the distinctive clip of heels or the solid thud of boots, so probably sneakers or flats. The silhouette of a petite female darkens the clouded glass of my office door.

I freeze when she stands there taking slow breaths. After a few seconds, she knocks lightly, and the knob turns with a soft click.

She's younger than I expect. Just a kid. Fifteen, maybe sixteen. A lank curtain of greasy strawberry blond hair hides one side of her pale face. The knees of her grubby jeans are ripped, but her tennis shoes look almost new. Given the state of her clothes, and that she's in my office instead of a classroom, she's likely a runaway. She's certainly wiry and skittish enough to be one.

She twists the hem of her frayed gray T-shirt, eyeing me warily. "Are you Charlemagne Kramer?"

My spine straightens. No one's called me by my real name in years. So how's this kid know it?

"Just Charlie." I gesture to the chair in front of my desk, and she shuffles over to it, perching on the edge. "So…you know my name. What's yours?"

Her bottom lip quivers until she clamps down on it with pearly teeth.

I sniff. There's a hint of spearmint toothpaste on her breath. Homeless people aren't known for their good dental habits, so she probably hasn't been on the streets long if she still brushes her teeth. Probably used the perfume to cover up the lack of deodorant. Likely no money to pay me, though.

I glance at the wall clock. Still a few minutes before

Jimmy's supposed to arrive. Enough time to pass her off onto someone else.

She shifts in her seat, crossing her arms.

"Come on, kid, this has to go both ways." When she glares at me, I sigh. "Look. You obviously came here for a reason, right?"

Her lips briefly purse.

"I need a name." I roll my chair over to the mini fridge and pull out a water bottle. I offer it to her. "Please."

She takes it, squeezing hard enough to make her dry, cracked hands pulse white. "Jane."

I'm tempted to ask if her last name is Doe but stop short. "What can I do for you, Miss Jane?"

"I need you to find someone. A friend. He's been taken."

"If he's been kidnapped, then you're better off going to the police."

"I *can't* go to them." She huffs, shaking her head. "They'd think I'm crazy."

I take out a notepad and pen from a drawer. "Well, tell me, and maybe I can convince them. I know people on the—"

"No." The girl whips out a white business card and tosses it on my desk. "They said you could help me. It's not... It's not a normal kidnapping. He wasn't taken by someone, but by *something*." Her expression hardens, but her words come out as a whisper. "He's not the first, either."

I pick up the card.

Ah, hell. Not one of these again. Written across it in rigid black letters are my full name and office location. An old calling card of mine for those dealing with trouble of the supernatural variety from when I went through a charitable streak. It's been years, maybe a decade, since anyone's brought one to me.

My brow furrows. "Where did you get this?"

"A friend of a friend. She said she got it from one of your old buddies." She huffs again. "So, will you help?"

"I don't do that sort of work anymore." At least, I try not to unless I'm getting paid… The last time someone approached me with a card, and I worked for free, I ended up nearly eaten by giant spiders and lacking sensation in my legs for a week. I don't need another monster or demonic presence hunting me down. Still, the kid came to me. Even if I won't take the case, I should put her in touch with someone who will and won't charge for it. I can do that much.

"But tell me anyway. What happened?"

She glances at the carpet, twisting her shirt again. "That's the thing… I don't know exactly."

My eye twitches as the ache in my left temple worsens. "Okay, let's try this: what makes you think your friend was taken by something? How do you know he didn't just skip town?"

"Because he kept having this really weird nightmare where he was riding a horse into the water. And he just looked so…so drained and weak. Like he was wasting away."

I tap my pen on the desk. That does sound potentially supernatural—maybe a succubus or some sort of malevolent water spirit like a nykur or kelpie—but I need more to go on than a hunch. "You said your friend wasn't the first. How many have gone missing?"

"One more. My other friend, Angel."

"Walk me through what happened to them."

Her mouth opens, but she doesn't answer immediately. When she finally does, her words are slow. "Angel had the dream for two weeks…then she was gone. TJ started having the same nightmare six weeks after that. He disappeared two weeks later…just like her. Does that mean something?"

"Potentially." I scribble down the info. Eight weeks

total between the kidnappings could mean it's cyclical. It also helps narrow down the list of culprits. Water spirits feed randomly, which means it's probably some high-ranking demon or nigh-indestructible monstrosity from the Old World. "How long has TJ been missing?"

"Over five weeks." Her voice trembles, turning thick. "I looked everywhere for him. For both of them. I…" She wipes at her eyes, smearing tears across her flushed cheeks. "What if it's too late?"

My insides squirm uncomfortably. "You did the best you could, kid. Coming to me, that was the right decision." I clear my throat. "Do you have anything that belonged to Angel or TJ? Jacket? Watch? Ring?"

"Oh, uh…" She digs around in her pockets and pulls out an old silver quarter. The face has been rubbed so much it's hard to tell it's George Washington. Somebody's good luck charm. Not that it did its owner any good.

She hands it to me. "This used to be Angel's."

"Great. Hang onto it, kid." I flip the coin toward her, and she catches it. I scribble a note for Jimmy Wong then twist around, yanking my coat off the back of my chair. "We're going on a field trip."

She stands abruptly. "We—we are? You mean you'll find them?"

I shrug on my coat, ushering her out the door. "No guarantees. And this isn't me taking the case, either. This is me figuring out if it's worth my time." Or someone else's. If the pattern Jane described is accurate, then her friend doesn't have much time left.

I write a mental list of all the people I now have to call and apologize to and reschedule appointments with. So much for a regular day at the office.

She cracks a tremulous smile. "I'll take it."

***

Half an hour later, we pull up beside the freshly mowed lawn of Trip's house. The car stinks of fast food after stopping at a drive-thru to grab the kid a meal—it's clear she hasn't had a decent one in a while—but at least she's fed now.

She nibbles on the last of her fries before stuffing the greasy container back into the bag. "Thanks again," she says while exiting my car.

The paper take-out bag crinkles when I take it from her and toss it into one of the trash bins lining the quiet street. Besides a couple of old ladies eyeballing us from behind lacy curtains and a golf cart driver shooting me a curious glance as he putters down the road, no one pays attention to us. "Come on, kid."

When we near the front door, her steps slow to a shuffle behind me. "Where are we?"

"A friend's. I want him to take a look at that coin of yours." Whether Trip can summon Angel or not will tell me if she's still alive or dead.

Jane cocks her head, clearly puzzled.

I rap on the door then adjust my sleeves and collar so they look crisper. "Just trust me, kid, this'll help."

She shrugs. "Whatever you say. You're the detective."

A burst of familiar smells and sounds leak from the house when Trip opens the door. Old dusty books, dead flowers, and the steady ticking of a grandfather clock. Lemony perfume, sugar, and the joyful hum of a woman's voice.

Trip startles and adjusts his thick glasses, blinking owlishly at me. The buttons of his blue shirt struggle to contain his girth when he laughs. "Charlie?"

"Been a while, Trip." I point to the kid. "This is Jane. She needs your help."

Trip offers her a wizened hand. "Jude Tripson. How

can I be of service?"

"It's best if we discuss it inside." I grin, eyeing his bulging belly. "What's Martha been feeding you?"

He pats his stomach. "A little too much of everything."

"I heard that," Martha calls from the kitchen. She emerges into the living room, wiping her flour-caked hands on her apron. Her face lights up. "Charlie!"

Before I can stop her, she waddles over and hugs me, squeezing me tighter than I'd expect for someone well into her eighties. When she releases me, I step inside and close the door behind us.

Jane settles onto the plastic-covered couch with Trip while I take a musty armchair. She tells Trip everything while Martha busies herself in the kitchen, and before long, the sweetness of warm sugar cookies fills the air. Martha brings out a plate of them and sets it in front of Jane before disappearing into the laundry room.

Once Jane's finished speaking, Trip extracts an unfamiliar book from a cabinet.

I sniff. Made of human leather. And given how faint the scent is, it's probably centuries old. "Interesting choice for your collection. What's this one for?"

"Oh, the usual," he says with a casual wave. "Not getting any younger, after all."

So, less energy spent on his part. Unsurprising, given that even simple spells wear him out quickly now.

He flips through the tome, settling on an illustrated page featuring smoke spiraling out of the mouth of a human skull. He coughs into a fist. "The incantation's a little tricky, but I think I can manage it. Jane, I'll need that coin you mentioned. And blood from you, Charlie."

"Of course."

"Excellent." From a drawer, Trip takes a sheet of paper and draws a circle of symbols on it. I don't recognize any of them, despite the fact that I've seen him do hundreds of summonings over the last sixty years. Then again, I'm not supposed to since it's not my job. Resurrecting souls is his specialty, not mine.

He sets the paper on the coffee table, beside a vase of withered roses and violets. Chanting under his breath in a guttural language, he places the coin at the paper's center. His voice deepens, and white smoke begins to rise off the symbols and the coin. "Now, Charlie."

Gritting my teeth, I slice deep across my wrist with my pocket knife. I squeeze my hand into a tight fist, letting the blood drip onto the coin and paper until the wound closes up a few seconds later.

Jane flinches. "Was that really necessary?"

With a handkerchief, I wipe away the blood. "All magic costs something."

"Hold on, *magic*?" Her eyes widen. "Like what wizards do? That's all re—"

The smoke hisses and thickens, turning a dark red, then black.

Her mouth falls open, revealing her half-chewed cookie. "You weren't kidding... Magic...real magic."

"What'd you think we were doing? Party tricks?" I grumble.

"Charlie." Trip glares at me like I'm one of his misbehaving grandkids. "Be nice."

"This is so cool!" Jane breaks into a wide smile. She looks at me, brows lifting in hope. "Can you do magic?"

"No." My voice comes out gruffer than I intend to.

She cocks her head, blue eyes full of questions. "Then how'd you heal so fast?"

I turn to Trip. "How long's this supposed to take?"

Trip closes the book, humoring me with the answer I already know. "Depends on whether anyone's there or not."

Jane scoots to the edge of her seat, pointing at the

smoke. "Something's happening to it!"

The outline of a young woman's head appears. Short, tight curls frame a heart-shaped face. A broad nose and thick lips form. Her eyes open slowly as if she's groggy from too much sleep. "Where...am I?" Her gaze jumps from face to face. "Who are you?"

"Angel, it's me. It's Jane. Are you okay?"

The smoke flickers, but Angel doesn't move. Then her lips part into a soft smile. "Jane."

"We need to ask you some questions, Angel, before time runs out." My stomach sinks. Whatever's going on, one victim is dead. Determining TJ's fate will require more investigation, however. "You went missing, and no one's been able to find you. Where are you?"

"I..." Angel's eyelashes flutter wildly. "I don't know. I can't remember."

"Give yourself a moment to think about it," Trip says in a soothing voice. "You might only get snapshots."

The image wavers. Curls of smoke rise off her cheeks in wispy tendrils. "There was an old woman. No...not a woman, but it looked like one. I thought I'd dreamed it, but..."

"Jane mentioned you were having night terrors," I say. "Do you remember them?"

Angel nods. "I was riding a horse, and it took me into this lake. I tried to escape, but it was like I was glued to its back. We sank deeper and deeper into the water, and I couldn't breathe. There was so much pressure. Like someone sitting on my chest."

My breath hitches. The woman. The riding of the horse. The chest pressure. I should've figured it out earlier. "Thank you, Angel." I nod at Trip so he'll dismiss her, but he doesn't catch it, too busy watching Jane marvel at her friend's smoke face.

"Angel, if you tell us where you are, we can come

find you," Jane says. "We can save you and TJ."

Angel shakes her head. "I'm gone, Jane. There's nothing to find but a body."

"Bo-body? I thought—" Her head whips to me, eyes burning with fury. "You lied!"

"I did not. I didn't know she was dead." Not for sure, anyway.

Angel's image fades, and the smoke vanishes. The last of the blood and symbols disappear with it, leaving a blank paper.

Jane rises and storms out. The slam of the front door rattles the house.

"That was…dramatic," I murmur.

"The girl just found out one of her friends is dead." Trip peers at me over the rim of his glasses. "And her other friend may have met the same fate. How did you expect her to react?"

I gesture to the front door. "Not like that."

"Charlie…" Trip sighs as he puts his spell book away. "Sometimes your lack of sensitivity astounds even me. Try to be a *little* kinder to her, please."

My face heats. Being empathetic has never been one of my strong points, but he's right. She's just a kid after all. More importantly, she came to me for help. "I'll give her a few minutes to cool off, but I can't wait forever. I know what took her friends. There's still a chance to save the boy if we move quickly."

Trip eases himself back onto the couch, knees crackling. "Perhaps you should fetch Jane before you enlighten everyone, then. As you said, we need to move quickly."

I drum my fingers on the armrest. I hate it when he uses my own words against me.

Trip glares.

"Oh, all right, I'm going." I rise slowly, taking my

time to reach the front door.

"Excellent, I'll make us some lunch," he says cheerfully. "Monster hunting is always more pleasant on a full stomach."

Outside, Jane sits on the curb by my car, snapping off blades of grass and letting them scatter in the breeze.

I hop onto the trunk. "You didn't run."

"You didn't take the case yet. I *can't* run." She rips up more grass. "I could've handled it, you know."

"Handled what?"

"What happened to Angel. Omitting details is still lying," Jane grumbles, throwing a puff of green confetti at my shoes. "I'm not stupid."

I chew the inside of my cheek. "Never thought you were, kid." She's certainly smarter than I was at her age. More determined too.

She glares at me. "So what now?"

"Well, I was going to take your case, but if you'd rather have someone else..." I climb off the trunk and head for the house, keeping my pace casual. "I know what it is that took your friends."

Jane's sneakers scuff the asphalt. "You're serious?"

"You really think I'd joke?"

"No..." She appears by my side. "So what is it?"

"In a minute. There are a couple of things we have to sort out first."

***

Jane slides into the back seat of my car, tugging at the collar of her new oversized T-shirt. "Was it really necessary for me to shower *and* change?"

"Pleasant smells are less distracting." I jerk the steering wheel, pulling into the street. "Easier to find your friends that way."

Trip turns around to her, wearing an apologetic smile. "I'm sorry about the ill-fitting clothes. I thought my granddaughter's things would fit better than Martha's."

"They're fine, and thank you," Jane says, tucking a wet strand of hair behind her ear. "You're sure she won't miss them?"

"Not at all," Trip chuckles. "She has more than enough outfits. Too many, in fact."

"Oh. Good." Jane's face appears beside my right shoulder. "So what is it that took my friends?"

"It's a mare."

"Like a horse?"

"No, as in where we get the word 'nightmare' from. Mares sit on your chest while you sleep and suck out your life force. The dreams are subconscious warnings initially— like what Angel and TJ experienced—before turning into your worst memories. This one must be new to the area, or else, there would've been a lot more missing people by now."

"Can you get rid of it?"

"Charlie killed one a long time ago." The corners of Trip's mouth crinkle into an impish grin. "When was it? The seventies?"

My teeth clench. "Yeah." The eighteen seventies. Back when I was a Pinkerton agent in New Orleans and took a case from a Voodoo queen.

"But that was over forty years ago, and you're like thirty. You couldn't have been alive—" Jane cuts off. "Just how old *are* you?"

"Old." My grip on the steering wheel tightens.

Jane glares at me in the rearview mirror. "Do you ever give straight answers?"

Trip chuckles. "Charlie's rather sensitive about his age."

"What's the big deal? If you're a necromancer—"

"Resurrectionist," Trip corrects. "Necromancer makes it sound like I'm raising the dead for nefarious purposes, which I most certainly am not."

"Oh...well, if you're a resurrectionist, then what is he?" She cocks her head. "Are you a vampire?"

A low, rumbling laugh escapes my throat. "No. Not even close. And vampires aren't like what you see in the movies."

Jane scoots as far forward as her seatbelt will allow. "*Really?*"

"Zombies aren't any better. Or witches. Or—"

"Not this again..." Trip rolls his eyes. He's heard me rant about how Hollywood screws up depictions of creatures like me too many times. "Please don't get him started."

"If you're not a vampire..." Jane says slowly, "are you a werewolf?"

The muscles in my jaw stiffen. Idiot. Set myself up for that one.

Trip sighs. "You might as well tell her."

"Fine," I spit out. "You got me, kid. Happy?"

She leans into the space between Trip and me, grinning. "Shouldn't you have a unibrow and hairy palms? I thought werewolves were supposed to be furry even in their human form. Can you change at will? Does it have to be a full moon? Are you allergic to sil—"

I slam on the brakes, making Jane yelp and Trip clutch his chest. Other drivers behind me honk, a couple of them flipping me off as they speed past. I pull the car over. Turning around, I squeeze the central console. The plastic splits with a loud *crack*. A piece of it digs into my palm, but I ignore it.

Trip puts a light hand on my shoulder. "Charlie—"

I raise my hand, and his body deflates against the seat. I know she's just curious, but the past isn't something I want to discuss. All it leads to is pain.

Jane's face turns paper white. "I-I-"

"No more questions." My voice comes out as a deep growl. More animal than man. "Got it?"

Trip's mouth puckers in disapproval, but he stays silent.

She nods, eyes lowering, then scoots to Trip's side of the car. Her knees come up, and she hugs them.

Great. I scared her. Something I'm sure Trip will lecture me on later.

After a few more moments of awkward silence, I flip on the radio and weave my way back into lunchtime traffic. No one speaks until we reach my house.

I get out and lean on the door. "Stay here. I won't be long."

Trip mumbles something while Jane just stares out the window, her back to me.

Sighing, I jog to the front door and jam the key in. Inside, I make my way to the supply room at the back of the hall. I pull a couple flashlights from the utility cabinet and stuff them into my jacket pockets before moving on to the weapons rack. Gunfire is too loud and might draw attention, so hack and slash it is. I take my machete. Coated in silver and blessed by the heads of multiple religions, it should work against the mare.

Rummaging through the electronics drawer, I eventually find a battery pack and matches. People aren't the only things mares can suck energy from—phones, laptops, tablets—granted, they can't draw much, but it's enough to sustain them if they can't find a fresh victim for a while. Finally, I grab a bag of flour because, as good as my eyes are, I can't see mares when they become invisible.

Someone knocks lightly on the front door. Trip would've just barged in, so it's got to be the kid. I poke my head out. "What?"

She points to the car with a shaky hand. Trip's head

is slumped against the window with his eyes closed. His face is slack and glasses askew, but his breath fogs the window, so he's clearly still alive.

I sigh. "Please, tell me he didn't try another spell."

Jane shakes her head. "We were talking, and then he—he just passed out." Her voice quivers like a plucked string. "Is he going to be okay?"

"Yeah. Summonings tend to sap a lot of his energy, but sometimes there's a delay." Maybe letting him tag along wasn't such a good idea, though. "Come with me. A little food and drink should perk him back up."

She nods, following me into the kitchen. Chewing on her lip, she shifts her weight from foot to foot. "What now?"

I point to the fridge then to the pantry. "Grab some water bottles and energy bars."

Jane eyes me warily as she passes. She snatches water bottles from the fridge then moves on to the pantry. Her shoulders stiffen, and her elbows stick to her sides, making her look small.

Still scared of me, then. I massage my temples then clear my throat, making her jump. "Kid, in the car—I didn't mean to frighten you. Just...my history isn't something I like to go into."

She stares at the linoleum, hugging the water bottles to her stomach. "Is it because of your family?"

"I—" The words die in my throat.

"Trip said you had a wife and a daughter..."

"I did." My voice goes quiet. Of course Trip would try to explain and make me look better.

She finally meets my gaze, frowning. "Did something bad happen to them?"

"No. They left." Because of me. Because of my lies. My heart clenches. "It was for the best."

"Oh..." she says softly. "That must've been hard."

"It's okay, kid. It was decades ago."

"Do you ever wonder about them? How they're doing?"

"I try not to." Something I usually fail at unless I stay busy.

She stares into the pantry. "I had someone once too…my grandpa, but he died."

"Is that how you ended up on the streets?"

She shakes her head. "My mom got custody of me. Everything was fine for a while, but then she got a new boyfriend. She started using again to please him…called me a liar when he came onto me…so I ran."

"I'm sorry, Jane." My hands curl into fists. What kind of parent chooses their latest fling over their own child? Jane's mother is lucky I'm a century wiser and not so tempted to break down her door and—

"It's Samantha, actually," Jane whispers.

I snap out of my darkening thoughts.

"I thought she or the government might send someone after me, so I changed it… Does that sound stupid?"

"Not at all, Samantha."

Wrappers crinkle as she pulls energy bars from the pantry. She offers them to me. "Is, um, is this enough?"

"Plenty." I motion for her to follow me, sucking my teeth. I'm so used to making snap judgments I didn't consider *why* she might be on the streets. Once the mare is taken care of, I can help find her something more permanent. Maybe even let her stay in the old house for a while… Someone might as well use it since I never do.

When we reach the car, I throw the supplies in the trunk while Samantha hops in the back seat. She unwraps an energy bar and waves it in front of Trip's face, making me chuckle. When that doesn't work, she shakes his shoulder.

As I slide into the driver's seat, she sits back and huffs. "Is he usually this difficult to wake up?"

"Give me one of the waters." That spell must've really done a number on him. I dribble a bit of water onto his face.

Some of it goes into his mouth, and he snorts violently, springing back to life. He adjusts his glasses, blinking at Samantha and me. "Sorry, dozed off."

"Uh-huh." I start the car then input the address Samantha gave me earlier into my phone.

He wipes at his cheek and mouth. "Did I drool, or was this your doing, Charlie?"

I grin.

***

For the next two hours, Trip keeps Samantha enraptured with tales of our past adventures from when we were on the force together in the fifties and sixties. And while I don't like him spilling so many of my secrets, it gives me enough uninterrupted thinking time to plan out how to find the mare.

Mares like to drag victims back to the dark, dank places of the world. Abandoned buildings, caves, sewers... Places they'll be undisturbed while they feed. Trip can use Angel's quarter to track her last movements, though it'll mean a lot of walking for us.

When we arrive at the location Siri insists is correct, I exit the car, squinting in the late afternoon sunlight. With only two or three hours before nightfall, we'll have to be quick. Trying to kill an angry mare will be hard enough without the kid and Trip.

Samantha leads us down an empty alleyway.

My stomach roils at the pungent intermingling scents of mold, rotting garbage, decaying rat carcasses, and stagnant puddles. Not even cockroaches would want to stay here. And tempting as it is to smear a glob of Vick's VapoRub under my nose to ward off the worst of the stink, I might miss something important if I do.

"Please, tell me you didn't walk all the way from here to my office," I say, sidestepping one of the rainbow swirls of oily water pockmarking the street.

Samantha glances back at me, her face flushed. "I hitchhiked some of it. Couldn't take a bus." She turns out her pockets. "No money."

One more reason to get her out of here once this is over. "How long did it take you?"

She shrugs. "A few hours. Come on, it's this way."

Samantha leads Trip and me into the heart of a decades-old abandoned business park. When we reach a set of rusted doors, she turns to us, biting her lip. "There used to be more of us, but once TJ went missing, they got spooked and left. I'm the only one who lives here now…"

Past the grinding doors, we weave around old machinery and broken windows to reach a half-dozen ancient mattresses covered in ratty blankets that reek of sweat, pee, and vomit. Several shopping carts full of junk—smashed televisions, mismatched shoes, dirty plush animals leaking stuffing, and more—line the moldy, water-stained walls. The urge to vomit rises in the back of my throat.

"This is home." Samantha plops onto one of the makeshift beds, sending curls of dust into the air. "What's left of it anyway."

I glance around. "This is a terri—"

Trip puts a hand on my arm. "Samantha, do you still have that quarter?"

She nods and fishes it out of her pocket, then hands it to him.

He licks his lips. "Give me a moment."

Trip closes his fist and mutters in the same guttural language from earlier. When nothing happens, he tries again, shutting his eyes tight. The creases of his face deepen, his voice turning harsh and gravelly. A soft blue glow emanates from his hand like a pulsing star. Smoke leaks between his fingers, pooling at his feet to form ghostly shoeprints. They move around the space, often overlapping, before heading toward the building's entrance.

Trip whispers more words, and after a moment, the trail vanishes.

"Aww, it didn't work..." Samantha's shoulders fall along with her voice.

"Actually, it did," Trip says, handing the quarter back to Samantha. He wipes at the sweat beading along his thinning hairline. "We'll need your phone, Charlie."

I take it out. Normally, we'd just follow the trail, but Trip seems to have something else in mind. "What's this all about?"

"Leaving the prints visible might attract attention, so I disguised them." Panting, he rests his hands on his knees. "We should be able to track them using your phone's camera."

"Ah, clever as always." I frown when he turns a shade paler. "Are you going to be okay?"

He waves me off. "Yes, yes, fine," he says in a proud but strained voice. "Just a new spell—it's more powerful than I expected."

"Right... Samantha, you mind helping him? I don't want him keeling over."

Trip *harrumphs* at me but doesn't protest any further when Samantha takes his arm.

The three of us follow the glowing blue footprints displayed on my phone's camera. The phantom tracks zigzag down alleyways and loop around backstreets. Luckily, this area is empty. Other than the rare homeless person, we don't run into anyone, which means the mare is probably close by.

It isn't until several passes through the same areas later—and multiple breaks so Trip can rest—that the trail eventually turns to drag marks. I plug my phone into the battery pack as we follow the neon smears into an abandoned building. Dust motes catch and spark in the final rays of sunlight filtering in through the empty window frames and rusting walls. I sniff then cough. A mix of faint sweetness and rotting meat drifts on the current. Decaying flesh. It's far enough away that Trip and the kid won't have picked up on it yet, but I don't want Samantha seeing the bodies of her friends.

"Trip, a word."

Samantha releases Trip, her gaze narrowing on us. She puts her hands on her hips. "What's going on?"

"I'll tell you in a minute. Go stand over there." I point to a corner far enough away that she won't be able to hear easily but close enough that I can still keep an eye on her.

She groans but does as I ask, facing the wall like she's a five-year-old in time-out.

Trip wears a grim expression. "You smell something, don't you?"

"A body. At least one."

"Angel?"

Slowly, I nod.

Trip glances at Samantha then back to me. "Do you think the boy's still alive?"

"Possibly." Mares don't usually move bodies unless something or someone disturbs their nest. But with the stench of death so overpowering, it would be easy to miss a living person.

"What do you want to do about Samantha?" he whispers.

"Keep her here. I'll go on ahead and report back." I keep a steady pace until I'm out of Samantha's view then break into a jog. As long as there's sunlight still in the sky, I don't have to worry about being attacked by the mare, but that will change soon.

"Hey! Where are you—"

"Stay with Trip until I say it's safe."

"But—"

"Dear, help me sit, would you?" Trip asks in a wavering voice, his footsteps turning to shuffling. "I'm feeling a touch dizzy. Do you have any water?"

Good. That will hopefully keep her occupied until I figure out what we're dealing with.

Samantha's shoes slap against the concrete behind me. "I'm going with you."

"What part of 'stay there' didn't you understand?" I whirl around. "I don't know what I'll find—"

"Yes, you do." Her hands clench into fists. "Whatever it is, I can handle it."

I sigh, rubbing my forehead. And I thought Trip was stubborn. Maybe telling her will keep her away. "You want full honesty?"

She nods.

"There's a body," I mutter. "Maybe two."

"Both of them are dead?" Samantha breathes.

"I won't know until I take a look." I pull a flashlight from my pocket and offer it to her. "If you really want to come, I won't stop you, but staying here doesn't make you weak or mean you care any less about your friends."

Slowly, Samantha reaches out and takes the flashlight. Her hand shakes. She pushes the flashlight back into my palm, face falling. "I can't…"

"And that's okay." I take her by the shoulders, turning her around. "Trip needs a babysitter anyway."

She laughs, and the bubble of tension between us pops. "I'm going to tell him you said that."

"Good. He could use a reality check. I won't take long." I start heading deeper into the building.

Sniffing occasionally, I weave past barrels of

chemicals and duck under broken pipes with rusted-off valves. As I enter one room, a wall of intense smells crashes into me. For several minutes, all I can do is gag on the stench of death. When I stop trying to heave up lunch, I shine a flashlight into the pitch-black space between two massive boilers at the room's center.

A decaying hand sticks out from behind a metal column. Despite seeing thousands of dead bodies over the last five hundred years, it's not something I've gotten completely used to. I listen for the mare. Silence. Not even a cooing bird or scurrying rat or chittering insect.

Satisfied the mare isn't here, I crouch beside the body. There's no evidence of earlier insect activity, just dried tissue and bone. Even the maggots and beetles don't want to be here.

Angel.

Just Angel.

Which means the mare isn't feeding here anymore, but it's close. They don't have the strength to drag victims very far. Finding it and TJ before dark, though… We may not have enough time.

I call in the body, making sure to get a hold of the right people on the force. They'll know how to handle it discreetly.

I head back to find Samantha sitting on the concrete beside Trip. She jumps up when she sees me then helps Trip stagger to his feet.

"Is it the nest?" he asks with a grunt.

"Was. I called it in. They'll be by soon to—er, clean up."

He nods.

"So they're both dead?" Samantha's voice is so quiet it's startling. Her bottom lip quivers.

"Just Angel. TJ's been moved."

She stares at the floor. "I guess that's something."

"How well do you know this area?" I ask.

"Well enough." She shrugs. "I've been out here a few months."

"Which building's the oldest?"

After a moment of lip-chewing, Samantha points to one of the large black voids in the pink-hued sky. "That one. TJ said they used to make dolls there until a fire burned down half of it."

I stare at the decrepit structure rising into the twilight like some ancient rotting cathedral. Half of it has caved in, exposing charred wooden beams and piles of dislodged bricks. No one smart would go in there. "Let's go."

***

Once we've exited the building containing Angel's body, I toss my car keys to Samantha.

She fumbles them. "What're these for?"

"Take Trip back to the car, and wait for me."

He shakes his head. "If the mare's not in there, we put ourselves at risk."

"It would come after us?" Samantha squeaks.

The darkening horizon is rimmed in purple now. A few more minutes, and it'll be night. "Get as far away as you can. I'll keep it busy."

"And if it decides to avoid you and go after us instead?" Trip waves at himself and Samantha.

Stubborn old man. "It hasn't woken yet. I can still get the jump on—"

Footsteps echo deep within the burned building. I draw my machete. So much for surprising it.

I grit my teeth as bricks and metal scrape against one another. Beneath the faint layers of old charred wood, melted plastic, and burnt fabric is the scent of moss and decaying pine needles. Grass and damp soil.

Trip pushes his drooping glasses back onto his nose. He stands tall, slowing his breaths. "You can't rescue the boy and fight off the mare at the same time. Let us help."

"Yeah, we're not useless, you know," Samantha adds in a determined voice. "TJ's my friend. I can't just leave him."

I glare at them. What mares lack in strength, they make up for in speed. If they return to the car without me, and it attacks them, I'll never reach them in time. I'd be able to better protect them if they came with me, but that presents its own risks. When neither of them back down, I hand Samantha a flashlight and the bag of flour. "If you think the mare is near, throw this at it."

"Anything else?" She takes both items.

More bricks slide within the building, closer this time. A faint new smell emerges. Body odor. It's old, so not from Trip or Samantha. The boy. He's alive.

I glance at Samantha. "Silver burns mares. If it grabs you—"

"Touch it with Angel's quarter?" she finishes.

I nod. She catches on quick.

Trip pulls a cross necklace free from beneath his shirt collar. He kisses it. "I'm covered."

Samantha frowns. "What about you?"

I hold up my machete. "Better than a silver bullet."

"Silver bullets are real?" Her eyes widen. "Those actually work?"

"Yeah, but they suck. Expensive, and they always go wide." Still hurt like hell, though.

Metal rattles and groans deeper inside the structure, moving further away from us.

"Keep behind me, kid, and don't separate from Trip." Martha will have my head if anything happens to him or Samantha.

With Trip and Samantha in tow, I follow my nose

into the abandoned building. Eerie silence greets us.

We push forward, past blackened walls and charred, unrecognizable equipment, before reaching a large chamber—probably the main factory floor, though it's hard to tell. The stink of body odor intensifies, coming from one of the corners. I crouch near a slim gap in the machinery. The sole of a worn shoe appears in my flashlight beam. I point. "There."

Samantha slides over the top of a conveyor belt before I can stop her. Doll parts tumble and bounce along the floor. "TJ? TJ!"

I wince as I follow her, the shrill sound grating on my ears.

The boy's chest rises and falls shallowly, his pale face gaunt and limbs skeletal, but he's alive. Barely.

Trip toddles over to a different conveyor belt and grabs a long sheet of thick plastic. "We can drag him away on this."

Samantha reaches out toward TJ but stops, drawing back. "Why won't he wake up?"

"Mares put people into a sort of coma after isolating victims." I scoop up TJ and carefully cross the conveyor belt, then place the boy on the plastic sheet. "Easier to feed on them that way."

The scent of earth and dying leaves grows stronger, but I still can't pinpoint it. Stars wink at me through the gaps in the ceiling as I rotate.

"There are ways to wake him," Trip says when Samantha hesitates again. He grabs the plastic sheet. "But we need to get him out of here first."

"Go." I keep my flashlight aimed at the ceiling above them, slowly highlighting different slabs of rusting sheet metal.

Samantha and Trip start to drag the boy away, but it's a slow process. By the time they've gone ten feet, Trip's face is red, and he's huffing.

Above them, a sheet of metal drops an inch. Oh no. "Move! Get back!"

I sprint forward, but I'm not fast enough.

Samantha screams as she and Trip are knocked onto the floor.

An intense pressure shoves me backward, forcing the air from my lungs.

Samantha scrambles to her feet, disoriented but unhurt. She throws a handful of flour in front of her. It floats to the ground. She tries again and gasps. The white powder remains suspended in midair, sticking to the hunched back of the mare. The bag slips from Samantha's hands, and she freezes, gaze glued to the creature.

Trip is sprawled out on the floor. Outlined by the cloud of flour, spindly fingers wrap around his neck. The mare recoils, hissing at the cross necklace, then grabs his head.

I bring my blade to its throat. "Let him go."

Trip moans, blinking slowly. One of his lenses has cracked, and there's already a large purple bruise running down the side of his face. And that's only the damage I can see.

The mare shakes the powder off its back. Its mouth opens into an ugly, unnaturally wide smile. A sound like an old woman's death rattle echoes off the walls. "You came here to steal my food and kill me. Why would I release him?"

I put more pressure on the knife, leaving a faint sizzling line. "Because I won't kill you if you let him—let all of us—go."

"Lies," it hisses. The long fingers clutching Trip's head constrict further as the rest of its thin skeletal body appears. Trip groans in pain, placing a hand on top of the mare's. Its large eyes turn to slits. "Do it. See what happens."

My mouth twitches, but I keep quiet. With Trip's life

on the line, I can't kill it. Not yet. I draw back my knife a little. "What do you want?"

"Food."

"No," I growl. "You flee the area, or I'll kill you."

Samantha takes a small step forward, the silver quarter in her hand catching in the beam of my flashlight.

The mare's gaze darts to the side. Two of its jagged nails slide across Trip's face to hover over his eyelids. "Take another step, girl, and I gouge out the old man's eyes."

I grind my teeth. I can't wait it out until morning when it will have to sleep. The boy is barely hanging on, and Trip isn't doing much better. "What if we made a trade? You want food. I can make that happen."

"Are you crazy?" Samantha's voice cracks, her face white.

The mare focuses back on me, the muscles in its sharp features softening ever so slightly. "A trade?" it purrs.

"Let the other three go, and you can have me instead."

Samantha trembles. "Don't."

It releases a harsh cackle. "One human for three easy meals? No."

"But I'm not human. Not entirely. Look." I pull my machete away from its throat and draw the blade across my palm, ignoring the stinging pain. Blood bubbles, oozing from the cut, and Samantha gasps softly. Though slower than usual, the wound knits together abnormally fast enough to get my point across.

"You could feed off me for years. Maybe decades."

It eyes my machete. "Throw it away."

I toss the blade to the side.

Slowly, the mare turns to Samantha, its knotted hair falling onto its haunting features. "Take them. But if you come back after that, I will make yours a slow, painful death."

Samantha glances at me with tear-rimmed eyes.

"Do it." I try to smile, but my mouth falters. "I've lived too long. Seen too much. It's okay."

Trip will send someone after me. We've both made enough friends and done enough favors for people over the years. As long as the kid doesn't do anything stupid…

The mare releases Trip. His head thumps dully against the dirt beneath him. It hisses at Samantha; she jumps. She grabs Trip's arms, tugging him onto the heavy plastic. Though she strains and grunts, she makes slow but steady progress, dragging him inch by inch toward a large hole in one of the walls.

My whole body tenses. She's smart. She won't do anything to endanger her friend or Trip.

The mare scurries over to me, clasping my face with its cold hands, and everything goes black. Dread builds in my tightening stomach. An uncomfortable sensation passes over me. Like my gut being shoved up into my ribs—but then it's gone just as quickly.

Light stings my eyes. Grass tickles the back of my bare arms, my legs. Insects buzz and wiggle through something wet and gooey nearby. A sickening smell reaches me. No… No.

I sit up, wiping at my mouth. My hand—more a boy's than a man's—comes away bloody. I can't look. *Won't* look at the mangled body I know is there, but my head turns anyway. Jean Dubois. The village butcher. My first kill.

Before I can even scream, I'm yanked out of the memory and into a new one, as if a cord is attached to my belly button.

My old house. The one where I'd planned on living a normal life with Alice and Lisa. Bright sunlight pours through the open kitchen windows, highlighting the red-gold curls of Alice's bowed head. She has her back to me, hands gripping the edge of a counter. "Is it another woman?" Her words are soft, but there's no anger behind them. They lance my heart like barbs.

My throat tightens, strangling the truth I want to tell her but can't.

She turns around, tears threatening to spill down her cheeks. Her bottom lip trembles as she sinks to the floor beside me, putting her warm hands on my thigh. She squeezes gently. "You can tell me. I can take it. Please...whatever it is, we can work through it."

I look away, unable to stand the pain in her eyes. I should've told her why I always disappear every month like clockwork—why I don't look any older than the day we married or how I recover from injuries so quickly—but I didn't. My mouth won't let me, forcing me to keep my silence just as I did that day.

She sucks in a shaky breath and stands to straighten the wrinkles out of her dress. Without a glance back at me, she walks out of the kitchen, heels clicking down the hall. The bedroom door closes softly.

I wince when the sobbing starts.

The scene swirls, and a new memory begins to play out. I'm still in the kitchen, but it's later that day now. I peek through the blinds at five-year-old Lisa trotting after Alice to the car, her strawberry blond curls bouncing with every happy step. I urge my legs to move, to stop them, but I'm glued to the spot, merely watching, clueless that Alice isn't planning on staying at her mom's for a night to think things over. That this is goodbye forever.

"Mommy, why isn't Daddy coming?" Lisa throws a glance over her shoulder in my direction. There's no distress in her voice, just curiosity.

Alice loads the suitcases into the trunk, sniffling. "Daddy's got to finish up something for work. He'll meet us later."

"Oh..." Lisa climbs in the back seat.

"How about we go shopping?" Alice's voice threatens to crack, but she manages a watery smile. "Just you and me."

"I'd like that." Lisa grins up at her then waves at me. "Bye, Daddy!"

There's an unholy scream above me, and Lisa's face dissolves into the mare's.

Samantha has an arm around its neck, awkwardly stabbing it in the chest with my machete. It rears back, and she slides off, landing with an "oof."

I stagger to my feet, head spinning. I'm not sure whether I should be impressed by her bravery or angry at her stupidity. "What were you thinking, kid?"

"I don't know!" She slides the machete across the rubble toward me. "Just kill it!"

The mare snarls at Samantha, skittering along the wall like a beetle. It crawls through a hole in the metal onto the next floor.

I climb up the machinery and follow the trail of black blood, cursing when I nearly lose my footing and rusty steel stabs into my leg.

The mare swipes at me, but I duck. Metal shrieks as claws tear through it.

The floor beneath me creaks, and a section crumbles. "Kid, get out!"

I can survive a lot of things, but a building collapsing on top of me is probably pushing even *my* limits.

The mare lunges, and I jump back. Another piece of ceiling falls as it begins to circle. "Werewolf," it growls. "You are a predator like me. You hunt; you kill. How can you side with humans?"

I step lightly, keeping toward the outside walls where the frame might be stronger. "Come a little closer, and I'll tell you."

It barks out a laugh and pounds its fists on the

ceiling, shaking loose more metal and wood.

My foot catches a hole and punches through it, bringing me to my knees. Ah, hell.

It pounces, and the ceiling groans, giving way. I grab it by the throat as we fall. There's a scream, but I can't tell from where or whom. Samantha? The mare?

Chunks of concrete, metal beams, and bricks crush my back, an arm, and a foot. Pain surges along my core to my limbs. I struggle for air. With my good hand, I push up, muscles threatening to give out under the extreme weight.

The bricks and beams slide off, and I cough, choking on the dust.

The mare shrieks and twists beneath my other hand, trying to right itself.

I keep squeezing until its cries stop, and the body goes limp.

"Kid? Trip?"

"I'm okay!" Samantha yells. Her voice is definitely outside the building. Thank God. "Trip and TJ are okay too! I got them out!"

I hack at the creature's neck, wincing with every swing until the head has separated from its body. I should burn what's left of it, but this'll do for now.

Cursing through gritted teeth, I limp through the rubble and dust. The pain is slow to subside, but at least the feeling in my cradled arm is returning. I'll have to reset a few bones so everything heals correctly.

The air tastes like blood and grime. The hazy outline of a slim female appears ahead of me. Samantha. Trip and TJ lie nearby.

"You could've gotten yourself killed pulling that stunt," I snap, hobbling over to Trip.

"And you could be a little grateful. You're welcome, by the way." Samantha pushes my hand away when I reach out to check his pulse. "I already checked them. They're alive." She frowns at me. "Are you going to be okay?"

"Next time, listen to me. The mare could've killed you—"

"But it didn't. And it's not like you had a plan."

"I *did* have a plan," I growl. "I just didn't share it because the mare would've heard."

"Well, how was I supposed to know that!" She plops down next to me, fiddling with her sleeve. "I'm glad you're alive," she murmurs. "When you were under...it looked painful. *Really* painful."

I grip her shoulder with my good hand. "I'm fine, kid. I'll heal."

"That's not what I meant." She pokes one of the bones bulging unnaturally in my forearm.

"Ow!" I cradle my wrist, glaring. And people think *I'm* rude.

Her smile disappears. "Did you see the horse and ride into the lake?"

"No, worse." The old kitchen floats into view, then a frowning Alice. I cringe, shaking off the memory. The house transforms into its usual neglected state. I've got more than enough properties around the country. Maybe it's time I let go of this one. Let someone else have a chance at happiness there. I couldn't do right by Alice and Lisa, but I could for Samantha. She's certainly proven herself deserving. "Kid, about you and TJ..."

Trip coughs.

Well, so much for that conversation.

He pulls off his glasses and sits up slowly. The side of his face is blue-black, and his shirt is ripped and stained with blood but not enough to worry me. Martha, however...

He squints at the building. A couple of beams snap in half, and another section of the structure collapses. "Oh my..."

"The mare's dead. Samantha got you and the boy

out. How are you doing?"

"I'll be better after a gin and tonic, but nothing's broken, only bruised, which is more than I can say for you, Charlie." He grunts, struggling until Samantha helps him to his feet. "I suppose you'd like me to help you set your bones?"

"If you don't mind."

He pats Samantha's hand, smiling. "You have mine and my wife's thanks, dear. And Charlie's, too. Even if he'll never admit it."

TJ groans, turning onto his side.

"You're awake!" Samantha drops down beside him and throws her arms around him.

He blinks at me and Trip. "Should I not be? What's going on? Who're you?"

"It's a long story." Samantha helps him up.

Crickets begin to chirp in the distance. I smile at the small sign of life. Of things returning to normal.

"Thanks for everything. I've got it from here." Samantha puts TJ's arm around her neck. She turns, slowly guiding him toward one of the buildings.

"Where are you going? At least let us patch you up!" Trip calls.

She glances at us over her shoulder then at TJ, whose stomach rumbles.

"Will we get something to eat?" he asks. "I can't remember the last time I ate…or anything, really."

"Don't worry; we'll get you something," I say. "Probably best if you two hang around for a few days."

Samantha leads TJ back to us. She eyes me. "You're serious?"

"What? You think we'd just help you with your mare problem then send you packing? I'm not *that* mean." I start limping toward an alleyway. "So…you still plan on living in that crap heap?"

She glares. "It's not like we have another option."

"What if you did? I've got this rundown place across the state line. Nothing fancy—haven't used it in years—but it has all the basics. Be better than what you've got now, anyway."

"You want us to live there?" Samantha's voice jumps an octave.

"I've been meaning to fix it up, and you, well…" I swallow the lump in my throat. "You did good, kid, getting both of them out. Least I can do after everything."

She blinks several times. "I…think I'd like that. TJ?"

He smiles. "It would be nice to be in a house again."

"Great. Good." I turn and limp away when the silence turns awkward. "Glad we got that settled…"

Trip chuckles. "Now, what shall we do about dinner? Energy bars are a start, but TJ will need more than that."

Samantha cocks her head at her friend. "Pizza?"

He gives an enthusiastic nod.

I grin. "Pizza it is."

What's in a Name

Heather Hayden

A rough gravel path stretched before Lani, the same long walk she took from the bus stop every day. It was late, and dark, and cool. Her well-worn hoodie couldn't quite keep the autumn chill at bay. Clutching the fraying straps of her backpack, she stepped briskly down the lane, already picturing a hot cup of tea and a portal to another world—that is, the fairy tale she'd picked up earlier that day from the library.

As she left behind the thin pool of light cast by the bus stop's streetlight, Lani glanced at the moon. It was bright tonight, enough that the mica in the gravel sparkled with each step she took. She smiled. Fairy dust, her mom used to call it. Back before Mom got sick. The smile vanished.

Small creatures rustled about in the undergrowth. Somewhere in the distance, a barred owl called out. When she was younger, Lani used to repeat the call back, sometimes "talking" with an owl for an hour or more before the cold or her mother's voice chased her inside. At sixteen, after working an eight-hour Saturday shift at a local burger joint, with homework still to do before bed, Lani was too old for such childish pursuits.

The owl called again then fell silent.

Something shifted in the corner of her eye, and Lani jerked her head around, eyes widening. The movement had been too big for a fox, too low for a bird with outstretched wings. It might be a deer. But no. The shape carved in shadow was too bulky for a deer.

Bear, something small and fearful whispered, even as common sense told her that no bear had ever been spotted in this small town in southern Maine. Lani stepped back, her breath catching in her throat. Should she run? Make noise? Her hand crept into her right jeans pocket, seeking the pepper spray she always carried. It wouldn't do much good against a bear, but its cool round canister offered a slight comfort.

For a second, she caught a glimpse of eyes that glowed orange from reflected moonlight, then the creature turned and darted into the trees. The heavy thump of its paws and the crackle of dry leaves and twigs shook Lani out of her stupor and sent her dashing down the path.

Her heart slammed against her ribs in time with her racing footsteps. Despite the heavy backpack thumping against her back and her aching legs, she didn't slow down until she reached the front door. Throwing it open, she darted inside, slammed it shut, and threw the deadbolt across with a sharp gasp.

Closing her eyes, she leaned against the solid wood of the door for a moment, breathing in the calming scents of beeswax and lavender. Mom must have lit a candle earlier—they soothed her.

Soft shuffling came from the tiny kitchen, and Mom peeked out the door, her face drawn with worry. "Lani...? Is...everything okay?"

Forcing a bright smile, Lani walked over and hugged her mom. "Of course! How was your day, Mom? What did you have for lunch?"

Mom's hesitation told Lani all she needed to know. Concern swept away thoughts of the creature in the woods as she focused on a more immediate problem. "You didn't eat anything again?" Lani tried to keep her voice calm, but worry snapped the last word in half. "Mom…"

"You know these new meds—"

"Mom, you need to eat." Lani slid her backpack off and dropped it on the floor by the small table.

The tuna salad sandwich she'd left for Mom's lunch sat in the fridge next to the cream-cheese-and-tortilla pinwheels Lani had made yesterday. Pulling them out, she turned around.

Mom sat at the table, head bowed over an untouched glass of water. Her eyelids drooped, and bags hung heavy under her eyes. Dr. Frey had prescribed her meds months ago, something to help with the pain and let her sleep, but they didn't always work. Nothing did. Nothing would, until they figured out what was wrong in the first place.

Lani took a shaky breath and brought the two plates over, pasting a smile on.

"Here." She waited until Mom picked up a pinwheel and nibbled on it before taking a seat.

Mom took a sip of water then set her glass down. "You're too good to me, Lani." Her voice was thick, either from a dry throat or tears. Likely both, given her shimmering eyes. "You shouldn't have to work this hard. When your father—"

"Dad's not coming back." Lani choked down a bite of tuna salad, not wanting to continue this conversation but knowing it was inevitable, as regular as the cuckoo clock that hung on the wall.

"He will." Mom's voice was thin, as thin as her limp brown hair. She took another bite then pushed her plate away. "I need to go lie down."

"Just a little more?" Lani pleaded, but her words fell on deaf ears as Mom shuffled out of the kitchen. The next bite of tuna salad tasted like wood ash. Maybe she should have played along, just until Mom finished her dinner…no.

There was no point in encouraging her delusions. Dad wasn't coming back. He'd never planned to. If he had, he wouldn't have left in the middle of the night, taking the car and half their savings, while Mom was in the hospital.

Lani forced herself to finish the sandwich then set the plate of pinwheels in the fridge for tomorrow.

Once the dishes were washed and put away, it was time to do homework. The cuckoo clock's little bird was Lani's only company. It popped out with a sharp "coo-coo" twice before Lani finally set down her pencil and stretched. She stood and was moving toward the sink to refill her glass when a deep howl rang out from the woods.

Her heart stopped for a second, freezing her muscles until the glass felt like a heavy stone in her hand. "What was that?" she whispered, the sound of her voice giving her enough courage to move toward the sink and peek out the window.

Darkness met her gaze beyond the thin square of light left by the kitchen window. The urge to double-check the front door shivered through her bones, and she retreated to the foyer.

The door was locked and bolted firmly shut. Everything was quiet, except for the occasional hoot of an owl. Lani took a deep breath, trying not to think about the creature that had confronted her on the path on her way home. Or the fact that she would need to walk to the bus stop in the morning, same as always.

Another long howl rose, this time closer to the house. Lani darted back into the kitchen and its welcoming light, wrapping her arms around herself. That wasn't a coyote, and there weren't wolves in Maine. Maybe someone's dog had gotten loose. But she'd never heard a dog howling around here before.

Again, she peered out the window, wishing she could see whatever it was.

Something shifted just beyond the edge of the light, shadow on darker shadow. Lani's breath caught in her throat, and she gripped the edge of the sink with numb hands. Whatever it was, it was right outside.

The creature moved again, stepping into the light. Limping, actually. It favored its front left paw, and a soft whimper drifted through the glass window. It looked like a dog—maybe a Newfie?—huge and black, and clearly in pain. Lani's heart twisted in her chest. *Poor thing. Where's your owner? Maybe I better call animal control.*

As she took a step back from the window, the dog raised its head. Large eyes glowed orange, flickering almost like fire in the dim light. Its gaze seemed intelligent as it caught her eyes, almost like it was pleading for help. Another whimper reached her ears.

Animal control might not get there before the dog ran off. *Should I try to coax it inside?* Lani hesitated, but the high-pitched whine cut through her misgivings. *I can't just leave it out there.*

Lani ran for the front door. She slid the deadbolt back with a sharp *shick*, and the lock followed a split second later. Taking a deep breath, she patted the pocket with the pepper spray and stepped out, leaving the door slightly ajar—if she needed to run, she didn't want to pause to open it.

"Hey, boy," she called softly as she turned the corner of the house, not wanting to scare the dog away.

It turned its massive head in her direction, even bigger up close than it had appeared from inside the safety of her house. Heart shuddering in fear but compassion pulling her forward, she took another step, holding out one hand in a placating gesture.

"It's okay," she crooned. "I want to help you." Her gaze flicked over the dog. Thick, shiny coat; clearly well-fed—it appeared in good health, besides the injured paw or leg.

The dog took a step back. She blinked, frowning. For a second, it had almost seemed like its paws were glowing. *That's impossible.*

The dog lunged at her.

Shriek lodged in her throat, Lani dashed for the house. She wasn't fast enough. The dog's teeth latched onto her arm, yanking her off balance. She hit the ground with a thump, the air knocked straight from her lungs. Gasping, she jerked her arm.

The dog released her, sending a wave of pain down her arm. Something warm trickled along her skin, and she hissed. It'd drawn blood. Visions of doctor's visits and shots danced in her mind. *I shouldn't have come out here. This was stupid. So stupid!*

"I apologize for hurting you." The voice was deep, words almost buried in a gravelly growl.

Lani scrambled to her feet as the dog backed away. "Who's there?" Her eyes darted around, searching for whoever had spoken but never quite letting the animal leave her gaze. "Is this your dog? Please tell me he's up-to-date on his shots." A few yards separated them now. If she ran, would she make it to the front door? Lani risked a step backward.

"Wait!" The dog took a step toward her.

Using her good hand, Lani yanked out her pepper spray, squeezed the trigger, then dodged to the side and ran for the house.

A heavy weight slammed into her back, knocking the wind out of her as she hit the ground. Lani tried to scream, but there wasn't any air. Twisting, she tried to push the dog off, certain that at any moment teeth would sink into her flesh.

"Pepper spray is an interesting choice of defense against a hellhound." The voice came from directly overhead, and Lani opened one eye. All she could see was the dog, its head only inches from her own.

"Call off your dog," she choked out.

The dog shook its head. "You don't understand. *I'm* talking to you."

Lani stared. It sounded like the voice was coming from the dog. Had she hit her head? She'd have to see a doctor for that, too. The medical bills were racking up. Not to mention how worried Mom would be when she found out Lani got hurt again trying to help an injured animal. *I'm sorry, Mom. If I make it out of this alive, I'll be more careful.*

"Look, I'm sure you have questions, but can we continue this discussion inside?" The dog glanced over his shoulder. "It will be safer. For both of us."

Is it really talking, or am I hallucinating? Lani wished she could rub her aching head, but both arms were pinned by the dog's massive paws. *Let's just play along for a moment.* "Why on earth would I let a strange dog into my house after it bit me?"

"I need help. Isn't that why you came out? To help me?"

"If you wanted help, why did you bite me?"

"So we could communicate. It's only temporary, just until the wound heals."

Gritting her teeth, Lani snapped, "Who gave you the right to do that without asking permission?"

"I couldn't exactly ask your permission without biting you, now could I?" The dog laid his ears back. "I did my best to make it a small injury."

"Why *me?*"

"You're the only person who's come close enough for me to bite them." The dog stepped off her back, whimpering as he put weight on his sore leg. He glanced over his shoulder again. "Can we go inside? There's someone after me, and I'd rather not be caught in the open like this."

There was a sharp note of fear in those words, and it sent spikes of ice prickling through her skin. Lani got to her feet, slowly this time. Her arm throbbed, but curiosity was trying to bubble to the surface. She'd read countless stories of talking animals, but she had never imagined actually meeting one.

"Will you help me?" The dog's ears drooped, clearly expecting a negative response.

Lani surprised both of them by saying, "All right. But no more biting and no barking or howling or any sounds whatsoever. If Mom saw you, she'd freak out."

"She can't see me unless I let her, and you're the only one who can hear me speak. Unless I bite her as well. Which I won't," the dog hastened to add. "No more biting. I promise."

She still hesitated, but a twig snapped somewhere in the darkness of the forest, and the dog cowered away from the trees and shadows. Another whimper rose in his throat, this one filled with fear rather than pain.

Something out there had terrified this dog, and Lani didn't want to meet whatever it was. "Come on." She hurried around the house to the front door, casting the occasional glance back at the trees.

The dog trotted after her, soft whimpers accompanying each step of his injured paw.

"Shhh." Lani pushed open the front door and stepped aside to let the dog trot by. Her arm ached as she eased the door shut and locked it. "I better not regret this."

"Your assistance is appreciated." The dog followed her into the kitchen. In the tight space of the room, he seemed as big as a horse.

Sitting down, he raised his injured paw. "I stepped on something sharp earlier today. You humans leave a lot of trash lying about in the woods."

"It's illegal to dump, but yeah, people do it anyway."

Lani fetched the first-aid kit from the bathroom, pausing outside Mom's room. Gentle snores told her that her mother was asleep. That was one concern out of the way, at least. Whether or not Mom could see the dog, Lani talking to herself would be more than enough cause for alarm.

She came back in to find the dog nosing the fridge open. "What are you doing?"

"There's food in there."

"Not for you." In the light of the kitchen, the wound on her forearm really wasn't that bad, more a deep scratch than a puncture. Wincing, Lani rinsed it in the sink with warm water and soap then dried and bandaged it. Some ibuprofen would be nice, but she'd taken the last two earlier that month and hadn't had time to pick up more.

The dog was still sitting patiently with one paw raised. As Lani approached, she sniffed the air and glanced at the stove. "Is something burning?" Nothing was on the stove, and it was off. The toaster had died two months ago, so it wasn't that.

A quiet whimper came from the dog. "Your floor is wood. I'm suppressing my fire, but I can only do so much."

Lani glanced at the floor as he shifted his paws and realized there were scorch marks in the wood. She drew in a sharp breath. "You can't go about burning people's floors! Mom's going to kill me." She ushered the hellhound to the bathroom and into the tiny shower stall. It was barely big enough, but at least the metal base would be more burn-resistant. Plus, the detachable shower hose would let her wash the dog's wound out easier than she'd have been able to at the kitchen sink.

The second she turned the water on, the dog bounded out of the shower, bowling her over. She landed on her butt, almost smacking her head on the sink, and dropped the shower head, which started spraying water everywhere. Muttering a curse, she yanked the handle to the off position and glared at the dog. "What was that about?"

"I hate water. Hellhound, remember?"

"I can't bandage your paw unless the wound gets rinsed out."

The dog looked from her to the shower and back again. "You are certain it is necessary?"

"Are you going to *melt* if you get wet?" Lani asked, half sarcastic, half serious.

A slow shake of his head as his ears laid flat on his head.

"Well?" She gestured toward the shower, wincing as the scent of smoke reached her nose again.

With a quiet clack of claws, the dog hopped into the shower again, all but tiptoeing around the small puddles of water. "Make it quick."

Lani pulled on the medical gloves she'd grabbed from the first-aid kit and laid a towel down for any inevitable splashes. Then she grabbed the dog's paw.

Yanking her hand back, she blew on her fingers. "You're hot!"

"Hell. Hound." The dog blinked at her, curling back his lips. A glint of teeth. "I can't keep my flames suppressed forever. Hurry up, would you?"

"I've half a mind to kick you out of here," Lani muttered, but it was half-hearted. Hellhound or not, the dog was injured, and she couldn't just send him away in hopes someone else would help him. She turned the water on low and grabbed his paw again. The fur and flesh were cooler this time, and she turned the paw over gently to get a look at the cut. It was crusted with dried blood and dirt, making it difficult to see how deep the actual wound was.

"This might hurt," she warned then began running warm water over the wound.

A soft growl was the only response.

It took some time, but eventually she got the wound

cleaned. It bled slowly, leaving a red trail down to the shower drain, while she prepared the bandages and antiseptic. She looked up just as the dog was about to lick it. "Don't you dare!"

"It hurts," the dog whined.

"I know, but licking it will mean I'll have to wash it again." Lani picked up the paw and dried it off with a towel, grimacing as the red stain soaked through. "I'll have to hide this in my laundry, or Mom will want to know what happened," she murmured to herself as she set it aside and grabbed the gauze.

"Are your...flames going to burn through this?" she asked, unwinding a length of stretchy fabric.

"I will suppress them if it is necessary." The hellhound twisted his head and sniffed the gauze. "What is it?"

"A protective bandage. It'll help keep the wound clean." Lani began wrapping the dog's paw.

Once done, she let the dog jump out of the shower, rinsed down the stall, and bundled the towels together. Looking down at herself—soaked, stained, and sore—she sighed. "I'm going to go change. Stay in the shower—wait, no. You better come with me." Mom usually slept through Lani's late-night showers, but they'd made enough of a racket she didn't want to risk her mother walking in on a giant dog, even if he did claim to be invisible.

Leaving the dog standing on a damp towel in her bedroom, Lani took some clothes to the bathroom and changed. She returned to find the dog curled up on the towel, asleep.

Her room wasn't huge, but the dog's bulk took up a good part of her floor. She reached out then hesitated, not wanting to touch the sleeping animal. "Hey." She repeated herself a bit louder after there was no response. "Hey."

"I need sleep," the dog grumbled, but he raised his

head. "What is it?"

"I bandaged your paw, but I didn't say you could stay here."

"Should I walk about the forest, ruining your efforts?" The dog's ears had a tilt to them that somehow conveyed amusement alongside his tone. "I won't set your house on fire while I'm sleeping, if that's what you're worried about."

Lani bit her lip then shook her head and turned out the light. "Fine, but you need to go first thing in the morning, paw or no paw. If Mom catches you in here, we're both toast." Despite her warning, a slight smile tugged at her lips. She'd always wanted a dog. Too bad they couldn't afford to keep one. Vet bills, kibble, everything else a pet needed—they didn't have the funds for that, not when she could barely keep food on the table for themselves.

The thought of food reminded Lani of the dog's interest in the fridge earlier. With a groan, she went back to the kitchen, pulled out the plate of pinwheels, and brought it to the room.

"Here," she said, flicking on the light and setting the plate down near the dog's head. "Wait, are some foods poisonous to hellhounds?"

"Of course not." The dog licked up several pinwheels at once, making short work of the leftovers. He snorted, licking his chops. "No meat?"

"Sorry," Lani said, but her heart wasn't really in it. Rubbing her eyes, she turned out the light again and slipped into bed. *I'm going to wake up, and this will all be a weird dream.*

***

Sunlight stabbed Lani's retinas as she opened her eyes, and she winced. How had she slept so late? And on a workday, too. Grabbing her phone, she checked for her alarm. It was off. Had she turned it off in her sleep? Muttering a curse, Lani staggered out of bed. Her arm ached, and she rubbed it absently, freezing when her fingers touched the bandage wrapped against her skin.

"It's about time you woke up." The deep voice, almost a growl, vibrated down her spine. "Your mother has been walking around the house. She even knocked on your door once. I was worried she was going to come in. I might be invisible, but I'm not a ghost."

This can't be happening, Lani thought, even as her eyes dragged themselves up from the bandage to the massive black shape crammed in one corner of the room beside her tiny dresser, as far from the door as possible. She sagged against her bed. *It wasn't a dream.*

"If Mom's up, you need to be quiet," she whispered. "We can't let her find you here."

"She can't hear me. I told you that already. The bond between us allows communication."

"Well, no growling or whining or barking." Lani gathered her work uniform from the dresser's cluttered surface, keeping her voice low. "I have to go to work now. Mom won't come in my room, but there's no way I can sneak you out now, and if you make a sound she might investigate. I'll let you out when I get home tonight." She winced, glancing around the room for something suitable. *I hope he's housetrained.* "I might have some old newspapers around here..."

"Hellhounds have no need for *newspaper.*" The dog's ears slanted back, and he glowered at her. "You're going to leave me here alone all day?"

"I could have left you outside last night, but you begged to stay." Lani snatched a hairband from her dresser. "Now shush. I've got to go. And no burning the carpet!"

***

Anticipation and worry skittered up and down Lani's arms like ants as she stepped off the bus. The doors hissed shut, and the bus rumbled away in a burst of acrid exhaust, leaving her alone at the end of her lane.

Squaring her shoulders, she marched down the road. It had been a shorter shift today, and the sun was still high enough to let her see the path. Gravel and dry leaves crunched under her feet, and wood smoke tickled her nose. Their neighbor, Mr. Milton, waved from his porch. She waved back but kept walking, not in the mood to chat today, even with their kind old neighbor.

Mom was asleep in her bedroom when Lani arrived home, but the sandwich Lani had left in the fridge was gone. Breathing a sigh of relief, she rushed to her room.

The hellhound raised his head as she walked in. "Finally. What took you so long?"

Lani resisted the sudden impulse to throw her backpack at him. "I had to work. I guess they don't do that where you come from, but here, it's the only way to make sure Mom and I have a roof over our heads and food on the table."

"Food?" The slightly plaintive yet hopeful note in the dog's voice poked at Lani's conscience. Of course the snack she'd given him yesterday wouldn't have been enough for a dog that big. Thankfully, she'd thought ahead.

Reaching into her backpack, she pulled out a bulging paper sack. "I figured you'd probably prefer just the meat, so I snagged some burgers for you on my way out. They're almost expired, but I didn't think hellhounds would get indigestion."

Almost before she had finished talking, the dog had leapt to his feet and stepped forward, nosing the paper.

"There's no fillers or anything. It's local. Well,

localish." She upended the bag onto the plate from the previous night. "Bon appétit. Once you're done, you can leave."

The dog gulped down a bite and raised his head. "Would it be possible for me to stay a little longer?" He held up his bandaged paw and gave a soft whine. "It still hurts a lot."

She narrowed her eyes at him. "You promised."

"Actually, I never did."

"And even if he had, you can't expect a hellhound to keep a promise." A rich, deep voice, chocolate to the dog's gravel, came from the doorway of Lani's bedroom.

She whirled around, heart stopping at the sight of a tall man dressed in a black suit standing only a few feet away. "Who are you? What are you doing here?" Lani took a step back, raising her hands defensively. *Did I forget to lock the front door? I should have double-checked.*

The man straightened his tie, a startling splash of crimson against midnight. "No need for formalities. I'm here for my dog."

A low growl came from the hellhound's direction. The man's gaze turned toward the dog, and in that moment, Lani realized his eyes were the same bright orange as the hellhound's. Whoever this was, he wasn't human.

Lani stumbled back a step, the familiar press of her mattress against her legs less of a comfort than she might have hoped for. "I-I found him outside last night. He was injured. I just bandaged his paw..."

"Did you now?" The man threw a sharp look at her before studying the bandaged limb. "It seems you did. Interesting. I suppose your lack of screaming and general hysteria indicate that he bit you as well?"

Lani's hand flew to the bandage on her arm, an odd surge of protectiveness running through her. "Yes."

His fingers combed through raven-black hair, which

fell back in perfect order. "Well, then. Let's fix that." He snapped his fingers.

"Wai—" The hellhound's voice cut out in a sharp whimper, and the dog backed away.

The ache that had been nipping at her arm all day faded, and Lani tugged down the bandage to find the wound gone. Not even a scar remained.

Rather than pleasure, a wave of fear slammed against her chest, knocking the breath from her lungs. Not only was this man not human, but he was clearly powerful and in a dangerous way. Where had he come from? Her gaze darted to the hellhound. The obvious answer was the most terrifying one.

"What do you mean, you don't want to come?" The man glared at the dog. "You don't have a choice in the matter."

Lani studied the dog's hunched posture, flattened ears, drooping head. He'd said he was running from someone. Had it been this man? Granted, she didn't know much about hellhounds, but she'd seen dogs act like this before. Dogs that had been abused. Her teeth ground together. *Don't get involved, Lani. Whatever is going on here, it's not part of normal reality. Just let them go, and forget about it.*

But she couldn't. *Hellhound or not, no one deserves that kind of treatment.* Squaring her shoulders, she took a step forward, her breath squeaking in her throat as she moved between the dog and the man. "He doesn't want to go with you."

The man gave her a look of dark amusement. "Is that so? And what can you do about it?"

"I…" Her voice shook, but she dug her fingernails into her palms. "I won't let you take him."

The man laughed out loud. Lani winced, thinking of Mom, sleeping peacefully in the next room. If she woke up and walked in on this strange meeting…

"How interesting. Humans don't tend to act so calmly around demons."

So he is a demon. Lani's mouth went dry. *What was I thinking, confronting him like this?*

A soft whimper from the hellhound gave her the courage to stand her ground, albeit on shaky legs.

"You're amusing." The man smirked. "And I have little use for a hellhound who shuns his duty. So I'll give you a chance to win him from me."

Never deal with the devil. The snatch of song, of warning, echoed in Lani's mind even as her mouth shaped a single word: "How?"

The man grinned broadly. "Judging by the reading material scattered about this room, you have a liking for fairy tales. So I will make this simple. If you can figure out his name, he can remain with you."

"His...name?" Lani's stomach dropped as she realized she'd never even asked the dog if he had a name. She rubbed her arm. Asking would be easy enough, once he bit her again.

The man's smile sharpened, as toothy as a shark's and just as terrifying. "Once I leave, he's more than welcome to bite you again, but—" he turned to the dog "—if you so much as breathe a clue as to your name, our deal's void, and I'll collect her soul immediately. Do you understand?"

The dog whined and nodded his head.

"My soul?" Lani's mouth fell open.

"Ah, yes. Can't be a wager without you laying something on the table as well. So what will it be? Are you a heroine or a coward?"

Lani hesitated, glancing at the hellhound. "All I have to do is guess his name? That's it?"

"Yes."

"Is this some kind of three guesses, three days deal? Like *Rumplestiltskin*?"

"You can have as many guesses as you like, and you've got twenty-four hours to make them."

"Twenty-four? But the queen in *Rumplestiltskin* got three days!"

"Yes, she did, but you are no more a queen than I am a wizened old imp. I hold the power here, so I make the rules. Now, what will it be?"

Lani glanced at the dog then back at the demon. This couldn't be happening. Not to her. She was just a waitress, a nobody, a girl desperately trying to make ends meet.

She was also the hellhound's only chance at escaping this man who more and more struck her as someone who shouldn't have any kind of power over anyone.

The demon smirked. "Let's sweeten the deal a little more, shall we? How's dear old Mom doing? Not well, is it? Doctors don't know what's wrong, they just say there's nothing to be done? Only a few years left to wither away until she dies?"

Lani choked, her fingers curling into fists. "Leave her out of this!"

"Ah, but I don't think you want me to do that. After all, I know exactly what ails her. Better yet, I can cure her just as easily as I fixed your arm." He snapped again in demonstration. "So what do you say? Figure out his name, and not only do you win him from me, but you also win your mother's good health."

Could he really do it? A thin needle of hope poked at Lani's hesitation. She glanced at the hellhound again. He gave a slight nod, as if answering her unspoken question. In an instant, the needle became a hammer, smashing at the defenses she'd built up since the first time a doctor uttered the word "terminal."

"I accept the terms," she whispered.

"Wonderful!" The man clapped his hands. "Guess away all you like, and I'll be back when you guess right...or your time is up."

Then he vanished. No puff of smoke, no flash of light, no evil cackle. Just there one moment, then gone the next.

Lani's legs gave out, and she crumpled to the floor, choking as she tried to convince her frozen lungs to breathe. Shivers ran down her body, and she hugged her knees to her chest. It took a drip of water on her arm to realize she was crying.

A soft muzzle nudged her arm.

Wiping her eyes, she looked at the hellhound. "What are we going to do?"

He touched her arm again.

Grimacing, she held it out. "Please be gentler this time."

Even knowing what was coming, it still hurt. She gasped as his teeth scraped her flesh, yanking her arm back to cradle it as soon as he released his grip.

"Why did you agree?" Surprise and sorrow held equal weight in the dog's voice. "Why would you risk your soul like that?"

"Mom's dying," Lani said quietly. "If there's a chance to save her..."

The unspoken question hung in the air: if the demon hadn't brought Mom into the deal, would she have still accepted his offer?

Lani busied herself in taking a smaller sack from her backpack—she'd grabbed a burger with the works for herself. After placing her backpack by the bed, she gathered her pajamas with shaking fingers. "I'm going to go change."

"Wait—"

She shut the bedroom door on the hellhound's protest and hurried to the bathroom, practically diving into the shower. After drying and dressing on autopilot, she stared at herself in the bathroom mirror, meeting pale blue eyes that regarded her in shock. Why, indeed. What had she been thinking?

"Lani?" The soft call from Mom's room grounded her even as it filled her with more anxiety.

Brushing damp hair out of her face, she hung her towel and dropped her work uniform outside her room before knocking gently on Mom's door. *Please don't let her have heard anything.*

"Mom?"

"Come in."

Lani opened the door. Mom smiled weakly from where she lay in bed, both of their comforters piled over her thin frame. "How was work?"

"Fine. I brought a burger home, would you like it?"

Mom shook her head. "I'm not hungry." A cough rattled in her chest, and she fumbled for an empty glass on the nightstand.

Lani took it to refill and came back in with some crackers as well. "You need to eat something, Mom."

"You're such a good girl. What would I do without you?" Mom nibbled on a saltine before sipping some water.

What would she do? Lani's heart squeezed in her chest. Her agreement with the demon affected Mom as well. If she couldn't guess the hellhound's name in time, Mom would be left all alone. Tears stung her eyes. *Did I make a mistake?*

Her gaze fell on the picture frame resting on Mom's nightstand. The two of them stood wreathed in sunshine on a beach, waves frolicking behind them as they waved at the camera. Mom looked perfect in that frozen image—tanned skin, bright eyes, no sign of the illness that would strike only a few years later.

"Lani?" Mom's brow furrowed. "Is everything okay?"

She forced a smile and turned toward the door. "Everything's fine, Mom. I'll see you in the morning."

And in the meantime, I have a bet to win.

***

Lani's secondhand laptop whirred softly as she booted it up. The hellhound was curled up beside her bed, quiet after repeated attempts to speak with her failed. There was nothing he could tell her to help win this wager, and she needed to focus on the task at hand.

A quick search brought up plenty of entries related to hellhounds. Lani took a deep breath. "Okay," she whispered. "Let's figure out what your name is."

"I can't give you any hints." The hellhound's ears flattened against his head.

"That's fine. I'll try everything I can find...Cerberus?"

No response. Lani sighed. "I guess it was too much to hope it would be the first guess I made." She kept scrolling down the list of black dogs in folklore. "How about Barghest? Or Moddey Dhoo?"

Still no reaction. Lani took a sip of water from the glass she'd taken from the kitchen and settled in. This was going to be a long night.

***

Lani's throat was sore and her mouth parched, despite all the water she'd drunk. Her eyes burned from staring at a computer screen for so long, and her head ached from staying up all night. As much as her body longed for sleep, she refused to give in. Every second ticking past was another one closer to the deadline. *Or should that be soulline, since my soul's at stake?* She shook her head at herself and opened another tab of dog names to try. It was already six— she'd have to get ready for school soon. Or ditch.

"Locke? Barnes? Rogan?"

The hellhound shook his head and stretched, a quiet sizzle coming from the carpet as it fought in vain against the dog's hot claws. Lani wrinkled her nose at the smell of scorched cloth. "Watch the fire!"

"You're never going to guess it." The hellhound's voice was heavy with defeat as he sat back down on his freshly dampened towel.

Lani clenched her hands in her blankets, trying to hide their trembling. "I'm sure I'll stumble upon it eventually."

"You've tried thousands of names. Some of them are ridiculous—who would name their dog McRoger? There's only twelve hours left."

"I can't just—"

A thump came from down the hall. Lani flew out of bed, nearly tripping over the hellhound in her haste. "Mom?"

She darted out of the room to find her mother sprawled in the hallway. Mom's pale pink pajamas looked like a splash of paint against the darker wood. "Mom!" Her mother didn't stir, and Lani's heart slammed against her ribs. *No, not now, not now.* "Mom!"

Falling to her knees, Lani shook her mother's shoulder. "Mom? Can you hear me?"

"Lani…" Mom whispered, struggling to open her eyes. "I'm okay, just feeling a little weak today…"

"We should take you to the hospital—"

"No." Mom grabbed Lani's wrist. "Please, no. There's no need. I'm fine." She pushed herself up with her arm, fingers digging into Lani's flesh as she moved. A sharp hiss came from her lips, and she tried to stand but stumbled again.

Lani managed to cradle her, stop the fall from being more than a gentle return to the floor, but fear cracked her voice as she insisted, "The hospital. We have to. The doctor said if you have trouble moving—"

"I know what she said." Mom waved her hand then rubbed her temple. "Please, Lani. I'll be fine, just let me rest a moment. How about...how about you get me some crackers from the kitchen?"

Lani did as she asked but ducked into her room for her cell phone on the way back.

"Is something wrong?" The hellhound looked from her to the door. "Your mother?"

"Stay here. Stay quiet," Lani snapped. "I have to help her."

The hellhound backed away and sat again, head hunched down. She didn't have time to reassure him, wouldn't even know what to say. Each thud of her heart echoed the ticking timer in her mind, but winning the wager wouldn't do any good if... Lani shook that thought away and dialed Mr. Milton's number.

***

The drive to the hospital usually took fifteen minutes. Mr. Milton made it in less than ten. Lani helped Mom out of the car, and Mr. Milton insisted on helping escort her inside.

Rosie, the receptionist, picked up the phone the second she saw them. "Dr. Frey to examination room three." She repeated the message then hung up and gestured to a nearby nurse. "Alyson, show them to examination room three."

The pretty blond did as requested.

"Go home with Mr. Milton," Mom insisted once she had settled herself on a chair.

"Mom, I can't just leave you—"

"Go." Mom narrowed her eyes. "The doctor will be

here shortly, and there'll probably be a battery of tests. You have school today, young lady, and I won't have you missing classes just because I had a little fall."

"I'm not leaving!" Lani bit her lip. In the stark white light of the fluorescents, Mom looked even frailer than usual. *I should have done a better job making sure she ate. She's too weak; that's why she fell. This is all my fault.*

"Go." Mom raised a trembling hand and pointed at the door. "Please don't argue, Lani. I don't have the energy for it."

Lani shuffled forward and gave her a hug. "I love you, Mom."

"I love you, too, Lani." Mom leaned forward to hug her back and slipped off the chair. Her eyes slid shut as she collapsed on the floor.

"Mom? Mom!" Lani shook her mom's shoulder, but there was no response. She looked up at Mr. Milton, panic squeezing her chest. "Can you find Dr. Frey?"

He opened the door, but the doctor rushed in, taking in the scene in a glance.

Dr. Frey yanked her comm from her pocket as she moved to kneel by Mom. "I need a stretcher in examination room three." After tucking away the comm, she took Mom's pulse. "We'll get her settled in Room 104. Mr. Milton, I know you're her emergency contact, but I think it's best if only family comes with us right now."

"All right." He rested a hand on Lani's shoulder. "I'll go pick up breakfast for you."

She was grateful he didn't ask what she'd like. Food was the last thing on her mind right then.

Two nurses arrived with a stretcher, and Mom was gently lifted onto it. Lani followed them through the stark white halls to the hospital room. Once Dr. Frey and the nurses had gotten Mom settled, she asked Lani to go to the waiting room while they ran some tests.

Pacing back and forth, Lani wrung her hands with worry. The clock ticking over Rosie's desk only made matters worse, reminding her with each quiet click that she was losing time to win the wager. *I never should have agreed to it.* A thought occurred to her. *Did he have something to do with her collapse?* Tears stung her eyes. *This is all my fault.*

"Lani?" Rosie gave her a sympathetic smile. "Dr. Frey will see you in Room 104 now."

Lani dashed through the hospital, sneakers squeaking as she skidded around each corner until she reached the right door. She took a deep breath of disinfectant-laced air before knocking on Room 104's door.

Dr. Frey opened it and gestured her inside. "She's sleeping right now, so please keep your voice low," she whispered.

Mom lay on a hospital bed, the needle in her arm attached to a fluid bag on a stand. A monitor nearby beeped steadily, its green light darting up and down in a thin, zigzag pattern. Lani squeezed her fists tight, wanting desperately to run forward and touch her face, hug her, anything to reassure herself that her mom was still alive.

"We gave her something for the pain," Dr. Frey murmured. "But the prognosis isn't good. She has two, maybe three days left. We've done everything we can."

Every word was a quiet hammer, chipping away at Lani's heart.

"There has to be something!" Lani insisted, her broken whisper ending in a soft whimper. A shudder ran through her body, and she hugged herself tightly. She couldn't fall apart. Not now. Mom needed her. Hot tears dripped down her cheeks. *I can't leave her like this. But the wager...it's her only hope. Our only hope.*

"I'm sorry." Dr. Frey took a step toward the door. "I'll be back to check on her in a few hours. You're welcome to stay as long as you like."

Unable to pull herself away, Lani settled onto the chair beside the bed. A knock came at the door a moment later. She opened it and found Mr. Milton there, carrying a small paper sack.

"How is she?" he asked quietly. His solemn gaze said he'd already spoken to Dr. Frey.

Lani sighed and shook her head. "I'll probably stay here today. Thank you for the ride."

"I got this for you." He held out the bag. "Nothing fancy—an omelet and some French toast sticks. I'll pick up something for you to eat later before I head home. Is there anything you want?"

Catching sight of a furry black head peeking around the corner of the hall, Lani bit back a gasp and focused on Mr. Milton's question. "Maybe a burger?" She ruffled through her pockets, searching for cash that wasn't there. "I can pay you back once I get my wallet—"

"No need." Mr. Milton waved the offer away. "I'll be back in about an hour."

Lani stood in the doorway, watching him head down the hall until he turned the corner.

The hellhound darted over and slipped by her, walking straight to the bed. His claws clicked against the smooth linoleum.

"Watch it," she whispered, closing the door. "And how did you get inside? Animals aren't allowed in the hospital." Despite her worry, a stir of hope lightened her mood. With him here, she still had a chance to win. And she didn't have to leave Mom's side to do it.

"No one will see me." The dog sniffed the air. "Is that meat?"

Lani unwrapped the omelet and set it on the floor. "Here. I think it's ham and cheese." Her aching stomach convinced her to eat something, so she took a small bite of French toast as she settled into the chair.

The hellhound turned toward the bed, ignoring the food. He sniffed again, deeper. "She doesn't have long." The words were so quiet, she almost missed them in her chewing.

Lani swallowed twice, the bread catching in her throat. "What?"

"Her soul scent. It's growing stronger."

"What's a soul scent?"

"Hellhounds can smell people's souls. It's one of our many talents." He sounded proud of the fact then sobered. "Every living soul has its own unique scent that grows stronger as the person approaches death. Your mom—"

"You don't know what you're talking about," Lani cut him off. "She's going to be fine. I'll find your name, and then the demon will heal her." She pushed aside the paper carton, appetite gone.

"Marbas wouldn't have made the wager if he thought you would win."

"I won't lose!" Lani's voice echoed from the walls of the small hospital room, and she winced, glancing at Mom. Her mother didn't stir. "I won't lose," she repeated in a whisper, swallowing against the lump still caught in her throat. Tears pressed against her eyelids, but she blinked them back and pulled out her phone. 6:47 AM. A little over ten hours until the demon returned.

The dog licked up the omelet then lay down by the chair and rested his head on his paws. He didn't say anything. He didn't have to. *Her soul scent is getting stronger...* Lani shook the words away and connected her phone to the hospital's wifi.

"You said his name was Marbas?"

The hellhound's ears drew back. "It's not a hint."

"I know you wouldn't risk that." Lani typed the demon's name into the search box anyway, morbid curiosity getting the better of her.

Marbas. A high-ranking demon with various abilities,

from shapeshifting to teaching medical arts. The latter of which included the power to cure diseases—or cause them.

Lani drew in a sharp breath. "Do you think he caused Mom's illness?"

"I don't know. Does it matter if he did?"

"Not really." The end result would still be the same if she failed. Lani ran a search for demonic names, deciding to try a different tactic. People named dogs after angels sometimes, so maybe demons used a similar method.

In a voice just above a whisper, she began reading out names. It gave her something to focus on, even if it couldn't drown out the beeping monitor and Mom's quiet, measured breaths. The hellhound didn't move or make another sound.

When Mr. Milton returned, Lani's throat was dry. Her eyes were not. He handed her a box of tissues, a plastic bag of takeout and a few snacks, and a four-pack of ginger ale.

"If you need anything, *anything* at all, you call me," he said, patting her shoulder gently. "Got it?"

She nodded, unable to speak. Tears started leaking again, and he gave her one more pat.

"I'm sorry, Lani. I truly am. Your mother is a wonderful woman, and she's lucky to have a daughter as lovely as you."

Lani shuffled back to her seat after he left and set everything down on the floor.

The hellhound sniffed curiously at the bag then glanced at the bed. "She's awake."

"Mom?" Lani rushed to the bedside and clasped one of her mom's hands in her own. "Mom, I'm here."

Mom squeezed her hand gently. "Oh, Lani. Thank goodness. I had the most awful dream." She lifted her head a little and looked around the room. "Is Dr. Frey here?"

"Not yet. She said she'd be back in an hour or so."

Lani patted her mom's hand. "You should rest. I'll be right here, I promise."

"Did you speak with the doctor?" Mom's voice was tight, and sorrow etched wrinkles around her soft blue eyes.

"Dr. Frey said..." Lani choked on the words.

"I only have a few days." Mom closed her eyes and lay back against the pillows. "I'll call Clary later. Once I've rested a bit. I spoke to her a few months ago, and she agreed to take you in if..." Her voice caught and trailed off.

Aunt Clary? Mom's sister, who lived two towns over and never visited? Lani wasn't even sure she remembered what the woman looked like. "I don't want to live with Aunt Clary," Lani whimpered. "I want to go home with you."

Mom blinked and raised her hand, stroking Lani's cheek. "You look exhausted, dear. Try to get some sleep. I'll rest too."

"Yes, Mom." Lani stood, holding Mom's hand until it went limp in slumber. She set it gently on the bed and retreated to her chair, shaking from the sobs she was holding at bay.

The hellhound's orange gaze met hers for a moment before shifting to the floor. He huddled against the chair.

Her phone's clock warned her that it was almost nine. Eight hours left. Eight hours before she failed and lost her soul and left Mom to die alone in this sterile hospital room. Lani scrubbed away her tears and kept going through name lists. Everything, anything she could find that might be remotely right.

None proved correct.

Mom didn't stir again, even when Dr. Frey popped in now and then to see how she was doing. Lani went through half a box of tissues and most of the ginger ale. She gave the takeout to the hellhound, who licked the Styrofoam clean while his ears remained tilted toward her quiet voice.

Time swept by all too fast and all too slow at the

same time. Her phone beeped a warning as the alarm she had set went off. 5:00 PM. Lani's breath caught in her throat, and she sped up, whispering word after word as quickly as she could. She wasn't sure exactly when the demon would appear, but she couldn't waste a single second.

Between one blink and the next, her phone shut down.

"Out of battery?" Marbas's mocking voice asked. "No, I think you're out of time."

"She has five more minutes!" The hellhound leapt to his feet, fur bristling. "No cheating."

"I'm a demon. What do you expect?" Marbas walked over to the hospital bed as Lani sat frozen in her chair. He leaned over Mom and gave a small sniff. "That soul's on its way out, it looks like. How interesting." He turned to Lani with a sardonic smile. "Judging by your face, you know this already. So how about a little trade, since you failed to win our wager? I'll release your soul from the bargain in exchange for hers, and she won't have to suffer through the last few painful days she has left."

"What? No!" Lani shook her head, dropping her phone on the chair and jumping to her feet. "You can't have her!"

The hellhound growled beside her.

"Too bad. Her soul has so much more flavor than your young one." The demon breathed in deeply through his nose before releasing a great sigh. "Ahhhh. It's been quite the day. But now it's time to say farewell."

"Three minutes," the hellhound snapped.

"She's had twenty-four hours. It's unlikely she'll come up with your name in three minutes." Marbas chuckled. "You must regret not letting me take him now. Wagering your soul on a hellhound who ran away—isn't he nothing to you compared to dear old Mom? How does it feel, knowing you traded away your chance to spend your mother's last moments with her?"

Lani gritted her teeth. She would not cry in front of him. She would not give him the pleasure of seeing her heart break.

"Well, it's been fun, but look at the time! We really must be going." Marbas held out his arm like a man asking a woman to dance. "Come along, now."

"Lani…" Mom's brow was furrowed, and her eyes twitched beneath her eyelids. "Lani, no…" she whispered again.

"Ah, it seems like she's having a bit of nightmare. Something about her little daughter's soul being eaten by a demon—"

With a strangled yell, Lani shoved him away from the bed. "Leave her alone!" She gasped in a breath, tasting iron and salt and a hint of ginger. Her head ached, her chest ached…but for a moment, her mind was clearer than it had been since she met the hellhound, anger chasing away the exhaustion and fear and hurt. Chasing it all away, just enough for her churning thoughts to settle for one bright second. *Isn't he nothing to you?* The demon's voice echoed in her mind.

He'd been toying with her, all along. *The hellhound never had a name, did he?*

"You'll regret that." Marbas smirked, brushing off his coat as though she had soiled it.

What more do I have to lose? Lani took a deep breath and turned to the hellhound, holding out her hand. "Your name is Cerberus."

"What?" The hellhound cocked his head, confused. "That was the first name you tried, remember?"

"What are you playing at?" The demon almost sounded worried.

Lani turned to him, still holding out her hand to the dog. "Demons are always cocky in fairy tales. And they always wind up making a mistake."

"Excuse me?" Marbas raised an eyebrow and folded his arms, cockiness returning to his voice. "I never make mistakes."

"But you did. He isn't *nothing* to me. *You* treated him as nothing—no wonder he ran away. You never even gave him a name, so I'm giving him one now." Lani smiled as the demon's eyes widened. "He's Cerberus. The dog of the underworld, who is going to tear your throat out if you don't leave us be *at once*."

Marbas stared at her. "You dare threaten me? You have no idea the forces you are playing with, little girl—"

"You lost your wager," Lani cut him off. "And if you won't leave the easy way, you'll leave the hard way." With a trembling thread of confidence, she commanded, "Sic him, Cerberus."

The hellhound rushed forward, but Marbas vanished, reappearing on the other side of the room. He gave a short, mocking bow. "It seems I've been beaten this time. You'd best hope we don't cross paths again." The demon snapped his fingers and disappeared.

Lani drew in a shaky breath, unsure if she wanted to laugh, or cry, or both.

Cerberus came over and nudged her hand. "You figured it out." He sounded equal parts shocked and amazed. "I'm..." He hesitated. "Thank you." The words were a soft, hesitant growl, almost like he had never said them before.

Before she could respond, Mom called from the bed, "Lani!"

"I'm here!" Lani ran over and grabbed Mom's hand, laughing and crying all at once. "I'm here, Mom. I promise. And I'm not going anywhere."

"Neither am I," Cerberus said, pressing his soft bulk against her leg.

Mom squeezed her hand, a tear slipping down her

cheek. "I had another awful nightmare, but then at the end... Oh, Lani. I'm so glad you're okay."

Lani smiled. "Of course I'm fine! How do you feel?"

"I feel..." Her mom hesitated, as though considering the question more closely, then her eyes widened. "I feel fine. Wonderful in fact. And starving." She pointed at the bag of potato chips by the chair. "Quick, let me have a few before Dr. Frey comes in here and restricts me to porridge and steamed vegetables."

Laughing, Lani kicked the bag under the chair and reached for the phone. "I think I better have them page her so she can release you. Then we can go home and have a nice dinner!"

Home. With Mom. She really was going home. Lani made the call to the front desk and managed to hang up before the tears started, but then she dove into Mom's outstretched arms.

"I'm so glad you're okay, Mom."

Mom stroked Lani's hair. "Let's have Dr. Frey check me out first, but I do feel better than I have in ages. Maybe the medicine is finally working."

Lani smiled at Cerberus, who grinned back.

"I should probably wait to reveal myself, right?" the hellhound asked.

Eyes widening, Lani gave a small nod.

Dr. Frey arrived. The first thing the doctor did was draw some blood, and once she'd sent a nurse off with the sample, she began asking Mom all sorts of questions.

"I truly feel better than I have in a long time," Mom kept insisting.

At last, Dr. Frey shook her head. "All your vital signs appear to be normal. I can't give you a clean bill of health until we've run a few more tests, but I think you can go home tonight, as long as you come back first thing in the morning. Do you need a ride?"

"I'll call Mr. Milton," Lani offered.

Mom nodded her agreement, so Lani grabbed her phone and slipped out to the parking lot to call their neighbor. Mr. Milton was delighted to hear Mom was doing better and promised to come pick them up soon. Cerberus sat quietly by Lani's side until the phone call was over.

As she tucked the phone into her pocket, the hellhound stood. "I suppose this is goodbye."

"Goodbye?" Lani stared at him. "What do you mean?"

He looked up, orange eyes somber. "I am grateful that you freed me from his service, but I shouldn't impose on your hospitality any longer."

"Where will you go?"

"I...don't know." Cerberus's ears flattened.

Lani reached down and patted his head. "How about you come live with us, then? I'm sure I can convince Mom to let you stay. Provided you don't scorch the floors too badly."

The dog's ears pricked up a little. "Are you sure?"

She nodded and was rewarded by a rough lick of an overly warm tongue. Laughing, she wiped her hand off on her jeans. "Let's go introduce you then." Lani grinned. "Come on, Cerberus."

He trotted after her, tail wagging. "I'm never going to get tired of hearing my name."

"I'm never going to get tired of saying it."

Soul of Mercy

J.E. Klimov

I noticed my first strand of white hair about a month ago. I'm only fifteen.

Since then, it has multiplied like a plague. I roll my head against the bathroom's tiled walls. Strands of snow-white hair fall over my face, but I don't want to look at them. Ever again. A chuckle escapes my lips; a sudden change in hair color means nothing in the grand scheme of things, but as a high school girl, it is my worst nightmare right now.

A knock on the door snaps me from my thoughts.

"Gabby, what're you doing in there?" my little sister whines. "I need to go potty!"

"Use Mom's bathroom." I grab a box of hair dye. After a pause, admiring the model's lush ebony hair, I hurl it at the door. "Go away!"

My sister's stomping is a hammer to my head. Groaning, I stand and study my face in the mirror once more. I used to have thick black hair, but now...it's streaked with white! I sigh. This is my second attempt at coloring my hair, but it's as if the white strands repel the dye. Since I discovered that first rogue strand, the color has spread like crazy. At this rate, I'll look like my great-grandmother by the winter dance.

Raking my nails against my scalp, I imagine all the girls at school whispering behind my back. Not that they don't do that already. My drooping left eye and corner of my left lip give them enough fodder for gossip.

"Gabrielle Flores!" my mom's voice thunders. The shuffling of her slippers grows louder with my sister's pitter-pattering filling the gaps of silence. "You've been in the bathroom for an hour!"

I sigh and gather the plastic gloves and bottles of chemicals to dump in the trash. Yanking the door open, I find my mom tapping her feet, arms crossed. I shrug.

"Mom, I—"

"You share the bathroom with your sister. You can't hog it all to yourself." She stops abruptly and wrinkles her nose. "You were coloring your hair again, weren't you? You're too young to dye your hair!"

"Gabby's in trouble, Gabby's in trouble!" My sister skips around us.

Balling my hands into fists, I hold my head high. Even though I don't feel like crying, my left eye tears up. "I was just trying to cover the white hairs."

"Oh, chicky." Mom's voice softens. "I know it's hard, but you can't play hair stylist in the bathroom." She bites her lip as her eyes trace my wet hair before reaching out to examine it. "This is unusual, but I'm sure it's not serious. It could be genetics. Father's side," she says bitterly.

Father. I try not to remember what he looks like.

After a breath, Mom regains her composure. "Just think of it as something that makes you unique."

"I'm 'unique' enough as it is."

The back of her hand traces the left side of my face. "Bell's Palsy doesn't make you a freak. And the doctor says it'll resolve in good time."

My lips crimp into a frown. Well, half-frown.

"My dear Gabby, stop trying to fight it. I know it's hard, but you've got to learn to accept yourself, or else, you'll end up isolated."

Whimpering, I push past her and charge to my room. I slam the door and fling myself onto the bed. Mom doesn't get it. My idiot sister doesn't, either. Throwing my pillow doesn't help relieve my frustration. It's tough enough to fit in as it is. I don't even like being in pictures—there are always nasty comments on Facebook.

The sizzle of the frying pan seeps upstairs. My mouth waters at something fruity. Plantains, maybe? Turning my head, I see that it's eight o'clock at night. I've already packed for school and eaten dinner. Homework? Done. Normally, I'd join my family on the couch and watch soap operas. The snacks of choice usually were potato chips if my mom felt lazy; otherwise, it's fried plantains or yucca.

But tonight, I want to be alone. I pick up my cell phone and scroll through my classmates' feeds. Julia is spending her Sunday night with her senior boyfriend. She's one of the few popular girls who's nice to everyone. Meanwhile, Yuki is at the local coffee joint, working on the musical he swears will bring him eternal fame. The edges of my lips twitch. He's adorable, but he's in a totally different social circle. Cliques suck. I yawn. Every time I blink, my lids become heavier. Did the room get warmer? Straining as the exhaustion creeps into my brain, I set my alarm for tomorrow. I collapse on my back and let myself fall into darkness.

***

12:01 A.M. The red numbers burn my eyes as I prop myself onto my elbows. I turn my head; I swear someone has just poked me on my shoulder. Fully expecting my sister, my jaw tightens at the sight of...nothing. A chill rattles down my spine, and I break into a cold sweat. It must've been a dream.

Shock forks through me like lightning when my gaze

lands on the vanity mirror. Moonlight pours through the gaps of the window blinds, lighting the room enough to expose my paralyzed face. The reflection ripples.

A scream wells in my throat. When I open my mouth, a hand wraps over my lips. Shrieking as loud as I can, I flail my limbs. Lanky arms pin me down. It's not my sister or mom. Certainly not my deadbeat father who is countries away. Panic explodes in my chest as I struggle.

"Calm down. I need you to not scream."

The voice is ethereal, but that doesn't stop me from clamping my teeth on a finger. The stranger releases me and mumbles frantically. I roll off my bed and yank my nightstand drawer open. Once I feel the handle of my kitchen knife, I leap out and brandish the blade.

"Don't touch me. I'm calling the cops!" I shout.

The same chill from earlier furrows up my spine and steals my breath away. I rub my eyes. I rub them again.

An androgynous figure stands on the other side of the room, hands up. Hair cascades in tendrils past his shoulders, but it doesn't distract from the wings that span from one wall to the other. They are feathered wings but, at the same time, translucent.

"Uh, uh…"

"I'm Brock, and I mean no harm. However, I must talk to you."

He snaps his fingers, and a yellow glow covers my hand. My blood runs cold; a pins-and-needles sensation infiltrates my palms then my fingers. I gasp when my fingers unravel one by one on their own—I have no control. Once the knife falls onto the floor, the glow fades, and I cradle my hand as I glare at him.

His irises shimmer like opal. "I'm an angel sent to reveal your new life role—"

I shake my head to break the trance of his unnaturally handsome features. "No. That's ridiculous. And what kind of angel name is *Brock*? If anything, I would think Michael, Gabriel, or Raphael."

"Gabby?" Mom's voice cracks through the air.

I freeze. If she sees this strange man in my room, she'll go berserk. I'm sure, like me, she hasn't forgotten the dark days from years past. All those break-ins. The strangers who followed my mom and me home.

My mom kicks the door open, frantically scanning my room. She clutches her cotton robe, curlers askew in her hair, eyes filling with anxiety. As soon as she spots me, she sighs. "What's going on?"

I wipe my slick palms against my pajamas. Brock has vanished into thin air. "Nothing. I had a nightmare. Large spiders. Woke up and jumped out of bed."

"Oh." Relief spreads across her face. "Well, I'm glad to know you're okay. You know I worry..."

"Yes, Mom."

She says goodnight. Her gaze lingers as she shuts the door behind her. As soon as the click sounds, I sigh.

"This is why I need you to be quiet."

I jump in place, whirling around. Brock materializes before me with his arms crossed. My head spins, and I sit on the edge of my bed. I fight for words, but nothing comes out. Panic simmers in my veins once again.

"Why do you sleep with a knife?" he asks.

Those words grate on me, but I refuse to open the box of memories. "Aren't you a celestial being? Can't you read my mind or just know automatically?"

Brock shakes his head. "There are limitations to what I'm allowed to know."

I wave my hand. "Whatever. I lived in a rough town until I was twelve. Death threats. *Bullies*... Is that enough anguish for you?" I ask forcefully, hoping it will mask the tremor in my voice.

Memories filter in my head until they land on the

night my father and mother were shouting in a cramped kitchen. I was seven and clueless about what they were shouting about. I only remember that I wanted them to stop. When my father cocked his arm at my mom, I grabbed the first thing I saw: a knife. I leaped in front of my mom and pointed the blade at him. All he did was laugh.

Of course, he didn't stick around for long, but our apartment was constantly broken into. So, as I grew up, the knife became my security blanket.

Brock studies my face. "I'm sorry," he answers softly. He bends onto one knee and takes my hand. I try to jerk away, but his grip is firm.

"Let's change the subject. Do you know why your hair is turning white?"

I suck on my teeth, silent.

"Gabrielle, you are the new Soul of Mercy."

Silence; then a frog croaks outside. The right side of my lip twitches. "What?"

The angel nods. His robe shimmers with his subtle movement.

I scan my room filled with normalcy. My backpack's zipper is near bursting from the number of books in it. My gym shorts and colorful tees create a path to the laundry basket. The stack of graphic novels in the farthest corner is probably the most "super" thing about my life. "This is pretty anticlimactic. No ceremony or animal sacrifice?"

Brock cocks his head and scratches his chin. "You have a strange imagination. No. No sacrifice, and no pomp and grandeur. However, your hair will continue to transform. A human with the grace of angels…"

"I get to blast demons away with superpowers or something?" A tickle of laughter replaces my panic, although I'm not sure what's worse. I give in and burst into a chuckle. My stomach cramps up, but every time I try to stop, I see Brock's stoic face and break into laughter once more. "Am I some descendant of a high priest? Am I a reincarnation of...of—"

"I don't see the levity in this," Brock replies, stone-faced. "This role comes with critical responsibilities. Ones that prevent the human world and the spirit world from interacting. I chose *you* for the job, and if you do nothing, chaos will befall Earth."

This is too ridiculous to be true. I'm pretty sure I'm overtired or dreaming. "Sure, okay, 'Brock.' By the way, in the human world, there's this thing called 'consent.'"

Burrowing into my sheets, I continue to giggle. The room spins around me, so I come up for air and nuzzle into my pillow.

"You can't just go to sleep on me." Brock shakes my shoulders gently.

I brush him off. "You're not real. I'm dreaming. This is all a silly dream."

Fully convinced, I let darkness consume me without hesitation.

***

BEEP. BEEP. BEEP.

I slam my hand on the snooze button. As patches of clarity piece together like a puzzle, I recall my funky dream. When my alarm goes off again, I knock it from the nightstand. I inch my way to the edge of my bed. The clock stares back at me: six forty.

Glistening metal catches my eye. The kitchen knife is lying beside my alarm clock. My heart plummets into the pit of my stomach. I slowly lift my head and hold my breath... to find that I'm the only one in the room.

"Phew. I knew I was just imagining things." I tuck the knife away in a drawer.

Gossamer curtains dance in the breeze. I tap my

fingernails against the bed stand. *Wait.* The window is shut. As I creep closer to the window, a lump forms in my throat. It's early October, but frost nips at my fingertips. I jerk back but press forward again. As soon as I reach the cord, I yank the blinds open. White-hot pain streaks up my arm, sending me flying onto my butt. After examining my forearm, clear of any signs of injury, I finally swallow that lump. The window is closed, and the curtains have stilled.

"What the heck was that?" A shadow of fear washes over me as I entertain the possibility that it had to do with Brock's visit. "But that means what happened *was* real."

I flex my fingers, daring to find something different. "Does it have anything to do with the Soul of Mercy thing? Maybe I have powers now? Or worse…a curse?"

Fear slams into me with such force that I can barely stand straight. It crushes me so much I barely notice my sister rushing me to change, brushing my teeth, and then dragging me out of the house. Barely notice the concern in my mom's eyes. Barely notice the bus ride and school bells ringing.

Gripping my geography binder with white-knuckled intensity, I veer toward my locker. I rearrange my color-coded folders, selecting the ones I'll need for homework. A band of tension squeezes my head; I tried looking up Soul of Mercy on my phone, but the teacher caught me. I blow a strand of hair from my eye, reminding me of my predicament.

"Watch out! A skunk! Take cover, dudes!"

I close my eyes and grit my teeth. A cacophony of laughter passes over me like a noxious cloud of gas.

"Hurry up, or she'll spray us!"

I glare at them, but they only point. At my face.

"Don't look directly at her, or you'll turn to stone!" A boy in a varsity jacket slaps his friend on the back. He contorts his face, trying to mimic my Bell's Palsy.

"Leave her alone, Chad! Go spend your bro time with your jock buddies elsewhere!"

Blinking up in shock, I see Julia waving her middle finger in the air like it was one of her cheerleading pom-poms.

"Thanks." I slam my locker shut and lean against it.

Julia flips her blond hair over her shoulder. She bites her fingers when her gaze meets my hairline. "Wow. It's worse."

"Thanks," I say for the second time and shove past her.

"Wait, I didn't mean it that way!" she exclaims.

I wave my hand. "Thanks for defending me."

Beneath my gruff tone, I smile to myself. It's a weird phenomenon when a popular person pays attention to you. I consider it the high school equivalent of a celebrity berating a bully on my behalf.

I head to the back of the school, embracing the crisp air when I open the door. Students in gym uniforms cluster on the running track, baseball field, and tennis court. Janitors rake the leaves in vain as orange and red rain on them. My phone vibrates.

PRIVATE: Meet me at the dumpsters.

My brow rises as my eyes dart around the field, but I find nothing suspicious.

GABBY: Who is this?

PRIVATE: Destiny.

I roll my eyes. My friends must be pranking me. Unless the angel from last night is real. A sour sensation pools in the pit of my stomach at the idea. I just don't get it. Religious or not, the concept of real angels interacting with humans in the twenty-first century is absurd.

Slinking toward the far end of the building, thoughts roll through my mind like a storm. I've been laughing at this situation, but the "funny" is wearing out. If it is Brock, I'd be really dealing with supernatural stuff.

As I near a small alley between the main school and the athletic center, an arm reaches out. I loosen my backpack and wale on the attacker.

"Stop it!"

It's the same airy voice. Brock. My heart continues to thump in my chest while I settle my breath. I dig my heels into the dirt but allow Brock to drag me further into the narrow walkway. His hair is tied back into a man bun. Sweat beads on his forehead.

"You *are* real," I say breathily.

He shrugs. "That's rude. But yes."

"That means..." I rake my nails through my hair.

"You're still the new Soul of Mercy." His lips stretch wide, putting his pearly whites in full display.

We lock eyes. Brock goes from looking mystical like some unicorn, to almost...a normal teenager. Color has returned to his flesh, and he wears our school's sweatshirt and ripped jeans. His disguise could easily pass him off as a jock.

Placing my hands on my hips, I tap my foot. "By the way, did you have anything to do with the nasty shock I got this morning? It nearly gave me a heart attack."

"Hm. The powers that accompany the role are slowly coming to you, I see," he says, rubbing his chin.

"But why me?" I gesture to my face. "I can't possibly be a choice candidate. Look at me. I don't have the look of a superhero."

"It has nothing to do with looks. Gabby, there's nothing wrong with *you*." He takes my hands and squeezes them. "But there's a lot wrong with your generation."

"Excuse me?" I want to take offense, but he's kind of right.

Brock's head drops as he sighs. When he angles his face upward, his eyes bore into mine with a dark intensity.

"With each generation, it's becoming more difficult to find a pure heart, and even then, that candidate isn't guaranteed from temptation. The last Soul of Mercy turned on us. Gabrielle, despite how much of an outcast you feel, just know that you are the world's best hope to protect the divide between the human and spirit world."

"Well, I'm still young. You think I can handle such a serious role?"

Pulling his lips into a solemn smile, he says, "I sensed a resilience in you, and after hearing just a fraction of what you've been through from our previous conversation, I'm more confident than ever."

I slap my hand against my forehead and run it down my face. Brock is so insistent. "Why can't you perform the job? Or another celestial being?"

"Because this involves your world. I need a human counterpart," he answers in a matter-of-fact tone.

I sputter like a lawnmower, looking all around me for a camera to confirm this was some joke. "No. This *cannot* be real. How can I handle this when I have homework and—"

"Enough excuses." Wings rip from Brock's sweatshirt, glowing with white-hot intensity. He tenses and scans the sky. "You humans are all about 'seeing is believing' crap. Well, Gabby, you're in luck. We got a live one! You'll have to hold your questions for now."

"What the heck are you talking about?" I pry my hands free and hug my chest.

He tugs his collar and jerks his head. "No time. Let's go."

"Hold it. I've got basketball practice." I reach for his hoodie, but Brock leaps into the air.

He lands on top of a dumpster with feline-like grace. Before I can speak, he jumps into the sky. The rays of the sun blind me, but when I blink into focus, Brock is standing on the rooftop, hands on his hips. He beckons to me.

I swear my head is going to explode. "I can't do that!" I hiss.

Brock continues to wave. Heat erupts at the base of my neck. Tightening all the muscles in my body, I hold my breath and jump…one foot high.

"Told you," I said. Without skipping a beat, I peel down the alley toward the field. I need to get out of here, and maybe if I run fast enough, I can lose Brock.

A gale sweeps past me and trips my feet, sending me face-first into the pavement. My nose throbs, and metallic-tasting liquid saturates my lips. I pound my fist into the ground repeatedly.

With a deafening roar, the gale transforms into hurricane-like winds, sucking all the words from my mouth. The force lifts me off my feet and launches me into the air. The school soccer field shrinks, leaving students looking like moving dots. I somersault, the world rushing around me in a blur of colors. Pain explodes in my back when I land on the school roof.

Brock leans into view with an amused smile.

I wheeze. "I want to punch your face."

"That's not a nice thing to say to an angel." He extends a hand.

"Whatever." I dust off my jeans and gape at the view. "I clearly have no choice. Where to? No, first, tell me how I'll get around without sustaining lifelong injuries?"

Brock points to my backpack. "You need to let go of all your worldly things. They are what tethers you down."

Sucking in a deep breath, I say, "Well, if I have to go all in…" I drop my backpack on the roof.

"Cellphone, too."

"No."

"Yes."

I grumble as I tuck it in the front pocket of my backpack.

"No one is going to steal it from a rooftop," Brock adds with a touch of pity.

"Okay. Done. Now what?"

Brock sprints toward the edge of the building. I chase him, waving my arms wildly.

"What are you doing? You have wings, and I don't!"

He winks. "Just have faith."

Extending his arms, he falls backward, and I shriek. What if people see him? What are they going to think? Pacing back and forth, I chomp on my nails as if they were my lifeline.

An audible *whoosh* catches my attention; Brock swirls into the sky and shouts, "Hurry up!"

"Wait. Wait!" I pump my arms and tell myself not to look down. Don't look down no matter what. My foot catches the edge of the roof, sending me into a belly-flop of a freefall. My eyes squeeze shut, and I tell myself, *fly*.

I hear Brock's voice echo in my mind: *faith*.

An invisible rope tugs me against gravity's wishes. I windmill my arms, finding myself rocketing into the sky. The wind whistles in my ears. Adrenaline rushes through my veins, and I laugh. I didn't grow any wings, but I'm still flying, and that's pretty darn incredible.

When I catch up to Brock, he turns to me and smirks. "Not bad, right? Follow me."

He jets toward the sun, which is beginning its descent. Goosebumps cover my body as the temperature drops, but I focus on following the canvas of blood orange, pink, and purple.

"What exactly does a Soul of Mercy do?" A chill lances through my body. "Would I be responsible for actual lives? What about my own?"

Brock's expression voids all emotion. "When a person dies, they transition to the spirit realm; however, some pass away with a restlessness that prevents them from moving on. They wander the earth, seeking their closure...or vengeance."

"Ghosts?" I utter.

"Some call them ghosts. Others call them spirits. The Soul of Mercy's job is to put them to rest."

"Ghosts that *haunt* things." My stomach sours.

Brock narrows his eyes. His silvery hair whips in the air, free from the poorly made bun. "If that's what humans call it these days, then yes. What's important is that we must keep the realms separate. The more restless spirits populate Earth, the closer they bring the spirit world to humans. This can never happen."

I slap my hand to my forehead. "Ghosts don't exist!"

"And humans don't fly." He snorts, flapping his wings. The feathers glisten like diamonds.

"Touché." I pause, shoving a pile of guilt into the back of my mind. "Forgive me, but it's hard to be motivated in a role that's been forced on me like this."

"You'll find your purpose over time, but in the short term, I can offer to heal your Bell's Palsy if that'll persuade you to give this a shot."

My heart skips a beat. The edge of my right lip twitches, but I hide my excitement. "Okay, fine." I sigh dramatically.

After a few minutes, Brock slows and points at an industrial park. My lip curls; it's the creepy joint just outside of town. As we descend, my eyes follow abandoned building after abandoned building. Fluorescent light signs flicker as if welcoming me into a horror flick.

I crash-land on my knees, tears springing to my eyes. Brock helps me up and mutters a prayer. A warmth coats my injuries, and the pain recedes. I open my mouth to say thank you, but a dimly lit window catches my attention. A polished sign, "TechBar," hangs above. Judging by the modern design, it had to be a start-up too broke to afford a nice office space.

Screaming breaks my train of thought. My heart pounds in my chest as I squeeze through the metal fence. A driving force pulls me forward, eroding my fears. It's as if my legs are running by their own will. I hop a second, shorter fence and shimmy against the wall beside the window.

I use my sleeve to wipe grime from the edge, and I peer in. A young man with frizzy hair cowers behind his computer desk. The room is no more than 800 square feet, filled with cheap shelves and a store-brand desk.

"P-p-please. Spare me!" His voice cracks.

Narrowing my eyes, I can't understand why he's this petrified. The room is vacant; the only sign of disturbance is a broken picture frame of himself and another man shaking hands. When Brock appears at my side, he folds his wings and clears his throat.

I roll my eyes. "You made me miss practice for this? This man's probably having a mental breakdown."

"If you had *waited* for me…" Brock presses his index finger between my eyes.

"Hey. What the hell?" I exclaim.

He shushes me and mumbles indecipherable words. Instantly, my skin burns, but Brock locks me with his other arm. Squirming, I fight for personal space. The white-hot searing intensifies, and darkness sweeps over my eyes like curtains.

My first thought: *Brock just blinded me.*

When he releases me, I rub my eyes incessantly. Every sound, from the rattling of metal to the crunching of paper, is amplified in my ears, and an acrid stench I didn't notice before overwhelms my nostrils. The metal paneling feels like spears at my back. I double over, overwhelmed with the sensations, and gag.

"Who's there?" the baritone voice demands in a

guttural growl.

Forcing myself to my feet, my vision returns to me. *Better late than never.* I ram the door open and stumble inside. The man's eyes peer through his mop of hair.

"H-h-help me! Ghost!"

A disembodied laugh shakes the walls, sending the man into the fetal position. "Look at you! So pathetic," says the voice.

The man's laptop rockets off the table and crashes onto the floor.

"What will you do now with your precious start-up, Matthew?" the voice continues.

While I search for the source of the voice, Brock materializes by my side. I turn my head and say, "W-what do I do?" My left eye waters; in fact, my face breaks out into micro-twitches.

"Demand him to appear," he replies nonchalantly.

My nostrils flare. "Oh, so it's that easy, is it?" I punch his arm, but Brock doesn't budge.

"Don't worry so much. I'll help you." He flashes a warming smile, bolstering my confidence little by little.

A binder whizzes by, clipping my ear. I duck and scan the shelves. Books fly off like a waterfall of paper. Amidst the chaos, Matthew crawls past me and sprints out the door. My heart pounds as I slowly rise onto my feet.

I swallow the wavering in my voice. "Listen, I can't have you running wild…and, er, knocking things over." Turning to Brock, I shrug.

Tiles crack, snapping my attention back to where I think the ghost is. Two foot-shaped holes appear on the ground. The room stills, but ragged breaths come from the direction of the broken tiles.

Stomp. Stomp. Stomp. Stomp.

As the ruckus continues, wisps of mist dance around a humanoid form. The specter's tantrum reminds me a lot of my sister, and with that thought, my fear diminishes like a snuffed-out candle. The fog solidifies, rounding out a portly man with a patchy beard. Tendrils of smoke smolder from his shoulders.

I lock my knees and put both fists in front of me. He doesn't appear how ghosts are typically portrayed. Instead of translucent, he has a reflective consistency, almost like a mirror. My eyes are wide and bloodshot—at least, that's what his rounded belly shows me.

"Don't interfere with my business," he shouts. "I will not rest until I drive Matthew mad and TechBar is destroyed!"

"You seriously plan on hand-to-hand combat?" Brock mutters under his breath.

"I have no other option." I squeeze tighter until my nails break through my skin. "Unless you plan on helping me out like you promised?"

No answer. I charge at the ghost, but with a flick of his wrist, a shelf to my right shivers. Brock rushes past me in a blur of color. I look up; Brock holds the shelf in place. His hands radiate with a golden shimmer as he sweeps his arms to the left. The shelf mimics his movement and smashes onto the floor.

I open my mouth to thank him, but a shadow washes over me. Turning in horror, I see another shelf dive my way. Despite my efforts, it crashes down on me, crushing my ankle. I bite my tongue, clawing at whatever I can.

"Gabby!" Brock shouts. He swims his arms around, trying to keep debris from crashing into either of us. Brock's entire body is now encased with that glow.

Creaks and groans freeze my soul. I'm able to peer up to see the shelf in front of me aim for my head in slow-motion. I tug my leg, but my attempts to free myself are in vain. A loose brick crashes into the back of Brock's head, sending him face-down in the dust.

My heart thuds, and I whimper. When people say life flashes before your eyes, they aren't kidding. I see my sister and mom struggling to make ends meet throughout the years. I could've been more helpful. The constant illnesses that trigger my Bell's Palsy. I could've been less selfish. Bowing my head to accept my fate, tears leak from my eyes.

Shadow evaporates. Shouts exchange, followed by crunching wood. The weight on my ankle lifts. I roll onto my back to find Brock back on his feet, sweeping the objects away like they are as light as feathers. His face is flushed and stamped with a scowl.

I blink away the remaining tears and get onto my knees. Somehow, I have to put this *thing* of out its misery.

"Gabby, I can play baseball all day with this ghost, but I need your powers," he exclaims as he sidles up to me.

"*How?*"

"Whether it's by talking or with physical persuasion…you *need* to convince him to let go of his wrath. When a soul has nothing to hold on to, then it transitions to the afterlife for good." He angles his strong jaw at me.

Fluid rushes to my injury, and my legs have the consistency of jelly. I've had enough. I just need the same patience I use when dealing with my sister. "Why are you doing this?" I shout.

The apparition crosses his arms. "Hmph. Why would you care?"

Once again, the room stills until nothing but the hum of fluorescent lights consumes the silence.

I raise my arms and let them fall to my sides, sighing in exasperation. "Wouldn't you rather live your afterlife in peace?"

"I can't," he thunders. "I conceptualized the idea of TechBar! When I met Matt, I believed we made a great team on this entrepreneur adventure together. He…he betrayed me! Took all the credit!"

I glance at Brock, who jerks his head toward the ghost.

"What's your name?" I ask as I wipe beads of sweat from my forehead.

"Harold." He swivels around until his back faces me. His shoulders quiver.

I grimace at the name. "Who is still named Harold these days?" I mutter. "Ouch!" A wireless mouse collides with my head. Rubbing my scalp, I glare at Brock.

While his facial features are now relaxed, the glow remains. He gestures for me to keep talking. My cheeks sear with heat.

Dying to end this awkward exchange, I close my eyes and try to empathize with Harold. If any of my few friends stabbed me in the back…

"I would feel the same way," I say.

"What?" Harold faces me again. His eyes glisten over plump cheeks.

"You want revenge. Retribution. And because you died before you could satisfy your emotions, you can't move on." I hobble closer to him, swallowing the lump forming in my throat. "But hey, did you see him? Ran away like a coward. A true businessman requires courage, and this twerp doesn't have it."

I tense as the room trembles. Pain shoots up my ankle, and I curse inwardly. The room fills with his rich voice once more, but instead of a treacherous roar, it's laughter. I stare incredulously at Harold, who is holding his gut and doubling over.

My lips twitch, and my heart swells. I got my foot in the door. "Right? He's going to drive TechBar into the ground. Crash and burn, and you won't be there for the shaming! Imagine the headlines in all the newspapers."

When I reach out and touch his shoulder, a chill zips up my limb and circles my torso. My hands glow. Harold loses shape as a sourceless wind whips around us. Faster and faster the wind howls, tearing Harold into strips of smoke.

"Extend your right arm!" Brock exclaims.

I don't question, I just react. The smoke circles the ceiling for a few seconds then rushes at me. I shriek, but the tendrils crash and dissolve in the palm of my hand.

In seconds, the wind dissipates, along with Harold's laughter. The haunting cackle gives me goosebumps, but all I can do is stare at my hand.

"You did it! Not the traditional method, but I'm proud of you," says Brock. He claps and beams down at me.

I shake my hand as if a bug had landed on it. "Please tell me that thing isn't inside me? Please, no. No, please, no. No!"

"Calm down!"

His voice mollifies the monster of adrenaline shooting panic symbols in my brain.

"Where'd he go then? It looked pretty clear that he was entering *this* hand."

He brushes curls from his eyes. "Let me tend to your ankle, then let's head home."

Brock runs his hands over my foot, and I try my best not to kick him. I'm too ticklish for my own good. As I relax, he sits back, and his iridescent glow transfers to my injury. It feels like it's in a warm bath. I wiggle my toes; the pain is receding. My heart flutters at the miracle before me.

"Brock?"

"Hm?"

"Thanks for saving me from getting crushed." I pause. My left eye starts to water for no reason again. I flush with embarrassment. "It's the palsy," I say gruffly.

"I know." His tone is flat. Not in a bored way, but rather like it's a normal part of conversation. "A promise is a promise. Would you like me to heal it now?"

A tug in my chest holds me back. Scratching the

nape of my neck, I say, "It's no rush. Let's go home first."

I don't want to admit to Brock that it felt good to help Harold. And Matthew for that matter. If I can't prevent my life from being a ridiculous mess, this role can allow me to help others. My condition suddenly seems insignificant.

"Earth to Gabby!" Brock dusts his sweatshirt, eyeing me.

"I'm ready," I stutter.

When I clasp my hands around his, strands of my hair glow and float in midair. I feel my body weight disappear as we levitate together. My initial sense of confusion is replaced by awe. The emotion balloons in my chest, which sends me rocketing through the door and into the night sky.

"Am I sensing that you're warming up to the role?"

"Not really. I still have no idea what I'm doing." I clear my throat. "So, is this is a lifelong commitment?"

He nods. "I'm sorry that you feel your life has been disrupted, but the burden must fall on someone's shoulders."

"That means I can quit school and never do homework again?"

"Nice try. It's business as usual. You can call it your…part-time job."

"Yeah, right," I exclaim incredulously. "There must be thousands of disgruntled ghosts, and there's one me."

Brock's wings flap rhythmically, and they glow under the copious number of stars. "You also have me. For millennia, this pairing has always proved sufficient. Have faith."

I roll my eyes. Faith. Again. "Well, I'm sure adding 'Soul of Mercy' will make me stand out on my college applications!"

He politely laughs, and his eyes focus on the sky.

We fly for a few minutes without speaking. It's a lot

to process, but if I don't have to throw my life away, what's the harm in becoming the Soul of Mercy?

I inhale the crisp air and sigh. "So, there is an afterlife then? What's heaven like?"

"What do you mean?"

"Religion is an enigma to mankind. Some love it too much; some don't believe it at all. Some believe in one god, many gods, or just spirits. When my grandma died, my mom told me that she would go to heaven."

"Whatever is beyond death's door is for humans to discover on their own." He continues to scan the skies.

"What?" I squawk. The peaceful warmth that once crackled in my chest like a fireplace snuffs out. "You got to be kidding me. I'm supposed to put souls to rest, so I think it's a relevant question."

Popping and sizzling cut Brock off. Something red flies in my direction. I dodge the fizzing object, and it explodes, assaulting my eardrums. Fireworks. I slap my hands to my ears; I can't hear my own scream—just high-pitched buzzing.

A ray of cobalt explodes to my left, while a gold ball shatters into hundreds of pieces to my right. I teeter in the air and hold my breath at a moment of stillness. I fall. My stomach jumps up into my throat.

As I plummet, I desperately search every corner of my mind for how to fly. Every breath I take, I choke. When I realize it's hopeless, I close my eyes, cursing Brock and his stupid Soul of Mercy crap. It shouldn't have been me. It's been barely twenty-four hours, and Brock's going to have to select another sucker.

I slam into a buoyant mass. When I open my eyes, I scramble to look around. What broke my fall? The invisible force lowers me gently onto the middle of a softball field, where I collapse on my knees and catch my breath. It's the public park a few miles from home. Substantial in size, it also has a basketball court, small pond, community garden, and an acre of rolling hills. My partner is hovering above me, body aglow.

"Wow. Brock, thank you."

"You're welcome." The ground shudders when he lands. "Looks like we may have one more objective today."

I stare at my hands. "I guess so."

"Are you ready?"

His words trigger a deluge of emotions. All my life, I've felt sorry for myself and allowed fear to tether me down. The hardships, the bullying—it trained me to hide in a shell as a coping mechanism. But this calling gives me purpose, even a little confidence.

Blood-curdling screams shatter the air. Beyond Brock, a blond girl trips and face-plants on the ground. A boy follows suit, leaving behind a picnic basket, candles, and a blanket. The girl shouts something.

My heart skips a beat. "Julia?"

"You know her?" Urgency skirts around Brock's every word.

"Yup. From my school. Popular girl but nice. She must be with her boyfriend." I cover my mouth with my hand. "Oh, no."

"What's going on?" Julia shrieks.

At the source of the fireworks, neon green smoke orbits around a crate. A man with various badges pinned to his chest lies unconscious.

"Let's go!" Shoving past Brock, I hop the fence and crouch and run beneath the bleachers to reach the soccer field. Fireworks continue to fire in random directions, popping and raining fire on Julia and her boyfriend.

"Stop it!" I shout. My fists glow with my words, feeding off my adrenaline. It bolsters my confidence. I bet I look so cool.

The mist hisses, launching a firework my way. I dive,

feeling the heat singe my hair. I hop up and race toward the formless entity, dodging each blast one by one. My feet fly at incredible speed, and when I jump, it's like I'm on a trampoline. Julia isn't my friend by a long shot, but I refuse to let anyone hurt her!

I make one final leap and curl into a ball.

Smash!

I shatter the box, but it's too late. All the fuses are lit. "Shoot!" I scramble behind a thick oak tree. Plugging my ears, I brace for the explosion.

With a deafening roar, dirt and grass rain on me. I crane my neck to find flames licking the remaining greenery, and the swirling green smoke shakes with laughter.

I stand, growl, and face the apparition. "Show yourself. You're out of ammunition."

The cackling ceases to be an echo and transforms into thick, hearty laughter. The wisps turn into a tattered figure. Jade beading and embroidery cover her from neck to ankle. Her hair resembles willow branches, exposing one eye, her sharp nose, and a scarred cheek. Despite her decrepit countenance, this specter had to be near my age when she died.

"Leave me alone," she hisses. A tear, or an apparition of a tear, leaks with each syllable. "You're letting them escape!"

Hands on my hips, I rock on my feet. "Why would you want to bother two people having a good time?"

She unhinges her jaw to release an otherworldly cry. "It's because they're *bullies*, and they will get their due. All of them. Every popular homecoming queen and better-than-thou prince!" She points at Julia, who fumbles with her phone. With a snap of her fingers, sparks fly into the air. They land on Julia's phone, and it explodes—sending glass and shrapnel everywhere.

"Just look at her pink skirt and shiny blond hair! She

reminds me of the girl who stole my diary and read it out loud in class. The girl who showed up on my doorstep with a pig, saying it was my prom date! The girl who forced my head onto the mud and held it there for minutes!"

I kick clumps of dirt in the air. "You think just because you were bullied in the past means these innocent people should be blown up by fireworks?"

"Leave me alone!" the apparition exclaims.

The girl's neck stretches, knocks Brock back a few feet, and twirls around me. She binds my limbs as I jostle violently. Air squeezes from my lungs, and I swear my ribs are starting to crack. I try summoning my powers. My mind fills with fog.

Light slices through the ghost's form, which immediately disappears with a *poof*. Falling on my butt, I gasp for air. I search for her all around. She could show up anywhere, including from behind me…

I turn and swing my arm.

"Whoa, there." Brock stands tall, a scimitar in one hand. It emits a turquoise hue, and I admire it for a second.

"That's so cool—"

"Watch out!"

I duck. Arrows of shadow rain over my head. Brock brandishes his sword and halts the assault. Springing to my feet, I turn to face the tormented soul. My gaze darts between Julia and the ghost, and a pang of empathy resonates in my chest.

She coils her neck on her shoulders, rolls her eyes into the back of her head, and emits a foul screech that pierces my eardrums. I cover my ears, searching for a solution. Apparently, this ghost does not want to bargain or make peace of any kind. Rotted skin peels as she stretches to about seven feet tall.

Brock appears by my side. "This is a strong one."

The ghost lurches at us, mouth wide and filled with

sharp fangs. Brock strikes the ground with his scimitar, blinding me with a flash of light. I peek through my fingers and notice the specter clawing at a barrier around us. Every time she makes contact, ripples of blue flicker like stars in the night sky.

"Okay," he says in a strained voice. "You must contain her in the same manner as our old friend, Harold. This may be more challenging, but just pour your whole heart and soul into it."

"How?" I shout over the howling winds.

"A thought. Anything you use to motivate you." He grits his teeth, heels digging into the dirt.

I lift my right hand at the apparition. My face twitches, reminding me of my condition. "I am bullied all the time."

The apparition pauses to study me but resumes banging on the barrier.

A vibration pulses from my body. "I was made fun of before…before this *thing* on my face appeared, and I know I'll be made fun of when it goes away." The sensation forks up my arm. My hair glows brighter than the barrier, and I stare this ghost down. "But you can't let hatred control you!"

Brock's barrier shatters like glass, and the creature dives at me.

I steel my nerves and keep my hand raised. An invisible fire erupts in my palm, and I bite my lip.

Her eyes roll back, her irises fixed on my face. "What are you doing? No. I'm not ready!"

My skin burns, and I lift my other hand. "You chose to do this the hard way." Sweltering heat radiates, and I cringe, unsure how much longer I can take it. The spirit collides into me, and the sheer force shoves me back a few feet; however, the fading wailing bolsters my confidence.

Like a switch, the light, the heat, and the soul-crushing cries evaporate. I teeter on the spot as my hands cool. Scanning the area, I search for the spirit. Gone. I wiggle my fingers. Is she truly gone? I bite my lip, well, the best I can. I felt her frustration and anger. I can't even begin to count the times I'd plotted revenge or an escape from this hell.

A breeze brushes past me like a sigh. I smile. I brought this soul to rest, and at the same time, she made me reflect on my life as well. How will I live it before it's time for me to part this world? Do I want to roam the world in agony like she did, never knowing the power of forgiveness?

"That was amazing!" Brock leaps into view and pulls me into a hug.

I tense and scan for Julia and her boyfriend. "I-is this appropriate?"

Pulling away, the angel beams at me. I tilt my head; Brock's serious exterior has shattered.

"Thanks for helping me," I add. "But what about my classmates?"

"They'll forget everything come morning." Brock's scimitar disappears with a *poof.* "It's another one of my special abilities. That's why you and I will make a great team. You've got a lot to learn, but I see it. I see massive potential."

A lump lodges in my throat. Me? Potential?

Brock winks. "I knew I made the right choice." He ruffles my hair, his thumb grazing my forehead. "I still need to heal your palsy. Let me do that before I forget...or another ghost attacks!"

His gentle fingers send me into complete harmony. I close my eyes and recall my rough childhood. I then fast-forward to high school and the never-ending social tormenting. Now, I see my future: helping others in ways no one else can. Much like my palsy, each stage in my life will come and go, posing different challenges along the way. I am at peace with that.

"You know what? No thanks, Brock. I'll let it run its course." I brush his hand away. "I've accepted this part of me."

"I hope you'll accept this as well." He ruffles my hair again. Brock waves a hand in a circular motion until wisps form. They swirl and form an oval mirror. "See for yourself."

I gasp. My hair shimmers a celestial white and silver.

The mirror dissipates, revealing Brock, who rubs his chin. I clench my hands and release them. For once, I don't care what others think.

"I love it," I finally reply.

"I look forward to working with you, partner." His eyes shine like stars.

After a few beats, I reach out for a high-five.

Brock's features are addled. "What?"

"Never mind," I say with a chuckle. "It's getting late. I need to get my backpack and do homework."

***

My sister scuttles up the middle school steps before I stroll down the sidewalk. Oak trees stretch over me, casting a welcome shade. I crack a smile; today is the first day I'm not filled with dread on my way to class. Chatter grows louder as I approach school.

Brock? When we returned home last night, he took off into the sky. The heavens. Space. Whatever. He said he would visit later today to train with me before the next ghost comes around requiring pacification. The more I think about it, the more I warm up to this role...as long as it doesn't interfere with my grades. And basketball practice.

Perfume rolls up my nostrils. Julia passes by, laughing with a group of girls. She clutches her binder covered in stickers. Her tan gives her a sun-kissed glow, and her teeth are perfect. I stop, breaking into a cold sweat at the thought of last night's adventure.

"Julia?"

She turns and regards me with wide eyes. "'Sup, Gabby?"

Two girls flanking her scowl at me, as if I'm some failed lab experiment. I smile sheepishly.

"H-how are you?" I study for her reaction.

Julia shrugs then flashes me her famous smile. "Fine? Thanks?"

Everyone giggles. Julia plays with her skirt, and her face draws into a blank.

"Good…" I trail off. "Um. I just wanted to…thank you again for defending me yesterday."

"No problem." With a flick of her hair, she leads her posse into school.

I blow out a low whistle. Looks like Brock did erase her memory. Things are back to their typical, messed up high school caste system with no gossip of ghosts to stir up panic. I hug myself.

A pen knocks me in the head. Raucous laughter erupts from the same group of jocks from yesterday.

"Look! Ghost!"

My skin crawls, but a sense of calm washes over me. I bend down to pick up the pen and pocket it. "Thanks for the pen, *dudes*." I flash a Cheshire smile and pass them, enjoying their dumbfounded faces along the way.

All's Fairy in Love and War

Matthew Dewar

Warren dropped a plump marshmallow into his hot chocolate and regarded Ivy. "And then what happened?"

Ivy rolled her eyes, adding a sassy wave of her finger when she spoke. "She had the *audacity* to tell *me* that *I* was the one in the wrong."

The white marshmallow oozed into the rich brown liquid. Warren swirled it around, creating a contrast between the dark and light colors. "She does have a point though, doesn't she?"

Puckering her pink lips, Ivy sucked her teeth. She made several mumbling sounds before crossing her arms. "Yeah. But, it's okay for you to say it, not her."

Warren laughed. He really loved humans, especially animated ones like Ivy. Fairies tended to be too serious these days. "I hope you've now learned that if someone hacks your social media and posts a funny comment, it is unreasonable to cut off their ponytail."

"Funny comment?" Ivy's eyes narrowed. "You saw what Chelsea wrote about you. Disgusting."

"I've been called worse." Warren reached out and patted her hand. "I appreciate the gesture, but you didn't need to do it. Shouldn't have done it. Comments can be deleted."

"And her hair will grow back." Ivy tilted her head

and flicked her wavy, highlighted locks. "It was only, like, an inch or two."

They shared a laugh as the waiter came and placed a large slice of pumpkin pie between them. They each took a fork and dug into it straight away.

"Om, this is so good."

"I know, right?" Warren swallowed and placed his fork down while she continued to eat. He hated deceiving her, but he had his orders, and it was his duty to spy on her. "You're back to school on Monday, yeah?"

"Mm-hmm." Ivy swallowed. "I had to apologize to Chelsea, and I'm suspended tomorrow. It was so funny. Principal Beckers called Dad and then handed me the phone. I had to pretend like Dad was telling me off. He was like 'this is excellent, sweetie. I'm having some connectivity issues I need your help with.' He didn't even ask what I had done."

Glancing around the cafe, Warren took note of the few people nearby: a young family with a toddler in a high chair; a stressed manager working through her break on a laptop; a teenaged employee trying to text and appear busy at the same time. It seemed unlikely that anyone was eavesdropping. Still, Warren reached into his pocket and pinched some fairy dust from his satin pouch. "*Ciuin*," he muttered, casting a blanket of silence over them to add extra protection. "Oh yeah, your dad's project. How's that coming along?"

Ivy sobered, her shoulders straightening. "I wish I could tell you, but I signed a nondisclosure agreement." She couldn't maintain her composure anymore, and a huge burst of laughter escaped her lips. "Can you believe he made me sign one of those? Who am I going to tell? A terrorist? Steal his *intellectual property*? I don't think so."

Warren laughed, but her father had a point. Mr. Winters's project was extremely important. Each human on

Earth required eight trees' worth of oxygen a year, and pretty soon there wouldn't be enough left. This invention would act as a super-tree, capable of purifying the air and providing the same amount of oxygen as one hundred trees. With thousands of these inventions around the world, humans would have an unlimited supply of fresh air. But falling into the wrong hands could prove disastrous, as the invention could be weaponized to deliver poison or harmful toxins into the atmosphere.

Ivy blinked rapidly before removing a stray eyelash from her eye. "Well, it sounds like there's just one final thing left to do, and then he'll be finished."

"Neat." Warren took another bite of the pie. "So, what's this final thing?" he said in between chews.

"Knowing Dad, it's probably just connecting the Bluetooth or something. He's amazing with machinery and everything else, but, like, he is so bad with computers. He's old-fashioned that way. Avoids computers like the plague." Ivy speared the last bite of pie with her fork. "But enough about that." She swirled the orange morsel in front of her mouth. "Let's change the subject to something more interesting. Got any goss for me?"

"Umm..." Warren racked his brain. "A new kid started today. What's his name? Kalen?"

Ivy's eyes widened, and her smile doubled in size. She shuffled closer and whispered under her breath. "Yeah, Kalen. He's pretty hot, right?"

Warren's cheeks flushed. "No, that's not what I meant." He leaned back, putting some distance between himself and Ivy. "It's just strange to see someone change schools in the middle of the term. What's his story?" Warren wondered if the cafe owners had recently cranked up the heat. All of a sudden, the air in the room had become sparse and stifling.

Ivy downed the last of her drink. "I had a brief chat

with him today. He's nice." She stood and winked. "You should talk to him tomorrow."

"What did he say?" Warren followed her. "Tell me."

Ivy waved her hands in the air and lowered her voice as if to mimic a fortuneteller. "I do not possess the knowledge you seek. You will find your answers at the source." She rolled her eyes so only the whites were visible and dropped her voice an octave. "Speak to Kalen." She giggled and pecked Warren on the cheek. "Okay, bye, babe. See you later."

"You're a weirdo."

Ivy pulled her lips back and went cross-eyed. "I'm not a weirdo. You are."

The toddler at the table nearby burst into cackling laughter as Ivy darted out of the cafe.

Warren texted her: "Ugh. Just tell me pls."

She spun, loose hair twirling around her face as she shook her head, staring at him through the window.

Warren took a seat and finished his drink. He watched Ivy cross the road and head toward the bus stop. His mission was to befriend her and find out all he could about her father's new tech while keeping an eye out for potential Secret Division agents. Which is where Kalen came in. It was too convenient that he started at Ivy's school moments before her dad's invention was ready. Warren had scanned Kalen on the magical spectrum, searching for clues as to his true purpose, but Kalen's aura came up clean with no hint of anything magical or malevolent about him. But still, Warren had a hunch that there was more to him than met the eye. He didn't look like the type to work for Special Division—an elite group of government-trained spies who had defected and now worked for personal gain—but then again, Warren didn't look like a two-hundred-and-sixteen-year-old fairy working for the Universal Secret Intelligence Service, did he?

Leaving some money on the table, Warren exited the cafe, wrapping his jacket tighter as the crisp autumn breeze greeted him. He needed to get home and touch base with Orlaith and tell her how things were progressing.

***

"Is that everything?" Orlaith asked. A small real-time image of her floated in a cloud of fairy dust, flickering and sparkling with her every movement. Her black hair was pulled back in a severe bun, and her sleek black bodysuit gripped each muscle.

"Everything." Warren had recounted all that he knew about Mr. Winters's project. For now, he left out Kalen. A hunch alone wasn't worth mentioning. He needed to investigate further. This was his first mission, and he needed to prove himself to Orlaith, not be paranoid that every person who was slightly suspicious could be the enemy.

"Excellent, Warren. You've done extremely well. Now, I know you're only meant to be on surveillance, but can I ask you a huge favor?" Her voice was laden with sugary sweetness.

Warren stilled his heart, not wanting to come across as too eager. He scratched his nose before answering. "Yeah, sure, what is it?"

"Excellent."

As if on cue, a pixie rapped on his window. He opened it, and she flew in, dropping a vial of silvery liquid on his bed.

"Gormund has created this incredible elixir," Orlaith said as the pixie zipped out the window. "I need you to install it into Mr. Winters's machine."

Plucking up the vial, Warren turned it over in his fingers. He had never met Gormund, but he had heard stories of the expert craftsman. He was the only dwarf who had agreed to share his expert craftsmanship and work for USIS. "What is it?"

"It's essentially an atmosphere repair serum. When the machine is on, these particles will mix in with the emitted oxygen and help cleanse the atmosphere of carbon dioxide and pollution, hopefully reversing the effects of global warming."

"Fascinating." On the outside, he remained calm and composed. On the inside, he was doing cartwheels. Orlaith had entrusted him with more than just surveillance, something that would benefit everyone on Earth. This was why he joined USIS in the first place. To make a difference.

"Oh, and, Warren, one more thing."

"Yes?"

"I was right. We intercepted communications earlier that imply Special Division has sent an operative. They're either going to try to destroy the invention or steal it. Please be careful."

Warren bowed his head and sent silent prayers to the Tuatha De Danann, the gods from his homeworld, and especially Fand, Goddess of the Sea and Queen of the Fairies. "Of course, Orlaith. I won't disappoint you."

***

Warren sat at a quiet table near the back of the cafeteria. The other tables were full of students laughing, studying, or playing games. He was so used to spending all his time with Ivy he hadn't realized he never made the effort to make other friends.

His phone buzzed in his pocket, and he pulled it out, knowing it was Ivy.

"Have you spoken to him yet???"

He was in the middle of replying when someone stood over him, blocking the light.

"Mind if I sit here?" Kalen's smooth voice washed over Warren.

Warren glanced up into Kalen's light green eyes. "Uh, sure. I guess." He stuffed his phone back in his pocket.

Kalen sat down and peeled off the plastic wrapping on his sandwich. His cheekbones were rather pronounced, drawing attention to his eyes and symmetrical eyebrows. Short brown hair was styled up off-center. "It's Warren, right?"

Warren nodded, forcing himself to stop staring at Kalen. "Got much planned for the weekend?"

Kalen shrugged. His shoulders were broad, and his arms lean, much like a swimmer's. "Mom's working all weekend, and I don't know anyone here yet, so I'll probably just watch TV and play video games. You?"

"Same." Warren shifted his focus to the magical spectrum. Kalen's aura was bland. A dull glow encased his physical form like all humans. Not a hint of anything malicious or magical about him. Warren realized he had been staring for too long and, with a flushed face, looked away. "So, your mom. Is that why you moved here?"

Smirking, Kalen replied, "Yeah. She's a geologist. She's come out here to sample some soils and stuff like that for a while." He placed his sandwich on the table.

"I take it you're not here for long?" Warren's curiosity piqued. His phone buzzed in his pocket again, most likely Ivy with an impatient follow-up text. Maybe she was right in a way. Maybe it was attraction that made him interested in Kalen, not the possibility of him being a spy. It wouldn't be the first time he had fallen for a human.

"Yep, that's all it ever is. A term here, two terms there. I was homeschooled for a long time, but that was worse. Even though I don't have time to make proper friends this way, at least I get a bit of socializing."

Yelling broke out a few tables away. Kalen turned

toward the commotion, and Warren quickly swallowed the guilt of what he was about to do.

He pulled out some fairy dust and whispered, "*Firinnie*." He sprinkled the dust on Kalen's sandwich before quickly scanning Kalen one more time on the magical spectrum. He was still unremarkable. Well, unremarkable in the sense that Warren couldn't detect anything magical or otherworldly about him. But his muscles, chiseled jaw, and green eyes were definitely remarkable.

Kalen turned back around and rolled his eyes. "On the plus side, being homeschooled, I never had to deal with that," he said, jerking his thumb behind him. He picked up his sandwich and brought it to his mouth. He took a breath and then placed his lunch down on the table. "So I've told you my story, what about yours?"

Warren paused, willing Kalen to take a bite of his sandwich with his mind. "I moved here not so long ago. Mom wanted a change of scenery."

He motioned for Warren to continue. "Go on."

"That's pretty much all there is to it. My dad got really… He's not here anymore, and Mom couldn't stay in the house. We moved out here to get away from all the memories."

Kalen's hand reached out as if to comfort Warren, but he quickly snatched it back and let it fall beneath the table. "I'm so sorry."

"Don't worry about it." Even though it was just a cover story, he could easily draw on his own experience. He lost his real father a little over five years ago, and it was at his funeral that a mysterious fairy named Orlaith had approached him and told him of USIS and the hero his father was. When she offered Warren training and an opportunity to join the secret organization, he couldn't say no.

Warren inclined his head toward Kalen's lunch. "Did

your mom make that? It looks good."

Kalen's lip twitched into a smirk. "Yeah, she did. You can have it if you want. I had a late breakfast. I'm not that hungry."

The bell tolled to signal the end of lunch, and Kalen balled up his sandwich. Short of ramming a truth spell down his throat, it seemed like Warren was going to have to come to terms with the fact he was crushing on another human. "If I don't see you before, have a great weekend."

"Hopefully you do," Kalen said before disappearing into the crowd.

Aware he had a stupid grin on his face, Warren pulled out his phone to several messages from Ivy.

"Well? HAVE YOU???"

"WARREN???"

"Are you ignoring me?"

"OMG are you talking to him rn?"

"Hurry up and answer me!!!!"

Warren quickly replied: "Tell you tonight."

She replied almost instantly: "Ugh. You're so annoying. Dad's being a pain. Save me!"

Warren continued to message her as he made his way to history. He chuckled to himself at the irony of being taught history by someone one hundred and eighty years younger than him.

Without looking where he was going, he bumped into someone.

"Oof, I'm sorry." He glanced up and saw Chelsea's face, half-hidden by an oversized knitted beret.

"Oh, Warren, it's you." She adjusted her hat and chewed her lip for a moment. "I'm sorry for... I'm sorry."

Chelsea's aura was a blue mess of sincerity and reeked of self-loathing and shame. Her apology was genuine. "Thanks, but it's done now. Hopefully, we can put it behind us," Warren replied. "I'm sorry about what Ivy did to you.

That was so uncalled for."

Chelsea's gaze dropped to the floor. "I think it was called for. I was pretty horrible to you, and it's because I, um, I'm sorry." A few tears caught the light as they dropped from her cheeks.

Warren considered putting a calming spell on her but thought better of it. She clearly had a few things going on inside her head that she needed to sort through. Warren had an inkling what it might be, but he would let Chelsea be the one to share the information if she felt like it. "If you ever need to talk, I'm here."

"Thanks, Warren." Chelsea hid her face from him and quickly bustled off to class.

Warren deleted the message he had half-typed and quickly wrote out a new message: "You'll never guess what. Chelsea apologized. :)"

***

When school finally finished, Warren went straight to the house USIS had rented out for him and changed into his recon catsuit. There were two slits over his shoulder blades that allowed for a long-overdue stretch of his wings. The material remained silent as he moved, and with a sprinkle of fairy dust, he could turn himself invisible. It resisted extreme temperatures, was near bulletproof, and transmitted his location and vitals back to Orlaith and the others at USIS headquarters.

He pulled on jeans and a light sweater over his catsuit and made his way to Ivy's for dinner. In the few weeks he had known her, Friday night pizza had become a tradition, followed by a movie of her choice, usually a predictable rom-com or cheesy horror film. Even though he was there on business, he had begun to enjoy the evening spent with Ivy and her father.

Opening the lid to his pizza and enjoying the wafting aromas, Warren nodded to the empty armchair and third takeaway box. "Is your dad not joining us?"

Ivy fiddled with the TV remote, leaving greasy fingerprints all over it. "Nah. He said he's going to work on his speech for tomorrow's big presentation. I offered to help, but he didn't need it."

"Want me to take it down to him?"

Ivy glanced at the clock hanging on the wall. "Um, no. I'm sure it'll be fine."

A few seconds later, the doorbell rang.

"I wonder who that might be." Ivy jumped up and ran for the door.

"Hi, come on in," Ivy's cheerful voice carried through the house. "We're just in the living room."

Warren's cheeks warmed as Kalen entered, wearing tight black jeans and an oversized white t-shirt.

"Hello again." Kalen's face glowed as he smiled.

"Hey." Warren glared at Ivy, who shrugged with a mischievous smile.

"Come, take my seat," Ivy said, swapping the meals around so Kalen sat on the sofa next to Warren. Ivy took her father's armchair. "I hope you don't mind scary movies. I chose the most terrifying one I could. Don't be embarrassed if it gets too much, and you need to hold each other for support or anything." Ivy winked at Warren.

The movie started, and Warren slowly ate, acutely aware of how close Kalen was. He could feel the warmth emanating from Kalen's leg beside him, and he itched to place his hand on it when Kalen jumped at a particularly scary scene in the movie.

Halfway through, Warren realized that he had been more distracted than he thought. He had secretly hoped that Kalen would have made the first move, shuffled closer so their legs touched, reached out with a hand, or something.

Warren could usually tell, but maybe he was wrong about Kalen. It wouldn't be the first time he had fallen for someone who couldn't love him back. Actually, that was his specialty.

The movie finished, and Kalen clapped Warren on the leg. "Hey, where's the bathroom?"

"Just through there and on your left," Warren replied, enjoying the lingering touch of Kalen's hand on his leg and how his green eyes sparkled with the reflection from the TV.

"You're ridiculous!" Ivy hissed when the toilet door closed. "I am the best friend in the world and practically served Kalen to you on a silver platter, and you completely wasted that opportunity."

Warren gritted his teeth, both at the thought of what he had to do and at the reality of his situation with Kalen. "I dunno. I don't think Kalen is that kind of guy."

While Ivy rolled her eyes and groaned, Warren pinched some fairy dust and blew it in her face. *"Codlatae."*

She crumpled onto the sofa, snoring gently. While he was thankful for her friendship and would have loved a fun evening, he had a mission to complete. He took the fairy dust and tiptoed to the bathroom, waiting to put Kalen under the same sleeping spell.

But the bathroom door was wide open, and Kalen was nowhere to be seen.

He cursed under his breath. Special Division was here, and either Kalen was one of them, or he had been intercepted by them on his bathroom break.

Warren quickly stripped down to his catsuit and turned himself invisible. He searched the small house, but Kalen wasn't in any of the rooms. He cursed himself for getting so easily distracted. Descending the stairs down into the basement, he found Mr. Winters lying unconscious on the floor.

Kalen stood in front of the machine, which resembled a large bladeless tower fan. It was connected to a giant unit where the air purification process occurred, churning out high volumes of oxygen.

Spinning around, Kalen's translucent wings stretched out behind him. "I'm sorry, Warren. I can't let you do this." His fists came up in front of his face, and he bobbed on the balls of his feet.

Warren hissed. How in the *Tech Duinn* had he managed to hide his true form? "But your aura?"

"Pretty neat trick, hey? Oh and ah, nice try with the truth spell at lunch today. Almost caught me." He shook his head and mouthed the words, "Not even close."

Warren launched himself across the room, whipping out his dagger as he flew through the air.

Kalen feinted left but dodged to the right. He grabbed Warren's arm and used his own momentum against him, flipping Warren onto his back.

In a blur of movement, Kalen drew his own dagger and forced it against Warren's throat. "Pathetic. Have they had to cut funding for self-defense classes at Special Division?"

Straining against Kalen's weight, Warren tried to get the upper hand. "You tell me." Warren hated himself for allowing Kalen to distract him. He should have said something to Orlaith earlier. She could have sent backup that would have prevented this. His shoulders were pinned, and his strength was quickly fading.

Kalen hesitated.

Warren seized the opportunity and tore his arm out from under Kalen, punching him in the side.

Kalen grunted and kneed Warren in the gut, winding him momentarily. His eyebrows furrowed. "What are you doing here?"

"To stop you from destroying the machine." Warren

grunted.

Grabbing a handful of fairy dust, Kalen forced it down Warren's throat. "*Firinnie.*"

Warren had spent weeks with USIS trainers learning how to resist the effects of a truth spell. The lesson he learned? It was impossible. And no one except a god or goddess could manage such a feat.

"Who do you work for?" Kalen demanded.

"Universal Secret Intelligence Service," Warren replied, feeling the lightheadedness that came with the spell. Surely Kalen knew that, but his face betrayed a hint of shock. Warren's head swam with confusion. Who did Kalen think he worked for?

Narrowing his eyes, Kalen asked his next question. "Why are you here?"

Warren fought the effects of the spell with every fiber of his being. He strained against the pull of the truth. Clenching his jaw tightly to keep the words inside, he eventually lost the battle as a pain started to develop behind his eyes. "Surveillance mostly. And to insert a vial into the machine that contains a reparation spell. It's going to repair the ozone layer and assist the effects of the machine."

Kalen released his pressure on Warren's throat and sheathed his dagger. "I have some bad news for you. Orlaith is not who you think she is. I didn't believe you at first, but the truth spell and your aura confirm it." He shook his head. "What I'm about to tell you is going to sound ridiculous, so put me under your truth spell and hear me out."

Completely at a loss of how to respond, Warren simply followed Kalen's instructions. It was clearly a trap, but he had no other ideas at this point in time. "*Firinnie,*" Warren muttered as he gently blew some fairy dust into Kalen's face.

"What is your name?" Warren started.

"Kalen McTiernan."

"Why are you here?"

"I've been sent by USIS to stop Special Division from getting access to this technology."

Warren paused. Had Orlaith sent Kalen as well? Was this a test to see who was the better new recruit? "So you don't work for Special Division?" he clarified.

"No. You do."

Warren's face warmed at the accusation. "What?"

"Orlaith and a few of her loyal supporters left USIS to form Special Division. Some of her team are aware of who they really work for. Some, like yourself, have clearly been lied to."

Warren chewed the inside of his lip. It couldn't be true. "Why should I believe you? You have no magical aura, which I thought was impossible. Have you learned to fight the truth spell too?"

Shaking his head, Kalen replied solemnly, "I have trained with Scathach's living descendant. I was taught how to walk among the shadows and hide myself within the magical spectrum. Like you, I have no resistance to a truth spell."

Scathach was a warrior of legend. She used to train elite warriors in her Fortress of Shadows. He had heard rumors that she had a living descendent somewhere in the Himalayas who continued her work, but so far, no one had been able to corroborate the story. If that were true, it would certainly explain Kalen's unique ability to hide his aura. But that would also mean everything else he said was true. Could it be? Could Orlaith really be the enemy? Could she really have deceived him all this time?

"Warren, listen to me."

"No. Maybe you believe what you're saying is true. I believe what I said." He twirled his dagger between his fingers. "We need evidence to prove that one of us is right."

"You're right." Kalen chewed on his lip for a

moment. "Orlaith's serum. If it's poison like I believe it is, it proves she's really Special Division. If it's the reparation elixir you say it is, I will concede defeat, and you can bring me in."

Warren picked up the vial and considered the consequences of testing it. Orlaith couldn't lie to him, couldn't lie to all of USIS. Kalen was wrong, and he was going to prove it. Warren uncorked the serum, and immediately, his legs grew weak, his vision blurred, and his hands trembled.

"Quick. Put the lid back on." Kalen's voice was strained, and his veins stood out on his hands and neck.

Warren stoppered the vial and spent a few moments recovering. He fought back tears and rage. His body reacted to the iron and whatever else was in that serum. It would have killed every fairy in the nearby vicinity, including Orlaith.

"I'm so sorry." Kalen placed a hand on Warren's shoulder.

"It's not Orlaith," Warren whispered. "Gormund." He took a few steady breaths as the effects of the iron continued to wear off. "This serum would kill Orlaith too. Gormund is the dwarf who made it. I don't know why he wants us all dead, but he does."

Kalen sighed. "Yes, Gormund is well-known to us." His eyes were heavy with pity. "I think you know what's really going on here, but I'm happy to investigate this further with you."

Warren nodded. "The only thing I know for sure is that when I find out who is Special Division and who has been deceiving me, they are going to wish they never met me."

Kalen grinned. He inhaled but turned away and remained silent.

"Come on." Warren held out a hand for Kalen. Ivy

and her father would wake up completely oblivious to everything that had transpired. He sent a prayer to Fand and the rest of the Tuatha De Danann, asking for clarity, strength, and guidance.

"*Baile*," Warren said, powering the fairy dust in his hands.

***

Warren and Kalen appeared in an alleyway in downtown Manhattan. It was mid-morning, and the chilly air was filled with excited chatter, honking cars, and the smell of greasy street food.

Once invisible, Warren led Kalen to the enormous McDonald's in the center of Times Square. They pushed through the thronging crowds ordering a late breakfast to the restrooms and entered the handicapped stall.

"This isn't so different from the main access to the real USIS," Kalen remarked.

Every time Kalen mentioned the real USIS, it was like a knife twisting and stabbing Warren in the gut. In mere moments, he would have answers, and someone would pay for the deception.

Warren turned to Kalen, whose green eyes were regarding him with a mixture of caution and intrigue. If he were in Kalen's shoes, he wouldn't trust himself enough for what he was about to do, but Kalen had agreed to the plan, and this was part of it. "*Priosunach.*"

Kalen's arms stiffened by his sides, and his eyes glazed over. He was a complete prisoner, incapable of making any sound or movement unless Warren instructed it, but he could still see and hear things. Warren offered Kalen a silent nod.

Warren coated his hand in fairy dust and placed it against the wall. "*Dul isteech.*" The wall rippled, and he dragged Kalen into the headquarters of USIS—or Special Division—or whatever organization it actually was.

Heart hammering in his chest, this was his moment to prove himself and take down the evil that had attempted to corrupt him. If Orlaith was indeed Special Division, there was no end to the hate and loathing that Warren could muster.

On his way to Orlaith's office, Warren made a stop by Gormund's lab.

He knocked on the door, and there were a few moments of hustling and bustling about inside the workspace before the door chimed and slid open.

"Ah, you must be Warren."

"And you are the legendary Gormund."

"That I am." The burly man clapped him on the shoulder, his size blocking the view into the room. "I hear your first mission was a resounding success. Not a bad effort for a baby fairy like you."

"Orlaith knows talent when she sees it."

"Ah, I wasn't aware she was going blind."

"She's probably not wanting to fix her vision if she has to look at you all day."

Gormund grinned. "You know what, little fairy? I like you. How did it go with my serum?"

"Everything went fine. Special Division here tried to stop me, but I overpowered him." Warren winced at how untrue those words were. "Before I take him to Orlaith, I just wanted to ask if I could work with you sometime. As much as I love fieldwork, I think it would be interesting to learn some of the behind-the-scenes stuff from you."

Gormund huffed and scratched his auburn beard. "That's something you'll have to take up with Orlaith. She runs a tight ship, and everything has to be approved by her."

"I'll bring it up later. Take it easy." Warren grabbed Kalen by the elbow and pushed him deeper into Special

Division headquarters. So Kalen was right. It was Orlaith. She had lied to him this whole time. He wondered how many others knew and how many had been betrayed.

Warren led Kalen through the narrow hallway and toward the door at the far end with Orlaith's name on it in a shining gold plaque.

"Are you okay?" Warren whispered to Kalen, allowing him to answer.

"Yes. Are you?"

Warren kept his gaze strong in front of him, not trusting himself to look at Kalen. "Yeah." But no. No, he wasn't.

***

"Warren! You positively blew me away with your resourcefulness and ability!"

Normally, Warren would have lapped up her praise, but knowing the truth provided him with the armor to see her as the monster she was.

Orlaith turned her computer screen off and floated over her desk to kiss him gently on each cheek. "The target is secure, serum in place, and you even captured a Special Division traitor." She ran the back of a fingernail along Kalen's cheek. "And a handsome one at that."

Kalen couldn't move or speak, but his eyes glared at her with fierce intensity.

Warren ground his teeth and forced his shoulders to relax. "I'm glad you're pleased with my success. I'm looking forward to helping USIS get rid of Special Division once and for all."

Orlaith held out a finger. "Ah, that reminds me." She picked up a manila folder from her desk and presented it to Warren. "Thanks to your success, I have already organized your next mission. While I interrogate this one, I'm sending you off to Germany, where a physicist is close to unlocking the science of time travel. Think what we could do with that technology. We need it, and we need to keep it out of Special Division's hands."

The last thing Warren wanted to imagine was the potential devastation that would ensue if Orlaith had the ability to travel through time. She needed to be stopped. Today. "*Saoirse*," he said, releasing Kalen from the spell. He lobbed the serum at Orlaith, and together they sprinted out of her office.

Slamming the door shut behind them, trapping Orlaith in with the toxic gases leaking from the cracked glass vial, Warren caught his breath.

Nausea and weakness washed over Warren. Kalen's face was green. If this was the effect from behind a closed door, he hoped Orlaith was suffering the full effects of it inside.

"Idiot children," Orlaith growled as she kicked down the door. "You didn't expect me to poison the world and not have a backup plan?" She walked through the haze of smoke completely unfazed, fanning a collection of silver throwing knives in her fingers as she approached them with pure evil in her eyes. Wispy tendrils of the poison followed her out of the room, reaching and clawing for their victims.

Warren glanced at her on the magical spectrum and quickly returned to normal vision. Her aura was fortified with magical protection unlike he had ever seen. He had no idea what other tricks she had up her sleeve.

She pulled back her right arm to throw one of her knives.

Warren saw triple of everything, and his limbs failed to hold his weight. If the poison didn't kill him, Orlaith certainly would. In a last-ditch effort to survive, he summoned a handful of fairy dust with one hand and grabbed Kalen's leg with the other. "*Baile!*" he cried, and the room blinked out of existence.

They lay in a meadow of lush emerald green grass ringed by small shrubs and skyward-reaching trees. A dryad stared inquisitively at them from the shadows cast by the canopy.

The fog inside Warren's head began to clear as the minutes ticked by. When he had cast the teleportation spell, he expected to reappear in the house he was renting while on his mission, not his homeworld of Tir Na Nog, but he was so thankful to be here. Just being home energized him and helped some of the puzzle pieces fall in place.

Kalen groaned as he sat up. "Thank you for saving me. That was impressive. I was too weak to react in time."

"No problem." Warren fiddled with his thumbnail before meeting Kalen's eye. "You need to get back to USIS and tell them about Orlaith and Special Division. We can take them down and put a stop to it. Did you see her aura?"

He nodded. "I have never seen anything like that. How is that even possible?"

"I think I have an idea," Warren muttered. "Now she knows I'm onto her, she'll go after the machine. I can't let anything happen to Ivy or her father. I'll meet you there. Send everyone you can from USIS. If that machine is weaponized, we are all doomed."

"Be safe." Kalen's voice was laden with concern. The corner of an eye twinkled with the hint of moisture.

There was nothing safe about Warren's plan. In fact, it was the opposite of safe. But it was the only way he could see them defeating Orlaith and preventing mass genocide. It had to be done. "I will. You too."

Warren was well aware that this was potentially the last time he would ever see Kalen. But he had sworn an oath. And he might have sworn that oath under false pretenses and to the enemy, but that didn't mean his intentions weren't good or that he intended to abandon them. Orlaith would be under pressure to expedite her plan, which meant he needed to step on the gas too. He scooped up some fairy dust. "*Farraige,*" he said as he teleported away.

***

Birds chirped, and waves crashed onto the pebbled beach. Warren glanced around the deserted landscape and shivered at the veil of fog that signaled the boundary between the land of the living and of those who had passed.

He cupped his hands to his mouth and shouted, "Fand! I need you! Please!"

He waited. He had prayed to the gods ever since he was a young boy, and he believed that they listened and answered in their own way. This time though, he needed something very specific, and the only way to get that was in person.

"Fand! Please! I beg you. I have nowhere else to turn. I need you. You are the only one who can help me. As my patron goddess, please, hear my plea and answer my call."

He sat there for over an hour waiting for her, repeating his chant until he'd nearly gone hoarse. He would die on this beach before he gave up. And his friends would die back on Earth if he didn't get help.

A lone seabird glided toward him. His heart skipped a beat. Since losing her true love, Fand had devoted her life to the fae, and she had to help him now.

The white bird shimmered with golden dust as it drew nearer before transforming into the shape of a lithe woman. Tan sandals laced up to her knees, exposing strong, sun-kissed legs. A cowhide bodice cinched her waist as flowing white robes framed her figure. Her teal eyes drank him in, framed by luscious red hair and a white feathered crown. "To what do I owe the pleasure?"

Warren bowed. "Fand, I have summoned you because I require your assistance. There is a fairy, Orlaith, on Earth, who must have made a deal with a god. Her aura is unlike anything I have ever seen. I think the god or goddess is using her to kill all the fae."

Fand's eyes narrowed. "How is this possible?"

"I have—"

Fand snapped her fingers and cut him off, eyes turning gold for several moments. Her thin lips snarled. "I can't believe I hadn't sensed it before now. The magical spectrum is distorted around her. I do not know which of the Tuatha De Danann have caused this monstrosity, but believe me, I am looking forward to investigating this. No one threatens the fae without feeling the wrath of Fand!"

Warren cleared his throat. "I wish to make a deal with you. I need to stop her."

"There is no rush. You and the other fae on Earth can return to safety here, and together we can—"

"No. It cannot wait. Even if the fae abandon Earth, there are still people there who depend on me, whose lives are in danger from other threats that will eventually require my attention."

"Very well. A commendable attitude." Fand smiled sadly. "But I'm afraid I am unable to help you. There are current political activities going on amongst the gods that prevent me from interfering. That's probably why the fae are under attack."

Warren folded his arms. "I'm sorry, but I don't care about the politics of the Tuatha De Dannan. Fand, you have a duty to protect the fae, and I require assistance."

Fand sighed. "What is it with you fae and being so dramatic?" She threw her hands in the air. "Very well. As I understand it, there are concerns that a certain magical weapon is at risk of being stolen from its current location. Therefore, I will summon it here. Understand me when I say

I am not giving it to you. I am leaving it here on this beach. If you choose to steal it and use it while I am not here, and it is brought to my attention, I will have to exact an appropriate punishment on you. Do you understand?"

Warren nodded. "I do." Whether she was forced to punish him or not, someone had to do something about Orlaith and the god who was using her as their pawn.

Fand closed her eyes and began muttering under her breath.

Switching his vision to the magical spectrum, he watched as her aura pulsated with brilliant golden light. In front of her, the glow turned blinding white and solidified into a sword. Fand's aura dulled, but the light of the sword remained radiant.

As Fand uttered the last syllable, Warren switched back to his normal vision. She gazed down upon the sword laying on the pebbles. "Cliamh Solais, the Sword of Light, one of the four lost treasures of Eirean. It will be safe here."

Warren beheld the weapon with awe.

Fand's body shimmered as she returned to her avian form. "Good luck, young Warren. We will meet again soon."

Grasping the wooden handle shaped like a dog's bone, he pulled the sword from its scabbard. The shining metal glowed like a fluorescent light bulb. He had read stories of the four treasures, but never did he dream of holding one in his hand.

Sheathing the sword, he tied the scabbard to his waist. He had a god to kill.

***

Bile rose to the back of his throat at the scene in front of him. Too many bodies lay scattered about. Humans. Fairies. Gnomes. Two centaurs. Several witches. Their lifeless shapes burned into Warren's mind, but thankfully, none of them were Ivy's or Kalen's.

Ivy was in her father's armchair where he'd left her. Her chest rose and fell as she remained in a deep slumber. The sleeping spell would still be effective for another couple of hours, keeping her out of harm's way. Bounding down into the basement, Warren found Orlaith standing over Mr. Winters, who was working on his machine. Kalen's body lay crumpled near Orlaith's feet. Unconscious, but alive.

Orlaith snarled as Warren drew the sword. Light illuminated the dark recesses of the basement.

"Mr. Winters, run!" Warren pounced at Orlaith, slashing through the air. She ducked under the swinging blade, swiping at Warren's ribs with her silver dagger.

The dagger failed to penetrate his suit, but his ribs bruised under the pressure. Pain pierced his side with each breath and every movement.

Swinging his leg around, Warren drove a powerful kick at Orlaith's head.

She brought her arm up, blocked it, then latched onto his leg, twisting him.

Warren rolled with it, jumping into the air and freeing his limb. He landed, sword at the ready, and ducked under a jab from her dagger.

A second dagger appeared in her other hand, and she came at Warren with a fury of jabs, slices, and swings. He dodged each one until she ensnared his sword and yanked it from his grip.

The Sword of Light flew through the air to the other side of the basement, and Orlaith stood over him, dagger poised over his chest. "You're going to die one way or another. Shall I make it quick for you, or do you want to wait until the machine is primed?"

Warren coughed and winced at the pain spreading under his ribs. "Fand knows the truth. Whether I die or not, you've already lost. The god you serve will soon be imprisoned."

Orlaith laughed. "Fand will do no such thing." She shook her head. "The world is changing, Warren. Can't you feel it? The gods abandoned us long ago. But he cares. Balor is returning to us. He promises a new world order, and we can be at the forefront of this revolution." She tilted her head to the side and smiled sadly. "But you won't live long enough to witness it." She pressed the dagger into the soft flesh between his ribs and pushed down hard.

Silver entered his bloodstream immediately and began weakening his body and softening his mind. There was no pain, only a gentle warmth that cocooned him. His eyes grew heavy with sadness and regret. He was willing to die to save the world, but he couldn't even do that.

"I'm sorry, Warren. You are not important. Neither am I. We are a part of something bigger. Like bees that are nothing without their queen. Our gods are returning to Earth. Fand is one of our biggest threats. You fae would do anything for her, and we can't have pesky annoyances like you to deal with." She sheathed her dagger and turned her attention to the machine, fiddling with the mechanics.

Cold set in on his hands and feet, slowly spreading up his limbs. The sword danced in his vision; there were three, four, five blades. He blinked, and for a moment, he had clarity. He saw the sword and knew he could make it.

He took a handful of fairy dust and slathered it on his wound. "*Leigheas*," he breathlessly muttered. His skin tried to knit itself together; his platelets within his blood vessels attempted to clot and plug the wounds, but the damage was too severe. He had moments left on this world, and the sword was too far away. He willed the sword to come to him, to fly into his hand. But there was no such magic.

With a massive effort, he pushed himself onto his hands and feet and lurched to the sword. It felt ten times heavier than before, and he swung it over his shoulder like a baseballer stepping up to the plate.

Orlaith spun around and released a throwing knife.

Warren swung the sword at her, barely feeling her blade protruding from his chest. With a breathless cough, he fell to his knees, collapsing in a heap beside Orlaith's decapitated body.

***

Warren woke with a groan. He ran a hand along his bare chest and felt the scars from Orlaith's dagger wounds. They were tender to touch and stung as he tried to sit up. He looked around Ivy's bedroom and saw one of her dad's old shirts. He stood and put it on, just about to head off in search of answers when a bird flew through the window and shimmered into Fand.

Warren's heart raced. What did she want?

"Greetings, Warren."

"Fand." Warren bowed his head.

"I retrieved the sword before anyone knew it was missing, so you will remain punishment-free."

Warren wasn't aware he was worried about that until his shoulders relaxed. "That's good. Is everything okay amongst the Tuatha De Danann?"

"The council is a joke," she said, shaking her head. "You have inspired me, Warren. Balor will try again. I'm not sure when or how, but I will not sit idle while he destroys the world."

"That's great. I definitely couldn't cope on my own." Warren subconsciously massaged his wounds.

"And you shouldn't have to." Fand dissolved into a bird and flew away.

He walked down the corridor and followed the hushed voices chatting in the kitchen.

"Warren! You're okay!" Ivy ran to him and embraced him in a warm hug.

"Oh, ouch!"

"I'm sorry." Ivy jumped back. "I'm so sorry."

"It's okay. I'm still a bit sore."

"Yeah, you almost died. Don't do that again, please." Kalen playfully punched Warren on the arm.

Butterflies tingled inside Warren's stomach. "Do I have you to thank for the healing?"

Kalen grinned. "I guess I'll be able to think of some way you can repay me."

Warren smiled and turned his attention to Ivy. "Is your dad okay? Everything all right with the machine?"

"Oh, yeah. A group of your people were here earlier, and they flew him and the machine to some secret place. I don't know much, and I'm hoping you can fill me in." She raised an eyebrow. "Kalen says you work for the government?"

A rush of memories came flooding back. If it weren't for Kalen, he could have ended up much deeper in Special Division. Who knew what he would have been guilty of in a few months' time.

"Warren and I work together for the government, yes. We used to work in different departments, but I've spoken to my boss—" Kalen turned to face Warren with a big grin on his face "—and he'd be happy for you to come work with us."

Warren's heart thudded with happiness.

Ivy turned around and began boiling water. She opened up a cupboard and bent down to retrieve some mugs.

In a moment, Kalen was beside Warren, entwining his fingers with Warren's.

Warren took his hand and placed it behind Kalen's head and brought him forward until their lips touched.

Ivy's voice barely registered. "I don't know about you two, but I could really go for a hot chocolate."

Warren pressed himself against Kalen, feeling his muscular chest against his own.

"Are you ignoring me? I said, do you guys want a— oh, sorry. I'll give you some space," she said with an excited squeak.

Warren laughed and pushed Kalen away. "No, it's fine. And yes, thanks, I'd love a hot chocolate."

The McWaterford Witch

Hanna Day

"I'd like the Jolly Meal with extra jolly," Jane said from the backseat.

The drive-thru attendant, a middle-aged woman who was squeezed into a blinding neon green uniform that clashed with her sour expression, peered at the girls through the car window. The static from her headphones crackled as she leaned forward. "So, do you want the burger or the nuggets, kid?"

The car sat alone in the drive-thru of McWitchy's Burgers and Buns, a lonely fast-food place just off the freeway. Its distinctive purple A-Frame rooftop and windows glinted in the afternoon sun, making it stand out starkly among the evergreen trees.

Traffic jammed up the highway on their way to the campgrounds, and after four hours in the car, Mrs. Yamaguchi had finally given into the girls' incessant nagging for a snack. It was far too late for lunch and far too early for dinner, so in Jane's mind, it was a perfect time for a rest stop. Her stomach rumbled. Unlike Michelle's mom, Jane's parents never bought fast food, except for special occasions. They need never know.

"The cheeseburger, please," Jane replied.

"The nuggets!"

"Me too!"

Michelle and Katie, Jane's fellow Mountain Gals,

crowded around the backseat window next to the drive-thru window. Mrs. Yamaguchi, Michelle's mom, said nothing. One manicured hand drummed the steering wheel as she waved her other impatiently, the credit card flashing in the afternoon sun.

"I'll be at the next window," the attendant said, handing back the swiped card.

Jane's stomach grumbled at the thought of a juicy delicious burger and the toys in the jolly little box. Something about fast food was so appealing, even though it wasn't good for her. Too much sodium or something like that, according to her dad.

"Hey!" Michelle leaned over Jane from the middle seat to look out the window. "There's a playground!"

Jane twisted in her seat. Walls of glass trapped spiral slides and pirate ship netting.

"Let's go!" Katie shouted. "Can we, Mrs. Yamaguchi?"

"No," Mrs. Yamaguchi said, "we're not stopping. We're already late."

Michelle plopped back down into her seat. "Aw. I never get to go."

The cashier greeted them as they pulled up to the pickup window. She stuffed neatly wrapped packages of food inside bright green cardboard boxes, glaring all the while. Jane reached out of the backseat window.

"Your meal...with extra jolly." The cashier looked at Jane. A sad old lady doing a teenager's job. That's what Mom would've said. That's what she always said about the cashiers whenever they got fast food. The cashier glanced at the Cadre number stitched on Jane's vest.

"Thank you!" Michelle blurted out.

Jane suppressed an eye roll. She only said that because her *mom* was there. Michelle was one of those girls who said one thing in front of her parents but another to her friends. Nothing wrong with that, as Jane did the same, but so blatant? No, thank you.

Secretly, part of Jane hoped the toy would be the heroine from that new Disney movie. All the commercials advertised it. Though of course, she would never say that in front of everyone else. Toys were for little kids.

As Mrs. Yamaguchi rejoined traffic, Jane and the other girls opened their boxes. Grease coated the box's dark gray interior, leaving behind unpleasant spots on the cardboard. Her cheeseburger was wrapped in plain white paper, the grease spots nearly transparent and coating her fingers in a fine, thin film. She rummaged around the burger and stopped as something soft—like her grandmother's fur coat—caressed her. Warmth radiated from the fur and into her chilled fingers. Perhaps it was the motion of the car or the sugar buzzing through her head, but it seemed to move, curling between her fingers. For a long moment, she kept her hand in the box, afraid to grasp whatever it was and pull it free.

"What's this?" Michelle exclaimed, holding up a rabbit's foot. "Oh no! The poor rabbit."

"I'm sure it's fake," Mrs. Yamaguchi replied between bites of her quarter-pounder. "We used to have those when I was a kid."

"What did you get, Jane?" Michelle asked.

Jane investigated her Jolly Meal box. Silly to be scared of such a little thing. The wrappers shifted, and she stifled a gasp. Jane snatched the thing and pulled it loose. A small tiger's tail keychain dangled from her fingers. In the light, the fur looked fake, the orange too bright.

"Well," Katie said, "I like mine." She jiggled a horseshoe keychain. "Think it's fate?"

There was nothing Katie wanted more than her own horse. Her parents drove an hour out of the city, weekly, so she could attend riding lessons. If you got her going, she would never shut up about them. Quite frankly, Jane thought horses were ugly, pooped a lot, and were too intimidating to ride.

"Sure," Jane replied.

Jane placed the tiger's tail back into the greasy box. She unwrapped the burger and smashed it into her mouth. The slightly soggy bun and the hardened cheese still tasted good. She ripped apart a packet of salt and dumped it on the fries, which were lightly browned and fresh from the fryer. In between bites of her burger, she jammed fries into her mouth. Though she knew she'd had enough, when she finished her extra Jolly Meal with extra salty fries, she wanted to scream at Mrs. Yamaguchi to order more because they all were still extra hungry.

But that was bad manners, especially for someone who had volunteered to drive them to the campgrounds, and Jane had to be a good little girl. But good little girl didn't quite apply to Jane—she'd just turned thirteen! Not so little anymore.

Crystals of salt stuck to her fingers as she smashed the last soggy bits of bun and pickle into her mouth. Jane looked outside the window. Towering pines grew thicker as they drove into the woods, leaving behind the rolling countryside to ascend the mountains. Ominous gray clouds twisted and curled in the afternoon sky as though threatening a thunderstorm if she didn't behave. She slurped on her root beer and watched the trees zip by, the condensation on her paper cup dripping down over her fingers, getting the salt into unseen papercuts and onto the trash balled up on her lap.

***

Weeds and tree roots cracked the parking lot surrounding a gray industrial building. After dumping their trash into a large dumpster on the side of the building, Mrs. Yamaguchi led them inside. One of the first things Jane noticed was the overwhelming damp as if someone had left the windows open during the morning rainstorm. Jane glared at her brand-new hiking shoes. The heavy soles would surely squeeze the moisture from the shaggy carpet.

Jane tugged at the bandanna around her neck. "That's not a campground!"

"Sure, it is." Mrs. Yamaguchi heaved a suitcase from the trunk. "We're not quite there yet."

The pictures in the Mountain Gal handbook had painted a rather specific idea of camping in Jane's mind. Picturesque campgrounds with tents pitched in neat, perfect circles. Marshmallows toasted to a light golden brown, smushed together with graham crackers and dark melted chocolate. A roaring fire to warm the soul from the chill seeping through the trees. But her family never went camping. Too many mosquitoes, her mother said. Too cold, her father claimed. Too boring, her sister whined. But maybe, perhaps it could be just right for Jane.

"Come on," Mrs. Yamaguchi said. "They're waiting for us out back."

They left behind the damp room and went outside. Instead of the great big fire pit Jane had imagined, with blackened stones surrounding a warm crackling fire, one of those janky metal outdoor fireplaces rested on the concrete deck. Her fellow Mountain Gals sat on plastic chairs, all smiles as they ate hot dogs off paper plates. Jane thought of the camping cutlery hanging from her backpack. Guess there wasn't any need for those either.

"So glad you made it!" Miss Gamble leaped to her feet. "I was getting worried."

At twenty-eight, the Cadre leader looked more like a big sister than a mom. She had had her daughter at eighteen. A floozy, Mom always said, and at least a decade younger than all the other moms. Unmarried. Good thing she kept the baby. As much as Jane liked Miss Gamble, she couldn't help but echo some of the other moms' sentiments. She wouldn't have a daughter in high school like Miss Gamble. Jane didn't want the other moms to gossip about her like Mrs. Yamaguchi did.

"We got caught in traffic and had to make a pit stop." Mrs. Yamaguchi examined her nails, not once looking up at Miss Gamble.

"Well, I'm glad you're here now," Miss Gamble replied, swinging her arm enthusiastically.

"This is fine," Michelle said. "I mean, it's not like we're staying in a cave or anything."

Jane fought back a grimace. Nothing ever seemed to bother Michelle—things were always fine. Fine, fine, fine.

"Shouldn't we set up our tents?" Jane asked.

"Oh, we're not sleeping outside," Miss Gamble said.

"But…" Jane looked around. "I thought this was a camping trip."

"It is, Jane, it is!" The Cadre leader's smile faltered.

As the girls chatted around the pitiful excuse of a campfire, Jane sat defiantly in a chair, arms crossed over her chest. Joining the Mountain Gals was supposed to be a great way to get out of the house and in the dirt without getting yelled at. Join the Mountain Gals, Mom said; it'll look great on college applications. Yeah, right!

The fire didn't do anything to alleviate the muggy air, which smelled like the morning's thunderstorm. Everything from the air around her to the clothes on her back reeked of mosquito repellent. Smoke and embers curled into the air as the girls, fueled by marshmallows and hot chocolate, sang horribly out-of-tune songs, with some girls two or three beats behind the rest. Jane should know. She took piano lessons.

As they settled down, Miss Gamble stood, the

badges on her vest glittering in the firelight.

"Now that we're here, we can officially start the weekend! Everyone recite the Mountain Gal Oath!"

"We are the Mountain Gals!
I will be as solid as the rocks we climb.
And always reaching for the stars!
I will respect the mountains, tall and mighty.
Respect friendship—for together we summit to reach our dreams.
Mountain Gals belay one another to the summit
And we never leave each other behind."

Their chanting floated through the campsite, echoing on the concrete walls and into the woods. Jane had recited these words several times before, but always in the school gym at Cadre meetings.

Once the girls settled down, Miss Gamble stood once more.

"Tonight, we'll go to bed early and get up at three a.m. to watch the lunar eclipse. Does anyone know what happens during a lunar eclipse?"

Jane's hand shot up so fast she knocked Michelle's elbow. "A lunar eclipse is when the moon passes directly behind the Earth into its umbra. That gives the moon its reddish color like when the sky turns red during sunset."

"That's right, Jane."

"Ow." Michelle rubbed her elbow. "Watch it, Jane."

"Then we'll memorize the fall constellations, which qualifies you for the astronomy merit badge," Miss Gamble continued. "Be in bed by nine, girls! We've got a long weekend ahead of us."

"When are we going rock climbing?" Jane asked, thrusting up her hand again.

She wouldn't be a Mountain Gal unless she

conquered some mountain this weekend.

"We still have a lot of work to do with our knots and harnesses," Miss Gamble replied. "We'll do the indoor rock-climbing gym another weekend."

"Oh…" Jane tried not to let the disappointment seep through her.

"Don't worry; we're still going to learn a lot this weekend." Miss Gamble's face lit up. "Oh, I almost forgot!" She dug into one of her vest's deep pockets and took out a golden carabiner, one of those special spring-loaded hooks used for rock climbing. "This is for you, Katie."

"Yay!" Katie exclaimed.

"Wait," Jane said, looking at the carabiner. "Why don't we get one?"

"Katie sold enough macaroons to get one, but she didn't come to the last meeting to get it."

Right. Jane had been just six boxes short for that reward, but she had really wanted one. Besides, everyone knew Katie didn't do any *real* work. It was silly to feel this way about a little hook that probably wasn't even made for real climbing. Just something fancy to put on her backpack. But for some reason, it seemed wrong that Katie won it. All she wanted to do was ride horses, so what on earth would she use a carabiner for?

As the sun set over the crinkled brown trees, something stirred within Jane. Insects seemed to crawl all over her, but no clouds of bugs buzzed around her, and she hadn't touched any poison ivy. No rash. Just a deep, deep itch underneath her skin.

This wasn't a real camping trip, Jane decided. It was just as dull as being at home over the weekend. Trees circled their fire pit, their dried needles crunching under her sneakers, but she didn't feel scared like she would have out in the real wilderness.

Katie, it seemed, had too many s'mores. She pranced

around the dry grass, shaking her fiery hair like a horse's mane. Michelle twirled her purple bandanna round and round her fingertips, flinching when Katie stomped on a particularly large tree branch.

"Did you know?" Michelle asked in a quivering voice. "There's a witch around these parts?"

The itch attacked Jane's bottom. "No."

"She lives near that old town where we got gas."

"And what? She haunts the drive-thru?"

"Oh, come on!" Katie plopped down next to her. "You're not telling the story right!"

Jane crossed her arms.

"Another Cadre, back when the Gals started, used to camp here too." Katie clicked on her flashlight under her chin, the light transforming her eyes into sunken shadows. "One night, they went on a hike much like this one so they could collect the last of their flowers for their botany badge. As the blood moon rose, they saw something on the McWaterford Trail."

"So, was it a witch?" Jane asked.

Thirteen years old was too old for scary stories. The girls in high school—the ones in the other Cadre—they didn't talk about this stuff. They talked about boys. About college. About real life and real things.

"Let me finish!" Katie's eyes bulged slightly. "As the girls approached the apparition, they realized it was a spirit of the woods. The spirit held her bony wand high," Katie said, lifting her flashlight into the air, "and exclaimed, 'You have trespassed on my land!'

"Furious that the girls were picking her flowers, which she had grown from seeds to petals, the spirit sought to curse them by turning them into animals of the forest. But one of the girls was a budding witch, and before the spirit could finish her curse, the little witch reacted. This girl, she didn't stand for this kind of stuff. She shouted to the other girls, 'Oaths bind! Nothing but our oath will keep us safe!' Now, as this was their first ever camping trip, the girls still carried their stuffed animals with them, even into the deep dark woods. And nothing makes an oath stronger than sacrificing the things you love the most, so as the witch descended upon the spirit, the girls tossed their furry friends into the fire their friend had created with a snap of her fingers. One girl sacrificed a bunny named Carrots. A tiger cub called Calvin and Biscuit the stuffed horse also met a fiery death."

"I heard it was a unicorn," Michelle drawled.

"It was a horse," Katie replied, her lips drawing tightly together. "Because horses are obviously superior."

Michelle rolled her eyes.

"By sacrificing that most dear to them, the girls banished the spirit and she was never seen again around these parts. Every girl escaped—except for one. The little witch stayed behind to finish the binding oath and was never seen again." Katie paused for dramatic effect. "Some thought the spirit took her in exchange for the others. Or that the witch stayed to replant the flowers the spirit lost. In any case, the witch now haunts McWaterford. Sometimes, you can hear her screeching in the dead of night, and on the night of a fall moon, the witch appears on the trail." Katie's grin widened. "If you're not careful, she may just snatch you up to replace the friends she lost."

"That's a load of baloney!" Jane exclaimed.

"*You're* a load of baloney!" Katie shot back.

Jane sat quietly, tolerating the stupid urban legend as much as she could. Katie probably forgot the real story and got inspired by their trip to the fast-food place— McWitchy's, wasn't it? Those stuffed animals were the same as the Jolly Meal toys.

"This is so lame," Jane said, leaning in close to the others. "This isn't a real camping trip."

A spark of fear flickered through Michelle's eyes, though it was gone in an instant.

"Let's see the eclipse our own way," Jane said. "Out in the wilderness. Like we're supposed to. Not in someone's backyard."

"Is that a good idea?" Katie asked. "We'll get in trouble—"

"I don't care."

A Cadre leader called out to them. The girls trickled back inside the building and pulled their bags from the pile on the floor. Jane glanced up at the moon. It wouldn't turn red completely until later that night. Jane also couldn't stop itching her butt. Must have sat on poison ivy or something. Awesome.

The Cadre lined up their sleeping bags around the perimeter of the room, as though keeping watch over the empty space inside. As Jane stared at the ceiling, illuminated by night lights plugged into the wall, she wished she could see the stars. It was, after all, the reason why she had come.

She wriggled inside her sleeping bag, trying to find some comfort on the cold hard floor. The incipient dampness weighed down the room, and every breath felt like inhaling a mouthful of must. What was the point of driving hours out of the city for this? It didn't seem right that they were earning their astronomy badges inside a concrete complex.

She looked to either side. Michelle and Katie were already asleep, perhaps dreaming of the blood-red moon. Michelle still clutched her rabbit's foot as if for good luck. They clung to their stuffed animals, dragging them along on a camping trip when they were nothing more than dead weight. Did they really expect to carry them all the way to the top of the mountain when they started climbing for real? Hard as it was, Jane had left her old friend Snowball at home. She got over it, and so would they.

Jane leaned over Katie's sleeping bag after the Cadre leaders started snoring. The other girl had thrown the golden carabiner carelessly over her backpack. One kick would send it spinning to the floor. Jane reached for the oval-shaped hook as she thought of all its different uses for climbing mountains. She wasn't in the business of selling hundreds of macaroons just to get one. Selling macaroons wouldn't get her up a mountain. She clasped the carabiner and stuck it into her pajama pocket.

"What are you doing?" Katie whispered, sitting up in her sleeping bag, her curly red hair tossed over her face.

It took all of Jane's might not to flinch. The darkness hid the red flush creeping up the side of her neck. A rushing sound filled Jane's ears, so loud she almost couldn't hear what they were saying. She swallowed and collected herself. It wasn't as if Katie would miss out on anything. If Jane had gotten something horsey, she would've given it to her. She'd make up for it later.

"Let's go outside," Jane said instead. "I was just getting up to go unless you're too chicken."

They whispered so as not to wake the leaders asleep on the other side of the room. Katie's rustling made Michelle stir.

"You can't talk the talk," Jane said with a slight sneer, "and not back it up. It's witching hour. You afraid of the witch?"

"Why should we go?" Michelle whispered. "It's cold outside. I'm fine here."

"Come on, you didn't want to come in the first place," Jane whispered back. "This isn't fine, and you know it." She threw her hands out to the room to emphasize her point, drawing Katie's attention to the windows. "I don't believe in witches or ghosts or ghouls, but I do believe in science. That's real."

Michelle looked at Jane with wide eyes for a few

moments before oozing out of her sleeping bag. They tiptoed across the room, the dull bathroom light illuminating their escape.

The fresh air reinvigorated Jane as she pushed the front door open. The stars spun around them as they crept into the darkness. They tromped and stomped through the undergrowth, turning off their flashlights when they heard an animal scuttling in the distance.

"What was that?" Michelle grabbed Jane's arm.

"Just a squirrel."

"Didn't sound like a squirrel to me."

Jane shined her flashlight into the woods.

"Do you even know where you're going, Jane?" Michelle asked.

"We're going north."

"North?" Katie put her hands on her hips. "What does that mean?"

"Eh?"

"Going north...you know..." Katie waved dramatically. "What's north?"

"Into the woods." Jane didn't want to stray too far. No one had given them a map, so she didn't want to get lost.

She knew *all* the constellations. The Little Dipper pointed toward Polaris, which pointed north. Unlike *some* people, she had read the handbook before this weekend. Though, as she peered up at the night sky, she couldn't locate the faint star as the moonlight washed everything away in its cool white light.

"I want to go back," Michelle whined.

Jane spun around. "What?"

"I was fine back at camp."

"You're always fine!" Jane threw her hands in the air. "Fine, fine, fine. That's all you ever say!"

"What's wrong with being fine?" Michelle demanded, plucking a stray leaf from her hair. "I could be sleeping!"

"Because you won't get anywhere being *fine*."

Even as Jane spoke, she was acutely aware that these words did not belong to her. Never be content being mediocre; don't be content with being *fine*, especially if things were not fine. This inability to spring to action, to want something more than was provided, irritated her.

"Well, we won't get lost, for one thing," Katie piped up. "Since you know *everything*."

"So? What are you going to do?" Jane asked. "Summon your imaginary horse to take us back to camp?"

"You're a jerk, Jane!" Katie exclaimed. "You're *always* a know-it-all! You've been mad ever since I sold more macaroons than you."

"I'm not a jerk!" Jane spat, her nails leaving red lines on her arm as she scratched at a bug bite.

But Katie *had* sold more macaroons than Jane had, and she had cheated because her mom took the order form to work. No one had helped Jane with anything. She'd spent weeks knocking on every neighbor's door, talking about how the proceeds would help her get up a mountain, but came back with orders only from friends and family. She wanted to be one of the youngest Mountain Gals to summit the world's tallest mountains, but no one seemed to care. Not even her friends.

"Do you hear that?" Michelle whimpered.

But Jane couldn't hear anything. She was focused on her itchy butt. In fact, Jane began to scratch all over. Small red bumps rose on her skin as the itching intensified to a white-hot burn. Coarse, thick hair erupted on her cheeks, her arms, in all the places where hair shouldn't be. Her hands had melded into three thick fingers.

No, not fingers. Paws. She had paws.

She plastered her hands to her face and screamed. The world loomed over her as her shoulders hunched. Long fuzzy gray ears grew out of Michelle's head. Katie's face elongated, and her eyes moved to the side of her head as if someone was squeezing it like playdough. In seconds, the transformations were complete. They were no longer three girls but a tiger, a rabbit, and a horse. Jane opened her jaws to shriek but could not produce any sound. Michelle, a rabbit, scurried in terrified circles around paws and hooves. Jane stamped her paws in frustration and let out a low growl. Her tail flicked back and forth in that same irritated manner her cat did whenever she tried to pet him.

Jane's mind raced furiously as she tried to recall the series of unfortunate events. No matter how many times she blinked her yellow eyes or licked the black lips of her new muzzle, she couldn't quite understand what had happened.

Birds honked as something crashed in the distance, their dark shapes flitting across the moon. The trio turned. At first, Jane couldn't quite decide what she was seeing. One of their discarded fast-food boxes, grown to the size of a small shed, tumbled through the clearing. The fur all along Jane's spine shot up as it stopped in front of them. A dark line spread from one end of the box to the other, and as its lipless mouth opened, she saw nothing but infinite darkness.

A roar cracked the air as Jane growled, her fangs glistening in the moonlight. The super-sized box considered them for a moment, still in its absurdity, then lurched forward and swallowed them whole.

Hooves, paws, teeth, and nails seemed everywhere as the girls toppled in the darkness. Jane dug her claws into the sides of the box, tightening her grip as the box shuddered in revulsion. What if she or Katie crushed Michelle under their massive weight? The box seemed to hop in great leaps, crushing twigs, leaves, even whole trees underneath it. And as Jane clung to its thick interior walls, she couldn't help but feel as if she were a cheap children's toy also, just waiting for a giant's child to pluck her from the box.

Light blinded her as the box tipped over and spilled them onto the floor. Jane snarled as a metal horseshoe stamped on her tail, snapping her jaws even as Katie backed away. Michelle's little pink nose wrinkled as her beady eyes bulged in their sockets. The familiar, achingly tantalizing smell of greasy, salty goodness infused the air. An 8-bit jingle echoed off the tiled walls and low-humming machines. Empty booths and tables stank of industrial bleach. The checkered linoleum floor glistened as if it had just been mopped. Too clean. The lights far too bright for this time of the night. A flutter ran through her stomach as Jane saw a large glass wall entombing a playground within.

A cashier walked to the counter from the back room. She surveyed the menagerie, her shadow flitting about unnaturally behind her.

Jane blinked in slow motion, her amber eyes focused on the woman in the gaudy uniform. Every single rational bone in her new body screamed at her as though desperate to tell her that this was all a dream, and she was just being irrational. But perhaps she *was* being too rational. Maybe that's why she had never won the carabiner in the first place. Jane propped back on her haunches and launched her heavy body into the air. Even with all the fur weighing her down, she felt as if she could take on the whole world. Or the witch who had cursed them!

Not only did Jane have paws, but she had claws. Very, very sharp claws. She opened her black-lipped jaws wide as she leaped at the witch.

The witch lifted a finger and pointed to Jane. With a clash and a cloud of smoke, Jane changed once again in midair. Her hands felt naked, devoid of claws that could hurt the witch who had done them harm. The witch stood near the garish plastic statue of the mascot: an old woman with green skin and a black pointed hat. She leaned against it, her hands crossed over her chest, a grimace gracing her face.

"I've been waiting so long for little girls to come back."

Jane stamped her foot. "I'm not a little girl!"

The witch pulled off her baseball cap and tossed it aside. She could have been a mother to one of her school friends down the road: a pale, middle-aged woman with gray around her temples, who didn't wear makeup to hide the crow's-feet sagging her eyes.

The witch grabbed the lapels of Jane's vest and pulled her closer. The soles of Jane's shoes squealed as she dug her heels into the floor.

"Be still, little girl." The witch's wild brown hair stuck to her sweaty forehead. A basket of fries, still dripping with hot oil, appeared in her other hand. She shook it at Jane.

Flecks of hot oil splattered Jane's face, making her wince. "What?"

To Jane's horror, the witch turned the basket over her head. Instead of boiling oil, a coolness trickled down her brow and onto her shoulders. The witch stumbled backward.

"You can't break the curse. Wasted magic!" The witch wailed, splashing the remainder of the oil across the spotless floor. "All for nothing!"

"I...can't break the curse?" Jane felt at her clothes and hair but felt no wetness.

The witch grabbed Jane by the wrist and dragged her to the glass playground doors. Her screams echoed off the empty plastic booths and concrete walls. Only the constant hum of the ice-cream maker and the crackling headset for the drive-thru window answered back. The witch hauled her up a flight of stairs, waving her hand over the playground. The ball pit, in bright primary colors, pulsated like a heart below them.

Cold sweat raced down Jane's back as the witch pushed her into the ball pit. As she sank into the pool of soft plastic balls, she flailed, searching for the floor to launch herself back into the air. Nothing but darkness greeted her. Balls cascaded around her as the playground flung her to the edge of the ball pit. Jane grasped the edge and pulled herself up, grimacing as she looked around. No way out except through a tube. After taking a deep breath, Jane clambered into it. The tubes seemed so much smaller than any other indoor playground she had been in and shuddered as she crawled, the ridges between sections of tubes pinching her fingers.

The hard colorful plastic walls closed in all around her, pushing her along as if the playground had swallowed a particularly large chunk of meat. Everything tilted, the playground tipping her deeper into the maze of tubes and slides. Jane slid on her stomach, throwing her arms over her head as she slammed against a bubble-window facing the back room. The kitchen sat still, the machinery shiny as if it had never been used. The witch stood in the back room, her hair falling out of its hairnet as she fussed over a bubbly, hissing pot of cooking oil. She held the metal fry basket, muttering to herself.

"Let me out!" Jane pounded a fist on the clouded plastic. "Hey!"

The witch turned and stomped away, cans flying off the walls as she threw her hands into the air.

Would Jane be stuck here forever? Always smelling of salt and grease and always slithering through the tubes?

Jane didn't know. All she did know was that her friends were in danger and she was stuck all alone in a children's play-place, too old to care for it and yet too young for any grown-ups to think she'd be interested in anything else. But why should she save them? Katie got more than she ever bargained for—she didn't own a horse but *was* a horse. And Michelle could scamper off back to the campsite, back to her mom—where everything was fine. They were too complacent, never going beyond what was expected just because it was convenient. Would they even rescue her after what she'd done?

Jane's bones creaked as she moved to another tube, one where a plastic bubble looked up to the glass ceiling. Stars winked at her as the moon was just starting to go into the eclipse. Its white surface, mottled by the gray shadows of the man in the moon, now had a bloody tinge.

Her stomach gurgled. While this place smelled of cheap plastic and the sweat of excited children scampering up and down the playground, she was still in a fast-food joint. Jane pressed her hand against the clear plastic.

"Hello?" her voice echoed. "What happened to my friends?"

The ball pit shuddered. A low moan echoed into the glass room, crawling up the slides and vibrating like vocal cords. Squeaking noises emanated behind her. As she turned, the floor lifted her to a neon green tic-tac-toe panel embedded into the wall. Its blocks spun rapidly, the block colors blurring together. After a few seconds, they screeched to a halt. Jane raised an uncertain hand and pushed the middle panel. Instead of the usual Xs and Os, a girl's silhouette appeared. A witch's hat twirled into the top right square. Jane flicked another, and the witch responded in kind. Another two moves.

Tie.

Another low rumble shook the playground. A long corridor surrounded by thick plastic netting rose to her right. Thin poles with circular platforms, spaced about two feet apart, led the way to the other side. Thick green boggy water flooded the floor, bubbling, burping, and burbling a foul stench—as if an animal had died and rotted in the water—and made her eyes water.

"Aren't you going to show me the way out?" Jane called out. "If I go, will you free my friends?"

A breeze drifted through the hallway, bringing with it the cool autumn air. Jane hopped onto one of the platforms and grasped the metal pole, her heart jumping into her throat as she wobbled and weaved her way to the exit. The bones of the playground shifted, rearranging themselves to accommodate her. The tube on her right transformed into a slide. She adjusted her tangled shoelaces, crawled over to the mouth of the tube, and slid down into the darkness.

The slide twisted in great big loops, reminding her of the first time she'd gone down a closed water slide. Nothing but the sound of rushing water and the occasional flash of light as the open sections flew over her.

Jane tumbled out onto a hard mat and skidded onto the linoleum floor. The glass door to the main restaurant cracked open. She walked past the tables, past the booths, and toward the counter and the back room. The building fluctuated, expanding and contracting like a lung, forever cursed to inhale victims and breathe out magic. She glanced at the witch mascot, grinning at her with its fixed plastic smile, and froze.

The statue held a big clear display case containing toys you could get if you bought the Jolly Meal—or whatever it was around here. A small horse pranced around, so tiny Jane could barely hear the neighing, and a rabbit dug uselessly at the bottom of the case. Jane's breath fogged the plastic as she examined them, her heart racing. Jane's hand raced over the plastic, trying to find an opening, anything to get them out.

Once, while playing outside in the snow, Michelle had screamed when another kid had pushed her into a playground tube. Some boys had thought it'd be funny to shove her in there and stuff up the ends with snow. She couldn't handle closed spaces. Jane rushed to one of the tables and grabbed a chair. It swiveled around but didn't budge. One of those fast-food chairs stuck to the table.

Jane's eyes fell to the counter and into the kitchen beyond. Could she steal a knife from the witch and pry the display case open? What else could she do?

Chicken nuggets and French fries sizzled in oil, while burger patties cooked on an unattended grill. Hovering knives chopped lettuce, tomatoes, and pickles. Ice-cream machines churned out an endless parade of chocolate ice-cream cones. Jane took a step and winced as her sneakers squeaked on the floor. She tiptoed toward one of the knives, one of those big, broad ones her mom never let her use. Much too easy to chop off a finger with, my dear.

She grasped the black handle. The knife struggled within her grasp like a live wire before it twisted out of her hands. Metal whistled through the air as every single knife in the kitchen abandoned its task and rocketed toward her. Jane shrieked as she threw her arms over her head. Cold sweat flushed through her as knives whizzed past and dug into the wall behind her. Some bounced off the kitchenware. Boiling water bubbled over the side of a big pot and hissed as it hit the flames beneath.

"How did you get out?" The witch appeared at the other side of the kitchen, meddling with the fry baskets.

"I played a game." Jane straightened her back. "The playground let me out."

Jane's eyes dropped to the floor. Delicate blue flowers formed an island of natural color in a sea of grease, the fresh earth beneath them dark and deep. They trailed across the floor, their thin vines curling at the tips, searching for tree roots to latch onto. Fireflies flitted over them, landing on the wide, broad petals for a respite before swirling into the air once again. Jane swallowed. "I'm sorry I can't break the curse, Miss Witch."

"Sit!" The witch pushed outward with her hand, jerking Jane backward into a chair that appeared out of thin air. She thrust a potato peeler into Jane's hand. "Peel the potatoes, girl, or I'll throw you back in the ball pit and make sure you stay there."

"Why?"

Gooseflesh prickled Jane's skin as the witch zoomed up to her. "If you can't free me, then make yourself useful!" The witch's voice boomed as her eyes grew dark and wild.

Jane flinched. The peeler wasn't any kind of weapon. No hope of using it to take down a woman with magic. It trembled along with her whole body.

"Unless," the witch sneered, "you *are* a useless, selfish brat."

Annoyance bubbled inside Jane, eating up what fear she had. How could the witch say that? She wasn't useless.

"Will peeling potatoes free my friends?"

"If you can't break the curse, then I'll need to find another who can."

Jane sat and began peeling. With every scrape, she felt, even more, a prisoner. She held no real power here—the witch's magic discombobulated her. She worked away at the potatoes, not sure why she was following the witch's orders. She already had so many chores. Jane do this; Jane do that. She supposed she wouldn't mind so much if people asked her what *she* wanted to do.

Like, she'd be *happy* to clean up after dinner or to pick up her room or take out the trash, but her parents always asked at the most inopportune time. Of *course*, she'd get around to cleaning her room. Of *course*, she'd clean up the dishes. But it was always the tone that bothered her—as if assuming she wouldn't do it. Never ever asking her, please. Jane looked up from her lumpy potato. She'd assumed the witch was nothing more than a sad old lady who couldn't get a real job because, surely, anyone who worked in fast food had to be a loser. But she hadn't asked to be bound here, to be forced to build a place around herself in a desperate attempt to attract Cadre members to free herself.

"Why couldn't I free you?" Jane asked.

The witch paused, her hands aloft, as if in the middle of some spell. After a long, long moment, she continued her spell-casting. "You're not a true Mountain Gal. You've betrayed your oath."

The carabiner felt like a bulging tumor in her pocket. Jane looked at the floor. It was hard to admit it, for she wasn't certain she believed it herself, but it was her duty to be kind and never abandon her friends. Mountain Gals valued these qualities, and she wouldn't be a good Mountain Gal if she abandoned her friends. And to do that, she needed to free her friends, her sisters, of the witch's curse.

"Guess I deserve this," Jane admitted. "I stole from one friend. I said bad things to another."

"I shouldn't have imprisoned your friends." The witch sighed. "I was angry at you, and now, I have only a little magic left."

A yawning chasm seemed to close between them, and the witch did not seem so cold or mysterious as she once did. The witch sat heavily on another chair.

"Why did you build this place?" Jane asked.

"The sisterly bond is an old, old magic, but it wasn't nearly strong enough to banish the spirit of the woods. My friends escaped, but I stayed behind to finish the spell. At first, I tried to stay where I was, haunting the woods and searching for a way to break the curse, but times changed. Mountain Gals no longer walked through the woods, so I waited." The witch spoke with the heavy resignation of one who hadn't had the opportunity to speak of such things in a long, long time.

Jane had seen it before, back when she was earning her community service merit badge. For a whole week, she had visited an old people's home, singing camp songs and playing games with them. She was glad her own grandparents were still alive and well and not stuck in one of those homes. For as she played Chinese checkers with a woman in her late nineties, she had seen the pain of being trapped in an aging body, no longer responsive. Jane didn't want that for herself. Not ever. Staying thirteen forever was a *great* plan.

"Trash blew into my forest. Ephemeral advertisements promised fast food as if they too had magic. I saw what had to be done. I sensed the campfires in the distance. Cadres return every year, so I created this restaurant as I felt the cities encroach upon the forest, hoping some girls would stop here, and one would free me."

The whole restaurant trembled. The oil stopped hissing, the knives stopped chopping, and the ice-cream machine ceased whirring. The wind blew away the witch's baseball cap and headset, leaving behind only graying brown hair. The collar of her shirt untucked itself from its neat folds and turned upward, swaying with the wind. Perhaps no one had ever dared to ask her such things. To ask her what she wanted, rather than assume. Jane wouldn't know. All she knew was that she wanted to be free of this as well as the witch.

"You bound yourself to the land instead of the spirit," Jane said. "You gave up that dearest to you."

"I misunderstood the true cost," the woman replied. "Sacrificing our stuffed animals...they weren't really dear to us. Not like we thought they were."

A thought crossed Jane's mind. A Cadre wasn't needed to break the curse now—because the witch herself was a Mountain Gal, one who had forgotten her oath. No matter how old, how wrinkled, how much the witch didn't look like a Mountain Gal, she was one. Oaths were strong, even the bad ones.

"Come on," Jane said. "How much of your magic do you have left?"

"Why?"

"We can't break the curse by ourselves—but we can break it together."

Jane took the carabiner out. The little leather strap, punched with the Mountain Gal logo, reminded her that she didn't deserve this. It wasn't just for mountain climbing—Katie could have used it while riding horses. Hooked it onto a harness or to the saddle. Jane had done a terrible thing and needed to make it right.

"Please," Jane said. "Let me make things right."

The wind intensified, whipping Jane's hair out of its ponytail and across her face. The magic flowed through the building, touching everyone and everything. Roots burst from the grout and tore apart the floor. Plastic booths melted into the checkered tiles, swirling around and around until nothing but the wavering grass remained. Katie and Michelle, little girls once more, lay in the grass, surrounded by the blue flowers, their wide eyes staring at the blood moon above them.

Jane spun slowly, watching the last of the restaurant dissipate into nothingness. Skeleton frames of the building towered into the sky. Piles of concrete materials were scattered around the clearing. A rusted mixer lay in the dead grass. Forgotten shovels rested against the crumbling drywall.

"This belongs to you," Jane said, holding the carabiner to Katie. "I'm sorry. To both of you."

Katie's eyes darkened, and for a moment, Jane wondered if she would ever forgive her. Then, she reached out and grasped the carabiner. It glowed, its soft golden sheen illuminating the clearing. Jane looked up at the moon, now in its full eclipse.

"Grab hold," Jane said, gesturing for the witch and Michelle to come closer, "and recite the Mountain Gal oath!"

Their fingers overlapped one another as they grasped a side. The spring-loaded release hook always seemed so unsafe, but now, she felt as if the heaviest mountain would not be able to break it.

"We are the Mountain Gals!
I will be as solid as the rocks we climb.
And always reaching for the stars!
I will respect the mountains, tall and mighty.
Respect friendship—for together we summit to reach our dreams.
Mountain Gals belay one another to the summit
And we never leave each other behind."

Then Jane saw it. Twigs twisted in tight curls around the spirit's bony shoulders and framed a sharp, narrow face sitting on top of a writhing dress of shadows. Jane could see how, in the dim moonlight, a group of terrified girls could have seen malice. The spirit turned to Jane. Small bundles of gnarled wood replaced her sunken eyes. As Jane looked at the lifeless eyes, she realized that the bond would only last as long as it was true, and honest, and fair. And to hold contempt in her heart would never make her happy.

"I'm the spirit of these woods, born of moonlight and a doe's breath and the susurration of autumn leaves in a winter breeze," it spoke in an echoing voice. "On this night, as the heavens bleed, so you shall be free of your curse."

The spirit's jaw creaked open. A gale tossed the witch to the ground, and just as the restaurant had melted before their eyes, so did the uniform. A faded purple uniform hung loosely from her bony shoulders. Patches of dirt clung to the white polo shirt and khaki shorts.

"I'm free..." The witch stirred. She gazed at her hands, at the sky as if she had never seen them before.

A trail of blue flowers sprouted in the spirit's shadow as it turned back into the darkness. The girls helped the witch to her feet. If Jane didn't know any better, she would've thought the witch was a Mountain Gal leader. But calling her a witch...that was a silly thing. Jane looked up at the woman and held out her hand.

"I'm Jane. What's your name?"

This Really Bites

Maddie Benedict

Tyler Lowell gripped the handle of his lunch cooler. Today was the day. He was finally going to talk to her.

He went over the words he'd planned as he walked along a sunlit path through the expansive mid-city park. He kept on the lookout, hoping he'd come across the park ranger on one of these paths; he'd seen her in passing several times before on his daily walks.

Finally, Tyler spotted her coming his way. His heart leaped with both nerves and delight. She looked so pretty and professional in her park ranger uniform, with her yellow ball cap and her brown hair in a ponytail.

As she neared, Tyler briefly lifted a hand. "Uh, excuse me…you're the local expert on parks, right?"

She paused with an accommodating look on her face, thumbs in her belt loops.

Open with an indirect compliment—check. "I was just wondering if I'm allowed to picnic here."

She raised her eyebrows a little. "Sure, there's no regulation against it. As long as you don't leave any litter."

"I just figured it's better to ask permission than forgiveness, right?"

She looked faintly amused. "Oh, is that how that saying goes?"

That's right, keep her talking. Make it a conversation. "The only problem is, I brought way too much lunch. Would you care for some of it?"

She paused. Then her mouth rose into a bit of a savvy smile. She glanced at his cooler. "What kind of snacks you got in there?"

She's interested! Tyler kept his tone casual. "Oh, you know, the usual: salad, sandwiches, juice boxes."

"Tempting…" She continued to meet his gaze, voice playful. "But unfortunately, I'm not allowed to fraternize when I'm on duty."

Make another offer! "What if I walk the same way you're going while you continue your patrol, then?"

She pursed her lips, adjusting the bill of her cap. Then she nodded. "That would work."

Yes! As they turned to stroll along together, Tyler switched the cooler to his other hand so he could surreptitiously wipe his clammy palm on his pants.

"Do you always go trolling the park for dates?" the ranger prompted.

Tyler gave a sheepish chuff. "No, I just come here on my lunch hour to get away from the hustle-bustle. And I happened to notice you making your rounds a few times too."

She studied him more closely. "Oh yeah, I think I've seen you around before."

He brightened, straightening. "You remember me? It's only fair that I give you a name to put to a face, then. I'm Tyler."

"Linda."

A classically pretty name. "So, what's it like being a park ranger? Do you meet a lot of bears and cougars?"

She laughed. "I wish! We don't get many of those around here, being in the middle of the city and all. But it's still big enough that it has its own ranger division like the one in Central Park."

"Have you ever had to hunt down a rogue animal?"

"Only with a tranq gun. I don't hunt for sport." A squirrel was hopping along on the grass, and Linda smiled at it. "I love animals. That's why I'd never eat one."

"Oh, I'm a vegetarian, too," Tyler remarked.

She eyed him sidelong. "Really? You're not just saying that to get on my good side?"

"No, really. I've never eaten a scrap of meat in my life. That's why I'm so scrawny, see."

Linda chuckled. "Ah, you're not that bad."

His chest swelled. *She complimented me back!* "Those sandwiches I mentioned are totally meat-free, too. Sure you don't want one?"

She smiled apologetically. "Hey, my job might be a walk in the park, but it's no picnic."

Appreciative mirth rose in him. *Gotta love a girl who can make puns.*

They drifted to a stop where the path forked. "But I'm on this beat every Wednesday," Linda added. "Between…twelve and one."

With a growing grin, Tyler watched Linda as she turned and went down the other path.

Lightheaded with success, Tyler headed out of the park before his lunch break was over, returning to the tech company building across the street. It was his first job out of college. Not the kind of place his ex-roommate Jax would've worked—but despite Jax being the jockish type, they'd become good friends in the dorm. Tyler turned pensive. Jax had mysteriously dropped out just before graduation, and Tyler hadn't heard from him since. From time to time, Tyler still wondered what had happened to him.

When Tyler got back to his desk at the office, he started unpacking the sandwiches to eat while he worked.

His rangy buddy Dwight came by, his lank black hair gleaming in the pale fluorescent lighting. He had a habit of moussing it—as if that would make him look cooler. He folded his arms atop the cubicle partition when he saw Tyler's cooler was still full. "Oh no, did she turn you down?"

Tyler looked up and preened. "On the contrary, I've got a date with her next Wednesday."

Dwight's face broke into a wide grin. "All right, man!" He gave Tyler a high-five. "Way to use your nerd charm! Maybe there's hope for the rest of us after all."

***

That night, Tyler took a taxi to the park to look at the stars, since the sky was still clear over the city for once. It would be a good spot to bring Linda on a date sometime. He became so mesmerized by imagining it that before he knew it, it was past midnight. On his way back, Tyler kept to the lit paths.

A shape emerged into the light of a nearby lamppost. Dark brown fur bristled thick and ragged, but it wasn't a dog. Its eyes gleamed golden. A wolf.

Tyler froze. What were you supposed to do when you encountered a wild predator? Play dead or make yourself big? Or did that only work with bears?

The wolf started growling.

Eyes wide, Tyler slowly backed away.

But with a bark, the wolf lunged after him. Tyler whirled and bolted. His heart was pounding as fast as his feet, but he didn't get far before the wolf leaped at his back and bowled him over. Tyler hit the ground, the breath knocked out of him.

He rolled onto his back, lifting one arm to shield his face. Pain shot along his forearm as the snarling wolf sank its teeth into his skin. He cried out in terror. *I'm going to be mauled to death!*

Tyler struggled frantically to kick the wolf off. His knee caught it in the underbelly, and the grip of its jaws let up. He wrenched himself free, curling up into a ball with his arms over his head. At least that way, he could protect his internal organs.

He cringed, tense and waiting in the darkness for the scrape of claws on his back. But a minute passed, and nothing happened. There was only silence.

Cautiously, he shifted his arm and peered out from behind it. The wolf wasn't there. Tyler lifted his head then rose up on one elbow, looking all around. No sign of it. Relief flooded him.

He scrambled to his feet, wincing at the hot pangs in his forearm, then dashed for the park exit.

Tyler cradled his wounded arm. He couldn't believe that had just happened—or that he'd survived. But he needed to do something about the bite.

As soon as he made it to the road, he waved down a cab and told the driver to take him to the clinic. But if Tyler told them it'd been a wolf, would they believe him? What was a wolf doing in the park, anyway?

He had to report this to the proper authorities before the wolf attacked someone else. His heart jumped. Would Linda be all right? He hoped she wasn't on duty at night. He only knew her Wednesday beat; even if he went to warn her tomorrow, it could take him hours to find her. And he didn't want to go back into the park alone, lest he encounter the wolf again.

Tyler started shaking. *The shock must be setting in.*

When he got to the clinic, he took a seat in the hall and had to wait for the better part of an hour before he could get in to see the doctor.

The doctor peeled back Tyler's sleeve to examine the bite mark. When Tyler told him what had happened, the doctor glanced up. "A wolf? In the middle of the city?" He sounded skeptical. "Are you sure it wasn't just a dog?"

"Dogs don't have yellow eyes!"

The doctor's brow furrowed, and his mouth drew into a thin line. He probably got all kinds of crackpots spouting claims that were just the product of overactive imaginations or hallucinations. "Well, whatever it was, you should inform Animal Control. If it would bite a human, it could be rabid."

The doctor cleaned and bandaged Tyler's wound, then gave him a rabies shot and sent him on his way with instructions to return three more times over the next two weeks for follow-up shots.

Tyler called Animal Control, and the representative assured him that they'd set up a perimeter around the park and coordinate with the park rangers in the morning.

By the time Tyler got back to his apartment, all he could do was simply flump down on the bed.

***

Tyler shuffled into the dim en-suite bathroom the next morning, still groggy.

Glimpsing himself in the mirror, he did a double take. There was a quarter-inch growth of new stubble on his chin. Tyler leaned closer, lifting a hand to touch it.

"What the...?" He'd shaved just the day before. It couldn't have grown that much overnight. Then he noticed the hair on his head looked shaggier than it had been. Frowning, he sank his fingers into it. He'd have to get a haircut soon.

After shaving, he carefully slid his shirtsleeve on over his bandage and took the bus to work.

He'd been at his desk for about an hour when he began to feel a prickling sensation along his arm. He absentmindedly scratched at it, but when the itch became too aggravating to ignore, he pushed back the cuff of his sleeve—and stared. His forearm was now streaked with long dark hairs. He'd never been a particularly hairy guy. Were his hormones finally kicking in? He'd never heard of it taking this long. He was twenty-three, for Pete's sake!

When Tyler got back home that evening, he saw that some stubble had already grown back. The worry lurking with him worsened. He shaved for the second time that day—then went straight to his laptop and looked up medical conditions involving excess hair growth. After half an hour, all he found was hypertrichosis, but rabies shots didn't have that side effect, and he wasn't on any other medication.

That, and he came across a link to…lycanthropy. That gave him pause. The impossibly rapid hairiness had only developed after he'd been bitten by a wolf.

Could it be?

Tyler shook his head, scoffing. *Of course not!* What was he thinking? Werewolves only existed in fiction, where they belonged.

The following day, he heard on the news that the park was open again, since the rangers had found no sign of a wolf in it. Tyler was sure there had been a wolf, though; he had the bite mark to prove it. If it really wasn't in the park anymore, where could it be? What if it was now roaming the streets of the city?

"In other news, the search continues for the unknown perpetrator believed to be responsible for several gruesome killings in nearby Slate City—"

Tyler switched off the TV. He didn't need to hear more bad news.

Over the next few days, Tyler got hungry more often, even an hour or two after a meal. He had to eat nearly twice as much to appease his appetite. Was this another symptom related to his hair growth? It was like going through puberty all over again!

One night when he came back from the supermarket, he made it through putting away the groceries before he realized he hadn't turned the lights on. Tyler paused and looked around. He'd been able to find his way easily, without bumping into anything, as if he could actually see the furniture as lighter shapes in the blackness. Frowning, he went over and flicked on the light switch anyway. He must have just been familiar enough with the apartment to navigate it instinctively.

Oddities aside, Tyler was still counting down the days until next Wednesday. He made sure to be on the same path as before, on time, to meet Linda. They walked together and got to talking and found they had a lot of interests in common: astronomy, board games, and techno music among them.

But Tyler started eyeing the surroundings with some unease. He hadn't been back here since the night the wolf bit him. Was it still around somewhere?

Tyler attempted to sound casual. "I, uh…heard you guys were searching the park for a wolf."

Linda frowned. "There *was* a reported sighting last week, yeah. But we haven't come across anything yet. It's a big park. It could just be a stray dog or a false account. It better not have just been some chump prank-calling us and causing all that fuss."

Tyler held a rather guilty silence.

"I don't even know how a wolf would get in here, through the whole city. Still, we're advising people not to go walking in the park at night."

Tyler rubbed his left forearm. *No kidding.* Though it had only been a week, the bite mark had mostly healed up. "So do you think we shouldn't keep meeting each other here?"

Linda looked over at him with a smile. "I wouldn't say that. I'm a ranger, after all; as long as you're with me, I'll protect you."

Tyler quirked his mouth wryly.

"Besides, even if there was a wolf, maybe it's moved on by now."

He gained a little reassurance from that. If it still had been here, they would have found some trace of it after a whole week. *Right?*

In the days that followed, Tyler started noticing everyday smells that had been too subtle for him before: someone's wool clothes on the bus, the stale, rain-dampened sidewalk, even the fruity gum under a bench across the street. He had no idea how or why he had developed this enhanced sense, but it didn't go away.

He even overheard gossip in the office, only to find the whispering culprits halfway across the room. He could hear the bus driver chewing a mint and later someone typing on a keyboard in the neighboring apartment. It started to drive him a little crazy, despite how he tried to ignore it. The world had already been loud and smelly enough before!

One time, Tyler opened his en-suite door—and it broke off one of its hinges. Dismayed, he tried to prop it against the wall, but he ended up dislocating the doorknob too. *It can't just be shoddy installation.* He lifted his hands off and had to go about everything even more gingerly than he usually did. The other perceptions might have just been his imagination, but this was something physical.

Tyler was so concerned that during his last follow-up visit to the clinic, he took a chance and told the doctor about all his recently developed symptoms. The doctor said he'd never heard of a disease presenting all those signs. There was hormone therapy to hinder hair growth, but that might be more trouble than it was worth. Tyler insisted they do a blood panel to rule out any serious conditions, although the results wouldn't be ready for about a week.

Tyler soon got tired of shaving twice a day and decided to give up on it altogether. By the end of the second day, he had a half-inch scruff covering his chin. But at least, it didn't seem to get longer than that, which was a small consolation.

The third time he met with Linda, she eyed him curiously. "Forgot to shave?"

He scratched at his beard. "Yeah, I guess I'm trying to grow it out."

"Well, it suits you. I like a little scruff on a man, anyway."

Tyler grew a grin. "Really?" Maybe it was good for something after all if Linda was partial to the rugged outdoorsman look.

Five days later, Tyler got a call from the clinic reporting that his blood test had come back free of any disease markers—and in fact, he seemed to be in perfect health. It was only a slight comfort that there was nothing medically wrong with him. But that still didn't explain his symptoms, and the only other possibility was something he didn't want to think about.

***

Tyler awoke to tight cramps in his gut. He sat up with a groan. His skin prickled all over. He clambered out of bed, toppling the clock on his nightstand onto its back. The numbers glowed 12:00. Tyler squeezed a hand on his bare side. This was worse than just indigestion. Was his appendix bursting? He shuffled across the carpet, crossing the square patch of pale moonlight that streamed in through the window. He staggered against the bureau opposite the bed, knocking off a lamp. His whole body was sore like all his muscles had been put through an intense workout.

He dropped to all fours, panting. It felt like his face was falling off. At the same time, it was as if he was being pulled up by the ears. He squeezed his eyes shut. His legs seemed to be shrinking, and there was the sensation that thick hair was sprouting from every inch of his skin. All his bones ached as if they were being either stretched or compressed.

Then it was over.

Tyler caught his breath in the sudden reprieve.

Then he lifted his head to look at the standing mirror and saw a brown wolf staring back at him.

He stayed stock-still, dazed. How had a wolf gotten into his apartment?

Then he realized it was the only reflection there.

When he lifted his arm, the wolf's foreleg lifted.

He *was* the wolf.

Holy crepe! He meant to shout it, but it came out as a lupine yelp as he stumbled back a few steps.

This couldn't be happening. He must be in a dream.

Maybe he could pinch himself to wake up. Not that he'd ever tried to see if that worked before. Then he looked down at his forepaws. How was he supposed to pinch himself when he had no fingers? Tyler lowered his head and nipped at his own foreleg with his canines. But despite the sting, the nightmare didn't end—even when he tried several more times with increasing desperation. He heard whimpering noises and realized they were coming from him.

Tyler turned, and a clattering struck the floor; he looked back to see his tail had swept his phone and keys off the footstool at the end of the bed.

He circled again. *This is crazy!* What was he going to do? If any of the stories were to be believed, there was no cure to change back into human form, other than waiting it out.

The light of the moon caught his eye, and he looked up. He drifted to the window that opened onto the fire escape and settled onto his haunches.

He drank in the sight of the full moon, and an overwhelming urge built in him to howl at it. And, tossing his head back, howl he did. He longed to go outside and run under the moonlight, to feel the wind on his fur. But the balcony only had a ladder, and there was no way he could climb down that in his current state. He doubted he could even turn the apartment doorknob to get out the other way.

Besides, he couldn't risk being seen as a wolf roaming through the building. At best, they'd call Animal Control. At worst...there could be some hunter with a shotgun down the hall who might fancy himself a hero. And Tyler also couldn't let himself loose on the city. He still seemed in control of himself, at least—and he hadn't felt any desire to eat people yet—but if he really was a werewolf, there was no telling what might happen.

A brisk rap hammered on the door, and Tyler whipped his head around. "What's all the racket in there?" the superintendent's voice called through the wood. "No pets allowed, Lowell!"

Tyler's heart raced. The man had better not use his master key to come in! Tyler ducked under the bed and made sure he was far enough in that his tail was out of sight too. But if the super entered, he'd still see the mess and undoubtedly look around for a dog. Tyler stayed silent and just hoped the man would go away. His wolf ear twitched toward the door when the super's footsteps receded down the hallway again.

Relaxing, Tyler crawled out to pad across the carpet. But he still had nowhere to go.

He started pacing. He was officially freaking out now. The minutes dragged on and turned into hours, and the panic in him grew. Why wasn't he waking up? His dreams never lasted this long. This couldn't be real. But the creeping dread began to sink in. What if it was? Would it be permanent? He couldn't spend the rest of his life as a wolf! It couldn't have come at a worse time. He was just getting his life together—he had a good job and a decent apartment, and now he was on his way to having a girlfriend. What would Linda think if she knew? No girl in her right mind would date a werewolf! This could ruin everything!

Tyler growled. And so did his stomach. He darted to the kitchenette, but the pads of his paws slipped on the smooth tiles, and he ended up skidding into the cupboards. He collected himself and stepped more carefully to the fridge, claws clicking on the floor. He reached for the fridge handle—only to remember his paw would be useless for opening it. How frustrating it was to not have human hands.

Eventually, he managed to push the magnetic door open from the side with both paws and poked his snout in. He took the frill of a bread bag in his teeth and pulled it out, then clawed it open to get at the slices inside, which he wolfed down. Tyler brought out a plastic peanut butter jar in his jaws then sank his fangs into it and ruthlessly ripped out a panel from its side. He stuck his muzzle into the hole and gobbled up everything he could get at. Next he batted out a carton of milk, and it burst open on the floor, sending the white drink pooling out where he could lap it up.

Tyler devoured everything he could get his paws on, until finally he'd eaten his fill. Feeling pleasantly drowsy, he left the fridge open and drifted back into the other room with his head low, then hopped onto the footstool and the bed. He turned around and laid himself out there, then set his muzzle down on his forepaws.

After a brief nap, he opened his eyes, but to his disappointment, he was still a wolf. There went his last hope that it was something he could wake up from. Then again, he'd had dreams before where he'd woken up, but he'd actually still been dreaming.

A few hours later, dawn lightened the sky out the window. Tyler's skin prickled again, and he sat up. It felt like his body was stretching out, his fur receding into his skin, but it was painless—even refreshing. When it was done, he looked down at himself. To his immense relief, he was human again. He wasn't wearing anything, though. His pants had slipped off when he'd first transformed. That could become inconvenient. Tyler hastened over to the bureau and got out another pair to put on. Then he went back over to the mirror to make sure he really was all back to normal. No more fur, no more wolf ears. But his stubble was just as scruffy as ever. Scratching at it, he gave himself a wry grin. He never thought he'd be so happy to see his lanky physique again.

***

Tyler started awake to his techno ringtone. He lifted his clock. "Oh, geez." It was ten in the morning already! He scrambled out of bed to pick up his phone from the floor. "Yeah?"

"Hey, man, what's keeping you?" Dwight asked. "You'd better get here before the boss notices you're an hour late!"

"I know! I'll be right there!" Tyler threw on his clothes, and there was a knock on the door just before he yanked it open.

"About all that noise last night," the superintendent began firmly. "I hope you don't think you can keep a dog here under my nose." He peered suspiciously past Tyler's shoulder into the disorderly room.

He thought up a quick explanation. "Uh...yeah, a stray mutt followed me home, but he was more trouble than he was worth. Don't worry, it was a one-time thing. I dropped him off at the animal shelter already." Tyler sidled past the man and hustled off to the elevator.

Tyler stayed up that night, dreading that the same thing would happen again. Sitting on the edge of his bed, he watched as the clock turned twelve and braced himself.

That's when it had happened before. But nothing changed. Once it was getting close to one o'clock, he began to relax. Maybe he only turned once a month, when there was a full moon. That was the traditional myth. Or maybe it had been nothing but a dream after all. Or some mix of sleepwalking and a psychotic break, anyway, since the room *had* been trashed when he awoke.

He still saw Linda the next Wednesday. She finally gave Tyler her number, and they started talking on the phone for hours every day after work until they became quite close.

On Monday at midnight, Tyler woke to the same prickling sensation. He shot upright. *No! It's too soon!* It had only been a week! But there was nothing he could do; he turned into a wolf again—this time without any of the aches, at least. He sought to somehow leave evidence that he was actually a wolf, and it wasn't just in his head so he could verify it in the daytime. Like taking a photo of himself—but he couldn't work his phone's touchscreen with his paw. Then he thought of leaving an impression of said paw in something like clay, but he didn't have any lying around. He settled for a cheesecake—and indeed, the imprint was still there the next morning. The reality of it finally sank in. This really was his life now.

Then it became every night that Tyler started turning, from midnight to dawn. He tried to make sure he woke up on time, but the lack of sleep meant he often ended up napping on the job later. His work performance lagged. He even enlisted Dwight to wake him whenever necessary.

He still managed to make it out at noon that Wednesday to meet Linda in the park; that was one appointment he wasn't willing to break. When he was with her, he felt like himself again while they just talked about their lives and thoughts.

At one point, Linda paused under a tree, and Tyler turned back around to her. She was admiring his thick locks, then she reached up and sank her fingers into them. "You know, I can't resist shaggy hair," she remarked. She lifted her other hand to play with the ends of his hair. Linda inched her face a bit closer, and Tyler started smiling with anticipation. He leaned in too, and they shared a tender kiss. When he met her eyes again, she looked like she'd be amenable to another one. But then Tyler drew back, remembering himself with a twinge of guilt. He disentangled her fingers and lowered her hands.

"Uh...I'm a bit shy about PDA," he murmured. He couldn't in good conscience let her get involved with him, not when he was a werewolf—and when she didn't know it. He shouldn't have even continued seeing her at all after he'd found out for sure.

Linda watched him with an amused smile. She linked her fingers with his, holding his hand as they resumed strolling. After a moment, Tyler gave her hand a little squeeze too.

Though he'd had no problem staying awake while with Linda, by midafternoon, he was dozing with his head on his desk again—until Dwight shook his shoulder.

Eventually, Tyler decided to try tiring himself out in his wolf form so he would be ready to get to sleep afterward, like walking a dog that had too much energy. He took the subway to the park before midnight then found some secluded bushes to conceal himself in, where he took off his clothes and tucked them away. After he transformed, he trotted out into the open.

With his wolf eyesight, he spotted a gray rabbit sitting huddled in the grass, motionless but for its twitching nose. A juvenile impulse sent Tyler charging at it. Its long ears perked up, and it launched into a bounding run. He kept after it, head low and four legs pumping. He became exhilarated by the thrill of the chase, the sheer freedom of movement as a wolf.

Then he realized the rabbit probably didn't consider this just play—it must be terrified of him, thinking him a predator. Tyler slowed to a stop. It wasn't like he actually wanted to eat it. He'd never tasted meat in his life, and he had no craving for it now, even in his wolf form. He was grateful for that because it meant he wouldn't be tempted to prey on humans either. Although, he would've expected the condition itself of being a werewolf would bring with it the uncontrollable desire to eat flesh; that's what most fiction had established to be the case. Then again, he'd never heard a story about a vegetarian being turned into a werewolf and what that would be like.

Eager to test out his wolf form, Tyler turned and lolloped off through the dark. He ran around in the park for hours, working all his muscles, weaving between trees and leaping over rocks, hopping up and over benches or prowling in the bushes. It was almost fun acting like an animal. He was one in body, but he still thought like a person.

He still had to avoid being seen by the occasional homeless person or drunk—the only ones who were wandering the paths this late. But long before he saw them, he could smell their unwashed clothes or cheap booze.

After getting his fill of exercise, Tyler paced along with his nose low to the ground.

He caught a whiff of a musky scent and lifted his head, sniffing. Grass rustled, and a pack of seven wolves emerged from a stand of trees ahead. He stared at them, unsure if he should run. Were these regular wolves? Fleeing might just prompt them to chase him. If he stayed, would they consider him one of their own, or would they be able to tell something was different about him?

They came padding over to him in a ragged formation. Then he heard a gruff voice—but not with his ears. It spoke in his head. *There you are, newbitten.* Somehow,

Tyler was sure it came from the shaggy brown wolf on the left. *We've been waiting for you to come out and play.*

With a twinge of unease, he took a step back. They were definitely werewolves. And they knew he was one too. What did they want?

We're about to go on the hunt, a tawnier wolf added. *There's plenty of small game to be had here in the park, to keep our skills sharp. Join us!*

But as they got closer to him, their glowing yellow eyes narrowed. They slowly circled him, sizing him up. They were larger than him, and they all looked so strong and intimidating. For the first time, Tyler was aware of how wiry he was in his wolf form.

You smell like prey, their thoughts hissed.

He's a leaf-eater! one grayish wolf put in.

A big auburn wolf fixed his gaze on Tyler. *It's time you embraced your true wolf nature. Become one of us!*

Ears laid back, Tyler whimpered. *No.*

It was a feeble thought, but they heard it anyway.

The others started growling. *No one resists the Alpha!*

They began closing in on him, snarling, and Tyler cringed where he stood. If they attacked him, there was no way he'd get out of it alive, even if he'd known how to defend himself.

Wait!

A dark brown wolf stepped forward. Tyler recognized him—not just as the wolf that had bitten him that first night—but his voice, his *essence* was that of his former college roommate.

Jax? he wondered, disbelieving. His fur was even the same color as he remembered Jax's hair being.

Let me talk to him, Jax went on to the others. *I'm the one who turned him; he's my responsibility.*

The circle grudgingly parted to let the two of them confer aside.

Listen, don't try to be a lone wolf, Jax told him. *You might not like the idea of following orders, but being part of this pack will afford you more security and brotherhood than you've ever known. You won't get a better offer.*

That's not it! I don't want to tear into live animals with my bare teeth. I'm not an animal!

Yes, you are!

No, I'm not! I'm just a guy in wolf's clothing!

Believe me, our way beats the alternative. Most other packs prey on humans. We're one of the good ones.

Tyler stared at Jax. *Why did you do this to me?*

His jaws parted in a wolf grin. *When I recognized you in the park after all these years—and so soon after our pack moved here—I realized it was the perfect opportunity. I wanted us to be friends again, and for you to experience the life of a werewolf too. I know it's the best thing that ever happened to me!*

Tyler's hackles bristled. To think, it hadn't just been some random, unavoidable animal attack, but that his own friend had purposely singled him out for this cursed existence... *You had no right! I didn't ask for this! I never wanted to be a werewolf!*

Well, you are one now. You'll come to realize what an honor it is to be chosen.

I don't want to be part of a gang. Tell them to leave me alone! Tyler turned aside.

Jax was unfazed. *I can buy you a few days to think about it. But then I know you'll make the right decision!*

Tyler took off into the trees, leaving the pack far behind. The sky was beginning to lighten. He had to get back to his clothes before dawn came.

He charged into a clearing but stopped short when he spotted a figure off to one side. Linda. She raised her tranq gun. Tyler stared at her, frozen. *Don't shoot, it's me!* he wanted to plead. But as Linda looked into his eyes, she hesitated, squinting. She lowered the gun slightly, and Tyler loped off into the woods again. Once he was out of her sight, he let out a breath. If he'd been tranqed, he would've turned back into his human form with the sunrise, and then his secret would have been out!

***

After the close call with Linda, Tyler wasn't sure he'd be able to act like everything was normal if he met with her again. She'd seen him in his wolf form. *She* didn't know it had been him, but still.

It was wrong to keep stringing her along. He had to make a decision. Did he dare tell her? What if she had him committed? Should he just break up with her for her own good? But shouldn't he leave that choice up to her? He'd deliberated for days and still hadn't come to a conclusion. He couldn't afford to see her until he did.

When he didn't show up next Wednesday, his phone rang. It was Linda. He eyed it guiltily but didn't answer. She called a few more times over the next couple hours. Then a text popped up on his screen.

"Didn't see you today. u ok? Not coming down with something, I hope?"

It might be simplest to just drift out of her life. But he didn't want to stay away. And it wouldn't be fair to her to end their association without an explanation. Especially if she liked him as much as it seemed.

After a while, a chirp announced another message from her.

"There've been more wolf sightings in the park lately. Is that why you didn't meet me there?"

It was agonizing to keep ignoring her, all the more so because he imagined how it must have seemed to her and what she must have been feeling.

A few minutes later:

"That's probably better. I even saw one the other day. That's one of the things I wanted to tell you. Call me when you can."

Frustrated dissatisfaction built within him. He'd never had to keep secrets before this happened to him. He cared too much about Linda to go on deceiving her. She was going to find out eventually anyway. Either she would actually stand by him in spite of it—and it would be better that she heard it from him—or she'd understandably opt out of continuing to see him, and it never would have worked in the first place. His condition wasn't going away. It was time to come clean.

That day after work, Tyler headed into the park and tracked her down, following the tangerine scent of her hair conditioner.

When Linda saw him, her expression lightened. But once they neared each other, she said, half-teasing, "Have you been avoiding me?"

"Yeah," he admitted. "I've been avoiding everyone." Tyler stuffed his hands in his pockets. "Listen, there's something I've got to tell you." He took a deep breath and lifted his eyes to meet hers. "I'm a werewolf."

Linda looked at him very oddly for a long pause. "Is this some kind of roleplaying fantasy of yours or something?"

"No, I mean it," he insisted. "I turn into a wolf every night—fur, paws, tail, and all. I can show you, but it only happens after dark. And we should do it somewhere we can be alone."

She turned her head to eye him sidelong. "Are you trying to get me to come back to your place?"

Tyler shook his head, face growing hot. "It's not like that!" He gave a frustrated sigh, desperate to make her understand. "Remember that brown wolf you saw by the trees, Friday morning?"

Linda frowned. "How did you...?"

"That was me. Thanks for not tranqing me, by the way." He offered a small smile. "I'm not a danger to anyone, trust me."

She looked down. "I do trust you, Tyler. I just hope for your sake that you're not as crazy as you sound."

"You'll believe it when you see it. Meet me here in the park just before midnight."

They got together at 11:50 p.m. in a secluded area but in the light of a lamppost so she'd be able to see it clearly when he transformed. Linda wore jeans and a form-fitting gray hoodie. She looked even nicer in off-duty clothes.

"Now, once I change, I won't be able to talk, and I won't turn back into a human until sunrise, so...don't freak out and shoot me or anything, all right?"

Linda raised her eyebrow. "Lucky for you, I didn't bring my gun," she replied wryly.

"Good. But I'd also prefer it if you didn't go running off to report me to anyone, either," he went on. "Promise you won't?"

"Whatever you say," she agreed dubiously.

Tyler nodded then proceeded to pull his shirt up over his head.

Linda looked a bit taken aback. "Why are you taking your clothes off?" She eyed his bare chest with some interest, though.

"Sorry, but it's either this or they get torn."

She shook her head. "You are *so* weird," she scoffed.

Tyler put his toe to his heel to push his shoes off too but left his pants on.

After standing around for a while, Linda crossed her arms. "Is something supposed to be happening?"

He was looking over his shoulder at the park's post clock. "It will, any minute now." The hands reached twelve, and all his hairs stood on end. Fur bloomed from every pore of his skin, and his body morphed until he stood on four legs as a wolf.

Linda's mouth slowly dropped open, and she backed away. "No way..." she breathed.

Tyler watched her, worried she'd run screaming from him. He sat on his haunches so Linda knew he wouldn't make any sudden moves. He kept his muzzle down, trying to look as harmless as possible.

Then Linda paused, studying him. "You *are* the wolf I saw before." She took a small step toward him. "No wonder something about those eyes reminded me of you." She ventured the rest of the way up to him then cautiously extended a hand, lowering it onto his head.

His ears dipped to the sides, and he half-closed his eyes. All the tension left his body at the soothing feel of her smoothing his fur.

"It really is you, isn't it?" Linda murmured.

Tyler tilted his head to nuzzle against her leg. It was a relief to know she wasn't afraid of him.

Once she seemed to have gotten used to him being around her in his wolf form, Tyler took a few steps away and looked over his shoulder at her, waiting until she understood his suggestion and followed. They went for a walk together with Tyler padding along beside her like a loyal dog. Linda watched him with a smile of wonder and often rested a hand between his ears. They played around too, running and leaping about and dodging around trees like a fantasy adventurer with her animal companion. Judging by Linda's grin, she found it as fun as he did.

Eventually, they settled down on the grass, and Linda talked to him for hours, looking into his golden eyes and stroking his fur. But later, she ended up reclining on her back and falling asleep with one arm tucked under her head. Tyler stayed up to keep watch. After a while, he gently laid his muzzle on her midriff, which rose and fell slightly with her soft breaths. Affection welled in his heart. He was so lucky—not only that she was dating him at all, but that she didn't even mind that he was a werewolf. Who else but a park ranger would think that was cool?

Once the stars began to fade, Tyler nudged Linda's face with his nose. She stirred and lifted her head abruptly, then smiled in fond recollection, setting a hand on his head. "I still can't believe my boyfriend is a wolf."

They revisited the place he'd left his clothes, and Linda turned her back so he could put them on once he became human again.

Tyler cleared his throat. "Okay, I'm decent."

Linda turned back to him and beamed. "It's good to have you back," she said softly and wrapped her arms around him.

He held her too, marveling that showing her his wolfish side had actually brought them closer together.

***

Tyler was preparing supper in his kitchenette while the small TV on the counter related the news in the background.

Upon hearing something about the park, he looked at the screen to see it showing a tarp-covered body. He snatched the remote and turned up the volume.

"...the site of a grisly murder," the newswoman went on. "The victim appears to be a homeless man who lived in the park. As of yet, he is otherwise unidentified, due to the extent of mutilation to what remains of the body. Officials believe it was an animal attack—but the question remains, what kind of animal in the city could have done such damage?"

Tyler got a sinking feeling. The only thing it could have been was...a wolf. He grabbed his phone and called Linda. The tightness in his chest relaxed when her voice answered. "Linda here."

"Hey, I just heard about the body on the news. Are you all right?"

"Yeah, I wasn't there when it was discovered. But we're going to continue investigating along with the police."

Tyler suppressed his worry. "Just don't go into the park after midnight, okay?"

"Why? Do you know something?"

He balked, gaze drifting down, so filled with hesitation it was like he was holding his breath. The longer his indecision lasted, the more the tension made him disinclined to speak.

"It didn't have anything to do with you, did it?" There was an abrupt edge to her voice.

Tyler lifted his head. "Of course not! I'm still in control." But he couldn't keep it from her now. He tried to think of a way he could phrase it over the phone. "But…there are others like me. A pack of them lives in the city."

"What?! Why didn't you tell me?"

"But they wouldn't do this!" Tyler went on. "They only hunt animals."

There was a pause. "How sure are you of that?"

Not sure enough.

Over the next week, there was a new murder every night, some even in alleyways in the city. It definitely wasn't an accident. Tyler decided to do some investigating of his own. He used his phonebook app to look up Jax's number and anxiously drummed his fingers on the dining table as he waited for the line to connect.

"Y-ello?"

"Hey, Jax. It's me."

"Tyler?" Jax sounded surprised but delighted. "It's good to hear from you, buddy! Have you made your decision?"

Tyler furrowed his brow. "No, that's not what this is about. Have you heard what's been happening in the park?"

"That wasn't us, man." His tone was sober. "It must be another pack. You know, the kind I was telling you about? We've caught a few glimpses of them encroaching on our territory. The boss doesn't like it, but we've been steering clear of them. They're probably the ones from Slate City."

Cold dread gripped Tyler's stomach. It was even worse than he'd feared. "They came here?" he breathed. "Do you know who they are?"

"Nope. Wouldn't know 'em if I saw 'em—in *daylight*—if you know what I mean. Would if I smelled them, though," Jax added thoughtfully.

"Is there any way we can stop them?"

"Nothing to do but go up against them. But I doubt they'd get scared off. They'd make it a fight to the death." Jax was silent for a moment. "There's more of them than there are of us. We could really use you on our team, bud."

Tyler sighed in aggravation. "You know I can't."

"They're killers, Ty! They won't have a problem offing us too!"

Turmoil filled Tyler, urgency warring with resistance. He couldn't abandon all of them to be murdered by the others—but he couldn't make himself a fighter either. "There must be some other way," he insisted. "Do they have any weaknesses?"

"You mean like silver bullets? Nah. That's a bunch of hooey. Regular bullets would still do the trick, though."

Tyler tried to think of an alternative. If they could somehow find out the werewolves' human identities…maybe they could tie them to the crimes that way and convict them as people. There was only one place they could be sure to find them. "Tell the pack to meet me in the park this Thursday. After midnight."

The next day, Tyler met with Linda, and together, they worked out the rest of the plan. It would mean revealing the existence of werewolves to the authorities, but it was the only way.

On Thursday night, she drove him to the park in her ranger van. On the way, he transformed into a wolf in the passenger seat. Linda brought her tranq gun as they headed into the park together, but she stayed back in the trees while Tyler cautiously continued forward to meet the waiting pack.

One of the wolves started growling. *I smell a human.*

And tranq darts! another added.

Why did you bring her here? the auburn-furred Alpha demanded of Tyler. *Do you mean to betray us?*

Some of the wolves lunged toward Linda, but Tyler darted out to block them. *No! She's here to help!* When they paused, Tyler looked each of them in the eye. *Listen, this new pack is a threat to us all. You want them gone, right? But you can't defeat them on your own. I have a plan. I'll help you get rid of them, on one condition. You'll let me stay a lone wolf.*

The Alpha stared at him for a long minute, golden eyes glittering. *And what might this plan of yours be?*

While you tackle them, Linda will tranq them so they can be put in a cage. She'll wait until your pack is long gone before calling in reinforcements. Then we can make sure they never terrorize this city again.

Alpha eyed the copse Linda was in. *It better work,* he said grudgingly. *If it does—and only if it does—then we have a deal. Honor among wolves.*

Tyler's heart leaped with success.

The wolves stiffened as the wind brought a scent of raw meat. They turned to face the new pack that emerged on the far side of the clearing. There were nine of them, and they were all larger and brawnier, with dark brown fur that was noticeably redder.

Linda slowly came up beside Tyler, tranq rifle held at

the ready.

The werewolves started toward the intruders, and the two packs drifted to a stop a few yards apart.

This is our territory, man-eaters, the Alpha growled. *Leave the city, or we'll make you leave.*

The other pack leader curled his lip in a sneer. *You think you runts scare us?* He turned his eyes to Tyler. *And what is this I smell? A leaf-eater? You're a disgrace to the wolf form. And your only other backup is a human girl with a toy gun? You're the ones who won't leave here alive.*

The man-eaters charged, and Alpha's pack leaped to meet them. They collided in a vicious flurry of snarls and teeth and fur and claws. The smell of blood and fear soon filled the air, stinging Tyler's nose. Several ganged up on the man-eater alpha to bear him down and leave the others without direction. Linda took aim, and as soon as they had him subdued, Tyler told the wolves of Alpha's pack to back off, so Linda had a clear shot at the right target. They did the same whenever Alpha's pack had one of the man-eaters pinned.

The opponent wrestling with Jax bit deep into his neck then threw him off. Jax hit the ground with a whimper, and Tyler's gut lurched. Then the man-eater charged at Linda while she was reloading.

No! Tyler raced toward them, fear gripping his heart.

The man-eater leaped at Linda, toppling her onto her back and sending the rifle flying out of reach.

Oh God, if it bit her, she'd turn into a werewolf too…

Tyler collided with the werewolf, knocking it off Linda, and they landed in a tumble. Snarling, the wolf surged up and sank its teeth into Tyler's foreleg. He let out a pained yip and tried to claw at the wolf with his other paw, but the wolf didn't let go. It was going to tear him to shreds!

Then the wolf went limp, slumping to the ground.

Tyler looked around to see Linda propped on one elbow, tranq gun pointed their way. Tyler's ears sagged with relief and gratitude. She must have been able to tell them apart, even in the dark.

Tyler limped over to rejoin her side as she got to her feet. She targeted the other man-eaters, and they resumed their strategy until every last one was sedated.

Alpha's pack licked at their wounds. Tyler checked on his own leg, but it was already beginning to heal, even faster than the original bite on his arm had.

At Tyler's request, Alpha's pack went to sniff out where the man-eaters had left their clothes. When they brought back the nine pairs of pants in their jaws, Linda searched the pockets for wallets. They had driver's licenses in them, so they now knew who all of the men were.

While the others dispersed, Linda used her radio to call in the other park rangers so they could help her load the wolves into the large iron cage in the back of the van. Tyler lingered; he didn't want to leave her alone with the man-eaters.

Linda looked at him and smiled. "Go on, Tyler. I'll be fine. These tranqs are strong enough to keep an elephant knocked out for hours." She patted her rifle, which was still pointed at the wolves. "And I still have some left over, just in case."

Tyler met her eyes for another moment then turned and loped off into the trees. But just before he reached the horizon, he looked over his shoulder. He stayed hidden in the thicket and watched until the reinforcements came before he withdrew to a far corner of the park.

***

Tyler met with Linda the next evening, outside the ranger station near the park. "How'd it go?" he asked, rather anxious. "Is the investigation underway?"

Linda's mouth twisted wryly. "Not quite. Representatives from some government agency I've never heard of showed up and confiscated them. Apparently, we're not the only ones who know about werewolves."

Tyler stared at her, filled with even more unease.

"Don't worry, I didn't tell them about you," Linda went on. "Or even the other pack. They're long gone by now."

Tyler softened. But a trace of uncertainty gnawed at him. "Are you sure you still want to date a werewolf?"

Linda stepped closer and looped her arms atop his shoulders with a contented sigh. "Why wouldn't I? You're the nicest werewolf I've ever met." She leaned in and gave him a kiss.

Tyler looked at her with a growing smile, his hands resting on her waist. "So, how would you like to go have a great big salad at The New Leaf?"

"I'd *love* to," Linda declared. They turned to stroll away together, each with an arm around the other. "I hear they have great turnovers."

The End

Gallery of Lost Souls

Madison Wheatley

"Would you turn that crap off?" I demanded, sliding into the driver's seat.

My partner, Detective Andrew Yataro, frowned at me from the passenger's seat of the police cruiser. I'd only been inside Mystic Donuts for a few minutes, and by the time I'd returned to the car, he'd already put on that awful rap "music" of his.

"It's my car, dude." I passed him a paper bag and a steaming coffee mug. "Aren't you a little old for that noise anyway?"

"You wound me." Yataro threw a hand over his heart as if in pain before switching the radio station back to classic rock. He opened up the paper bag, releasing the sweet aroma of buttery cinnamon sugar. "Judge me for my music, but I'm judging you for perpetuating the 'cops eat donuts' stereotype."

"Just try them."

Yataro arched an eyebrow, but he reached into the bag and popped one of the donut holes into his mouth. Within seconds, his eyes were shut, and a childlike grin spread across his face.

"Told ya." I typed an address into the GPS.

"You sure they didn't use magic to make these?" Yataro mumbled around the donut.

I felt my jaw tense up. "Like I've said before, not everything good in this world is a result of mages and their wonderful powers. Normal people are perfectly capable themselves."

Yataro held up a hand defensively. "I didn't mean it like that. I just meant, like…" He fell silent, and his cheeks flushed. "Donut?" He waved the bag.

I shook my head. He hadn't meant any harm with his comment, but it certainly struck a nerve. It knocked me right back to my childhood, those years surrounded by mages but unable to manage a simple spell. Years of disappointing my parents and being mocked by my siblings.

Everything had changed during my eleventh-grade year when I went to live with my uncle, a prominent member of the police force. He had enrolled me in the police academy, where I'd excelled, and for the first time in my life, I didn't have to worry about measuring up to someone with magic.

Until Commander Jamison announced the Magical Investigation Program. This beta project paired mages and commons together to investigate supernatural crimes. With my knowledge of the magical world, Jamison saw me as an obvious choice for one of these teams.

That's where Yataro came in. Despite his being younger than me, his magic made me feel insecure. I kept having to remind myself that, with or without magic, he's still just a kid.

Swigging the last of my coffee, I turned down the radio. "You read up on our missing vic?"

Before he could answer, I passed him a manila file folder labeled "MAXWELL, TYLER." He opened it and looked over the photograph of a young male high school student with a messy Afro.

"Ah, a Tanglewood Prep kid," Yataro said. "Lucky."

"What, you actually *miss* high school?" I switched on

the car and began following the GPS to the boarding school for magically gifted students. "Just thinking about that hellhole makes me sick."

"No way! But it would've been nice to have graduated from Tanglewood instead of Southwest High."

"I don't blame you." I smiled, thinking of my own high school's bitter rivalry with Southwest. "Liberty High had some pretty nasty cheers about you guys, especially after you vandalized the statue of our mascot."

"Well, those were clearly more barbaric times. Though to be fair, with a mascot like the Wild Donkeys, you guys were basically *asking* to be vandalized."

"Touché."

The GPS directed us through the heart of the city, down a dark alley lined with buildings and a group of scruffy-looking people smoking cigarettes. The digital voice announced we'd reached our destination.

"Stupid GPS." I squinted at the display then back up the sad-looking street. "Don't suppose you could magic this thing into working properly, could you?"

Yataro grinned. "We're here."

I waited for the punchline, but then a distant memory from my childhood burst into my mind. When my partner slid out of the car, I followed him. Outside the safety of my car, the street felt aware, almost hungry. The sensation of invisible eyes crawled across my skin, a feeling that had once terrified me as a child.

Yataro closed his eyes, and he chanted to himself; the words were familiar, similar to those my father had uttered when he split open the world as I knew it, revealing a hidden world—the magical university my older sister Nakia would soon attend.

The school all my siblings would attend. All but me.

For what seemed like ages, nothing happened. Then there was a shift in the air like a rogue wind blowing in from some warm, far-flung country. The warmth settled itself around me, sank into my skin, and before I knew it, my eyes shut as I surrendered to the strange, invisible embrace.

I opened my eyes to an entirely different world. It was the same street, same city, but it had dropped its facade of abandonment, revealing instead a clean, well-kept campus. The abandoned buildings were now student housing. The vacant lot was now a manicured lawn dotted with sculptures and shrubbery.

I caught a glimpse of Yataro. My amusement must have been painfully evident because he just stood there with this whimsical look on his face watching me react to the strange transformation.

"What?" he said. "You've never seen a spatial transformation spell before?"

"It's been a while, okay?" I turned away, caught up in the memory of watching Nakia disappear to seek out a bright destiny I could only dream of.

"Joyce? You all right?"

I whipped back around and forced a smile. "C'mon, we've got work to do."

***

I didn't really know what to expect when walking into a magic high school. On the one hand, Tanglewood was just like any normal private school. Students trudged from class to class, clad in purple polo shirts and dark gray skirts or dress pants. Teachers stood outside their doors, warning them not to linger in the halls.

On the other hand, it was just like in the movies. When the warning bell sounded, a few freshmen summoned a wavering beam of light that pointed them in the direction of their next class. Not far from us, a couple girls whispered about their failed attempt to create a successful love potion.

A staff member led a belligerent-looking young man to detention, lecturing him about how just because he *could* magically disable the firewall on his computer doesn't mean he *should*.

A bulletin board outside the counselor's office was plastered with pictures of Tyler Maxwell. The photos surrounded his missing person's poster, on which the anonymous tip hotline number was highlighted in yellow. Even though I'd already seen Tyler's picture plenty of times, something about viewing him in this new, candid light— painting in art class, goofing off with his friends, cosplaying as a comic book superhero—made my heart stop. I couldn't take my eyes off the display, and as I scanned photo after photo, I began to feel cold inside.

"Hey, the principal's waiting for us," Yataro said, approaching me. He looked at the bulletin board and then to me. "What's wrong?"

"Just thinking. You remember the Changeling Case, right?"

Yataro's eyes narrowed, and he stepped a little closer. The final bell rang, and he cringed at its harsh tones. "The what?"

"A few mage kids went missing several years ago. It was just before I joined the force, way before the MIP was founded. The police had no idea what happened." The cold feeling in my chest intensified, making goosebumps rise on my flesh as I conjured up that long-buried memory. "Just thinking about how afraid everyone was. How afraid Tyler's family must be now."

Tyler's eyes burned into me from the photographs. I turned away.

"You think these cases could be related," Yataro mused, still looking at the pictures.

"I wasn't involved in the first case, so I can't say," I said, starting toward the main office. "I wish I had been, though." After watching the news, my mom covered the house with so much repellant magic that not even the mail carrier would set foot near our front door for several weeks, all out of fear that some mysterious killer would steal away my baby sister in the middle of the night. "No one should have to be afraid of losing their child."

***

Yataro and I met with a group of staff members connected to Tyler Maxwell: the headmaster, a guidance counselor, and the head of Tyler's dormitory. We started off in a conference room in the dorm, where the staff gave me a breakdown of their lead—a lead that the "regular" police hadn't been able to make headway with.

"Dr. Carmen Westfall," Mr. Jimenez said, handing me a packet of papers stapled together. "Tyler's senior mentor." The guidance counselor's red-rimmed eyes shone, and he cleared his throat as if in an attempt to keep from crying. Then he looked up at me. "You probably don't know this, but in magic schools like ours, seniors participate in a mandatory one-semester apprenticeship with a skilled mage, practicing their craft in the outside world. Tyler's an artist, so I naturally paired him up with Dr. Westfall, an art therapist."

I looked at the top paper on the packet, which had been printed off Dr. Westfall's website. A header in a slick silvery font read, "Silvercoast City: Discover the Healing Power of Art." In the upper left-hand corner of the homepage was a professional photo of a middle-aged woman with wavy auburn hair and a warm smile.

"Tyler loved his apprenticeship at first," Mr. Jimenez continued. "Said he finally figured out what to do with his life after college." A dark look crossed the counselor's face, and he ran a hand through his salt-and-pepper hair. "But eventually he started coming to my office, complaining of nightmares and anxiety."

"And you think this is a result of his working with Dr. Westfall," Yataro said, scrawling important facts on his little notepad.

"Why?" I asked.

Mr. Jimenez shook his head. "I should've put two and two together earlier, before he...disappeared. Looking back, I realize his dreams were all the same. When he'd describe them, it was like he was describing a painted landscape, but one with weird colors and designs that made him uneasy for some reason he couldn't pinpoint." The counselor's gaze shifted between us, shame evident in his features. "But the thing is, Tyler had always been a little anxious, so I figured these dreams were triggered by his parents' recent divorce or maybe his upcoming graduation."

Iris Cloudfield, the headmaster, spoke up, "Evidently, Dr. Westfall was brought in for questioning?"

I nodded. "They said she was clean. Her alibi checked out."

She looked at her colleagues and threw up her hands, defeated. "This Westfall is the closest thing we have to a lead. We'd greatly appreciate your giving her a second look."

The dormitory head raised a chubby hand. "Maybe you can search his room for clues. Again, the police did it, but you know how commons are. Always overlooking things."

Yataro chuckled, but I pursed my lips to keep from making a smart comment in return. *Just smile and nod, Talisa. Smile and nod.*

***

Tyler's room was clearly that of an erratic artist. From the decorated walls to the cluttered floor, there was hardly a space on his side of the room that was clean. I found myself dividing the room with an invisible line; Tyler's roommate's walls were bare, and all his belongings were kept in perfect order.

"Maybe Tyler's still in here," Yataro joked. "Perhaps in that person-sized laundry pile?"

I glanced at my partner, suppressing a smile. "Don't you have some magic you could be doing?"

"Yes, ma'am." He saluted me.

Shaking my head, I began to photograph Tyler's bedroom, eyes scanning for anything that appeared out of the ordinary. A series of ink drawings caught my attention. Plastered on the wall above his pillow—which was pinned under a pile of textbooks—were portraits of costumed superheroes in flight. Unlike everything else in Tyler's room, these drawings were arranged in a neat square. Curious, I reached out to touch one of the pictures, but before my fingers could even graze the paper, I felt something like static electricity rip through my arm.

"Dammit!" I cried out, yanking back my arm. I turned to Yataro, whose golden talisman was hovering a few inches above his cupped hands in preparation for a spell. At my outburst, the sphere dropped onto his skin, and his face wrinkled in irritation.

"What?"

I pointed to the offending drawing. "It shocked me!"

Stepping over composition notebooks and action figures, Yataro joined me at the bed and smiled when he saw the arrangement of photographs. "You don't say." He also attempted to touch one of the pictures but quickly yanked his hand back in pain when he got too close. "Joyce, can you get the lights?"

I turned off the lights and, when I returned, found Yataro sliding the pile of textbooks to the floor and lying on the pillow as if preparing to go to sleep.

"What are you doing?"

"Just watch." He gripped his golden talisman in one hand then snapped his fingers with another, uttering a two-syllable spell at the same time. "Now look at the pictures."

At first, I didn't notice anything. As my eyes adjusted to the darkness, though, I began to notice the superheroes moving, slightly at first, like slow-motion images against a paper backdrop. Within a few seconds, they were flying in and out of frame, shooting inky laser beams from their eyes, capes billowing behind them.

Another childhood memory bubbled to the surface of my mind. "Are these what I think they are?"

"Guardians," Yataro said, sitting up in the bed. "You've heard of them?"

"My sister Nakia used to have nightmares all the time. She'd put her horse drawings above her bed, insisting that they'd protect her from the bad dreams." I frowned at the still-moving images. "Hers never shocked me, though."

"That's one hell of a protection spell. Let's find out what dreams these guys were defending him from."

Gripping the talisman and chanting a spell, Yataro waved a hand over each of the pictures. Within a few moments, the ink drawings faded away. One by one, ruddy splashes of color bled from the center of each sheet, spreading slowly outward from the center. Gradually, blurry shadows and shapes began to take form.

"Are those...trees?" I asked.

"I guess?" Yataro cocked his head sideways and leaned closer. "It's hard to tell. Everything's out of order, like a puzzle."

The longer I stared, the more sense I was able to make of the mixed-up images. Indeed, it was like we were examining the scattered pieces of a puzzle, one that depicted a strangely colored forest at twilight. Rust-colored tree trunks stood tall against a sky that faded from pink to purple to black. Deep blue leaves twitched as if blown by the wind.

In the lower right-hand corner, a dark brown shape curled up at the base of a tree trunk. I photographed the disjointed image with my cell phone.

"Is that a person?" I asked, pointing at the shape.

"I don't think so. Looks more like a dog or maybe a rock."

"If we could put these pieces in order without getting zapped, that'd help."

Fidgeting with the spherical talisman, Yataro took a step back. "I'm sure Tyler will forgive us for breaking his protection spell." Inhaling deeply, my partner shut his eyes and waved his free hand over the magical drawings while chanting yet another spell.

A few seconds passed, and nothing happened.

"Did it work?" I asked.

Yataro ran a hand through his hair, his cheeks turning red. "Not yet. You would have heard, like, a hissing sound."

"So, *like*, can you try again?" I said, imitating his inflection.

"Just shut up, okay?"

My eyes widened, and I instinctively stepped toward him. "Did you just—?"

"I'm sorry," he said. "I just…need to focus."

I backed away from him, arms crossed. Foot tapping, I watched as he repeated each of the steps but slower, more deliberately. This time, we did hear hissing, as though the invisible barrier were shriveling in a magical fire. Within half a minute, the sound died down.

Yataro breathed a sigh of relief. Reaching out to grab one of the pictures, he opened his mouth to say something but was cut off by the sound of lightning ripping through the air. The barrier smacked Yataro back with repellant magic, throwing him against the desk, where his body slid to the floor in a cartoonish manner. He groaned, rubbing his temples.

"So I take it the barrier's still up." I bit back the urge to smile.

"Just a little."

***

No sooner than we'd left Tyler Maxwell's room did the bell ring, dismissing students from class. Within seconds, we were surrounded by rowdy teenaged mages, but Yataro was in such a state of melancholy he barely seemed to notice.

"I can't believe I couldn't do that spell!"

"Don't sweat it," I said, barely avoiding a collision with a boy who was more focused on his smartphone than where he was going. "It happens. Right?"

Yataro was practically stomping down the hall, and I had to work to keep pace with him. "Not usually. Not to me. It's like I—"

Before he could finish his thought, he was thrown back by an invisible force. For a moment, I thought he'd smacked into another protective barrier, but that idea proved to be false when a female student materialized in front of us, rubbing her head as if in pain. As her invisibility spell wore off, she flipped back her dark bangs and looked at Yataro, bewildered.

"*Andy?*" Her voice was shrill, and her words seemed to catch on her braces. "Is that you?"

Yataro didn't give her a second look but brushed past her with such gusto that I feared he'd knock her over. "Sorry, ma'am. Don't know what you're talking about," he said as he walked away.

For a moment, I stood there bewildered at the exchange. Once I caught up with Yataro, I asked, "That girl…do you know her?"

Yataro laughed. "No clue who she is."

"She knew your na—"

"Nope! No one calls me 'Andy.'" He cringed, pushing open the exit doors and holding them for me. "'*Andy.*' Such a gross name, right?"

I opened my mouth to object, but he quickened his pace, beating me to the cruiser. I knew he was hiding something, but I decided to let it slide. For now. After all, we had bigger concerns. I unlocked the cruiser, and Yataro slid in and slammed the door shut. I followed, forcing a barrage of questions to the back of my mind.

Back in my seat, I reached to turn on the ignition.

"Hold up. I have to get us back…like, *back*-back. Remember?"

I'd forgotten how Yataro had transformed the dark alley into a boarding school. I held my breath as I waited for him to complete the spell and didn't relax until we were back in the trash-littered alley once again.

"Good," he breathed. "At least I can do some spells right."

"At least you can do magic, period." The words flew from my mouth without my permission as I pulled the cruiser back into the street.

Yataro whipped his head toward me, looking stunned at my bluntness.

"Just saying. You don't know how lucky you are." The envy and resentment that had had decades to accumulate simmered in my chest, threatening to explode. So I changed the subject before my partner could respond. "So we got pictures of the nightmares. The forest. Thoughts?"

"It looks like something out of a painting. The art style's nothing like Tyler's. It's much more skillful."

"Something like his mentor would have done." I shrugged, fingers curling tightly around the steering wheel. "Either way, it's the closest thing to evidence we have. Let's hope Jamison likes it."

***

Commander Jamison was overjoyed when he saw the photos. Before I could ask what the big deal was, he pulled a tablet out of a drawer and pulled up a series of photos taken of Dr. Westfall's paintings. Each brushstroke, each shadow, each color was similar to those depicted in Tyler Maxwell's captured nightmares. To me, her artwork didn't seem particularly scary. Why, then, was it the subject of such awful dreams? This question made Carmen Westfall worth looking into.

So that afternoon, we loaded into the cruiser again for another long drive. Throughout the trip, Yataro was completely silent, eyes closed in meditation as he waited for his magical energy to be restored; after all, neither of us wanted a repeat of the incident at Tanglewood Prep.

Carmen Westfall's studio was a townhouse on Sholes Boulevard, home of the wealthiest of the wealthy in Silvercoast City. Standing in the shadow of the towering white stone, I thought of the creaking floors and mildew of my own apartment, and my heart sank.

Yataro whistled.

"Ready to drop out of the force and start art therapy school?" I asked.

Yataro followed me up the staircase leading to the wide French doors flanked by bay windows. "Me? Even attempting anything remotely artistic would more likely *cause* trauma than fix it."

A few moments after the doorbell chimed, the door opened. A woman appeared in the doorway, her auburn hair tied back with a gold hairband. She wore a sunlight-colored floor-length dress, and an eight-pointed star dangled around her neck—a talisman.

"Dr. Carmen Westfall?" I said.

Her wide green eyes glanced from me to my partner.

"Yes?"

I flashed my badge, and Yataro followed suit. "We're Detectives Talisa Joyce and Andrew Yataro. Magical Investigation Program. We're here to speak to you about your mentee, Tyler Maxwell."

She crossed her arms. "Yes, I've already spoken to the police."

"I understand. We just have a few follow-up questions. Do you mind?"

"Come in." She stepped aside and led us into the living room, her long skirt swishing as she walked.

The interior of Carmen Westfall's apartment was striking, almost an assault to the senses. Brightly colored walls clashed with dark hardwood floors. A golden spiral staircase and an old-fashioned elevator connected each of the three stories. Expensive-looking paintings—mostly landscapes—from various time periods decorated the walls. Again, I felt small and impoverished standing in Dr. Westfall's huge living room with its colorful furniture and throw rugs and so much art.

"Can I get you a drink?" Dr. Westfall asked, gliding in front of us like a fairy.

"No, thanks," I said.

Yataro shook his head.

Dr. Westfall sat down on a loveseat. We sat across from her, and Yataro pulled out his notebook and pen.

The doctor kicked off her sandals and tucked her legs underneath her. "Well, like I told the police the other day, I haven't heard from Tyler since well before he went missing. They took my alibi and ran my background check and everything."

"Yes, I know. We're not trying to accuse you of anything," I said. "We did come across something in Tyler's room that we were hoping you could help us understand."

Some of the frustration in her countenance melted

away, and she leaned in slightly. "What might that be?"

I pulled out my phone and showed her the photo I'd taken earlier. "This is what Tyler had been dreaming about before he disappeared."

"He tried to block it with a Guardian spell," Yataro added.

Dr. Westfall stared at the photo, expressionless. "Huh."

"I know your artwork is similar." I slid the phone back into my pocket. "We wondered what might have frightened him about this image."

She shrugged. "He never mentioned feeling uneasy about my art."

"So, what, none of your work is magical?" Yataro asked.

Dr. Westfall scowled at him. "When did I say that?"

"What he meant is, we know the kind of work you do. You're an artist, a therapist, and on top of all that, a mage." The tension between the two made my heart race as I tried to steer the conversation. "I don't know much about how magic works, but I know that sometimes magical items can have...adverse effects?"

Dr. Westfall's scowl gradually flattened. "Fair enough." Standing, she added, "If it would make you feel better, browse my gallery. Look as long as you want; use whatever spells you think necessary. I guarantee my work doesn't carry any *adverse effects*. Certainly, nothing that would make a bright kid like Tyler want to disappear."

We followed Dr. Westfall's swishing skirt out of the living room. I shot an accusatory glance at my partner, who responded by mouthing, *I don't like her.*

Honestly, there was something about her I didn't like either. I couldn't put a finger on it, but it was there nonetheless.

She led us to the second floor then through a wide

hallway covered in paintings—hers. They all depicted gorgeous, almost alien landscapes sprawled out on canvas in sharply contrasting colors. Orange skies and purple cornfields. Too-large stars and diminutive mountains. Twisty yellow rivers cutting through seas of navy blue trees. Not only that, but the images moved: waves crashed onto sandy shorelines; trees swayed in the wind; shadows twitched beneath towering trees. I slowed my pace as I passed each of the paintings, captivated by their strange beauty. Despite my disinterest in art, the paintings awakened in me a sense of wonder, and questions floated through my head like champagne bubbles. *Where is this supposed to be? What would it be like to live in a place like this?*

"Here you are," Dr. Westfall said, her bare feet padding ahead of Yataro and me.

"They're incredible." Yataro's wide eyes darted from one canvas to the next. He took the golden talisman off his neck and held it in front of each painting, quietly chanting a magic-detecting spell.

The doctor smiled at Yataro as she crossed the gallery floor.

"So how'd this mentor-mentee thing work anyway?" I asked her. "What kind of work did Tyler do with you?"

"Observation, primarily," she replied, watching Yataro move around the gallery. "He also assisted with group therapy sessions and researched different techniques."

"What kind of techniques? I honestly didn't know art therapy was a thing until this case."

Yataro halted in front of a chaotic ocean scene with purple waves crashing against a bright yellow shoreline. Within seconds, his countenance stiffened, as if he'd suddenly remembered some terrible memory. I opened my mouth to ask if he was all right, but Dr. Westfall interrupted me.

"Now that you mention it, Tyler practiced some

therapeutic techniques with me. If it'll help, I can show you his work."

"It's worth a look."

"My office is right this way." She continued down the hall toward a closed door. I turned to make sure Yataro heard, but he was still staring at the painting.

"Yataro?" When he didn't respond, I called his name more sharply.

My partner turned to us slowly, his eyes glazed over. "Sorry." Tearing himself away from the landscape, he approached us with heavy feet.

***

That evening, Yataro managed to talk me into taking us to a diner not far from the station, the Starlite Cafe. We sat across from one another in a secluded booth and debriefed. I sipped coffee while Yataro swiped through the pictures I'd taken of Tyler's art therapy work: a canvas covered with dark, clashing colors and jagged lines; a self-portrait, the eyes wide and sad and the lips drawn tightly together; a sketch of a smiling elderly lady sitting on a porch—his grandmother, Dr. Westfall explained—and a painting of his unsmiling family of four. This last painting was covered over with mean fracture lines, giving the impression that it was breaking like glass. As I'd photographed the artwork, it had made my heart sink.

"Poor kid." He slid my phone across the table.

"This doesn't really help, though," I said, picking up the phone. "All it shows us is that he's got a broken family, which we knew from the counselor's statement."

He drowned his pancakes in blueberry syrup. "Something's not right."

"And you're sure your amazing mage powers didn't pick up on anything?"

"Why, they most certainly did." Yataro straightened up and wiped syrup from the corner of his mouth. "Get this: there's a spell that makes the paintings *move*."

"Fascinating. Anything else?"

"Nothing."

I downed the rest of the coffee and slid it to the edge of the table. "Then how come you had to stare at that one picture for a billion hours?"

"It wasn't a *billion* hours."

"Seriously, why?" Thinking about how transfixed he'd been made me uneasy.

"There was just…a depth to her work," he said with a faraway look. "I don't know…just something about it drew me in."

"Ah, so you like the artsy girls, then?"

He looked at me, embarrassed.

I winked. "Got it."

Yataro covered his head with his hands. "I do *not* like that pretentious snob."

"Right, *sure*."

He groaned. "You're the worst."

That's when something weird happened. As he moved his hands, I noticed a strange sort of motion on his face—a twitching, but one that seemed to be happening in slow motion, like the movement in Dr. Westfall's paintings. The crimson in Yataro's face was replaced with a sickly pale color.

"You okay?"

"Yeah." Yataro slid out of his booth. "Just…need a smoke break."

"Want me to join you?"

"No!" His eyes widened as if he was surprised at his own sharpness. "I mean, no. I just need some time to myself. For…magic reasons."

He stormed out of the cafe, practically knocking over

a couple of teenagers on his way. I thought about respecting his wishes and leaving him alone. *What's the harm in a guy taking a quiet smoke break?*

But then…something was off about the way he looked before he left. With the day's work done, I could finally pay attention to that nagging feeling I'd been ignoring ever since his weird encounter with the girl at Tanglewood. And it made me remember…

That time when Nakia tried to sneak into an R-rated movie…didn't she use an appearance-altering spell?

I jumped up from my seat and took off after Yataro, dropping a couple of twenties on the table.

When I got outside, Yataro had a box of cigarettes and a lighter in his left hand. He wasn't using either, though. Instead, he was whispering a spell, punctuating it with profanities when the magical light refused to spark from his right hand.

"Hey!" I clasped his shoulder, and he whirled around, taken aback just as I'd hoped he would be.

With his concentration broken, his aging spell fell away. The once tall twenty-something was replaced by a boy. He couldn't have been any older than seventeen. His clothes looked comically big on him, and his face was paper white with fear.

"I knew it!" I jabbed a finger at him. "I knew something was off about you!"

Yataro's eyes drifted toward his feet. "I can ex—"

"I mean, what almost 30-year-old man listens to Lil' Pump?"

"Joyce, I—"

"And what do you think you're doing smoking!" I snatched the lighter and cigarettes, shoving both into my coat pocket. "I should arrest you…impersonating a police officer, acting as a con artist—"

"Joyce, please!" He held up his hands like I was

about to shoot him. "You've gotta listen to me."

Listening was the last thing on my mind as I prepared to tear into this punk kid who had deceived me for so long. But before I could say another word, I sensed eyes on me from within the diner. Turning, I saw people watching the exchange between us. With a sigh, I grabbed him by the arm and led him toward the police cruiser. "Fine. You've got until we get to the station to give me one good reason why you shouldn't be behind bars, and it better not be a sob story."

***

As sob stories go, Yataro's wasn't bad. Poverty, a demanding stepdad named Jeremy who just didn't *get* him, a school in which mages were the minority—all these factors led him to con his way into the police force and manipulate us all with his magic.

"I just saw an opportunity and took it." Yataro sounded like he was on the verge of crying, and this only made me cringe. "I'm failing my classes. I'm not gonna get into a good school, which Jeremy loves to point out. I'm not gonna get anywhere in life, not without money—real, grown-up money."

"But how?" Despite my anger, I was somewhat impressed. "How can you be a full-time student with a full-time career?"

"I have a process. A complex process involving a few lies and a lot of magic."

"Which is why you're having a hard time with basic spells."

"I'm stretching myself thin." His voice cracked, and he put his head in his hands, tugging at his hair as if to tear it out. It was hard for me to believe that this frightened boy was once a man capable of magic that I envied.

"The girl at Tanglewood..." Little by little, the pieces clicked together in my mind.

"My cousin," he explained. "She knows me well enough to see through the spell."

There was a long pause. When we pulled into the parking lot of the SCPD, I looked at him. "So what now?"

"I dunno. We're in too deep, don't you think?"

A bitter laugh burst from my chest. "*You're* in too deep, kiddo! This is all you."

"I meant, like, we're in the middle of a case. Wouldn't it be awkward if I just disappeared from the staff?"

"You mean, *like*, wouldn't it be awkward if I arrested you?"

His face flushed again. "No, I meant—" He sighed. "Let's just finish the case. Okay?"

I gestured to his ill-fitting "grown-up" clothes. "Not with you. I want the other guy back."

"I can bring him back, I promise!" Yataro practically yelled. "I just need tonight to rest."

I pondered Yataro's proposition. On the one hand, he'd betrayed me—betrayed the entire SCPD with his little scheme. Sob story or no, I couldn't deny that fact. On the other hand, maybe we were in too deep? Maybe halting this investigation to arrest Yataro and find a new partner would do more harm than good? Maybe for Tyler Maxwell's sake, it was best to continue.

I leaned in close. "No more mistakes. One slip-up, and you're done. And after this case is over, you're going to resign. Got it?"

His eyes dropped. "Got it."

***

I dropped Yataro off a few blocks from his house. As the teenager trudged down the sidewalk toward the darkened, decrepit apartment that resembled my own, I let the flurry of emotions resulting from this revelation do battle within me.

"This is what I hate about mages," I said to myself.

I thought about how Nakia had cheated and "magicked" her way through school. How she used magic to get ahead in life, even when she didn't deserve it. I thought about how whenever I told my parents about her scheming, they brushed off my concerns as "jealousy."

As the sun set over the city skyline, I rolled that word over in my mind: jealousy. As a law-abiding citizen, was it right to be jealous of other people's ability to deceive? *Shouldn't I be grateful that my hard work and tenacity have gotten me this far?*

Shouldn't I?

***

No sooner had I stepped into the SCPD building than Commander Jamison called Yataro and me into his office. I immediately worried he had somehow found out about Yataro's scheming and that I'd be in trouble for covering him.

"Have a seat." Jamison gestured to a chair across from his desk. As I made my way to the desk, I noticed that the one vein in the middle of his forehead hadn't popped yet: a good sign that he wasn't angry. Not at me, at least. Soon after, Yataro timidly stepped into the office, looking just as tense as I felt but also very grown up. Jamison's countenance remained unchanged, and the tightness in my chest dissipated.

"I wanted to touch base with you both about the Tyler Maxwell case," he said, leaning in closer and running a hand through his snow-white hair. "You find any dirt on the therapist?"

"Something about Dr. Westfall's art made Tyler uneasy," I said. "Yataro swept the place for suspicious spells, but the place was clean. Our questioning didn't really lead anywhere helpful."

Yataro reached into an inner coat pocket to retrieve his notepad. He flipped to the page where he'd scrawled yesterday's notes. "Would you like to take a look?"

Jamison nodded and took the pad, but he couldn't mask his own shock at Yataro's terrible handwriting. "Geez, my teenage son has better handwriting than you do."

The color drained from Yataro's face. Shaking my head, I couldn't keep from smiling at his paranoid terror.

"Well, I called you because there's been another missing person's case filed. Two, actually. Rachael Ward and Camilla Franklin. One's a college student, and one's a bigshot CEO. Different ages, different locations. But they've got one thing in common."

"Mages," Yataro said.

"Right. Powerful mages, too." Jamison leaned forward in his seat. "Anyway, turns out they'd been seeing a therapist before their disappearance, too."

"Dr. Westfall?" I asked.

"The very same," Jamison said. "Alibi or no, there are too many red flags surrounding this woman. I think it's time to take her into custody."

I nodded. "We're on it."

"I know you two are perfectly capable, but be careful with this one. She's slippery." Jamison stood and pulled a small key from his pocket. Turning around, he unlocked a small safe. "Take these with you." He reached into the safe and produced two Disruptors. He tossed one to each of us. I examined the weapon; it was similar to a taser, but instead of shocking the victim, it would emit a painless pulsing sensation that would render a mage unable to cast a spell.

"Good luck," Jamison said.

***

"Well, here goes nothing," I said once we were alone in the parking lot. "May your body remain free from spontaneous bouts of puberty."

"Ha!" There was something about that one-syllable laugh that made Yataro sound utterly insane. "I'm all good, Detective Joyce. I'm all good." He reached under his shirt and pulled out at least ten medallions of varying shapes and materials hanging around his neck. "Clearly, the one talisman wasn't enough to keep the spell active."

"Damn. All that for one spell?"

He opened the car door and slid inside. "Don't worry! I promise, no more screw-ups. I won't let you down."

I got into the car and started the ignition. Pulling away from the station, I asked him, "Does something seem...off about this case to you? Too easy?"

A brief pause. "I guess?" he said. "I like easy, though, so..."

"Maybe I'm paranoid, but I feel like we're being led into a trap," I said, my voice low.

"I wouldn't worry about it," he said. "Like I said, I swept the place for harmful spells and got nothing. Dr. Westfall may be up to something, but she's also immensely proud, maybe too proud to hide her work."

My fingertips wandered over the cool surface of the Disruptor. "I hope you're right."

***

When we arrived at the townhouse, all the windows were dark. However, Dr. Westfall's car was still parked in the driveway, so we ascended the stoop, hoping for the best.

I pressed the doorbell, whose pleasant silvery chimes were followed by a long silence. Frowning, I pounded the door. "Police, open up!"

Still no response. "Try the door," Yataro whispered.

I turned the knob, and sure enough, the door swung open. Sinister darkness bathed the townhouse interior, making cold sweat bead on my brow. Tentatively, I stepped inside, and my partner followed close behind, closing the door behind him.

"She's here," Yataro said. "I can sense it."

"Where?" I instinctively drew my gun, and he followed suit.

He scowled in concentration before answering, "Everywhere. It's like she's somehow managed to take control of this entire house."

I flicked the nearest light switch, but the lights stayed off. "I'm calling for backup," I said, pulling out my radio. But when I pressed the button, I heard nothing but static.

"We shouldn't be here," Yataro turned around and started for the front door. He jiggled the knob then heaved his body against the heavy wood paneling. It wouldn't budge. "Nice. Evidently, we're trapped."

My heart dropped into my stomach, and I ran to the nearest window. Chest tightening, I flicked open the lock and tried with all my might to pry open the window. When that didn't work, I tried another window, which proved just as ineffective.

"I've seen this magic before," Yataro said, suddenly at my side. "And I know the counterspell. Problem is…"

"*Problem?*"

He reached into his shirt and fished out one of his talismans, the golden sphere with an array of magical symbols on it. "You know what this is for, right?"

"It's like…a battery, right? It stores magical energy."

"Right." He stuffed the sphere back into his shirt. "For a spell like this, Dr. Westfall would need something similar."

"The necklace?" I said, remembering her star medallion.

"Probably not. A talisman could be anything, and a spell like this would take a great deal of power. Not to mention, she's found a way to keep me from detecting her magic. That takes a hell of a lot of power. Whatever this talisman is, we've got to find it and destroy it. It will reverse the spell's effects."

A sound like howling floated from the top floor, making us jump. The silence that followed made me grit my teeth. I tried the radio again, but it still yielded nothing but static; Westfall's work, no doubt.

As the howling continued, we ascended the spiral staircase to investigate. It sounded heavy and sorrowful, more human than animal. We followed the sound into the gallery Dr. Westfall had shown us yesterday. Wall lights illuminated each of the bizarrely-colored paintings, the only light we'd seen since entering the townhouse.

"There's no one here," I said. "But who was making that noise?"

Yataro stood stock-still in front of the painting again, that tense, pale look creeping onto his face.

"This again?" I said.

Yataro held up a finger to quiet me, not even glancing in my direction. "There's something…"

The howling resumed, and the door to Dr. Westfall's office swung open. Every fiber of my being screamed, *No, no, no, do not go in there*, but I couldn't shake the feeling that I must have missed something when I was in that office yesterday.

"Yataro!" I hissed. "Snap out of it."

I don't think he even heard me. Part of me wanted to run over and shake him, but my feet were moving toward the door without my permission, like some force was luring me in. The more I tried to fight it, the stronger the compulsion grew, and the more my mind tried to rationalize the decision to leave my partner alone. *If there are clues to be found, they're in that office. Yataro will snap out of it... He did last time.*

But as I entered the pitch-black office, I was struck with an overwhelming sense of vulnerability. A feeling of nakedness. Yataro had said he sensed Dr. Westfall's omnipresence; now I felt unseen eyes peering through me. Predator's eyes, waiting for the right moment to strike.

I tried the light switch, but this one proved useless too. I reached for the small flashlight tucked into my belt and swept it around the room. "What did I miss?"

There wasn't much to see. Walls coated in colorful canvases. Tables and chairs surrounded by easels and containers of art supplies. Shelves laden with books. A mahogany desk and leather plush chair.

The desk held something I hadn't noticed the last time I'd been in this room: a picture frame. I picked it up and was surprised to see a photograph of a much younger Dr. Westfall carrying a small child on her shoulders, their faces frozen in laughter.

She has a kid?

Something shifted in my periphery. I whirled around in time to see the office door closing, slowly at first but increasing in speed. I jumped over the desk, knocking over a few items in the process.

"Yataro!" I shrieked as I crossed the office floor.

Frozen in front of the painting, my partner turned at the sound of his name. He opened his mouth to speak, but no sound came out.

Within seconds, he was gone.

The door slammed shut. I banged against it with my fists, tried to wrench the doorknob free, screaming the whole time.

Because he hadn't just disappeared.

It was like…his body had collapsed into dust. A shimmering, smoky dust that had immediately been sucked into the painting.

***

After trying for what seemed like hours to call for backup, I stuffed the two-way radio onto my belt, cursing whatever spell continued to block our communications. I kicked and fought to free myself from the office, but eventually exhausted myself. In the end, that familiar sense of uselessness came crawling back. I'd kept Yataro's secret because I thought his magic would prove useful. Instead, I'd managed to put us both in danger. Yataro's disappearance was on my hands.

The only thing I could think to do was search Westfall's office for her talisman, but that, too, proved fruitless as I couldn't detect magic the way Yataro could. Still, I fished through drawers and lifted rugs and tried to find anything that looked remotely magical.

I was so caught up in my useless search, I never heard the sound of bare feet padding down the corridor. When the door wrenched open, I jumped and whipped the Disruptor out in front of me. Gray light from the gallery flooded the room, making me squint.

Dr. Westfall smiled coolly, unfazed by the Disruptor being pointed at her. Even without makeup and wearing a paint-splattered hoodie and jeans, she looked just as elegant as she had the day before. And a hundred times more confident.

"Detective Joyce. I thought you might come back."

My finger twitched over the Disruptor's trigger. With a flick of her wrist, Dr. Westfall made the entire room tremble. My legs gave way, and the weapon flew out of my clammy hands as I held the desk to steady myself. I stooped down to grab it, but as soon as I touched it, it collapsed into something like black dust that quickly dissipated. I then reached for my gun, but it too collapsed into dark powder.

Despite my unarmed state, I approached her with clenched fists. "What have you done with my partner?"

"I don't know what you're talking about."

"He disappeared!" It was all I could do to keep from slapping her. "He was sucked into one of your paintings!"

Her eyes brightened, and her lips curled into an eerie half-smile. Without addressing my accusation, she stepped into the gallery.

Jaw clenched, I forced myself to follow her, despite the fact that every cell in my trembling body screamed that fighting this mage unarmed was madness. I took slow, deliberate steps to keep from bolting for the door. *He's my partner,* I told myself. *I can't abandon him.*

The doctor stopped in front of Yataro's painting. It didn't take long for me to notice the new addition: a dark figure wading in the waves. Magic made the water rise and fall, and I could faintly see the figure waving to me from the other side, like a glitchy digital image.

I glared at her. "Let. Him. Go."

She didn't avert her eyes from the canvas. "Believe me; I take no pleasure in this…" Her mouth formed a thin line, and she turned away from the painting. "I'm sorry."

Sensing danger in those last two words, I stepped back a few feet from her, my hand slapping the empty holster. There was a high, electrical hiss, and my heart skipped a beat as Dr. Westfall's hands glowed with blue tendrils of lightning, poised to strike.

I was about to be killed, and the only way to avoid it was to make her talk. My mind raced, the sound of Dr. Westfall's lightning making my head swim. Then I remembered.

"Wait!" I held up my hands. "Is this about your

daughter?"

My entire body tensed up against the inevitable lightning strike, but it never came. For one long pregnant pause, Dr. Westfall stood there, eyes shining. Finally, her hands dropped to her side, and the relief that overcame me was so strong I had to fight to keep from collapsing to the floor.

"She vanished," Dr. Westfall said, her voice small and feeble. "Just vanished in the middle of the night. Your police did no good. I begged, pleaded for them to keep looking. Used all the magic I had within me to search when they gave up."

"Was she…" A memory of my mom's fretful protection spells flashed in my mind. "Was she one of the Changeling kids?"

Dr. Westfall nodded slightly, and my blood ran cold. "My magic alone isn't enough to find her. I needed to create a talisman unlike any other. A collection of other powerful mages, from whom I can draw magical essence. Only then will I be able to track down my child and bring her back."

"Kidnapping, though? There has to be another way." I regretted my words as soon as they left my mouth.

"There is no other way!" Sparks flew from her fingertips and struck me on the shoulder. I was thrown against the wall, my skin burning with pain. "You're no mage. You don't understand!"

"You lose your daughter, so you kidnap other people's daughters? Other people's sons, wives, friends? How is that right?"

Dr. Westfall loomed over me. Lightning crackled in her clenched fists. "No one is more important than my daughter. No one."

My shoulder screamed in pain as I planned my next move. Yataro's words from earlier echoed in my mind. Destroy the talisman…reverse the spell.

I reached into my coat pocket for the lighter I'd confiscated from him. Flicking it on, I wrenched Yataro's painting off the wall and held the little flame close to one of its corners.

The lightning died in Dr. Westfall's hands.

"Sorry," I said, holding the little flame close to the canvas. "Don't mean to make you nervous. I know you must have worked really hard on this doodle."

Her eyes darted from me to the painting and back again. "That *doodle* holds the soul of your partner. Your friend. It would be a very bad idea to burn it."

"It's just a picture," I said, mustering as much nonchalance as I could manage. I moved the flame closer to the canvas.

"Do what you want!" Dr. Westfall held up her hands. "It's your partner who will suffer. His whole world will be bathed in fire."

"Or it'll release him, more likely. I know what happens when you destroy a talisman." Still, my stomach churned at the thought of turning Yataro's painted prison into a fiery inferno from which there was no escape.

But there was that look in Dr. Westfall's eyes. Eyes that were too wide, too bright. There was the shrill quality in her voice, even as she assured me that I was about to set Yataro's world ablaze.

No. I may not have had magic, but I knew a lie when I heard one.

I held the lighter to the center of the painting, right where Yataro's silhouette was painted. She rushed toward me, knocking the canvas out of my hand. But it was too late. Dark blue smoke poured out of the painting, and silver sparks flew. The room shook again, sending canvas frames crashing to the floor.

An enraged scream exploded from Dr. Westfall's throat. I scrambled for the door, but invisible hands slammed it shut in front of me. I heard the sizzle of lightning and leaped out of the way just in time to avoid the strike.

A shadowy, smoke-encircled form emerged from the fallen painting. Looking as though he'd been oil-painted onto the backdrop of reality, Yataro rubbed his temples and stepped forward drowsily.

"What have you done?" Dr. Westfall shrieked. Her expression was wild, like she wanted to cry and rip my head off with her teeth all at once.

When Dr. Westfall's lightning caught my arm, it didn't hurt as badly as before. *Her powers must be fading!*

The blue smoke encircling Yataro fell away, revealing him in his true form—a teenager.

Dr. Westfall charged us. I held up my arms to brace myself against the assault, but star-silver light burst from Yataro's hands. Looking up, I saw a wall of light separating us from the mage; she was frozen in place like a life-size villainous action figure.

It was over. I wasn't going to die.

"You okay?" Yataro asked, studying me in a way that assured me I wasn't.

"I'm good." Except that my heart was beating too fast, and my skin was too cold, and my head was spinning, and I just needed to sit down. "We have to save the other mages."

"Nope," he said, guiding me toward the nearest wall. "I may not be a real cop, but I *am* First Aid certified. You're in shock."

"I have to help." I didn't have the willpower to put up much of a fight, though.

"You just got through saving both of our asses, and I would very much like you to not pass out." He took off his leather jacket and rolled it up. "Pillow?"

"Ugh, fine." I took the "pillow" from him and lay on the ground. "And watch your language, young man."

He smirked and stooped down to examine the burnt painting. "Good thinking. Weren't you afraid of burning me to a crisp, though?"

"Yeah, Dr. Westfall said something about that," I said, still fighting dizziness. "But Dr. Westfall is also a terrible liar."

He picked up the lighter and held it to another painting. "Either that, or you're a human lie detector," he said.

"Dunno about that," I said. "I didn't know what the hell I was doing half the time."

"You know what I hate?" Blue smoke and sparks poured out of the painting he'd set on fire. He moved on to the next one. "False modesty. Just take the compliment, geez."

I cracked a smile.

"You're not useless," Yataro said. "And I owe you one."

"I'll keep that in mind," I said as he moved to another painting. A shadowy figure began to rise out of the first one he destroyed.

"Mystic Donuts? My treat?"

"I need something stronger. Shame you're not 21 or older."

Yataro fished out his talismans. "I can fix that real quick!"

"Nope, sorry."

He clutched his chest. "You wound me, Talisa Joyce."

"Hey, don't grow up too fast, kiddo. You've got potential, but you've got a lot to learn. Give it time, and you'll be a real asset to the force."

Yataro smiled. "Well, I'm glad I got to learn from the best."

***

With the talismans destroyed and the mages set free, we were able to call for backup. Dr. Carmen Westfall was put behind bars for kidnapping Tyler Maxwell, Camilla Franklin, Rachael Ward, and several other mages. That one case put to rest at least ten missing persons cases, some of which had gone cold.

A few days later, we sent Detective Andrew Yataro on his way. He'd resigned, saying he wanted to go back to school—which wasn't a lie, really. Jamison was utterly bewildered, but Yataro assured us all that he'd be back once his schooling was done.

All was well, or so it seemed, but I couldn't get the story of Westfall's missing daughter out of my head. So late one night, I found myself in the high-security correctional facility, sitting on a bench, a phone in my hand, waiting for Carmen Westfall to appear. When she arrived, she didn't look anywhere near as powerful, dressed in her orange jumpsuit and magic-blocking arm braces, but her glare still sent chills up my spine.

Dr. Westfall sat and put the phone to her ear. "What?" she hissed, glaring at me through bloodshot eyes.

"I know I'm the last person you wanna talk to." I leaned forward, forcing myself to meet her icy gaze. "And I know our police couldn't help you before. But I think we can help now."

It didn't take long for the ice in Dr. Westfall's expression to thaw. A tear trickled down her cheek. "You can't do anything."

"Try me."

The Ghostly Loch

Mari L. Yates

Doyle O'Malley, the zombie proprietor of The Ghostly Loch, glanced up in the mirror behind the bar. It had been a long night, but it was finally closing time, and the last stragglers were making their way out into the cold, foggy streets of Albfest—Belfast's supernatural realm.

He watched a fairy slip into her leafy jacket and pick up her dandelion clutch before waving and heading for the door. That's when he saw it. Something was on the wall behind him that shouldn't be there. Doyle squinted at it in the mirror. Letting the tap handle snap back into place, he turned and slammed the half-filled beer down on the counter. "For the love of Death, Eoin! I gave ye one job!"

"I'm not paying you for half a pint, Doyle. Let's have the rest, then!" A wizened specter tried to slam his translucent fist onto the polished cherrywood bar and seemed surprised when it made no impact.

"Not now, Harlon. Can't ye see I'm yellin' at Eoin?" Doyle shoved the beer across to his last patron then lifted his remaining lip in a snarl as he turned back to his employee. His already rough accent grew thicker as he accentuated his words with a wagging finger. "I told ye to watch the door, Eoin. There's one rule. NO CHILDREN ALLOWED IN THE LOCH!"

The grayish-white poltergeist seated near the door

blathered out an excuse. "I haven't let any kids in here tonight, boss!"

Doyle stomped around the bar, coming to a shuffling stop near the booth closest to the door. He pointed a finger at the purple drawing on the wall. "Then how do you explain *that*?" He snatched a rag off the bar and slid into the booth to scrub at the stucco.

"Oh, that. Was probably the little breather who was in here earlier today." Eoin nodded as if he'd explained everything.

Doyle froze. The supernatural realm was protected by strong magic. Breathers, or humans, as they called themselves, couldn't just wander into the pocket dimension hiding in the middle of their city. They had to be escorted in by a resident.

"What breather?" Doyle twisted in the seat, rag forgotten on the table. "Who brought him? We weren't even open yet; why'd ye let him in?"

"It was a wee girl, actually." Eoin's forehead creased as he bobbed in the air. "She was alone, best I could tell. Didn't see anyone with her. She sat down right there, colored for a bit, and then the next time I looked, she was gone."

"And ye didn't think to come mention this to me?" Doyle leaned over the table and rubbed at the crayon trails with a finger. As he did, his thin cotton shirt snagged on one of his exposed ribs, and he plucked at it with his fingers. Even with Farrah recasting her "decay-no-more" spell each week, Doyle was losing more and more muscle lately, along with large portions of his skin. He avoided looking at the mirror on the opposite wall. He didn't need to see; he knew what he looked like: a typical, rotting-fleshed zombie. At least he still had his lips, so he didn't look like he was grinning at everything all the time.

"She didn't seem to be causing any trouble," Eoin

said. "A-a-and I figured maybe her host had asked you to watch her or something."

Doyle glared at Eoin and pointed at the table. "Because I'm in the business of babysittin' in the wee hours of the morning, right? Ye see her again, let me know. There's wax in the stain now and scuffs in the seat! I just had everything revarnished last week, Eoin!"

"I know, boss. I'm real sorry."

Harlon let out a loud belch. "I'll come by tomorrow and fix the table, Doyle. If I get the rest of my drink." He wiggled his glass.

"Do that." Doyle lumbered back over to the bar and poured Harlon another drink. He grumbled to himself and began washing the dishes. He tried not to think of the bloated mess his skin would become after being submerged in the water. His right hand was already looking a little ragged. Was that bone showing on his pinky finger? It made his stomach churn just thinking about it. He really should look into hiring more help around the pub. He shook his head; he couldn't do that without asking the Hyenas for help. Doyle turned to his spectral bouncer. "Hey, Eoin? No more little girls. I don't even want her in the pub. No children at all. Is that clear?"

"Yes, boss." Eoin nodded, making his way to the door. "I'll sit here and watch for her myself."

Several hours later, with his feet dragging more than usual, Doyle made his way over to flip the "open" sign around and twist the deadbolt. Granted, the lock wouldn't stop spirits from entering the place, but it was the habit of it. He'd owned a pub for all of his adult human life. And his entire undead life, come to think of it. He found it hard to let go of some things. The routine of closing up was one of them.

"Go home, Eoin." He waved his partially rotted left hand through the poltergeist bouncer napping near the door.

Not that Eoin did much in the way of actual security. At least, he hadn't let any little girls into the pub in the last twenty-four hours.

Eoin snorted and blinked awake, eyes going wide when he saw the place was empty. "You sure?" He yawned loudly, not even bothering to cover his spectral mouth.

"Yeah, I can finish up here." Doyle nodded. "See ye this evening."

The spirit grunted as he floated toward the back door. "I'll just make sure the place is all locked up first."

Doyle wiped off the tables and picked up a few stray glasses to dump in the sink to be washed the next day. There was a small snap as the last glass left his hand. Doyle looked down just in time to see his left thumb bob twice in the water before sinking below the soapy surface. He cursed and fished around in the water for the severed digit. When he held it aloft, he was dismayed to see that the bone protruding from the end was jagged and broken. There would be no salvaging it. He turned to toss it in the trash and froze. What was that noise? He cocked his head and listened for it again.

There was a rattle as the doorknob twisted, though the deadbolt stopped the door from opening. Doyle slowly walked around the counter and looked toward the door.

A little girl stared through the Loch's front door. A breather, no less. He could tell by the way the glass was fogging up in front of her semi-open mouth. She had her arms hugged around herself as if to ward off the cold.

Doyle blinked in surprise. He wasn't sure what he'd been expecting, but it certainly wasn't a child no bigger than an imp. Making sure to avoid the creaky boards near the center of the room, he crept closer to the door, wanting a better look at the little vandal. He peered through the glass into the early morning dawn. No little girl. He glanced down at the door; the ragged circle left by her breath was disappearing, just like she had.

***

"You have to help me, Farrah." Doyle held the phone to his ear with his shoulder as he restocked the bottles behind the bar. He'd explained about the breather's visit to the Loch the night before.

"I'd really love to, Doyle, but I'm not allowed in Albfest without Trevor's permission. You know that."

"Let me worry about Trevor," Doyle said with more bravado than he felt.

There was a long silence, then Farrah sighed. "Fine. Tell me what's been going on. You said something about a little girl?"

"There's a breather showing up in me pub and drawing on all the walls!"

"Calm down. You're certain she's not there with a host? I know you've always said you don't want kids in the Loch, but technically, under Trevor's new laws, you can't stop them from coming in with a resident."

"Eoin's been letting her in, apparently; she's just showing up at random times." Doyle shrugged, leaning against the bar and switching the phone to his other ear.

He listened to Farrah's chatter a bit more then disconnected the call, disgruntled that he couldn't convince the witch to come immediately.

***

Three nights later, Doyle heard a tapping at the downstairs window. He went downstairs to the pub and flipped on the lights. The same small shadow stood in front of the Loch.

Her wide eyes scanned the room through the window until she saw Doyle. She stumbled back a step and lost her footing, falling on the sidewalk. As Doyle watched, her face twisted and she began to cry, her thin wails leaking through the window.

Doyle started to head back to the stockroom. A breather lost in Albfest was none of his concern. He glanced at the window one more time and saw the little girl pushing herself off the ground, tears streaking her face as she tried to wipe off her skinned palms. Before he knew what he was doing, he was unlocking the door and stepping out into the street. He must be getting addled in his un-age, but she reminded him of himself at that age: bedraggled, lonely, and looking for any shelter he could find.

"What's yer name, lass?" Doyle gestured for her to come inside then checked both directions for any signs of Hyenas, the dreaded werecat gang that did Trevor McCormack's dirty work. The last thing he wanted was for them to see him offering shelter to an unaccompanied breather. Seeing nothing, he ducked back into the pub and closed the door, making sure it was locked.

The little girl had scurried into the warmer environment and now stood in the middle of the room shifting her weight from one foot to the other as she stared at Doyle with large, frightened eyes.

"Name, lassie?" Doyle couldn't keep the irritation out of his voice. He didn't hate children, but he didn't know how to deal with them either.

"C-c-cary." She stuttered her name and shrank back when Doyle walked past her to the fireplace.

"Alright, Cary. My name's Doyle. Why don't ye tell me how ye ended up in front of me pub and who you were with? I'll call them and get this whole mess sorted. Can't have you gallivanting about in…" He trailed off and took a better look at the little girl over his shoulder. She was wearing a thin sleeveless nightgown with what looked like a sleeping cat curled up on the front. It stopped mid-thigh, and the thin fabric wouldn't keep her warm in this weather.

Who had let her out on the street like this?

Doyle stirred up the fireplace with a poker, washing the area with fresh heat. "There now, that should make ye feel better." He turned back around and nearly dropped the poker. There was no one in the Loch with him. The wee lassie had disappeared.

***

For three blissful days, Doyle was able to forget about the little girl named Cary. A few times he found objects moved or a chair pulled closer to the fireplace, but he shrugged it off as his patrons being messy and went about his business.

On the fourth day, however, he found another table with crayoned artwork.

"Eoin, come, look at this."

His bouncer appeared at the back of the pub, an anxious expression on his face. "Yeah, Doyle?"

"Those are definitely crayon marks." Doyle pointed at the table. "I thought I told ye not to let her in here again."

Eoin's shading went from pale gray to solid white. "I swear, I didn't!"

"Then how do ye explain those?" He pointed at the purple streaks on the table. Doyle's eyes caught on another lilac mark on the wall. His beautiful, bone-white stucco wall. "Or that? There's a new scribble somewhere in me pub every time I look. She's been getting in here somehow."

"I-I-I…" Eoin shook his head and shrugged. "I don't know, boss. I'll figure it out."

"No, call Farrah. See if she can do something to keep the little breather out of my joint."

Doyle stormed out of the main taproom, leaving Eoin to deal with the mess—and ignoring the fact he'd let her in once himself.

When he returned an hour later, Farrah was walking around The Ghostly Loch. She muttered under her breath as she waved her burning herb bundle around the windows and doors. Tall for a woman, Farrah's long legs took her the length of the front window in two strides.

"Well?" Doyle crossed his arms. "Is the Loch in danger of becoming a weak zone?" He nervously awaited her answer. If the wards in place were losing strength, it was possible more breathers would find their way through. And the last thing Doyle wanted was for his pub to become some sort of hangout for fans of the supernatural. That had happened to Tom Finnegan over on the west side of the realm. Doyle shuddered, thinking about the eclectic mix of breathers and supernaturals that Tom now had to deal with on a daily basis. If something like that occurred, Doyle was more likely to attract the attention of the Hyenas, which meant Trevor McCormack, lycan mob boss extraordinaire, would be informed that business was booming. And then he'd insist on providing "protection" for the Loch. That wasn't something that would be right for the pub. No, Doyle preferred to cater to only the residents of Albfest.

"No, I can't really tell you how she's getting in." Farrah shook her head, setting her long blond hair to swinging. "Have you tried a pastry? I just made them this morning. Strawberry and cream."

Doyle eyed the dish on the bar piled high with sugary confections and grimaced. "No, thank ye. Ye know sweets don't agree with me. Or any food, really."

Batting her lashes, Farrah turned her face to him with a sparkle in her pretty blue eyes. She pouted and put her free hand on her hip. Her red-tinted lips trembled, and Doyle could tell she was trying not to laugh.

"I'll try one!" The little girl's voice came from behind the bar moments before she appeared. She clambered up onto one of the stools and reached for a sticky tart.

"Oh!" Farrah rushed over to the bar and lifted the plate before the girl's fingers could reach the flaky crust. She shook the herb bundle in the girl's face, causing Cary to sneeze. "These aren't meant for consumption by children." She turned on her brightest smile. "Can't have you flying away or turning into a frog, now can we? I'll have to make you a special plate of my chocolate chip cookies for your next visit. Would you like that?"

The little girl's face fell slightly, but she nodded and slid back to the floor. "I'm just going to go draw now." She walked over to the booth closest to the fireplace.

Doyle gritted his teeth, surprised to find he didn't want to immediately shoo her from the pub but more tempted to tell her to be careful not to get any more crayon marks on his walls. Instead, he found himself turning to stare at Farrah.

"What's in the pastries?"

The witch smiled at him sweetly, not quite meeting his eyes. "Oh, you know. A dash of this and a pinch of that."

"Farrah..."

"It's nothing, Doyle. Well, probably nothing. I just didn't want to take any chances. I'm new to the whole 'no child' diet. Ever since Trevor threw me out of Albfest, I'm actually having to use real sugar! Can you believe it? And cooking without casting spells on my oven; it's utterly mundane!" She rolled her eyes dramatically. Seeing Doyle's raised eyebrow, she sobered, picking at the front of her shirt. "I may have slipped up and used the 'stay forever' flour. I wasn't really paying attention."

Doyle glanced over his shoulder, doing a double take when he noticed the booth was empty. "Where'd she go? And why aren't any of your spells holding her out?"

Farrah frowned, drawing a quick rune in the air and blowing it across the room. When nothing happened, she sniffed the air like a hound catching a scent. "I'm not sure, but she's definitely not here any longer."

"Ye see what I'm putting up with?" Doyle slumped against the bar. "I can't do this much longer, I'm tellin' ye."

"Don't worry," Farrah patted his arm and grimaced when skin flaked away. "I'm going to figure this out. I think my mother had a recipe for keeping children away. It was from before she started eating them. I've never tried using that kind of spell before, but I'll give it my best shot."

"Thank ye, Farrah." Doyle gave her a tired smile.

She blew him a kiss and crossed to the door. "Of course, Doyle. What else are friends for, if not to help with breather infestations?" She giggled and let herself out.

Doesn't it take more than one before it's considered an infestation? Doyle sighed. *And what did she mean by Cary's next visit? Am I not paying her to keep the breather out of my pub?*

He looked back at the table, seeing a lone sheet of paper. Muttering to himself about having to pick up after a breather, he went over and snatched it up. He started to crumple the page, then something caught his eye. Doyle held up the sheet so it would better catch the light. His patchy eyebrows rose as he studied the childish artwork.

On the page was a purple line drawing, broken in several places, that he guessed was supposed to be a zombie. The head was drawn at an angle, and one hand was bent up next to the body while the other hung loosely at the figure's side. Was that...him? He turned the page, studying it from a different angle. The small stick figure smiling up at him from the badly drawn booth, that was definitely supposed to be the girl.

The longer he stared at it, the more his mouth stretched into a grin. He chuckled.

Staggering to the bar and cursing his loose ankle joint when it rolled, Doyle tucked the paper into the frame of the mirror behind the bottles. He leaned back and looked at it, his smile growing wider.

His little breather had drawn him a picture.

***

"Doyle? She's back."

Eoin waved one hand in the direction of the young girl climbing up into the booth in the corner. "I swear I did'na look away from the door this time. One second, it was you and me and Old Harlon, the next, well, it was the three of us…and her."

Doyle rested one hand on the bar and the other on his hip as he frowned at the girl. He grimaced as he watched her scuffed hand-me-down shoes dig fresh furrows into the varnish on the booth's seat. He'd lost count of how many times Cary had shown up and climbed onto that bench and pulled out that insufferable purple crayon.

She never said a word, never even looked at them. Just sat there humming to herself and scribbling her stick figure drawings. Limp brown hair hid her face from Doyle, but he could see the moth holes and frayed edges that dotted her worn flannel shirt and blue jeans. The space where his heart would have beat ached. He pushed a fist to his sternum, worried he was about to lose another part.

"What harm's she doing, Doyle?" Old Harlon followed his gaze and then took a noisy slurp of his beer.

"She's scaring off business, that's what." Doyle snatched up a rag and began polishing the bar, studiously ignoring the little girl with the faded Elmgrove Primary School patch on her torn denim jacket. "No one wants to drink in a bar with a…breather problem." He stole a glance at the little girl again. Business had never been great at the Loch, so while technically untrue, he found it easier to blame her than on his own reticence of working with Trevor and his gang. But that didn't stop his chest from hurting each time he looked at Cary.

Eoin floated over to the bar and lowered his voice. "Maybe if we just asked her what she wants, she'd go away?"

Harlon grimaced before swigging down the rest of his beer. He motioned for Doyle to refill his glass and glanced sideways at the bouncer. "You never did much haunting, did ye, Eoin? Doesn't work that way. It's not like breathers ask us what we want, get the answer, and, *poof*, we disappear." He shook his head and grinned. "What was it that tied you to Doyle, anyhow? I'd have thought a young lad like you'd be chasing some lass, hoping for a peek up her skirt."

"I don't see what that has to do with—" Eoin started.

"Breathers can't be reasoned with. That's why we haunt them." Harlon nodded at the girl. "That one there, she'd be a crier for certain. Her high, shrill screams for Mommy and Daddy would be a delight to hear."

Doyle nodded his agreement. "Aye, she'd be a prize for any supernatural to find. Late at night. Tucked into bed with her dolly. Not sitting in my pub at half past ten!"

He turned and studied the girl, taking a better look at her than he had before. Mousy brown hair hung in tangles to her shoulders, her threadbare clothing showed signs of patching, and she gripped that nub of purple crayon tightly in her fist. His unbeating heart swelled with pity as she stared back at him.

Old Harlon floated off his stool and glided closer to the girl. "What's your name, wee breather?"

"Cary." She seemed entranced by the specter, leaning over and waving her arm under him as if making sure he was really floating. "What's yours?" She looked at all three of them in turn.

Doyle bit back a smile as she struggled up onto the tall stool. He'd almost forgotten how much fun breathers could be. He thought about reaching out and giving her a boost but busied himself polishing glasses instead. He preferred as little contact with the living as possible. Even Farrah bothered him, and she was a witch.

"I'm Harlon. And that large, incredibly stupid poltergeist is Eoin. I understand you already know our dear zombie host." Harlon hovered over the stool next to Cary's and turned back to Doyle. "Another beer for me, barkeep. And a glass of milk for the child."

Doyle glanced out the window. It was raining again. Well, they were in Albfest, after all, and it mimicked the weather in Belfast round the clock. Couldn't be helped. He also remembered what it was like to be a penniless child out on the streets on Belfast's rainy nights. He sighed, knowing he'd been defeated. "All right, then. One drink." He quirked an eyebrow at her and tried to look stern. As stern as a mangy-looking zombie could, anyway. "And then ye're on yer way."

Cary nodded exuberantly, teeth flashing in a grin. "Yes, sir, Mr. Doyle!"

"Eoin, aren't you supposed to be watching the door? I'm not looking to start a milk bar for girls," Doyle snapped as he drew up the beer.

His bouncer cast an unreadable look at Doyle, smiled at Cary, and then resumed his post at the door with a soft laugh.

***

The buzz of conversation slowed then stopped altogether. Without turning, Doyle sighed, opened the mini fridge, and pulled out the milk, pouring some into a glass. He rotated to set it on the counter and saw Cary rooted in place near the front window, staring around at the assemblage of ghosts, zombies, fairies, demons, and vampires. He liked it better when the pub was empty during her visits. From the wide-eyed, terrified look on her face, so did Cary.

"Come on, lass. We haven't got all night." He glared around at his patrons until they went back to minding their own business. Pretty soon, the bar was humming again.

"Well now, wee one, come and see what Doyle scrounged up for you." Old Harlon grinned at Cary and raised his beer in salute.

"Hi, Harlon! Hi, Doyle!" Cary dropped her bag, shyness disappearing as she ran over to climb onto a stool. "What did you get, Doyle?"

Reaching under the counter, Doyle grabbed a small cardboard box, lifting it onto the bar.

"Crayons!" Cary pushed away the milk, scooting the box of colored wax sticks closer and flipping open the lid. "Look at all the colors!" She looked up at Doyle with a huge grin. "Thank you! How did you know it was my birthday?"

"I thought ye needed more than that wee scrap of purple; that's all." He shrugged, feeling his shirt catch on his newly exposed shoulder blade. "But ye're not to use those on me tables." Doyle slid a plastic placemat in front of her. "Ye want to draw? Ye use one of these. I'm done paying Harlon to redo work he's done a hundred times already."

"It's no longer just me own money he pays me with, either." Harlon chuckled. "Ever since Cary started coming in, the Loch hasn't been such a...ghost town." He cracked up at his own joke.

Cary frowned briefly then hurried back to her bag and pulled out a sheet of white paper. Bringing it to the bar, she carefully placed it on the placemat. Picking up the box, she ran her finger over the colored sticks, half-pulling one out before pushing it back into its slot. She furrowed her brow as she concentrated then selected a red crayon and started drawing.

"Where's Eoin?" She glanced at the empty stool near the door.

"It's Saturday. It's his day off."

"Ghosts get days off?" Cary sipped her milk, looking around the bar. "Is that why there's so many people in here? Do they all have today off?"

"Partly. And Eoin's a poltergeist, not a ghost." Doyle didn't say the other part out loud. Word had started to spread. Instead of scaring off the few regular customers Doyle had, news that he had a precious young breather haunting his pub had made the other supernaturals curious. They'd been coming in droves all evening. Which was odd for a Saturday night in Albfest. But he didn't want Cary to know that. He didn't want her to think she could come around any more than she already did.

It made Doyle nervous. Surely, this boom in the Loch's business would attract the attention of Trevor McCormack. So far, Doyle had been lucky enough to skate beneath the notice of the lycan mob boss. His pub did decent enough but not the kind of decent that made the Hyenas come along asking for their share. And there would be no polite refusal if the werecats showed up at his doorstep. Doyle had seen what happened to those who'd tried. Windows ended up broken, doors bashed in, and more than one family had been run out of Albfest.

No, having a werewolf and his gang nosing around the pub was the last thing Doyle needed.

He pushed the glass of milk closer, silently urging Cary to drink. It had become their habit over the past couple of weeks. She would show up, drink her milk, draw a picture or two, and then leave.

How she kept popping in and out was still a mystery, though. She just appeared. Sometimes near the bar, sometimes by the fireplace, and once in the men's restroom. Thankfully, that had been a slow evening. He wasn't about to explain to a wee girl that some of the undead still needed to take care of certain necessities.

"Have school in the morning?" Harlon asked conversationally. He lifted his drink to his incorporeal lips and sipped.

"Nuh-uh." Cary shook her head, refusing to look up. "Saturday, remember?"

"Then why are ye here?" Doyle crossed his arms and looked down his nose at her.

She shrugged. "Just am."

Tilting her head back and finishing her milk, Cary slammed her glass onto the bar like she'd seen Harlon try to do on several occasions. Doyle glared at her then laughed when she exaggerated wiping her mouth on the back of her hand and sighing loudly.

"Well, ye can't stay."

Harlon growled and tried to catch Doyle's eye. Ignoring the ghost, Doyle picked up Cary's empty glass and wiped down the counter in front of her. "We're awfully busy tonight, and I've not got room for ye to be sitting around taking up a seat."

She simply nodded, sliding back to the floor and dragging her feet over to her bag. She picked it up, slid the strap over her shoulder, and looked back at Doyle with a small smile.

He blinked, and she was gone. "I expected more of a fight from the wee lassie. She's not usually so compliant." He dumped her glass into the sink and frowned. "How does she do that, anyway?"

Harlon shrugged. "Maybe she's a witch."

"What?" Doyle leaned against the counter, propping himself up with one bony elbow.

"A young one, to be sure. But it's the only thing that makes sense." Harlon set his glass down and shook his head. "Only a powerful magic user could teleport so effortlessly. Didn't you say she just 'wishes' to be here and it happens?"

Doyle nodded, staring at the spot where Cary had

stood just moments before. Could it be true? Was she a witch? He wondered if Farrah would be able to tell them for sure.

"Harlon, if that be the way of it…"

The old ghost nodded sagely, not meeting Doyle's eyes. "Aye, I know what you're thinking." He leaned closer, eyes cutting side to side as he made sure no one was listening. "Trevor would love to get his paws on a young, pliable witch. Ever since Farrah refused to play by his rules, he's been dying to catch one he can control. We can't let that happen."

***

"The Jolly Sheep?" Cary's forehead scrunched as she a took a drink of her orange juice. "What kind of name is that?"

"I'll have you know me father owned a sheep farm. The thought of one of those wooly creatures getting into the lager always made me laugh." Doyle struggled to keep a straight face as he wagged a finger at her.

"Now ye see why I was haunting him!" Eoin cackled from his stool. "He wouldn't change the name of the place before either of us died, so I had to keep trying after! Tell me 'The Ghostly Loch' isn't a much better name for a pub."

"It is a better name, Doyle." Cary raised her eyebrows at him and spun her stool around.

"Hmph, changing the name certainly didn't get rid of ye, now did it?" Doyle chuckled and grinned at Eoin. "As for ye, lassie, ye'll be late for bedtime." Doyle gestured at her glass. She'd informed him on her last visit that she was "much too grown up for milk" now. "Drink up, and be gone."

Cary smiled and picked up a pink pastry from a nearby tray. Another one of Farrah's newly designed recipes.

"Mmm. Tell Farrah she got it right this time; these taste exactly like bubblegum!" She finished her treat, gulped down her drink, and slid from the stool. Coming around the bar, she hugged her arms around his waist and leaned her head against his chest. "I wish I could come to the Loch every night."

"Ah, lass." Doyle gently pushed her away. He was always self-conscious that Albfest's magic wouldn't mask the smell of his decomposing flesh. "Ye must stop talking like that. Ye know breathers can't live in Albfest."

"Farrah said she used to." Cary shrugged and headed for the door. "Maybe one day I'll be allowed to stay here, too."

Doyle had no doubt that it was possible. Cary had been coming into the pub for the better part of two years now. And in that time, she'd won over nearly every resident she'd met.

But they were still no closer to figuring out why Cary always appeared in Albfest. Or even where she'd end up when she did arrive. All they knew was that she always appeared somewhere near Doyle, even if he wasn't in the pub. She couldn't explain it either. Doyle had asked.

Doyle had stopped caring so much when it became clear it was only Cary and not a slew of school-aged kids popping up in his pub.

It hadn't been easy, keeping her continued presence in the tavern a secret from Trevor. Doyle had so far managed to avoid any contact with the mob boss or his cronies. The Hyenas had come sniffing around a time or two, but they'd not found anything they could report back to their boss. Doyle had thought all he had to do was make sure he kept his business low, and there would be no reason for any of Trevor's men to come snooping around his place.

***

Now, Doyle moaned as he watched Kendrick Dunne tap his fingers on the tabletop. Watching Kendrick interact with Cary made him wish he could go back two years and undo his invitation to let the vampire drink at the Loch. All his carefully laid plans could go up in smoke if the bloodsucker got a better offer. And with Trevor and the Hyenas carefully guarding the portals between Albfest and Belfast, the vampires' food supply was quickly dwindling.

Kendrick pulled out his phone and tapped the screen a few times before glancing around at the other patrons.

Dread crawled up Doyle's spine as he went into the kitchen to get Cary's order. When he came back out, Kendrick was leaning forward across the table, trying to catch Cary's eyes.

"You sure you don't have a spare crayon?" Kendrick gave Cary a hopeful look.

She shook her head, laughing at the twitchy vampire sitting across from her. "No, I left them with Doyle; I only carry the one I think I'm going to need the most." She held up the pretty blue stick before going back to her drawing. "I don't want to lose them at the..." It was the closest she'd ever come to telling them where she came from.

"It's all right, I get it." Kendrick, smooth as ever, waved away her reluctance and flashed a grin. He quickly hid it behind his hand when Cary drew back at the sight of his fangs. "Sorry. I know you're still not used to them."

"No, it's all right. I'm sorry." Cary looked from Kendrick to Doyle. "I'm trying not to be afraid of anything here, but sometimes I can't help it." She grinned up at Kendrick, her young eyes locking onto his.

Suppressing a snarl, Doyle shuffled in their direction. He'd have to remind Kendrick about the conversation they'd had: no using his powers on Cary.

Kendrick glanced up as Doyle put a basket of fries in front of Cary. "Say, Doyle. Don't suppose you have any

Type-A tucked away back there anywhere?"

Doyle shook his head. "No way, Ken." He glowered at the vampire. "And stop making eyes at the girl. She's not for you."

"Pig's blood? Cow? Anything?" Kendrick's voice rose in pitch each time he asked a question. His eyes darted to Cary and back, tongue darting out to lick his lips.

"The answer is no, Ken." Doyle gave him a stern look and gestured at the phone lying face down on the table. "Nothing other than beer. Not until ye can assure me that there's no way Trevor knows about Cary. In fact, maybe you should leave until you can bring me some good news."

The vampire cut his eyes toward Cary before shaking his head. "He's a lycan, Doyle. You know how they are. If they don't hear something themselves, they've got others who listen and report back."

Doyle gave him a suddenly wary look. "I'll be sure and have Farrah by to revoke your access to the Loch in the morning."

Kendrick opened his mouth to reply then shut it.

"What have you told him?" Doyle poked the vampire's chest with a bony finger. "What have you told him about Cary, Kendrick?"

The vampire's eyes dropped to the table. "It was lucky, her taking a shine to me on my first visit." He gave Cary a goofy grin. "You remember, don't you? You were drawing that picture of a snowman and wanted to know if there were such a thing as zombie snow people." He looked back and forth between Cary and Doyle. "When I went back to the lair, I told Trevor a breather had found a way into Albfest without a host. He rewarded me very well. I didn't go hungry for months. He's had me watching you ever since. I even convinced him not to send the Hyenas around as often as he wanted. I thought maybe it would be easier to get you to trust me." He licked his lips, and his eyes darted to

Cary's neck, then away when Doyle growled. "He's promised me all the blood I can drink if I can deliver him the girl. Trevor seems to think she's the key to keeping the portals open for good. Think of it, Doyle. *Permanent* access to Belfast. My kind wouldn't have to go hungry ever again."

The bell on the front door chimed, and Doyle glanced over his shoulder. Two Hyenas stood just inside the pub, tongues lolling from their mouths as they grinned around at the nearly empty bar. He glared at Kendrick, who looked up at him with red-rimmed eyes.

"I'm sorry, Doyle. The passageways have been really guarded lately. And I need to feed. I never wanted anyone to get hurt. If you just let him have Cary…"

"Lass, it's time for ye to leave." Doyle gave her a sad look and moved to block her from the Hyenas' view. "And Cary?" He glanced over his shoulder at his little breather. "I don't think it's safe for ye to come back for a while."

***

Doyle squeezed his eyes shut tighter when the door creaked open.

"See? He's perfectly fine." A deep, growling voice echoed off the walls.

"He's missing an arm!" Cary's indignant response sounded different. It wasn't the same little girl's voice Doyle remembered. "That's hardly what I call 'perfectly fine.'"

Cracking his eyes, Doyle saw Cary glaring up at Trevor with both hands on her hips. When had she gotten so tall? And so pretty? He groaned and pushed himself to a sitting position. What was she doing here? This wasn't supposed to happen. He'd never wanted the lycan to even find out about Cary. Then the mob boss had had him brought to this prison in the hopes that Cary would show up. Only she'd listened to Doyle and stayed away. How long had it been? He'd lost track of time in this windowless cellar.

"Leave her alone, McCormack." His voice sounded rusty with disuse.

"Doyle?" Cary's attention snapped to him, and she ran to the bars that made up the front of his cell, dropping to her knees and reaching through to grasp his good hand. "Talk to me, how are you feeling? Does…" She glanced at his stumpy arm, which had been broken off just below the shoulder. "Does it hurt much?"

Shrugging, Doyle squeezed her fingers. Her hand didn't fit into his like it had when she was little. "Not really. It'll make it a bit harder to pour drinks, though." He tried to smile, but his lip, torn ragged from one of the Hyenas' punches, refused to cooperate. "You got big."

Cary gave him a small smile and whispered, "I missed you. I couldn't stay away any longer." Her mouth set into a firm line, and she pushed herself to her feet. "Let him go." Cary turned to face Trevor once more.

"Now why would I do that?" The lycan raised a bushy eyebrow.

"Because if you do, I'll…" She gave Doyle a pleading look and mouthed, "Forgive me." She squared her shoulders and took a deep breath. "I'll tell you how to keep the portals open for good. Farrah and I have been researching it. There's something called the traveler's token. It's a medallion, and it's in the museum. You let Doyle go, and I'll get it for you."

Doyle and Trevor locked eyes, and the mob boss gave him a wolfish grin. "Done."

"No." Doyle shook his head. "Cary, don't. You don't know what kind of monster he is."

Cary swallowed hard but held up her chin as she looked back and forth between both men. "I have your word? You'll let him go?"

Trevor nodded once and held out a paw. "Aye, and

I'll even leave a few of the Hyenas to help out around the place if he wants, now that he's less able."

Doyle's heart sank as he watched Cary's hand slide into Trevor's clawed grip.

"Deal. I'll be back as soon as I have it." She was gone from the room almost before she finished talking. Vanished in the space of a blink.

***

There was a crash in the kitchen. Doyle glanced at Eoin, then, ignoring the startled looks of the Hyenas lounging around the pub, he charged through the door on his left.

Cary was lying on the floor, hands pressed tightly to her middle, her eyes squeezed shut. Blood seeped through her fingers.

"Eoin! Call Farrah, quick!" He grabbed a towel from the shelf with his remaining arm and knelt next to Cary. He felt the cold tiles of the floor through his jeans and knew that some skin on his knees would be gone tonight. He pushed the thought from his mind. That didn't matter right now.

"Doyle?" Cary's voice was thin.

"I'm here." He pushed the towel over her midsection and moved her hands out of the way, so he could apply pressure. "What happened?"

"I wasn't fast enough." Cary panted as she struggled to get up. "Security guard saw me and got a shot off."

Doyle pushed her back down with a grunt. "I never should have let ye do this. I should have found a way of stopping ye when ye left Trevor's." Doyle looked over his shoulder. "Eoin! Where is Farrah?"

"Couldn't...let..." Cary trailed off, eyes fluttering closed for a moment. She was pale. Too pale.

Doyle shook his head, cursing under his breath. It was a miracle that she'd even managed to travel back to the Loch.

"Doyle."

He looked down to find Cary's bright eyes burning into his.

"Make sure Trevor gets this." She shoved her right hand into his and uncurled her fingers, dropping a small amulet into his palm. "It's…what he…wanted." Her eyes unfocused, and she slipped into unconsciousness.

Doyle was vaguely aware of slender hands grabbing his arm and dragging him away from Cary.

Kendrick's voice was low in his ear. "There isn't much time. I can save her; Farrah won't make it in time." The vampire moved to look at Doyle with a question in his eyes. Doyle nodded once; he wasn't sure Cary would ever forgive him, but he couldn't lose her, not again.

***

"Well? Did you give it to him?" A familiar female voice snapped Doyle out of his thoughts.

"Cary?" He squinted into the dark hallway that led to the bathrooms.

She stepped out of the shadows, tall, lithe, and even paler than she'd been in the kitchen two nights ago. Her dark hair framed her face as she leaned against the wall. "The amulet, Doyle? Did you give it to Trevor?"

Feelings of relief and fear mingled in Doyle's gut as he moved to the bar, hanging onto it for support. He nodded, unsure if his voice would work without shaking.

"Good. I'll tell Kendrick. Hopefully either he or one of the brood can pilfer it back."

She looked Doyle up and down. The way her red eyes burned into him made him glad he wasn't still among the living. "Feeling well enough for a walk?"

"Of course." He shuffled toward her. "What did you have in mind?"

Gesturing at him to follow, she turned and headed for the Loch's back door.

She led him down Albfest's main road, stopping at the top of the hill. He looked back over his shoulder at the barely visible lights of The Ghostly Loch then faced the same way as Cary. She'd brought them to the highest point in the city, overlooking all of the sleepy, supernatural town.

They stood in silence for several minutes. Cary reached out and took his hand in hers, smiling.

"I'm sorry we couldn't find a better solution." Doyle let go of her hand and slipped his good arm around her waist to squeeze her to him.

Cary beamed up at him, her new fangs coming down as her teeth were exposed. "Kendrick said he felt like my being hurt was all his fault. Which it was." She chuckled. "And he needed to make things right. This is the best he could do." She twirled away from him, holding her hands up toward the moon. "It's lucky he came into the Loch when he did. Eoin couldn't get Farrah to answer her phone. And so what if I'm forever young? Isn't that every young woman's dream? Besides, I never liked being out in the sunlight anyway."

They both laughed.

"And what will you do now?" Doyle gave her a curious look.

"Kendrick and I were talking while I was healing. We think the amulet might be even more powerful than Farrah and I originally thought. We're going to steal it back." She glanced around before continuing "We'd like to put Trevor out of business while we're at it. But we'll need your help. And Eoin's and Harlon's, too."

She started walking back in the direction of The

Ghostly Loch.

Cary paused when she realized Doyle wasn't following her and looked back with a genuine smile. "Are you coming or not?"

Doyle smiled back at her, happier than he had been in a long time. "Yes, of course." He shuffled toward her and took her chilly outstretched hand in his. They walked back the way they'd come in silence.

When they reached the Loch's front door, Doyle squeezed Cary's hand. When she turned toward him, he winked and handed her the small stub of purple crayon he'd been carrying in his pocket for twelve years.

"Welcome home, Cary."

No One Delivers to the Sewers

Kristy Perkins

Deep in the sewers, beneath the mighty city, a torpid army gathered…

The city plans labeled it as the "central valve room," but there weren't any valves. Just a dark stench miasma, unnaturally slick walls, and rivers of gurgling filth that trailed lazily between ancient stone floors. A single beam of light sizzled through the air at the center, leaving hazy impressions of the restless crowd.

Tobias's low, gravelly voice boomed out of the shadows. "Together, we are mighty! We are becoming stronger every day, looking to a new world where beings like us are respected and feared. Soon, we will rise up and destroy humankind. Who's with me?"

Someone snorted and, judging by the splatting sound, spat out something slimy. Someone else giggled.

Tobias glowered at the assembled masses of his rodent troops—and one tied-up human photographer—and gave a long, heartfelt sigh.

He cleared his throat. "Look, guys, it's not that hard. You spread that nasty cold virus, make the humans sick, and when they're weak and helpless, we can take over the world. Remember?"

The rats weren't paying attention. Some were eating or poking their neighbors. Others were sniffing the air like they had something better to do. A few made a game of hopping over the river of sludge that crawled through the center of the room. One in particular, with a bite out of one ear, was chewing a ragged piece of paper. If not for their being comparable in size to a housecat, it would be almost impossible to know they were intelligent mutants. They could at least pay attention to the dominant predator.

The man in the back corner gave a terrified squeak. "Are those rats talking? Is this poison? Am I dying right now? Is this what happens when you die? I knew I should have gotten a gas mask!" He squirmed in his bonds

Tobias glared at the unfortunate paparazzo. Humans were so rude, among many other undesirable traits. Unfortunately, he needed this one alive to make sure the area could still be considered highly toxic. Humans reacted best to firsthand accounts.

"Seriously, what is going on? I just wanted to get pics for those crazy conspiracy theorists. I was going to edit some monsters in. Nothing was supposed to actually be down here!" He squinted into the shadows, craning his neck and trying to stretch out of the ropes.

Tobias growled, and the human froze. The tiniest whiff of smoke crept from Tobias's mouth and wafted into the lone beam of light that trickled down from the surface. The green toxic sludge was good for general ambiance, but there was nothing like sunlight for Tobias's big reveal.

The human's meager muscles strained at the ropes, and his damaged camera banged against the wall as it swung around his neck. There were bite marks on his arms, and his t-shirt had new holes.

Tobias slunk out of his corner, nice and slowly, inching his claws into view first. The light gleamed off the black scales of his forearms. He paused, flicking his tail into the light and then back. Just a glimpse of the barbs at the tip. A flutter of the wings, a build of the smoldering fire at the back of his throat, and then Tobias took the final step into the light, letting his head and full body come into view.

It was funny how time changed opinions. In his youth, Tobias had been the pathetic runt of his species. Now, as the only one left, he was a terrifying specimen, even if he was only the size of a horse. He was a fearsome beast. He was a creature made for skulking about in the shadows of humanity's underbelly.

He was a dragon.

The captive gaped. "You're...."

"Yes, I am." Tobias chuckled. The flames at the back of his throat crackled at the edges of his mouth. He waved a claw at the rats. "Take our guest to the main tunnel, and leave him. Drug him, and they'll just assume he's a rambling maniac and the air is toxic." He slammed his forepaw on the ground. "And tell the kraken to keep a better watch on the perimeter!"

The rats cheered. The majority scurried to drag the photographer out, leaving Tobias and the one-eared rat with the paper in the empty, smelly tank of an underground lair. Tobias sighed in their wake. Sewers were safe but miserable. The price he paid for allowing his plans to stagnate.

"Number Two, are you taking notes?"

The rat looked at Tobias nonchalantly, shifting the half-eaten remains of the paper behind his back. "No, boss."

Tobias sighed. "We have a buffet table for this reason, Number Two. Progress cannot be made if you and your kind insist on eating all the notes."

The rodent spat out a slimy ball and attempted to unravel the wad. "Sorry, boss. It didn't make it to my tum, so it should be fine. I remember what was on it! We're on track to steal some really nice speakers from those theater people in the park."

Tobias sighed and left him to it, stomping off to his office.

Number Two was reliable enough, as far as right

hands went. He had a penchant for scatological puns, but at least he put in the effort to learn how to read. Some of the rats figured the ability to speak and their increased muscle mass would be enough to get them ahead in life.

The mutant rats had been an interesting addition to his lifestyle a few decades before. The mermaids introduced them as fellow sewer dwellers. None of the older supernatural types were sure where the rats had come from, precisely, but at the time, there had been a dozen of them, and they showed no signs of dying off, so Tobias took them under his wing—literally, when it came to fending off the psychic cats hunting them, but usually in a more metaphorical sense.

For a while, helping the rats build a society had helped Tobias find his purpose in life, but his thoughts always turned back around to the problem of his species. He had hated most of them, but they were also gone, and memory was kinder about the abuses he had suffered.

Tobias's office was a plain little room off the main chamber. Just a bit of privacy away from the worst of the stench and a place to keep his treasures. Mainly a heap of the gold things he'd picked up over his lifetime but also odder things like pizzeria menus and books, one of which was the journal he used to record his memories of the glory days of dragons. His prerogative as the last dragon was to write down his memories in the way that he remembered. No matter how he tried to shift the narrative to make himself the hero, the loneliness always came through, and the journal ended up buried in the heap.

He carefully picked up the pen and delicately inscribed the letters on the paper:

The other dragons sucked.

The sentiment was valid a thousand years later. Pushing Tobias down in the mud, the constant insults—his clan had bullied him relentlessly.

The dragon elders had let them get away with it. They never knew what to do with him, the runt who wasn't meant to survive infancy. In the absence of a better plan, they set him up to fail at everything. Perhaps they'd never outright said he was useless, but that was certainly how Tobias remembered it.

Now, Tobias was the only one left, and he could write it so he was the hero and the others, fools.

Tobias cursed when his claws tore yet another hole in his day planner. He had tried using tablets, but his stupid finger knives sliced through those just as easily as paper, and besides, there was no wifi down in the sewer lair. It had taken him ages to get the ethernet cable installed in his private office, and Number Two had to do all the typing. Keyboards were more expensive than pads of paper.

More carefully this time, he picked up the little book with the tips of his claws and put it on his desk.

Give speech to mutant rats.

Done. Even if they had ignored him, Number Two knew enough about the plan to keep everyone on track. If Tobias didn't change his mind about the details again. The plan had changed hundreds of times since he'd first started plotting vengeance against the humans.

Check on dragon egg.

He could probably skip that today. The scientists still thought it was just a decorative rock, and they were following the same tests the last humans did, so it wasn't like they were going to figure it out tomorrow. Even if they did, they'd never imagine it was a dragon egg. Even the Alchemy Knights hadn't figured it out yet.

Tobias ignored the nervous tremor in his tail and the roiling in his gut. The egg was fine.

Clean tail, trim tail barbs.

He could also skip that one if he wanted. He'd done a full scale-polishing last week, and letting the tail barbs get a little ragged had a good effect on the few humans who made it that deep into the sewers. According to Number Two, they ran away faster when Tobias was a little jagged.

Wing stretches.

Why had he put all the boring things on Wednesday? Why hadn't he scheduled a terrorizing of the sewer workers? Or plotted a meeting with the mermaid clans to figure out the best routes for releasing the baby krakens into the wild? All the advice books said to space out business with pleasure.

Order from that sushi place on 10ᵗʰ.

Tobias rested his claw on that one. It didn't really count as fun per se, not like watching a cooking show or taking a good long prowl. It was still better than wing stretches, so he tapped the phone and commanded it to call Bao's Sushi. Modern technology was great.

Tobias drummed his claws, full of nervous energy as the man on the other end mumbled through a greeting. "I'd like to order the shrimp tempura roll and two spicy tuna rolls."

The muttering was only decipherable because Tobias knew the sequence that came next. He forced his claws to still.

"Yes, delivery."

Another incomprehensible mess of verbal sludge. Tobias wished endless torments on the mumbler. Non-native speakers had better diction.

"I'll pay with cash."

The next question was more of a tired grunt. Hope rose within Tobias that perhaps this person was too exhausted to realize what was happening.

"No, nothing else."

Tobias's tail jerked side to side before he settled his nerves. The next quizzical grumble brought them to the moment of truth. He could almost taste the tuna.

"Address is…it's just easier if I tell you how to get

here. Start in front of 17 Ebon Boulevard. Face the front door, go to the alleyway on the left side..."

The voice changed from exhausted apathy to a suspicious rumble. Tobias's visions of that exquisite meal began to evaporate.

"No, I'm not homeless! I live underground. There's a sewer grate under a dumpster. Tuck the bag through the hole in the grate, and I'll put the money in a clean bucket."

A disbelieving flurry of insults. Tobias nudged the phone away, but that didn't help with the volume or quell the creativity on the other end. He had to give it one more try.

"No, I'm being serious..."

A derisive laugh.

"Please, I just want some su-...-shi!"

They hung up. Tobias sighed and rested his head on the desk, letting acid tears of frustration fall and burn through the metal. No one delivered. And it wasn't just the grate, either. He'd tried having them come through the main sewer entrance or delivering to the park at night or somewhere else he wouldn't be seen, but no. No one wanted to deliver, and the rats didn't understand how to steal good food.

It didn't matter how many times he tried and failed; each time stung the same as the last. Tobias curled up in the corner, tucked his wings in tightly, and settled his head on his forepaws for a long sulk.

Number Two stumbled into the office. "Hey, boss. We got the lighting fixed in the south tunnel. Charlie wants to start on the heaters for the nursery since he's got some babies coming soon, but I wanted to check with you first."

Tobias shook his head. "That sounds fine."

Number Two crinkled his nose and set down his ratty clipboard by the door. "What's up?" He made a snuffling noise. "Aww, boss, you called another restaurant?

You know they're never gonna deliver. Why keep torrenting yourself?"

"Tormenting, Number Two."

The rat scratched his rump. "No, I'm pretty sure it's torrenting. You know, when you watch the cooking videos, and it makes you sad?" More scratching. "No, wait, that's flooding. Surging? Rivering?"

Tobias sighed. He slumped back on the floor. "What's the point?" he wailed. "I outlived the others, but now I'm alone. It's the worst, Number Two! Taking vengeance on humans is only good for so much. And I can't even properly enjoy their wonderfully creative food."

"It's fine. You're gonna be okay." Number Two patted Tobias's cheek and drew his hand away, hissing from the acid burn. "We'll check on the dragon egg. Oh! Or you wanna look at the menus for that new bakery on 52nd Avenue? You know, Wallflour? Come on. It's got a pun for a name, so it can't be that great. The guy based it off his own name. Henry Wallace. A few okay pictures can be almost as good as the real thing, right? You'll feel better once you look at food that's not garbage. Come on, boss. That's it. Over to the computer."

Tobias allowed himself to be led to the glowing screen, cheered more by the rat's efforts than the tantalizing photos of delicate pastries he would never be able to taste.

***

The clan elders panicked when the hunters didn't come back. So they sent me to investigate because I was the only one capable of finding out what happened.

Tobias stared critically down at his own words, large but neatly written, no rips in the paper. With his earlier breakdown, it was easier to throw out his plans for the day. Vengeance would come easier in a day or so. In the meantime, since he couldn't console himself with decent food, he could at least write about his sorrows.

My fellows were long dead. Dragon scales peeled away, claws sawn off, even eyes gouged out and placed in jars, all deposited on cart after cart to be taken away as spoils. Disgusting, but at least the humans didn't waste any part of their fallen foes. Some even made jewelry out of the scales, like it was a badge of honor.

Tobias blocked out most of the memory. The battle had been long over, but the corpses were so massive the humans were still grimly despoiling them.

Our clan was not the only one to suffer attacks like this. Humans had finally figured out how to stand up to dragons, and they were striking back en masse, not giving their foes a chance to regroup or flee. Not a slaughter as much as retribution, plotted by a group who eventually called themselves the Alchemy Knights.

It had taken a few centuries to appreciate the skill and ingenuity involved in so thoroughly eliminating dragonkind.

They never managed to catch me, though. Humans are so odd sometimes. Incredibly innovative, but they can't see what's right in front of them.

Tobias thought of the egg at the lab and scowled. It was hard to tell sometimes if he resented humanity more for the murder of his kind, or because after it was done, they forgot dragons had ever really existed.

"The Alchemy Knights are back!" Number Two squealed in excitement. "Those doofuses are gonna get it this time!"

Roused from his thoughts, Tobias swiped blindly with his claws. Number Two dove back out the door. Most of the rats knew better than to come into Tobias's little office without warning, especially when he was in an introspective mood. His embarrassment at being caught off guard quickly offset the adrenaline.

Tobias cleared his throat and settled back down onto

his tidy heap of treasure. "You're sure it's them?" His tail twitched in anticipation.

"Yep!" Number Two poked his head around the door then waddled back in. "They've got their badges and everything. Ancient societies are the best. They label stuff, but in a classy way, and they always have stuff we can pawn to pay for the internet."

Fair point. So perhaps a few more of those visitors ran into trouble. Not many humans came down that far into the sewers, anyway. Too busy investigating Bigfoot on the surface, the attention hog.

***

Tobias hung from the ceiling by his claws, his muscles relaxed, listening to the approaching invaders.

"Ugh, Henry. I can't believe you talked us into heading into the sewers. This is gross. You know that, right? Just because you're desperate for a change in pace, it doesn't mean the rest of us should have to suffer."

Female humans could be so shrill. Tobias held back his groan and let the group of Alchemy Knights pass under him.

Like Number Two had said in his crude way, they had pins on their coats, dragon scales set in gold. Six knights, and all armed with the ancient swords their ancestors had used to hunt dragons. Why, Tobias didn't know. A gun would certainly kill him more easily than one of those decrepit sabers.

There was snuffling in the darkness. The rats were beginning their assault. The humans froze.

"What was that?" one of the males squeaked.

Tobias crawled toward them, pulling himself across the ceiling with his claws, letting them graze across the cement. The whisper of noise made the humans stir uneasily.

The rats snuffled a little louder.

"I think we're on the right track," a human whispered.

They moved onward, huddled together like sheep.

More rats funneled into the tunnel behind the intruders. Whichever hapless knight looked back would see pairs of red eyes that never ceased their staring. Sure enough, a few seconds later, someone yelped, and the humans picked up the pace.

Perfect. Alchemy Knights in name only. Fools who had seen grandpa's journal and thought, "This is cool," without any regard to what it might actually take to kill a dragon.

Tobias smirked and followed on behind. The humans were running by the time they made it to the main room. A few had drawn their rusty swords. Tobias chuckled deep in his throat and dropped to the ground, landing neatly on his paws.

The humans spun around in awkward circles, trying to spot him. One nearly fell in the culvert, which burbled ominously.

"Hello!" Number Two bounded in front of them and waved cheerfully. "If you'll just direct your eyes to the looming specter of my boss, we can get started." He stepped aside and gave a tiny bow.

Tobias snorted, letting loose a puff of smoke. Number Two's cheery address always confused the humans and destroyed the ambiance.

He stalked into the middle of the room, roared, and gave a quick blast of fire. A woman's jacket caught fire, and she shrieked. Tobias sighed. "You scream like a rat, madam." He knocked her into the central waste stream with a flick of his wing.

Two of the men tried to run and crashed into each other. One toppled into the wall and knocked himself unconscious, while the other fell into the sludge next to the woman. The infant krakens did their best to tangle the two up, but they just slimed everything up and made it impossible for the humans to climb out of the muck. Not that the babies cared. They flailed and wiggled and burbled happily.

Tobias wanted to laugh. Those pathetic excuses for dragon hunters deserved what they got and far worse.

The rats mobbed the third man, tearing his jacket to shreds. The other woman tried to fight but broke down in a fit of coughing. The rats took advantage and tied her shoelaces together. When she fell down, they tied up the rest of her with nylon ropes stolen from an unfortunate plumber.

Which left one last human, standing all by himself in the center of the chamber. He was the shabbiest of the lot, with holes in his clothes even without the rats. Tobias stalked in a loose circle around him. The poor fool had a sword, but he clearly hadn't thought he would have to use it. He swiveled to keep facing Tobias, but he didn't try to attack or run. He looked terrified, his body held tense, his eyes betraying him.

Tobias leaped at him, knocking the man over. He got in one desperate swing before Tobias pinned his arms with his claws. The dragon scale badge was torn off with the man's sleeve. Tobias took a deep breath, ready to melt that sword with his fiery breath.

He froze, the tantalizing aroma of bread filling his nostrils. The flames in his throat choked him. There was some awkward coughing and a lot more smoke for a minute. He sneezed out the ashy backwash.

When the smoke cleared, Tobias leaned in closer. The website photo had been pretty clear. There were the cheekbones, the slightly uneven eyebrows. Even the hair was styled the same.

"You're Henry Wallace?"

The man stopped trying to wiggle free, his mouth wide open. Was he about to scream in terror or to rally his cohorts for an escape attempt? It didn't matter which since he kept looking at Tobias's mouth and then his claws and then his mouth again. Whatever he'd been thinking, he was stuck on a loop now.

Tobias chuckled. How strange that, in a world of talking rats and faeries and so many other odd creatures, these folks still expected a dragon, of all things, to be a mute beast. Then again, the original dragon hunters hadn't exactly left detailed records.

Tobias tried again. "Henry Wallace. You opened up the Wallflour bakery on the surface." He didn't want to sound too eager, but a hint of a purr got into his voice anyway.

Henry sagged under Tobias's claw, blinking rapidly. "Right. That's me." The man was trying to search his pockets for something to save himself. It was a lot of unnecessary squirming, and Tobias allowed it so as to make the man feel more comfortable with the situation.

It would be so easy to hurt this man. A moment's vengeance for a lifetime of persecution. Or he could push down his most dragonish instincts and finally be happy for a time.

The years of boredom pressed down on him, and he made his choice. "If I spare you and your friends, would you be willing to deliver?"

Henry wiggled out to a sitting position and scratched his head. "What?"

"If I let you and the other knights go, will you deliver some of your baked goods to a prearranged location for me?" Tobias cleared his throat. "I'll pay, of course. Cash." He nudged Henry back to the wall. Not pinned anymore but not in a position to run away without being roasted.

The rats took their cue and let their own captives up.

With some coaxing, the baby krakens shoved the two in their clutches onto dry ground, and the conscious humans were herded and rolled until all five of them were in a tight clump. They didn't try escaping, beaten—and chewed—into submission at that point. Number Two showed up by Tobias's side with a pen and paper.

"What is going on here?" Henry asked helplessly, craning his neck to see how his friends were faring.

"You're negotiating for your lives in exchange for regularly supplying me with various baked goods." Tobias curled his tail so the barbs flicked against Henry's arm.

Henry gulped. "I can do that. But aren't you a dragon? Don't you want...?"

His question faded like the thin trail of smoke that wisped out of Tobias's mouth.

Tobias sat up straighter, fluffed his wings out. "Excellent!" Tobias was happy, and he couldn't be bothered with keeping up frightening appearances. "Number Two!"

"Boss!" The rat stuck out a piece of paper with surprisingly neat handwriting on it. "I got the directions to the delivery slot," he said in his squeaky little voice. He waved it around near Henry's hand until the man took it. "The alleyway looks super evil, but we don't let anybody shady take up living there, so it's actually pretty homey. But you'll probably want your guys to be up on their tent us shots."

"He means tetanus."

"Naturally." Henry got to his feet and made an attempt to dust himself off. "I don't suppose there's anything you care to tell me about your dietary requirements."

"Dragon stomachs are quite resilient, so no allergies."

Henry nodded. "Any else I should know?"

Tobias leaned in close. "Don't bother fishing for

information. I'm still entirely capable of ending our bargain here. I can always send my rat army after you."

Henry gulped. "What about those things?" He gestured at the flow of sewage, where the little krakens were splashing around.

"Oh, they'd make their way to the ocean. The mermaids might cause trouble, but as long as you don't plan on taking any cruises, you'd probably be safe from them." Tobias's smile showed all of his teeth.

"Okay." Henry nodded his head slowly.

"So we're clear, if you don't abide by this agreement, I'll have to hunt you all down and eat you instead." Tobias growled low in his throat.

Henry whimpered.

Number Two laughed. "Good one, boss!" He scurried up a pipe and over to Henry's shoulders, and patted him lightly on the head. "He wouldn't eat you. The boss hates human meat. But there's lots of nasty things that don't involve eating."

The baker gulped again, wavering under the weight of an infant-sized rat climbing around his head.

Number Two gave Henry's head a firm hug. "This is really something, you doin' this for the boss. He's been desperate for some good food that's not downriver garbage. Sometimes he toasts it up real nice, but you can always tell it was dunked."

Henry's hands were clenched into fists, and his skin was pale. A rat the size of a cat hugging your head will do that. It threw Tobias off, too, when it happened. Even if he was a runt the size of a carthorse, his kind didn't do hugs.

"Oh!" Number Two finally hopped down when the quivering shoulders made it hard to stand. "Boss, that reminds me. The crematorium was pretty generous this time, so I was thinking we could get those curtains with the stars on them for movie night?"

Henry shook his head. "Is this actually happening, or did I inhale something?"

Tobias shrugged, flapping and stretching his wings to settle down on his haunches. "A little of both."

The humans were escorted out, mostly unharmed. Clothes torn, more than a few scratches, but that was to be expected where rats were concerned. Henry kept looking back, oddly disappointed. Of course, Tobias kept their badges.

Just a little reminder that while he might be desperate for a good scone, he was still a dragon.

***

Tobias waited a few days before testing his newfound connection, giving the rats enough time to finish installing the new security room. Those first delivered cupcakes were a summer sunrise on a full stomach of mutton. Absolute perfection.

"Next time, I'm going to order a whole cake," he told Number Two through a mouthful of crumbs.

The rat nodded amiably. "Sounds nice, boss. But what about the plans?"

Tobias smiled at his little companion. "Oh, I'll get to those eventually."

"Sure, boss."

Tobias scowled. "I haven't forgotten. I'm not giving up an entire lifetime's goal just for some sweets. Some wonderfully decadent treats." He delicately picked up another cupcake. "How did the delivery boy react to the alleyway?"

Number Two sighed. "It was that Henry guy. Guess he didn't feel like subletting his employees to the dumpster."

"Subjecting."

"I like mine better." Number Two scratched his

undamaged ear. "But that's weird, right, boss? That he would come himself and not send someone else? Should we be doing tests here?"

Tobias laughed it off, but he did keep a careful eye on how his stomach felt for a while, just in case they did try poisoning him. After three days, he figured it was safe, so he ordered something else. Not a whole cake, but a selection of scones. Waited again, to ensure that they hadn't somehow changed their minds, and then ordered. Fresh every time, and, if not hot, then at least easily warmed by his breath. Delicious. He could have replaced his entire treasure heap with baked goods quite happily.

The deliverer was always Henry Wallace himself. Tobias initially assumed it was because the man didn't trust Tobias, but apparently, Henry had trouble keeping delivery boys. Henry would wave to the cameras they kept in the alley sometimes and would greet the rats he saw.

After a month, Tobias had finished as much of Wallflour's menu as he could afford and was halfway toward completion of the first step of his anti-human plan. Not the disease plan, but the new plan. It was a bit more complicated and involved a few large-scale bank robberies, but Tobias was confident that the rats could pull it off.

Then came the day when it all went wrong. Tobias was sitting in their security room. It meant no new curtains for the intended movie room, but with the renewed human interest, they'd all deemed it wise to install a security system.

Something was wrong with the cameras, and the rats couldn't figure out what. The cameras kept turning on and off, focusing on the wrong things, and not accepting input from the computers. The whole situation made him uneasy.

Number Two burst into the security room. He gave Tobias a perfunctory nod, but he was scratching himself all over. "I hate to be the bad news bear, but our spies heard there's somethin' up with that egg. It's got all shaky, and the scientists are freaking out. Is it supposed to do that, boss?"

Tobias reared up. "You know very well it is not. Show me!" he roared.

Within a few minutes, the rat logged in to the lab security cameras. Sure enough, the egg was twitching. Tobias sank back on his haunches. With equal parts dread and wonder, he said, "It's hatching."

"Well, that's oblivious enough," Number Two muttered. "But what do we do about it? Boss? Boss?"

***

Once, Tobias had written about what happened to him after the Alchemy Knights thought they'd achieved victory. In some ways, he found it easier to detail the raw viscera of disemboweled dragons than to record his own malaise. He'd spent a few centuries in desperate straits, but after that?

He'd hidden the words away in the deepest part of his hoard, but sometimes they still flitted into his mind like hatchlings.

At first, I wondered if a few other clans might have survived, but no. All I ever found were a few scattered bones. There was the triumph at being the last, which I expected. There was the desolation at being alone, which I had feared. But there was also the boredom, which was entirely unexpected.

I never missed the others for themselves, but I missed the struggle to prove myself a real dragon in their eyes.

Then I found the egg. Dragons had become so mythological that the humans didn't actually know what it was. I was in a panic for weeks, trying to figure out what to do with it. I could have left it to the humans. They liked babies, and there was a decent chance they wouldn't kill it when it hatched.

Raising it myself was out of the question. I told myself that over and over as I burned down a museum and encased the egg in molten metal. It'll survive for centuries like that. Just a temporary solution until I can figure out a way for us to survive without burning down whole cities.

The egg had knocked the kilter off Tobias's already unbalanced life. Its very existence demonstrated that dragonkind might have a chance at rebuilding. Tobias never found any other eggs, but he'd never looked all that hard, either.

How many years ago had Tobias written that? He wasn't sure. The internet hadn't existed yet, so there was no easy way to search for others. So he'd stayed where he was, not really doing anything other than watch the egg pass from museum to lab and back.

He was the only dragon left, even if it was just for his corner of the world, and as such, he had to be the most dragon-y dragon to ever dragon-ize. And all he remembered of his kind was their violence, how they'd pillaged and plundered and fought and shoved his face in the mud over and over.

Vengeance was the only thing he could think of that would make a suitable legacy. With the mutant rat population growing by the day, he had an army, and he knew he could outsmart the bullies of the world. So his thoughts turned from protecting the egg to recreating the world as it had once been.

Except he was still bored, and he absolutely needed better food than garbage.

***

"...so there's still a week before anything happens. That's what you said, boss. There's time to get the egg out of there before anyone finds anything out. Easy-squeezy." Number Two hissed through his teeth. "Come on, boss, please, stop crying. The puddle's going to eat through the floor. And my foot." The acid tears sizzled as they pooled on the floor, giving off a sharp vinegar smell.

Tobias sniffled, attempting to snap out of his thoughts and refocus on the present moment. "I don't understand what went wrong. That egg should have stayed dormant until I was ready for it to hatch." He belched fire. "I'm not ready to be a father!"

"Sure you are," Number Two said, dancing around the encroaching pool of acid. "You just have to make it a prioress. Even take a foot back from this whole army thing you've got going on down here."

Tobias puzzled through the phrases. "Assuming you mean priority, how can I do that? You need me to guide you."

"Aww, boss, we don't need you. You think about it a little, and you'll know that. It's nice having you around and all, but we've got our whole clan and all. We'll do fine down here, humans or not." Number Two patted Tobias's nose. "But don't worry. You're still in charge and all. We'll keep working on the whole revenge thing if you really want us to. But it's good if you go and save the baby."

There were so many reasons why Tobias absolutely needed to stay in the sewers. He could feel them all filling up his brain, raising his stress levels and pushing him to a panic attack. Or at the very least a very good excuse to huddle in a corner and order two dozen brownies immediately.

Number Two climbed on his shoulder and physically pried open Tobias's eyelids. The rat then leaned over so he was about an inch away from Tobias's eyeball. "Boss, you gotta go. It's your clan."

Tobias had a protest rising in his throat like a fire, but then it died entirely. Number Two was right. Whether or not the dragon egg was an actual literal descendant of the clan that had once been his, it didn't matter. He'd sworn to avenge his kind. That made all dragons his clan.

"And maybe you can get those Alchemy Knights to stop messing with our cameras," Number Two added.

"What?" Tobias roared.

Number Two didn't flinch, but he did lean back from Tobias's fangs. "It's definitely them chopping the system. I was gonna tell you, but you seemed so happy bossing everyone around looking for the answers."

Tobias snarled and stood up, Number Two clinging to his horns. "So that's why the egg is hatching. I'll kill them."

Number Two kicked him soundly in the nose. It shocked Tobias into sitting back down. The rat slipped to the floor and stood squarely in front of Tobias. "No, you won't."

"They're a threat to my existence," Tobias bellowed.

"They're curious." Number Two stared up at Tobias in a way that made him seem that much taller. "You like humans. You admire their noodles and planes and muffins. You pretend to be mad because they offed your clan, but you didn't even like those guys."

Tobias blinked. He shrank down a tiny bit. "You noticed all that?" he said in a small voice. He couldn't really deny it. Humans were all the same size, and they couldn't fly, so they came up with all sorts of wondrous things to give themselves advantages. As a runt, he couldn't hate that, no matter how hard he tried.

"Boss, you've been working on these plans of yours for longer than I've existed, and yet when it comes to doing them, somehow you always find a reason to squeak out." Number Two leaned against Tobias's forepaw. "I can use my pointers to count how many humans I've seen you kill. You don't want them dead; you want them embarrassed. And you want them to give you food."

Tobias had a feeling like indigestion in his stomach and didn't particularly like it. But the rat was right. "Fine. But

I'm still having a discussion with the Alchemy Knights."

***

Slinking around alleyways and back streets was a lot easier than Tobias thought it would be. His scales reflected the streetlights like a car, and as long as he kept darting quickly enough, he could fool untrained eyes.

The city was different aboveground, and he got turned around once or twice, but he finally made it to Wallflour. It was three in the morning, but bakers got up obscenely early to create their wares. Henry Wallace was no exception.

Tobias spent a few fretful minutes peering in the darkened windows, scanning the area for signs of life, when the car pulled up. He leaped at the door as soon as it began to open. His claws screeched across the metal as he landed, pinning his foe between the doorframe and the door.

Henry yelped and grabbed for something in his pocket. Tobias slammed the door again, but it was too late. Henry sprayed his eyes with pepper spray.

Or at least, he tried. Most of it got up Tobias's nose, which made him sneeze, which left a trail of singe marks across the car door. Henry yelled something incoherent and pushed against the door.

Tobias shoved back. "Why are you spying on me?" he growled.

"Why do you think? You're dangerous. A dragon living right underneath a large population of humans seems like a good way to end up with a lot of people dead."

It was infuriatingly rational, and Tobias spat a glob of fire on the ground. "What did you do to the egg?"

"The what?" Henry tried to squirm back into his car and failed. "You know, I don't care. At least let me get my day started. Flour's flammable, so if it comes down to it, just roast me and get it over with."

Try as he might, Tobias could detect nothing but sincere ignorance about the egg. Number Two was right. Tobias backed away slowly and let Henry out of his car. The man scowled at him, ducked back inside the vehicle for a coffee mug, and then stumbled to the bakery door.

Tobias followed him. "I'm here to amend our bargain."

Henry scoffed, fiddling with his keys. "You're insane. I'm not going to help you get your hands on a weapon that could destroy humankind, or whatever the 'egg' is."

"It's not a weapon, you fool." Outwardly, Tobias remained surly and stoic. Within his thoughts, he groaned and mentally beat up that part of his brain responsible for his earlier slip. But Henry had messed with the cameras, and he might be useful. "It's a dragon egg. You're going to help me get into a scientific research lab, or I'll..." He trailed off, unable to come up with a good threat.

Henry fumbled his keys, made three attempts to pick them up, and then simply stood there with his arms crossed like it hadn't just happened. "There's a dragon egg out there?" He didn't sound murderous. A little stressed, but not like he was about to hunt down and smash an egg. "I'll help. No threats necessary." Henry scowled. "I'm here to make sure you don't turn savage, not to cause your extinction."

How odd. It didn't sound like what an Alchemy Knight might say, but he hadn't hesitated, and that sincerity was still there. Tobias nodded sharply like that was how he assumed things would go all along.

***

Tobias clung to the awning, cursing under his breath about the weak plaster. It was barely holding, and it was anyone's guess as to whether or not it would support his weight long enough to complete his mission. He was completely at the mercy of his human ally.

Ugh. Ally. What was he supposed to do if the terse plan he and Henry had come up with failed? Or if the human simply decided to betray him? It was well within human nature to be capable of such things, of abandoning a pledge and changing their minds and doing something cruel. Tobias had no way to know whether Henry would keep his word or not.

Henry Wallace had walked into the laboratory's main building ten minutes earlier, pretending to be there with a cupcake delivery. In the frenzy of the lab, he'd managed to slip in quite easily. The skills he'd been using on Tobias's security system would be helpful in extracting the egg, which was an aggravating piece of irony.

Tobias couldn't go in. He was a runt, but he was still a dragon, and he didn't want to clue anyone in that dragons still existed. The rats would never let him live it down. He hated having to depend on a human, but he couldn't risk it. Not until the cameras went down.

Just when he was losing hope, alarms broke the peace of the near-dawn hour. Tobias launched himself from the awning and spread his wings wide. He flapped hard until he was above the roof. When he spotted the skylight, he dove.

The window shattered beautifully, and Tobias came crashing down into the laboratory. It was filled with fumes and yells and coughs and crashes. The atmosphere filled his ears. It was almost enough to overwhelm him completely, but he forced himself to focus on the security cameras hanging limp and useless on the walls.

Tobias struggled forward, shoving aside the furniture. He'd watched from those very security cameras on a daily basis, so he had a good idea of where he was going. The final door was locked. He breathed fire, a quick burn.

Whatever the door had been made of disintegrated. Tobias stepped through the hole and went straight to the egg.

It was quivering constantly now, tiny shakes reverberating through the metal coating. The child inside was trapped and suffocating, all because he was selfish. Tobias bathed it in fire, trying to melt away the metal.

When he stopped, the metal was a dull orange that faded all too quickly back to gray, leaving the egg still completely trapped. The alarms were still blaring in the background, and there were shouts growing closer.

If Tobias didn't leave now, they might see him, but if he didn't free the egg, the hatchling would die.

Tobias sucked in a deep breath and blasted it with the hottest fire he'd produced in a century. He was a mighty clan leader, and he was going to save his kin. The iron melted away like liquid, dribbling onto the floor and creating a massive stink. The egg beneath glowed a brilliant yellow.

There was a series of shouts right outside. Tobias snatched up the superheated egg with his foreclaw and awkwardly ran with three legs. He charged through the gathering security personnel, skidded down the hallway, and crashed through the window at the end.

His wings wedged in the opening. He wiggled frantically, his heart skipping a beat. He'd never been too big for something before.

The plaster cracked, and he made it through. He extended his wings gracefully and soared off into the night, leaving no sign that he'd been trapped. Behind him, he left a thoroughly befuddled research team. No doubt, some of them would end up deranged conspiracy theorists who lurked in sewers for signs that they hadn't gone completely insane one night.

Tobias didn't really care because he was gliding through the air, his prize tucked safely in his arms.

***

Euphoria kept him gliding until he reached the sewer entrance, but the landing was a little awkward. Tobias hadn't properly gone flying in over a century, so his skills were a little rusty. The egg didn't make it easy for him, either. A piece of it broke off right before they hit the ground. Tobias frantically wrapped his wings around it and rolled across the ground to cushion it as best he could.

When he finally stopped rolling, Tobias groaned. His wings throbbed with bruises, and his foreclaw was in almost unbearable pain from holding the egg that was too hot even for a dragon's skin. He ignored it. There were more important things to panic about. The egg was fractured.

Examination showed that the cracks had originated from within the egg, and Tobias breathed a sigh of relief. He didn't want to cripple the little thing before its life had properly begun. He set it down on a pile of dirt and settled in to wait. Each time the egg cracked, it was like a gunshot.

Tobias's nerves hadn't been so fraught since the days of dragon hunts. What if this precious little one turned into a bully? What if he failed as a parent?

Not ten minutes later, Henry Wallace came dashing down to the tunnel. He skidded to a halt next to Tobias just in time to see the last piece of shell splinter.

The egg cracked open, and a tiny baby head poked out. The delicate frills of its head ruffled adorably, and the tiny fangs were on full display as the hatchling gaped at its surroundings. Its wings pushed the rest of the shell out of the way, fluttering feebly as it tried to gain its bearings.

The little dragon staggered out of the shell. Tobias vaguely remembered that a lot of instinct was involved in getting out of the shell, walking, exploring immediate surroundings, that kind of thing. He didn't have to do anything more than just watch. Right?

Number Two was right. His priorities were going to have to change. This little one needed him to be a parent, not a vengeful agent of the night. If Henry's cooperation was any indication, dragons would be far better off working with humans than annihilating them. It was time to throw out those traditions he'd held on to and create something new.

"Cute kid," Henry muttered, patting Tobias's shoulder awkwardly. He moved his hand off a split second before he would have been roasted.

"You think a dragon hatchling is cute?"

The child was a shriveled, crinkly mess, but it was a mess he was responsible for. He felt his heart swell at the oddly adorable little one.

Henry rubbed the back of his own neck. "Well, yeah. It's a baby. I guess I'm predisposed to see it as cute."

Tobias rolled his eyes. "Humans." He cleared his throat. "Just as a hypothetical, if you were to go back in time to meet your ancestors, what would you say to them?" He made every effort to remain still, to not shift into anything that might be deemed a menacing pose.

"I'd try to hold them back," Henry answered almost immediately, like it was something he'd thought about a lot. "Dragons were a plague, and some of them needed to die, but you're an intelligent species. Some of you must have been willing to negotiate. My forebears shouldn't have wiped you all out, just made it clear that we weren't going to be put down anymore." He relaxed as he spoke, and he met Tobias's eyes.

Tobias nodded slowly. Time would tell, but at that moment, he believed the human. "A diplomatic response, to be sure."

"An honest one."

Something came tumbling out of the tunnel behind them. Henry jumped, but Tobias had smelled Number Two coming and was only mildly surprised.

"Hey, you're okay! I'm glad you didn't get blasted or anything, boss."

"Number Two. Look."

The rat finally spotted the little dragon with a squeal that was sure to wake anyone in the area not already woken by the breaking egg. Number Two ran in circles for a full minute, came back to squeak over the hatchling, and then ran in circles again. Safe to say, he was pretty excited.

"This is the best day of my life!"

Tobias blinked. "Don't you have your own kids?"

"Well, yeah, but there's thirty of 'em. This is the only dragon baby in the world! You're not sad and alone, boss. We find a few more of these, you have a species again." He leaned in close. "Aww, it's a girl! Boss, she's already flaming." The rat jumped back to avoid the fiery infant hiccup.

They both watched as Number Two gently poked at the tiny dragon, coaxing her to her feet, prodding so she'd stretch her wings. Tobias shifted to keep the weight off his injured limb. Henry scratched his neck. There was an awkward pause in what Tobias was surprised to realize was a conversation.

Henry gave Tobias a sidelong look. "Are you reconsidering your plans to attack humanity?"

Tobias snorted. "Of course not!"

"I can pick up some sushi next time if you agree to hold off on your plans for global domination." Henry was grinning, the fool.

Against his will, Tobias's claws curled around the intangible tempura roll, and a purr erupted in his chest.

"I can get you some baby food, too, if you want. Or raw steaks if that works."

Tobias cleared his throat, spat out some smaller flames. Things were getting too comfortable. "I'll only consider this if you work for me and give up your surface job."

Henry sighed. "Sure, why not? As long as you pay me."

Tobias sneezed fire and stared.

Henry shifted uncomfortably. "The bakery's failing, and obviously, the dragon hunter thing isn't going that well. And I know you're good for the money." He gestured at the baby dragon, crawling after Number Two. "Besides, learning about dragons is all I ever wanted to do. No way working for you would be boring."

Humans. So strange, with their peculiar talent at finding the universal elements of life, even if it was completely by accident.

Henry gave him a worried look. Tobias cleared his throat, embarrassed at being caught staring at his former opponent. "We'll work out an equitable contract later. I'm sure—"

"Hey, boss! She tried to bite me!"

Such words were not usually spoken with such delight, but Number Two was not typical by anyone's imagination, even that of his own kind. With a longsuffering puff of smoke, Tobias trotted over to where his adoptive offspring was learning about her predatory instincts. Number Two needed rescuing. Henry looked on, shaking his head, a baffled grin on his face.

And thus, by the entrance to the sewers, in the suburbs of a middling to average city, two ancient enemies forged a bargain for the safety of the world.

A Particularly Powerful Lunar Event, a Completely True Story

Melion Traverse

I didn't expect that the guy who lived down the dirt road beyond my apartment was a necromancer. And I certainly didn't expect to make that discovery one late spring morning as I tested my new mountain bike on the road that cut a dusty scratch through the forest. But that's life, isn't it? You think the day will be normal, and the next thing you know, your dog is running off through a graveyard, and you're ditching the bike as you sprint after him.

It was just that sort of day to find a necromancer, and all because my roommate had texted me a picture of a great mountain bike that I thought I absolutely needed because adulthood seemed too near on the heels of my upcoming college graduation. But I digress.

The graveyard seemed a lone and tragic thing, like a thought that drifted away, and nobody cared enough to remember it was forgotten. I can't explain now why I thought that. Yes, the headstones were worn and tilting, but the plots all seemed well-tended with the tang of fresh-cut grass soft on the air. Still, the fingerprints of long-gone memories and something else, something intangible that no amount of tended lawn could erase, lingered over the place.

And my blasted dog was leaping all about chasing butterflies.

"Ranger!" I hollered, my voice sharp on the last syllable.

Ranger knew that tone, and he left off chasing the butterfly to come trotting to me with his tongue lolling and his face a perfect grin of canine satisfaction. Even when he knew I was mad, he couldn't be bothered to not be happy. Soon he had his paws up on my shoulders and was nuzzling my face, tail wagging a mile a minute. I buried my fingers into the thick ruff of his neck and pressed my forehead to his sleek head.

"You big idiot." I laughed. "You can't go frolicking in cemeteries—nothing good ever comes of that."

"Woof," he replied and dropped to all fours, ready for another caper.

Movement made me look up from the dog, and all my muscles pulled taut as dried leather. In my zeal to get Ranger under control, I hadn't noticed that a house was on the other side of the cemetery. I mean, I'm sure that I saw it; I just hadn't paid attention. So I certainly hadn't expected to see the male figure coming down the back steps.

I wished to God I had Ranger's leash with me so I could snap it on and run back to the bike, and we could bolt off down the road before we both got busted for trespassing. But I'd left the leash at home.

Strange, that. You know, if I'd brought the leash, my life would have been very different; it would have spun away in another direction that I can't say would be better or worse, only that... No, I can say it would be worse. Safer, definitely, but worse. While I watched the man striding toward me through the graveyard, it hit me somewhere in my ribs that my life was never going to be safe again, and the realization warmed like a spark of sunlight after a storm.

I gripped Ranger's collar and stood straight, any thoughts of running now cast far to the spring winds by that spark of sunlight.

The dark-haired man coming across the cemetery was older than me, but only by a few years. I'd just turned twenty-two (did I mention the mountain bike had been my birthday present to myself? I sometimes did that in those days because I wanted to at least have something, but that doesn't matter now—that will never matter again), and I still thought of any guy old enough to be out of college as a man and not a boy. Looking back now, I'd probably call him a boy.

The man stopped halfway through the cemetery, and the wind ruffled his dark hair and snapped at his flannel shirt. He stood studying me with his hands in his trouser pockets as though I were something he'd never seen before, and I stared back, uncomfortably aware that I was some strange girl in dusty jeans and sweat-damp t-shirt with a dog half-strangling itself, trying to tug free of my hold. Ranger never particularly cared for being restrained.

"Is that your dog?" the man finally asked and then, with a half-laugh, rolled his eyes—I could see that well enough despite the distance. Very green eyes. Green eyes I couldn't meet without heat rising to my face and betraying me. Good grief. What was wrong with me?

"Sorry, that's a dumb question," I heard him saying as I made a pretense of ordering Ranger to sit. "Of course that's your dog. I think I meant to ask what you two are doing out here."

I shrugged and tucked a strand of hair behind my ear. The wind blew it free right away and straight into my mouth. "We were out for a bike ride." I jerked my thumb over my shoulder to where my bike lay on the roadside. "I mean 'we' weren't—I was riding, and Ranger was running.

Because it'd be stupid if a dog were riding a bike. I mean, I guess there're all sort of videos with dogs riding bikes and surfing and things, but Ranger doesn't do that." *Shut up, Kara!* I shut up.

"Oh. Well, he shouldn't be running about in graveyards, at any rate," the man said, and I only remembered afterward that he smiled when he said it. If I'd realized that then, I wouldn't have used the tone I did.

"Yeah, I get that—it's why I chased after him," I spat out as I gestured to Ranger.

I turned back to the bike, dragging Ranger with me even though he clearly wanted to chase after more butterflies.

"My name's Jasper," the man called after me, and the tread of his boots on the fresh-cut lawn was a soft thud-thud in my ears.

I looked back as he came over, and my grip went even tighter on Ranger's leather collar even though I wasn't afraid. Well, I was afraid, but not in the way I probably should have been afraid of a stranger. What I mean is, I was the most dangerous thing out in that field, but for the first time in all my life, I realized that I'd found something even more dangerous than I was. Something that made my heart race and my hands sweat. I, well, one day you'll understand what I mean, or maybe you already do and just haven't told me.

"Does Ranger bite?" asked the man. Jasper. That still hardly seems the name for a necromancer.

"Uh, no. I mean, he would if he had to." Truth is, Ranger was probably the friendliest Dutch shepherd that'd ever been whelped. Maybe the long-haired ones are just that way—I can't say since he's the only one I've had. He was a big ball of fur and wagging tail, who saw the world as one great festival of new people to give him pats.

"Ah, well, you could, uh, you could let go of him,"

Jasper said. "He looks uncomfortable, and I can't imagine he'll cause any real trouble running through the graveyard in the daytime."

He sort of whispered that last part, and I know enough about saying things you'd rather not have said to catch that tone.

"What was that last bit?" I asked. Free at last, Ranger went right to him and began soliciting attention in a most shameless manner.

"Oh, nothing," Jasper said, but I knew he was making too big a display of petting Ranger to be telling the truth. But I also knew I shouldn't press the point—it doesn't get people anywhere when they do that with me.

"Do you own the cemetery?" I asked, latching onto the first coherent question that skittered into my brain.

"The cemetery? Yes. It's part of the property."

It hadn't been a very good question, looking back, but it took the conversation somewhere safe. Even talking about cemeteries is safer than talking about secrets, and I guessed right away that Jasper had secrets. Most of my life, I've known how to judge when a person has a secret. If I don't pry at their secrets, I know how to keep them from prying at mine, even by accident. You learn how when you need to survive.

I could tell that Jasper hadn't learned. But then, he was a man with a cemetery in his backyard.

You're wondering now why I didn't run off, thinking that I'd end up in that cemetery, aren't you? It's a good question, and I suppose it's something to think about whenever you meet a person down a country road who has a burial ground twenty paces from their kitchen window. But, well, I figured that if he tried anything, Ranger would be the least of his problems.

That's the thing about being a young lycanthrope: you forget that just because you can slip into another skin in an instant and lose your soft, weak human flesh somewhere beneath a coat of rough fur that you may not be the scariest thing anybody'll meet.

Turns out, I was not the scariest thing in that cemetery. But it would be a few days before I learned that.

***

Ranger bounced ahead of me as I opened the apartment door, leaving my bike chained outside. I'd finally called the dog away from Jasper and had returned home, but that encounter lingered like a last burst of sunlight fading into dusk—warm and haunting.

"Hold on! I've flashcards all over the floor!" called Deb, my roommate. "Gah! Ranger! Get off that!"

I rushed in to pull my dog away from the pile of flashcards scattered around the main room. Deb was in her final semester of German and was in desperate need of an A on the final in order to not tank her GPA. Already we had sticky notes on every household item identifying what was what in German, so I was hesitant about what new ploy she had concocted.

"*Wie gehts?*" she asked.

"*¿Que?*"

Deb sighed. "You know, you could try learning just a little bit of German to, I dunno, help out your friend."

"I can identify every appliance in the kitchen, does that help? *Der Toaster ist gebrochen,*" I said as I unwrapped a toaster pastry.

"What? When did that happen?" Deb appeared in the kitchen with a stack of flashcards.

"When did what happen?"

"When did the toaster break?"

"It didn't," I said. "But I'm trying to help you. It's about the only thing I know how to say in German. Okay, I could say, '*Die Mikrowelle ist gebrochen*,' or '*Der F—.*'"

"No, thanks. You've helped enough," Deb interrupted. She snatched one of the toaster pastries from the foil packet and gave me a long look. "Something happen while you were out?"

I shrugged. "No, not really."

"Mmhhhm," she mumbled through a bite of uncooked pastry, which, for reasons unknown to science, taste so much better untoasted.

I busied myself with shoving half my pastry into my mouth so that I wouldn't have to talk. It didn't forestall further questioning.

"What's his name?" she asked.

There wasn't really a point in denying anything. The thing about a person with fay bloodlines on both sides of her family was that she could just *know* things from subtle changes in posture or voice or expression, things too subtle for me to even think I needed to cover.

"Jasper," I said. "That's his name."

"Is he hot?" she persisted, a smile on her face.

"Oh, come on." I opened the fridge for some juice to wash down my toaster pastry.

"No, he's probably not. But *you* think he is," she teased. "I bet he's kinda dorky, huh?"

"Deb!" Where was the orange juice? Ah, there it was. She hated orange juice, so that meant I got to drink it straight from the container.

"And furry, too, I bet," she said, still laughing and enjoying every bit of the discomfort I tried to hide behind gulps of juice. "Lycans *always* go for furry guys."

"Heh, better that than the mopey ones you're always bringing around," I retorted. "Like Devin, who only spoke in grunts?"

"Broody. They're broody, not mopey," she said. "And Devin was just too sophisticated for you to understand." At that, we both broke out laughing. It was an old joke. The night Deb broke up with Devin for being too anti-social (even for a half-vampire) and for embarrassing her by insulting her friend (that was me), Devin had answered by standing in the parking lot, shouting about how he was too sophisticated for little girls to appreciate. Deb dodged a bullet with that one, for sure.

It was around then that I realized that I'd never even told Jasper my name.

"You're definitely hopeless, Kara," Deb said when I told her. Then she brightened and added, "But that just means you have an excuse to go see him again."

"What, are you nuts?" I had sat down at my computer to begin working on an essay. "I'm not just going to walk up to his house, knock on the door, and say, 'Hey, just dropped by to tell you my name.' That's too weird, even for me."

"Hopeless," Deb replied as she shook her head.

Besides which, I wasn't sure exactly what I thought of the guy who owned an old cemetery. I knew nothing of him except that detail and his name. And that he had a secret. Then again, so did I. Well, my essay wasn't going to write itself. I turned back to my computer and clickety-clacked my way through explaining the Jacobin roots of the French Revolution.

***

"Have a good evening," I said as I looked up from where I was sprawled before the TV (or *das Fernsehen*, as the label stuck to the frame read).

Deb adjusted her silver cocktail dress, tugging it into place as the lamplight glittered over the sequins. She was going to some Spring Fling dance thing, and I was trying not to be jealous that I was lying on the floor like a tufted rug.

My pelt at that time of year is always a little patchy and doesn't really flatter me at all.

"Lookin' good," I said. It was true. Tall and slender, she rocked that dress with some classy heels. I shifted to scratch at the fur on my neck with a hind leg. A large clump of fur worked loose and drifted to the floor. Ranger sniffed at it and gave me a severe look as though to remind me it wasn't him making this mess.

"Thanks. I hope John thinks so, too." Deb flashed a smile and then went serious. I recognized the look she was giving me. Half trepidation and half pity. Damn it.

"He's not a freak, huh?" I said, getting to my paws. Guess I'd be going to hide in my bedroom until Deb left. No point raising questions about how many dogs were in the apartment. And we certainly couldn't have people see me in wolf form and think we had a wild beast in there. That'd be bad.

"You mean he's *normal*, well, yes."

"Eh, I thought he seemed less broody than the last couple of guys," I said. Deb's answer was a laugh and a rude gesture as I retreated to my room, herding Ranger along with me.

Even after Deb left with her date amid nervous laughter and tight voices, I stayed in my room with my chin resting on the windowsill. The cool spring air wafted through my fur, and I liked how it tickled in my ears. But mostly, I just sat there, staring into the gloaming darkness and sniffing the rush of scents that always came with spring. Sweet flowers, sweeter grass, the tangy odor of deer. My window overlooked the greenbelt that stretched out behind our apartment. Somewhere beyond the deep shadow of the trees was the little house and the cemetery and a man who knew my dog's name but not mine.

"What's it matter anyhow?" I muttered. "I'm a lycanthrope." But both my parents had been lycanthropes, and *they'd* found each other. I glanced toward a picture beside my bed. It was from my high school graduation, and I was there in my cap and gown, and both my parents had their arms around me. We were all laughing, and I remembered that moment, the joke my dad told, the feeling that the world was endless and that I could do anything.

Two years later, they'd died in a car accident. Turns out that lycanthropes aren't scarier than drunk drivers.

Feeling absolutely sorry for myself, I turned back to the window and stared out into the world drizzled with moonlight.

It was a strange moon that loomed over the horizon and set the wisps of clouds passing across it aglow: a super-moon *and* a blue moon all on the spring equinox.

Had I not been moping, had Deb not left for the night, had it only been a regular full moon, had any of those things changed, I would have stayed inside, and everything would be different. But the wildness of spring and the pull of the moon and the loneliness of my empty apartment all rose together, and next thing I knew, I was loping out of the apartment with Ranger bounding ahead as though on a great frolic.

Yes, of course, it was stupid. I won't argue otherwise.

Wind ruffled my fur, and its coolness brushed through my body, freeing my muscles. I ran onward, galloping out across the greenbelt to plunge into the forest on the other side. I wasn't really sure where I was going, except that I knew I couldn't go the other direction because there were homes that direction. Even though I looked like a regular wolf, going near people was risky. But out this way was just forest, open land, and a winding dirt road that would lead past a cemetery.

It had been several weeks since I'd first ridden my bike down that dirt road, and I had gone back twice. Of course, I didn't mention it to Deb; I can only handle so much teasing, thank you. I hadn't seen Jasper either time, which was fine because I didn't know what I was going to say. Besides which, as I'd biked down the road again and stopped to stare across the cemetery at the house, I'd had the unsettling idea that what I was doing might be considered stalking. I mean, yes, the road was on public land, but it was still a little weird. I was already a lycanthrope, I didn't need to be a creeper, too. So I'd stopped.

However, with the moon calling to my blood, I didn't have many places to run where I wouldn't be seen. I loped down the road with silver moonlight shivering through the puffs of dust kicked up by my paws. Out of the tall grass, a rabbit dashed across the road, and all my nerves burned to run after it. I started to swerve off my course and follow its heedless plunge through the weeds before I remembered myself.

That's the benefit of being a born lycanthrope: I can control myself on full moons and don't lose my mind like turned werewolves do. Anyhow, I couldn't go chasing off after rabbits—it would be a bit psychopathic to come trotting home with bloody bunny corpses in my jaws. Deb certainly didn't deserve that sort of roommate.

Shortly after the rabbit bounded past, Ranger let out a shrill yelp and bolted back toward me. As he tucked himself down around my paws, I raised my head to see a herd of deer charging in the direction of the rabbit. Pelts sleek in the light, they moved like an undulating flood of flesh as maybe a dozen does raced past.

"You doofus," I muttered to Ranger. "Scared by a herd of deer? My brave protector, indeed."

If a dog can give an indignant look, Ranger certainly managed it as he leaped to his feet and shook himself. I gave him a nudge with my nose.

"C'mon, let's see what's happening." Something had startled those animals and sent them fleeing, and since I was out and wandering, curiosity had me by the nose.

We slowed from a careless run to a trot that let me focus on scenting the air. Ranger stayed so close beside me that I could feel him shivering. It wasn't long before the air turned a weird texture. No, I mean texture because that's the best way I have to describe it. It was heavy and tingling as though seared by lightning, even though the sky was almost clear. The atmosphere set my fur on end, and when I glanced at Ranger, I saw blue sparks flicker along his fur.

I'd never seen anything like it in my life, and I began to turn back to my apartment for Ranger's sake.

That was when my darned dog suddenly flung up his head, gave a heart-piercing howl, and bolted out across the fields.

"Ranger!" I hollered. "Get back here! Ranger!" Story of my life. But I really only had myself to blame. I plunged into the tall grass after him—at least in wolf form, I could catch up to him.

His snarls and barks filled the night. And then came a man's voice.

"Ranger! Back!" shouted the man. Jasper. Ah, blast. Although at the time, I was thinking something a bit more, uh, emphatically four-lettered.

I couldn't leave Ranger, and I couldn't transform into human form since it was a full moon, so that meant that if I wanted to save the dog I'd inadvertently endangered, I'd have to make myself known. The guy who didn't even know my name was about to know my lifelong secret.

With a last burst of speed, I broke through the tall grass and ran straight into the cemetery. What I saw brought me to a stumbling stop. There was Ranger, running frantically from one gravestone to the next, snapping at what I first took to be thick-stemmed plants waving up from the dirt. Then one of the plants grasped for my dog and missed him by inches, and I realized with a sick and hot horror that spilled through my guts that I wasn't seeing plants. Those were hands. Human hands were erupting from the graves.

Standing above it all was Jasper. The wind blew his hair back from a face that, even in the moonlight, was the pale white of panic. He held open a hefty tome, and across his shoulder was slung a shotgun. So, this was his secret. Not exactly what I'd expected.

"What in the hell is happening here!" I shouted. It wasn't a question.

"I—" Jasper broke away to stomp on a hand that was reaching for his leg. For a moment, he stared at me and then shook his head with a dry laugh. "So, you're a werewolf? What has this evening come to?"

"Did you raise the dead?" Was that even a question I was asking? What was my life even?

"No! My father did!" he answered, kicking another hand. It snapped off at the wrist, smacked into a headstone, and went limp after a couple grotesque spasms.

Ranger continued darting and barking, his face the perfect expression of doggy-rapture as though this were his equivalent of whack-a-mole, and I'd brought him out here to have a grand ol' time.

Jasper clapped the book shut, and the sound seemed to echo over the graveyard.

"Back to the house," he said and grabbed hold of Ranger with an easy swoop of his arm as though the dog were nothing bigger than a puppy. We all ran. I bounded up the back porch without touching the steps, and Jasper threw open the door as we all skidded inside. He deposited a very confused Ranger on the kitchen floor. Poor dog, his one great moment of joy had been stolen from him just as soon as he'd found something even better than butterflies.

"Can I get an explanation here?" I asked as I peered up over the windowsill to see a cemetery wriggling with limbs. Dirt heaved as though the ground were gasping for breath.

Jasper, meanwhile, rummaged about in a bookshelf, scrambling through various old tomes that filled the house with the rich smell of worn leather. As I looked around, most of what I could see was just stack after stack of books piled against walls, beside furniture, overflowing from bookshelves. It was like a library had opened the door and vomited into the house. Ordinarily, it would have been exciting. But under the circumstances, it was just another link in the weirdness chain.

"I thought that book would stop the spell from coming to pass," Jasper said. He nodded toward a leather-bound volume he'd left on the table. Dust rose from the pages of another tome that he flipped through before casting it aside. "But it wasn't that one. He lied to me! Which, of course, he would since he *wanted* this to happen. But I didn't know that he'd know that I *wouldn't* want this to happen. Damn it! Where would he have put it?"

"Um, can I help?" I asked, although I couldn't think of what I could do. Maybe call the police? Yeah, I could see how that would go. *Hello? Police? Yes, there are undead crawling from their graves. Can you send a SWAT team right away?* Yeah, not likely.

Jasper looked from the book in his hands to me to the disaster outside the window. Then he sighed and gave a defeated sort of shrug.

"I'm looking for a book that references something called the *Cantio Surgentis*," he said. "It's a spell to raise the dead, but it's not just for reanimating a couple of corpses—it's particularly for raising them *en masse* by using a buried talisman to focus power. There must be a reference in these books somewhere."

I glanced about at the insurmountable stacks of books. "Just start anywhere," he said as he saw my overwhelmed expression.

"I know it's a weird night," he added, "when I have a werewolf in my house and I don't even have time to be worried."

I picked a tome at random and started flipping pages as best as my paws could manage. Latin. Why was everything in Latin? Oh, look, one in what looked like Greek. I shoved that one toward Jasper. I could name every blasted appliance in my apartment in German, but I couldn't tell you a single noun in Latin. *Take Spanish,* they said. *It'll be useful,* they said. *Like hell it is.*

"Honestly," he continued, "I can't believe this is happening."

"Yeah, the dead rising wasn't what I was expecting this evening, either," I said.

"Well, that part I expected." He didn't look up as he tore his way through a book. "I suspected they'd rise at a particularly powerful lunar event. I've been staying here because I couldn't be certain *which* event would trigger their rising. Now I know. I meant more that I didn't expect that I'd have company."

I looked pointedly down at my lupine form, over to Ranger, and then in the direction of the cemetery.

"Having company is what you find weird tonight?" I said. Well, whoever heard of a necromancer being normal? I don't think that goes quite with the territory.

"Well, no," he said. "I mean more that I didn't expect that the one time I have company, it's when I'm trying to fight off a zombie revolution. I'd sort of thought that if I were to invite you inside, it would be for normal conversation and lemonade, or something. I make pretty good lemonade."

"Oh, well, that's good to know. Maybe we could serve some to the zombies?"

"Let's pretend for a moment that I'm aware that what's happening out there is not ideal, all right?" He stopped rifling through the book long enough to massage the bridge of his nose.

Oh. Here was a guy who'd wanted to invite me over for lemonade and I was being snarky. This would be why Deb always got the guy. Well, that, and fay can use some sort of charisma enchantment.

"Sorry," I said. "That wasn't a very constructive remark on my part. My name's Kara, by the way."

Jasper smiled. "Well, now I at least have the name of the person who sits on her bike at the edge of my property. That makes it a little less creepy."

"That's creepy?" I exclaimed. "Bro, you've got zombies crawling up from your backyard. You win the prize for creepy tonight."

"Touché. Now let's keep reading—it has to be in here somewhere."

Flip-flip-flippity-flip. I sneezed at the dust sifting off the pages. For every book I pawed through, Jasper managed four or five, yet the stacks of waiting tomes hardly seemed to diminish. I poked my head up to look out the window. Limbs wriggled from all the plots, and some graves, I saw to my horror, had the heads and upper shoulders of corpses pushing forth.

"Jasper! We do *not* have time for this," I called over my shoulder. "What are those things gonna do when they get free?" What a stupid question. As if I thought they'd come tap on the back door and ask for tea.

"Kill anything in their path," he said, and although his voice seemed oddly calm, a look at his shaking hands showed a man trying not to piss down his leg. I wondered whether, if I peed on the floor, I could blame it on Ranger. Or if anybody'd even care.

"O-okay." I winced at my high and stammering voice. "The book you were reading in the graveyard—why'd you choose that one?"

"Why? Because my father wrote it, and I know that it worked to cast the *cantio* because I watched him use it when I was a boy. He always said that it contained all his most powerful *cantiones*, back when I was growing up. And it *did* have a section on nullifying the *cantio*, but the section was wrong. Deliberately wrong, I'm sure, because my father was a very powerful necromancer who didn't make mistakes."

The book in question still lay on the kitchen table, and I dragged it down. More Latin. And some German! But nothing about refrigerators or washing machines. Was that French? I didn't know. Oh, bleep. Was that *hieroglyphics*? Seriously?

"How many languages did your father speak?" I asked in exasperation. At least, this book had pictures and diagrams that I could follow.

"I'm not sure, to be honest. I know five, and he knew more than I do. Many more, I think."

I skimmed through the pages until I found one with neat, spiky handwriting that read "*Cantio Surgentis*" and included an illustration of what appeared to be a blue crystal and another of a person holding a book and standing before headstones with lines emanating from the person. A half-risen corpse protruded from the grave in the drawing. Well, I'd found the right section. Pressing the book as flat as I could, I stared into the divide between the pages. Oh, well, that was interesting. I traced a claw down deep in the crease.

"Hey, Jasper? I think something was pulled from this book and replaced by this section." I motioned to the valley between the pages, and Jasper left off his search to investigate.

His mouth was a grim and terrible line as he studied the arrangement of pages.

"Yes, yes, somebody has," he said at last and turned to the window. "This is particularly bad."

I wanted to ask how this could possibly be worse,

but I held my tongue.

"He's buried the real pages with him. And the crystal. They're both with him." He gave a nod with his chin to the writhing burial ground. "Out there."

"Okay, that's gross," I conceded, "but it means we dig him up, and you have the pages."

Jasper shook his head. "It's not that easy. My father will rise along with all the others, and I can guarantee that he'll be even more powerful. This was his plan. He'll rise and have the instructions and the crystal that magnifies the power instilled by the *cantio*, and then we're all in for it."

For one long moment, we stared at each other, man and lycanthrope, while the spring wind battered on the windows, and the undead moaned out in the cemetery. Then Jasper swung the shotgun off his back.

"You dig, and I'll shoot," he said, and the resolve in his voice surged with an iron power even as his hands kept shaking.

We locked Ranger in the house, and the dog's howls sang into the night, but we couldn't risk a zombie getting a hold of him. As we marched into the cemetery, several corpses had already clawed up through the dirt so that they were free from the chest up.

"Lord Jesus, forgive me," Jasper muttered and racked the shotgun. I turned away as he pulled the trigger, and the gun boomed. The body exploded in a spray of parched flesh and fragmented bones. Again and then again.

His father's grave was set aside from the others by a couple yards. The headstone simply read, "Ezekiel Quinn Owens. 1960-2012." Nothing about being a beloved father or husband. But more surprisingly, the ground was still. I can't believe I just said that last part, but there we go—it had been that sort of night.

"A-are you sure he's buried here?" I shivered despite my fur.

"Yes." Jasper nodded. "I had him buried here according to his wishes, although he didn't get the headstone he wanted. All sorts of arcane writing on it. I figured that if I didn't let that get put over him, he wouldn't be able to do this." He gestured with a sweep of his hand.

"Maybe it worked so that he can't rise?" Hey, there was hope.

"Maybe." By his tone, my hope wasn't contagious.

I dug. Jasper ran to get a shovel, leaving the shotgun with me and sprinting away before I could point out that wolves make terrible marksmen. But he returned soon enough, and we both went to digging with the force of panic and adrenaline spurring us on. Now and again, Jasper would stop, pick up the shotgun, and stride out among the graves. There'd be a thundering blast, maybe two, and then he'd be back beside me with the shovel, tossing scoop after scoop of dirt.

The moon had risen high and washed the world in a jarringly soft light by the time we had a tremendous heap of dirt beside the grave. Both Jasper and I were coated in mud and loam, and I had it all in my nose and mouth and ears and eyes so that I kept spitting muddy trails of drool. I tried to forget that it was grave dirt.

"We have to be close." Jasper panted. High overhead, the moon had already peaked, and my muscles burned from paws to shoulders with the exertion of unending digging. At the time, I didn't know how tall Jasper was, exactly, but he'd struck me as tall enough that when he was neck deep in a grave, we should have been damned near standing on a casket.

I had just returned to a mad scramble of digging when I sensed Jasper stiffen. "Oh, Lord Jesus," he murmured. I looked up. A mud-caked pair of shoes and faded, grave-stained pants stood at the edge of the grave.

"*Salve, Filii,*" rasped a voice. I tilted my head back to

see a man who loomed like Death in the nighttime. The moonlight showed parchment-thin flesh and eyes that sank deep into sockets like creatures peering from a cave. Leather-gloved hands grasped sheets of paper and a silver chain, from which dangled a crystal that gleamed pale blue under the full moon. A silver-edged cane was tucked in the crook of one arm.

"H-hello, Father," Jasper answered as he moved between me and the corpse that was his father. He raised the shovel even though he'd never be able to swing it in the narrow confines of the hole. "You've got no power over us. I won't let you do this."

"It's not about letting, son," the moving corpse said, and he trailed his voice over "son" as though it were a laughable word. "I had friends bury me in the forest along with some others just for the occasion—you buried an empty coffin. While you were busy with a wild goose chase, we got free."

The shuff-shuffle of more feet scuffed over the ground, and several other figures joined Ezekiel Owens at the graveside, each of them more rotted and decayed than he. Each brandished long, rusty knives. This was not how I thought I'd go to meet my parents. In the best spirit of lycanthropic defiance, I snarled. None of them cared.

I'd found things more frightening than a werewolf.

"You have two choices," the corpse said. "You can agree to help me and find yourself at my side as both a dutiful son and as a very powerful young man who can gain access to any knowledge he wishes, to any woman he wants, to wealth and power that would be beyond your fathoming."

Ezekiel paused for a long moment while the offer lingered in the night air. The zombies held, waiting at his side.

"Or," he continued, fingers clenching his cane, "I can have you killed in that muddy hole, and you'll serve me as a mindless body, as an automaton of muscle and flesh, a thing beyond knowing and beyond caring."

"No. Not for all the knowledge in all the books that history has ever lost would I serve you," Jasper said, adjusting his grip on the shovel.

That was it. That was how we were going to die. No. I refused. Not with all my life before me. I planned to live.

"I accept!" I announced, and everybody just about whipped toward me.

"Kara! No!" Jasper hissed.

Ezekiel Owens's grin was a gut-churning rictus stretching his rancid flesh. "I didn't off—"

"No, you didn't offer it to me," I finished for him. "But your son won't do it, and you know that. You've always known that, haven't you? But you need somebody who can think and reason, right? Somebody who won't just be a zombie. There are things in this world I would give anything to have. And I can't perform magic, so I'm not a threat to your power, but I am a lycanthrope, and that can be quite useful."

"And what would you have in trade?" Ezekiel's smile slashed deeper into his face.

I couldn't bring myself to look at Jasper, so I stared straight up at the corpse in the suit, straight into those feral-animal cavern eyes.

"My parents. I want my family back from the grave," I said. "Give me that, and I will destroy whatever you want destroyed and hunt whatever you want hunted. I will be your hound."

The undead necromancer considered me. Bile bubbled in my throat.

"For your family, then? Very well," he said. "There will be a war for certain, and I can always use one such as you to win the werewolves over. Get out of that pit, lycan."

"Kara?" Jasper whispered, lowering the shovel. The

pain of a dozen knives was in that whisper, as though I had just ripped out his guts and let them spill to the muddy ground.

I leaped for the edge of the hole, lost my footing in the loose dirt, and crashed backward into Jasper, who went to his knees under the impact.

"Your gun," I hissed at Jasper as I struggled to gather my limbs under me. "Use your damned shotgun."

Then I made another leap and scrambled for solid ground.

Ezekiel Owens nodded at me, his face inscrutable. He turned to the zombies, and his voice came level and cold as he ordered, "Kill the boy, and leave me his body."

I drew back without thinking, hackles bristling.

"Oh, you find that a bit callous, lycan?" the undead necromancer asked when he caught my expression, a rough laugh in his voice. "Be prepared to sacrifice much if you wish to win this war. But when I triumph and—"

A shotgun blast cracked and then another as two zombies exploded. Atta boy, Jasper! I jumped away from Ezekiel as his son racked the shotgun again and raised it to his shoulder, barrel trained on the old necromancer.

"Idiot boy!" Ezekiel growled and raised the crystal. The talisman flashed a blinding blue like a star had erupted and sprayed a hundred years of light across the cemetery. Something like lines of lightning exploded across the ground, radiating from the necromancer, and the earth shuddered and heaved along the lines.

Jasper's shot went wide, a few pellets of buckshot scattering across Ezekiel's cheek in bloodless wounds. Light continued to pulse, and it flowed into the zombies remaining by the grave, illuminating them as though they were conduits of a terrible storm. Ezekiel shouted an order in a language I didn't know, and the zombies responded by grouping between him and Jasper.

The zombies advanced with knives poised.

The shotgun racked again. Another blast. But the zombies didn't even flinch. I didn't know when Jasper had last reloaded or how many shells his weapon held, but there didn't come another blast, and the zombies lurched closer.

Ezekiel gave his cane a deft flick and pulled the handle away from the shaft, revealing a long, thin sword blade. I was completely ignored while he fixated on his son.

I am a lycanthrope, and there is something I hate doing because it hurts—a lot. Also, it's never practical, and it reminds me of things I don't want to be and forces that stretch beyond my humanity. But as I watched an undead necromancer stride toward the other zombies with flares of light reflecting off his sword blade and a powerful talisman held aloft, I figured that night my ultimate skill was about to become very practical indeed.

A howl of fury and pain erupted as I pointed my muzzle to the moon. All of my muscles shivered and roiled beneath my skin. My back legs extended; my shoulders widened; the toes on my front paws elongated and stretched into sharp-clawed fingers. Muscles strained against my skin. A red sheen stretched over the world. In only heartbeats, I had become a beast from nightmares.

Ezekiel swung around just as I lunged. Before he could raise his sword, I had my claws in his throat. I snapped his neck in one move and then grasped his head in my hands. He slashed at me with flailing strikes that only scratched my skin. All my muscles heaved as I tightened my iron grip.

"Please! No! I will—"

His voice ended with a sharp crack as his skull crushed between my clawed hands. Before the husk of his body dropped to the ground, the pulsing light flashed out, and everything plunged into a darkness beyond shadows. But I could still see. I swung around on the zombies. I seized the nearest undead and snapped it across my knee and launched myself among the others with fangs exposed and froth spattering across my jaws.

Jasper clambered from the grave and frantically searched through his father's suit until he found the wrinkled pages. The young man rose to his feet with purpose as I swung zombies about, bashing corpse against corpse.

Snatching the talisman, Jasper's voice thundered over my snarls and over the growls of the zombies as he recited the words of the *cantio*. The syllables lifted and fell and rose again, power rippling through the words like living electricity. At the final shout, the talisman flared once more in a bright light that knifed into my eyes, and I turned from the sight of the young man with parchment in one hand and talisman aloft in the other with the wind billowing out his flannel over-shirt like a cloak. For that moment, his silhouette was that of a tremendous necromancer with an abyss of power at his command.

Like leaves gusting to the ground in an autumn wind, the zombies collapsed. And then, just as brilliantly as it had begun, it ended. The light snuffed out, and Jasper stood there with his chest heaving and sweat dripping down his face. And me? Well, I clutched a broken zombie in my claws as I surveyed the mess. I sheepishly dropped the body.

"Sorry about your father," I said, which seemed a rather weak attempt at comfort coming from a nightmare beast. But Jasper just smiled.

"He wasn't getting a Father's Day gift from me, anyway," he said. He shook his head as he looked at me and then back at himself. "So, you're a deranged hellbeast, and I'm a necromancer."

"Pretty much," I said. "But this hellbeast and necromancer just saved the world, I think."

"Yeah, I guess we did." Jasper nudged at a shattered body. "Come on, I'll clean this mess up tomorrow. Shall I make us some lemonade?" He extended his hand, and I reached out to him, letting his fingers intertwine with my claws. "We make a pretty good team, I'd say. Any chance you want to make a career of hunting undead? I hear that's a profitable line of work."

"After I graduate?" I asked as we walked to the house, his hand warm in mine. From the house, I could hear Ranger barking.

"Of course."

And that, since you asked, is the complete story of how I met your father and how we saved the world on our first date.

Author Biographies

Katelyn Barbee – No Rest for the Werey

Katelyn Barbee is a Phoenix college student by day and a writer by night. When not working on her fantasy series, you can find her at the cinema catching the latest flicks or enjoying a nature walk when the weather is nice. The story "The Thief and the Spy" was inspired by the many variants of Cinderella.

Her other publications include "The Miller's Daughter" in *From the Stories of Old*, "The Solstice Beast" in *Whispers in the Shadows*, and "The Thief and the Spy" in *A Bit of Magic*.

You can connect with Katelyn on Twitter (@WriterBarbee) or Facebook (Katelyn Barbee).

Heather Hayden – What's in a Name

Fueled by chocolate and moonlight, Heather Hayden seeks to bring magic into the world through her stories. A freelance editor by day, she pours heart and soul into her novels every night, spinning tales of science fiction and fantasy that sing of friendship and hope.

Heather has always been fascinated by the various "black dogs" of yore, from hellhounds to church grims. Like Lani, she grew up in the forest of Maine, though she's never seen any large black dogs lurking around her home. Her love for animals and the paranormal inspired "What's in a Name." This story is dedicated to Lady, Molly, and Princess Lollipop—all wonderful dogs (none of whom are capable of producing fire, thankfully).

Heather's other publications include *Augment*, a YA science fiction novel, and several short stories in the JL Anthology series. She is currently working on *Upgrade*, the sequel to *Augment*, as well as a gaslamp fantasy series titled *Rusted Magic*.

You can follow Heather's writing adventures on her blog (hhaydenwriter.com), Facebook (@HHaydenWriter), and Twitter (@HHaydenWriter).

J.E. Klimov – Soul of Mercy

J.E. Klimov grew up in a small suburb in Massachusetts. After graduating from Massachusetts College of Pharmacy and Health Sciences, she obtained her PharmD and became a pharmacist; however, her true passion was writing and illustration.

Ever since J.E. Klimov was little, she dreamed of sharing her stories with the world. From scribbling plotlines instead of taking notes in school, to bringing her characters to life through sketches, J.E. Klimov's ideas ranged from fantasy to thriller fiction.

The idea for "Soul of Mercy" came about when Klimov discovered her first white hair in high school. Her teenage ego was slightly damaged, but it inspired her to write a story to explore the mystical relationship between humans and angels. She scribbled the plot idea down and saved it for a rainy day…

Klimov has published two novels with Silver Leaf Books: the award-winning YA fantasy, "The Aeonians," and its sequel, "The Shadow Warrior". "Soul of Mercy" is her fourth short story featured in the JL Anthology series.

You can follow J.E. Klimov and stay tuned for news on her publications among other things on her blog (jelliotklimov.weebly.com), Twitter (@klimov_author), and Facebook page (@klimovauthor).

Matthew Dewar – All's Fairy in Love and War

Matthew's passion for reading and writing developed at a young age. Fascinated by all genres, enthralled by the endless creativity of imagination, and captivated by foreign worlds and intriguing characters, Matthew makes time in his busy schedule to write every day. If he's not reading or writing, you might find Matthew working as a physiotherapist, teaching group fitness classes, entertaining his dog, or dreaming of traveling to an exotic destination.

The idea for "All's Fairy in Love and War" came from Matthew's childhood love of fantasy and spies and his interest in Irish mythology.

If you would like to read more from Matthew, check out his book: Nightmare Stories, a collection of young adult horror fiction where twelve teens discover that happily-ever-afters only exist in fairy tales. Other works have appeared in From The Stories of Old, Between Heroes and Villains, Whispers in the Shadows, Of Legend and Lore, The Seven Deadly Sins Anthology: Gluttony, and The Seven Deadly Sins Anthology: Wrath.

You can connect with Matthew on Twitter (@WriterDewar), Facebook (Matthew Dewar Author), or at his website (matthewdewarauthor.wordpress.com).

Hanna Day – The McWaterford Witch

Hanna Day is a writer from Southern California with an interest in history, fantasy, and the deep, dark existential horrors of the unknown. When not contemplating the vastness of space or writing, she works in nonprofit fundraising.

"The McWaterford Witch" was inspired by her first-ever camping trip and cheesy horror shows.

She can be found on Twitter (@hannacday) and Facebook (@hannacday).

Maddie Benedict – This Really Bites

Maddie Benedict is a Millennial who has been writing fiction ever since she was little. She loves animals, and, unsurprisingly, she's a vegetarian, which she has been her whole life. She's never met a werewolf, but if she did, she'd only like the harmless kind.

"This Really Bites" is the second of several short stories she's written to date, and it's her first official publication. She has hundreds more ideas where that came from (and also where other ones came from), which she expects will keep her busy for the next century or so.

Madison Wheatley – Gallery of Lost Souls

Madison Wheatley is a fiction writer from Northwest Indiana. When it comes to stories, Madison is a fan of all things magical (and a little bit spooky). She shares her love of literature with the students in her middle and high school English classes, and she enjoys when they "geek out" over the books they're interested in.

Madison has always loved the idea of magic hiding out in plain sight—the idea that it could be obscured in some dark alley or in an unassuming abandoned building. This fascination fueled the creation of Silvercoast City, a place where the mystical and the mundane coexist. However, Madison is also inspired by stories in which people use their "ordinary" talents to save the day. Characters like Talisa Joyce appeal to Madison because she can relate to their journey from insecurity to empowerment.

You can read Madison's YA horror story "All That Glitters" in *Seven Deadly Sins, A YA Anthology: Avarice*. In addition, her YA flash fiction piece "Bad Thoughts" is featured in issue 8 of *The Passed Note Review*. Her current project is *Ambrosia*, a new adult psychological thriller with elements of horror.

You can connect with Madison on Twitter and Instagram (@mwheatleywriter) or through her website (www.madisonwheatley.com). You can also send an email to madison@madisonwheatley.com.

Mari L. Yates – The Ghostly Loch

While her novels are still unpublished, the quality of Mari's writing has been widely recognized: she was a finalist in James Patterson's Co-Author competition hosted by MasterClass in 2017 with her thriller, *Windows to the Soul*, and in 2014, she made it to the quarter-final round of Amazon's Breakthrough Novelist contest with her fantasy, *End of Order*. She is committed to the craft, having "won" NaNoWriMo each year since 2013. When not writing, Mari likes to read, go bowling, or spend time outdoors with her family.

She can be found on Facebook (@marilyates), Twitter (@meadowmirth), and her website (www.marilyates.com).

Kristy Perkins – No One Delivers to the Sewers

Kristy Perkins is a nanny, and a writer whenever she can find the time. Ever since she could write legibly, she has created stories. She writes fantasy and sci-fi stories to satisfy the need for more dragons and spaceships in her life.

If they existed, how would dragons adapt to modern society? That question, when combined with sewer alligator conspiracy theories and a general bewilderment with delivery services, spawned "No One Delivers to the Sewers."

Other short stories of Kristy's can be found in the JL Anthologies *Between Heroes and Villains* and *A Bit of Magic*. Follow Kristy on Twitter (@KristyEPerkins) or Pinterest (perkinswhatif), and check out her blog at (nocluewritingplatform.wordpress.com).

Melion Traverse – A Particularly Powerful Lunar Event, a Completely True Story

Melion lives with two dogs, one spouse, and a fluctuating amount of chaos. When not writing, Melion practices historical fencing and other martial arts, studies medieval history, lifts weights, consumes energy drinks, and wages the Battle of Dog Fur.

Melion's works have been published in *Deep Magic*, *Cast of Wonders*, *Cosmic Roots and Eldritch Shores*, *Havok*, and other magazines. Melion has also published under pseudonyms in *Cicada* and *Electric Spec*.

Find Melion blogging haphazardly at delusionsofsanityblog.wordpress.com.

About the Just-Us League

Hailing from all corners of the globe, the members of the Just-Us League share a common passion for words and worlds.

The League can be found on Facebook (@jlwriters), Twitter (@JL_writing), and our website (jlwriters.com). Follow us for updates, giveaways, and new releases.

Also by the Just-Us League

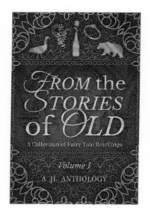

In this international collection,
new life is given to fairy tales, both classic and obscure.
Discover unexpected twists on old favorites,
and fall in love with new tales and worlds to explore!

Available on Amazon.

What is the difference between a hero and a villain?
This question lies at the heart of twelve unique tales about
those who wield superpowers—from flight to ice generation.
Follow these men and women as they set out to save
themselves, and the world, from the great evils around them.

Available on Amazon.

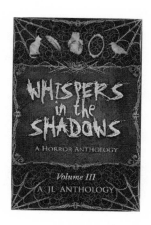

Even when we think we're safe, our biggest fears can be
revealed, our worst nightmares brought to life.
Keep the lights on and brace yourself for ten creepy tales of
horror and misfortune.

Available on Amazon.

New life is given to eleven old stories
in this second collection of irresistible fairy tale retellings.
Be transported to new worlds
and enjoy fresh twists on old favorites.

Available on Amazon.

The oldest story can be made new again,
changed and altered until it is reimagined and restored.
Follow these characters on their journeys
as eleven magical tales are turned on their heads
and seen from new perspectives.

Available on Amazon.

Made in the USA
Columbia, SC
14 November 2018